Praise for Vanish

"*Vanishing Daughters* is a creepy, moody, devious heartbreaker of a novel! Great characters and a compelling plot filled with twists you won't see coming. Darkly elegant!"

—Jonathan Maberry, *New York Times* bestselling author of *NecroTek* and editor of *Weird Tales Magazine*

"*Vanishing Daughters* plunges us into the nightmare that is grief, from which it feels impossible to wake. Pelayo constructs an elegant yet haunting house of memories, dreamlike vignettes quilted, and interweaves violence, true crime, injustice with dark fairy tales through part poetry, part prose. In this multilayered exploration of sleeping women awakened, *Vanishing Daughters* illuminates how our lives are inseparable from folklore, from our ancestors, even if unfair."

—Ai Jiang, Bram Stoker and Nebula Award–winning author of *Linghun*

"A marvelous fusion of fairy tale and haunted Chicago history, loss and the will to live on, age-old injustices and a drive to give peace to the past. Mysterious and spooky, *Vanishing Daughters* is as heartrending as it is spine tingling, a girls-gone-missing tale in which Cynthia Pelayo navigates grief to find purpose in our many deaths, one for every soul we've ever loved and lost."

—Nick Medina, author of *Indian Burial Ground*

"A lyrical, ghostly homage to the city of Chicago. One of Pelayo's finest."

—Erika T. Wurth, author of *White Horse*

"A cerebral thicket, growing tight around and keeping you. No matter how much we think we know, Pelayo shows there's always another stone to overturn in her Chicago tales. *Vanishing Daughters* bares the heart in its rawest condition, revealing how our human nature can erode the lines between past and present, between grief and obsession, and between dark fairy tale and ghost story."

—Hailey Piper, Bram Stoker Award–winning author of
Queen of Teeth and *All the Hearts You Eat*

Praise for Cynthia Pelayo

"A dreamlike modern fairy tale full of grief, longing, and murder, *Forgotten Sisters* is Cynthia Pelayo's best yet. Like the best hauntings, this one will linger in my head for a long time."

—Christopher Golden, *New York Times* bestselling author of
Road of Bones and *The House of Last Resort*

"Aspects of *Forgotten Sisters* glide past each other like ghosts as Cynthia Pelayo adroitly juggles past and present, reality and the supernatural, in this elegiac gothic novel. You'll be haunted long after you've finished turning the pages."

—Alma Katsu, author of *The Fervor*

"A gritty murder mystery about a house that drips with haunted histories and a river that carries dark secrets and dead bodies in its current, *Forgotten Sisters* is a mesmerizing, propulsive read that doesn't just bend genre, it transcends it."

—Rachel Harrison, national bestselling author of *Cackle* and
Black Sheep

"Personal, historical, and heart-deep. *Forgotten Sisters* captures the complicated sense of being stifled by home yet lost without it. From the eerie start to the unforgettable ending, Pelayo brings the chill of crime stories, grim fairy tales, and the gothic into a haunting mystery that will drag you into dark waters and never let go."

—Hailey Piper, Bram Stoker Award–winning author of
Queen of Teeth and *A Light Most Hateful*

"Guaranteed to make your heart thump and skin crawl."

—*The New York Times*

"Cynthia Pelayo's wonderfully eerie *Children of Chicago*, an ode to Humboldt Park and fairy tales and crime novels and Chicago's Latinx community, has ambition to spare."

—*The Chicago Tribune*

"Pelayo masterfully ratchets up the tension and the scares. Robert McCammon fans will be pleased."

—*Publishers Weekly* (starred review)

"With superior worldbuilding, a relentless pace, a complex heroine, and a harrowing story that preys off of current events as much as its well-developed monster, this is a stellar horror novel that fires on all cylinders, from the first page through to its horrible conclusion. For fans of dark fantasy based on fairy tales such as Seanan McGuire's Wayward Children series or novels by Helen Oyeyemi, with just the right touch of Sara Paretsky's V.I. Warshawski."

—*Library Journal* (starred review)

"Cynthia Pelayo combines police procedural with suspense, horror, and a fairy tale to give you a dark genre-bending tale, perfect for *X-Files* fans and readers who eschew cookie-cutter books."

—Alma Katsu, author of *The Hunger* and *The Deep*

VANISHING
DAUGHTERS

Other Works by Cynthia Pelayo

Stand-Alone Novels

Forgotten Sisters

Santa Muerte

The Missing

Chicago Saga Novel

The Shoemaker's Magician

Children of Chicago

Poetry

Poems of My Night

Into the Forest and All the Way Through

Crime Scene

Collections

Lotería

Writing Poetry in the Dark

The Hideous Book of Hidden Horrors

Slash-Her

Diabolica Americana

Were Tales

This World Belongs to Us

Poetry Showcase Volume VII

Poetry Showcase Volume V

¡Pa'que Tu Lo Sepas!

Lockdown

Both Sides

Campfire Macabre

Snow White's Shattered Coffin

Far From Home

Halldark Holidays

Twisted Anatomy

We Are Wolves

VANISHING
DAUGHTERS

CYNTHIA
PELAYO

THOMAS & MERCER

Text copyright © 2025 by Cynthia Pelayo
All rights reserved.

Published by Thomas & Mercer, Seattle

www.apub.com

Amazon, the Amazon logo, and Thomas & Mercer are trademarks of Amazon.com, Inc., or its affiliates.

ISBN-13: 9781662513930 (paperback)
ISBN-13: 9781662513923 (digital)

Cover design by Olga Grlic
Cover image: © IIdiko Neer / ArcAngel; © bike_4310, © CandyRetriever, © Nadezhda79 / Shutterstock; © ANHELINA OSAULENKO / Unsplash

Printed in the United States of America

*To all of us who have ever looked up to the sky
and wondered if there was something more*

She sleeps, nor dreams, but ever dwells. —"The Sleeping Beauty," Alfred, Lord Tennyson

Chapter 1

TIME: 1:43 a.m.
DATE: Friday, December 1

"Keys and gates and locks and thorns," I say. "But what's my name?"

I'm seated at the edge of my bed. My heart is racing and my hands are twisted around the comforter, as if grasping this fabric will keep me grounded and safe somehow. I did it again. I woke myself up screaming.

I don't know what happens in those moments; all I know is my body jerks, and I sit up quickly and scream.

Now I am awake and staring out the window, trying to piece together what that was. Was it a nightmare? Something else? These episodes started happening the night she died. I turn to the pink dream journal beside my bed and the white pen. I pick them both up, open to a new page, and write the date at the top:

December 1

I woke up again. It's 1:43 a.m. I feel scared. Like I want to cry. I can't remember what I was dreaming about.

I set the pen down on the bed beside me and flip to previous pages; they are all the same. Dates and times. Waking up in a panic. Unable to recount what it was that caused the terror and racing heart.

The only thing I can think of is that this is yet another symptom of grief.

The only source of illumination in my room pours in from the soft yellow glow of the streetlight just outside what is now my house. The sparkling snowflakes gently descending across the dark city sky look like soft silvery confetti. There's a delicate scent of rose lingering in the air. Very often with these aging historic homes, there's a familiar smell that hangs in the air. I noticed it when I returned home. I pushed the front door open, my suitcases at my side. I stood at the threshold for a moment, peering into the darkness, taking in the shapes and shadows welcoming me back.

When I set foot in the house, there it was, the smell of my child-hood, that of velvety roses.

I rub my temples. I'm struggling with memory. My thoughts are thick like syrup. I'm trying to pull myself away from the cloud of sleep.

I close my eyes tight and remind myself that I am here. It is winter. I am in my mother's—now my—house.

I open my eyes once again, directing my focus to the window.

In a way, I always knew I'd come back here. I love this house. This is a house of dreams. Multiple floors. Built-in shiny oak dressers that, when polished just right, show your reflection. Rich wood paneling. Chandeliers that hang in the living room and dining room, those pendants like fat sparkling diamonds.

As I walked through the house when I first returned, I noticed how with time the colors of the wallpaper had faded. Layers of dust collected above chandeliers, and spiders spun their fluffy webs along the edges of dressers. Even now, sitting here on this bed, I can feel the cold wind blowing in from along the sides of the old window. Of course Mother couldn't keep up with the demands of this house through the years on her own, with her modest salary.

I feel bad now that as the years passed, I failed to notice those details when I visited her when she was alive. I was just too wrapped up in my own life, working and writing.

There is no doubt that, with time, things change, but even with age, this is still a grand house. Without her presence here, though, this space—its rooms, hallways, and foyer—all feels so cold and empty.

Mother and I liked watching those silly murder mysteries on PBS. In many of them, the stately homes built of stone, their walls decorated with red-and-gold tapestries, dark oil paintings, or landscapes with blooming botanicals, had wonderful names like Styles Court or Swinly Dean, Gossington Hall or End House.

"Why doesn't our home have a name?" I remember asking Mother one evening as we both watched a murder mystery, the blue light of the television casting the living room in a dreamy glow. While our home was built of stone, its walls weren't decorated in tapestries, but we made up for it in paintings.

Mother smiled and then laughed. "The house does have a name."

It was in that moment that I realized people could keep information from their loved ones for years, decades even. Maybe it was unintentional, I tried to reason. I didn't want to believe that Mother kept this a secret from me all this time.

Why would she conceal the name of this house from me on purpose? Maybe it had just been a mistake? Something she had always wanted to tell me, or maybe she thought it was something I had already known.

Mother crossed her legs beneath her on the sofa and pushed her swooping blond curls away from her eyes and said: "Rose House."

It's so silent and pretty outside, but inside this house and inside me, these fast-spinning threads are tangling together.

Time passes.

I don't know how much, and all throughout this night I can still hear Mother's musical voice pinging in my head.

There are dreams that dissipate with the morning sun, and then there are dreams that linger. Mother called these dreams omens, messages, occurrences so otherworldly we could not simply shake them off with the sunlight, because those people we encountered and those conversations we engaged in felt just so real.

"Dreams hold much more meaning, much more power, than we wish to realize," Mother said.

And I guess I want to know why. What are dreams trying to tell us? What are my dreams trying to tell me? Even the ones I can't remember.

My head is full of fairy dust, but I see it now, materializing along the edges of my memory.

Black asphalt. Iron cemetery gates. A car the color of midnight.

In the distance I hear that voice. It's radiant, like the strumming of a harp. That voice. Her voice. It's still playing back in my head.

I rub my eyes, forcing these last lingering sprinkles of sleep and dream, which cloud one's thoughts, away from my mind.

I stand.

I feel the plush carpet beneath my feet, and I begin to pace. To think.

I stop and press the palms of my hands into my eyes. My arms are shaking. I take a deep breath, exhale, and relax my arms down at my sides.

What was it I saw just moments ago? Was that a dream? A hallucination? A memory of something I saw once? A movie? Something else?

What do we call a dream that seems so crisp, so clear? Because to call it a dream doesn't feel right. I feel like I was right there, a participant in all of it.

That's where I first saw her, this woman who materialized in my dreams, whom I had never seen before.

I look to my hands, and I can see her so clearly now, the woman who comes to me when I sleep. Her luminescent skin. Her sparkling blue eyes pleading.

"Please take me home," she said.

I remember her bright, lovely face. Her golden-blond hair pulled back in a high ponytail and her beautiful white gown.

My thoughts are swirling, wondering.

Am I her?

Is she me?

Am I someone else?

My hair is long and fair, but much longer than that of the girl in the dream. My face is much narrower too, not round and plump like hers. She reminds me of a young Grace Kelly.

I can't be her, but I know her. I'm connected to her somehow.

I feel like this is all colliding into a singular moment. Or is it collapsing? Falling stars shimmering against the black sky.

My eyes move to my cluttered desk. More notebooks and pens, some books, and my computer. The green-and-gold woodland-wallpapered wall catches my eye.

Loops and swirls and ribbons can be spotted deep within the pattern. In parts, along the edges of the wall, the paper is peeling back, curling in on itself, yellowing on the inside.

This entire house is a defiant act of decayed decadence.

I reach my hand out to touch the wallpaper, but I pause, remembering my mother's words: "This house, in this city, is special, because it is eternal and timeless. Things within these walls do not move like things in other houses."

I remember what I'd said to that. "It's like a time warp."

"Yes." Mother had nodded, her gaze looking up. "A time warp. But that's what makes this home special. The trees on either side, the plants and the pond and the greenhouse. This is our little fairy kingdom in this vibrant place. While things out there move with electricity and speed, in here there's a gentle shift that takes place like the delicate adjustment of a radio dial."

Mother took great pride in our garden, and people would come from all throughout the city to drive past our house, or walk along our sidewalk, to peer into our property and admire her work.

She'd said: "Our family planted these trees and planted these bushes and grew these roses and lavender and rue and marigold and hyssop. A great wooded garden for a great Victorian greystone mansion nestled along a grand, historic boulevard. The bold and bright colors of this house radiate against the bustling cityscape. Still, we must remember that everywhere there is light, darkness is always waiting to creep in, and for that we should take care."

The wallpaper in front of me feels like it's slowly moving away. I forget whether I'm breathing, and so I have to remember to inhale and count each breath—one, two, three, and four. And just as my heart rate settles, I am reminded that I will never hear her voice again. My brain is unkind to me. At that thought it feels as if the room shifts forty-five degrees and I am standing at an angle. Everything feels off.

I close my eyes and try to steady myself here, in this point in time, but there I go, falling under the spell of dream dust.

I see my mother, in a black sweaterdress. Her hair is smooth and long and down past her shoulders. Her eyes look dim and her skin lacks luster. She looks very, very tired, as she did days before her diagnosis, but still she smiles. I can smell her scent, the sweet, toasted perfume of warm vanilla.

She speaks to me, there, in that quiet space:

"Remember, my darling, that we are timeless, eternal, existing forever and ever. Sometimes patterns repeat, but sometimes a pattern must be broken in order to move the story forward. Remember that, and remember my love for you. My connection to you and to this house can never be severed. I know that. The house knows that. It is important that you know that as well. In this, our forever house. You and I are brightly colored contrasting pieces of fabric stitched together on our family quilt. We will always be together."

The scene disintegrates into a shimmering sheet of black. I open my eyes and I am right back here, in my bedroom. I focus on the wallpaper, green and gold, and I press my hand to it, feeling the embossed edges of golden leaves beneath my fingertips.

My heart is racing. I feel it in my throat.

"Remember." I press my palm against my temple. Trying to catch my breath. "What is my name?" I plead with the house. Why are some things coming so easily to me, but my name is just lost out there in the ether?

Everything else is there. Pictures steadily developing. The notes of a song forming. Flashes of dreams erupt along the edges of my vision, like crackling fireworks in the sky.

In my mind I see a pretty white dress and pretty white dancing shoes. These were her things, not mine, I tell myself.

My name.

I need to remember my name, but all I can think about are the images that form behind my closed eyes and that make no sense. Some are my memories, but some are not.

How is this a part of grief?

I'm scared to sleep. When I sleep, these are the things I see. And the only way to awaken from these dreams is first to remember that I'm dreaming and then to jolt my body awake somehow.

A steady hum begins somewhere deep within the house.

Is it the heating system? A fan? What is that noise? As seconds draw on, I realize it is nothing mechanical. Instead, it's a series of discordant creaks and cracks, stomps, and low murmurs, a doorbell, and then a scream and the sound of something falling.

None of those sounds make any sense. I am home alone.

I open my bedroom door. Cool air hits me, followed by the sweet smell of flowers. The long hallway just outside my room is much draftier than my bedroom. When I was a little girl, I'd get so scared to step into the hallway to go to the bathroom. This long stretch seemed so endless when the lights were off, like it extended on into forever. I felt like the moment I started walking down this hallway alone, I could be trapped in an eternal night. Wandering a never-ending path.

I close the door, and then in my room the walls come alive. There are pounding and scratches from behind the wallpaper, as if someone has been sealed behind the drywall, immurement. Sealed high up, in a turret, in a tower.

The sound fades. I approach the wall and press my left ear against it, listening. A slow, steady susurration, like the sound of leaves swaying in a forest, melds into the words:

"Bring her home. Bring her home. Bring her home. Bring her home. Bring her home."

I back away from the wall. A rush of clarity comes to my senses. The room seems brighter, and it's as if a spotlight shines on my life, and then the rest of the room goes dark, and the only light is the glow of my computer screen. A video clip is set to pause. There is my mother standing beside a monument.

I remember now.

Cemetery visits for her restoration work soon unfolded to her telling me stories of the people whose headstones and tombstones and mausoleums she cared for. Some died of sickness. Some of accidents. And of those, some killed by another; far too often no one knew what happened to them, just that they were found dead one day.

The room fills with floral scents. Jasmine. Lavender. Hyacinth. Gardenia. I remember now, the greenhouse just outside and our wonderful long summer days in the garden, the smell of earth and sunshine.

I look back to my computer screen, and I read the name of the great monument my mother is standing beside. There's no smile on her face. Her features are solemn. In the background I see them, gleaming granite headstones rising from the ground.

My thoughts, my memories, it's all a ball of yarn, unrolled and wrapped again.

The noises in the house soften. I sit in my computer chair.

A gust of wind rattles against my window. The low, vibrating moaning returns, like a chant, or a prayer, or something more. My eyes remain focused on the curtain. I see it now begin to shift and move, billowing as if air is blowing in, but the window is closed.

A hint of shimmering snow appears from beneath the fabric. When I push the curtain back, there is nothing. Not a single snowflake.

"What am I supposed to do?" I shout to the wallpaper and the glass light fixture above, the dark wood molding and the bronze doorknob of my bedroom door. "I don't understand what you want me to do!"

I sigh and lower my head into my hands.

My mother, the crunchy mom, believed in making everything from scratch—nut milks and homemade baked goods. She shunned harsh chemical cleaning supplies. She mapped out her daily movements based on the stars, sat in meditation in the garden each morning, and later in the day did yoga with the setting sun. My mother believed in beauty and energy, ghosts and the continuation of us all. Maybe growing up with that is what pushed me to want to believe in something else, in science and order, structure and rules.

I write about science. I write about what is real, and this, what is happening to me, is real, even though it feels like it isn't, I tell myself. I remember this now. My job in freelance. I'm a freelance writer. I write about health. I write about science. I write about the mind, even though my mind isn't working as it should right now.

Why?

I stand erect.

I utter that one word that's distorted my entire reality: "Grief."

A new picture appears on my computer screen. A movie plays, a camera navigating a dense forest. I feel like I am there, but that cannot be because I am right here in my bedroom, and not among those ancient, gnarled trees, but I feel them.

And then I am there.

I maneuver around moss-covered branches that twist and stretch toward the sky, as if commanding the blue expanse above to come down to earth. I hear the rustling of leaves and insects chirping and clicking. I see shafts of sunlight piercing through the dense foliage.

The ground beneath my feet feels soft, a carpet of fallen leaves and ferns and wildflowers. The air is damp with the smell of earth and musk and with hints of fresh, bright pine. There's a vibration of enchantments in the air.

I extend my fingers to a leaf, both wanting this and terrified for it to be real. *Is my brain breaking?* I touch the leaf and rub it between my thumb and pointer finger. It feels like leather.

How is this real?

"What's my name?"

As soon as I say those words aloud, I am back in my room.

I shake my head. It's a hallucination, one part of my brain tells me, but another part whispers that it's a time warp.

I hear the faint sound of music. The distant strains of something from long ago. A melody that seems to play in some empty ballroom somewhere. The music stops. There's a sharp whir, as if a radio dial is being adjusted.

The dial settles on a low, steady hum.

Vibration. Sound. Movement.

I press my hands against my ears, trying to silence the house, trying to make these dreams, these hallucinations, whatever they are, go away. I cannot tell where all these stirrings originate, from me or the house or some great beyond.

Reality can seem so big when we are in it, but when things occur that we cannot explain, it's as if we have lost our balance, like gravity no longer exists and we are tumbling in all directions, yet no direction at the same time. The rules of existence no longer apply.

It feels like an impossibility to move forward when someone you love has died.

I am pacing my room now. Rubbing my shoulders. The cold from the hallway has crept in.

The road.

Black asphalt.

The pretty girl in a white ball gown.

I'm trying to think. What were my mother's words? It's there, along the edges of my thoughts. Dream and sleep and a black car along a cemetery road. The automobile needs to stop, but it does not.

I hear a tapping against my window.

I pull back the red velvet curtain. There's so much red and gold in this house. This home feels like a fading, decadent dollhouse.

I see flurries blowing diagonally in the wind. Streetlights. The quiet boulevard. And tapping against my window is a rose vine. I press my palm against the cold glass, and I hear a voice scream in my head. It's a voice that's traveled through my dream into my waking life. It's a voice that defies time and space.

"Bring me home!"

I remember now.

My name is Briar Rose Thorne.

My mother died two weeks ago. This is my house. Our house. A forever house. A house that knows many secrets.

THE SLEEPING BEAUTY

by Alfred, Lord Tennyson

I.

Year after year unto her feet,
The while she slumbereth alone,
Over the purpled coverlet
The maiden's jet-black hair hath grown,
On either side her trancéd form
Forth streaming from a braid of pearl;
The slumbrous light is rich and warm,
And moves not on the rounded curl.

II.

The silk star braided coverlid
Unto her limbs itself doth mould
Languidly ever, and amid

Her full black ringlets downward rolled
Glows forth each softly-shadowed arm,
With bracelets of the diamond bright;
Her constant beauty doth inform
Stillness with love and day with light.

III.

She sleeps; her breathings are not heard
In palace chambers far apart;
The fragrant tresses are not stirred
That lie upon her charméd heart.
She sleeps; on either side upswells
The gold-fringed pillow lightly prest;
She sleeps, nor dreams, but ever dwells
A perfect form in perfect rest.

Chapter 2

TIME: 7:00 a.m.
DATE: Sunday, December 3

I'm in my pajamas. Flannel pants and a flannel button-up long-sleeve shirt and gray wool socks. Even so, the house is still too cold, and over my sleep clothes I wear my pink, white, and blue checkered bathrobe.

It feels as if the last few weeks I have existed in pajamas.

"Keys and gates and locks and thorns," I say, holding on to the curtain of my bedroom window, looking out onto the snow-covered boulevard.

I look to my bed: soft white pillows, a white sheet, and a heavy white comforter. My gaze moves to my nightstand, and I see the book I was reading just before sleep. Sleeping once felt like the safest thing to do, but now I don't trust it. Nighttime is deceptive. It promises me peace and comfort, but all it brings me is terror, in clips and scenes of my mother, and memories that don't seem like memories. They feel like visions plucked from the sky.

I should call Daniel. I know he told me to call anytime, message anytime, but this, what I'm dealing with, is so much for one person to bear. I don't want to do that to him, dump all my grief onto him. We've been together less than a year, and me dealing with the death of a parent isn't something that's usually expected in the typical chain of events that unfold in the beginning of a relationship. Still, he says he's committed and he's here. I'm glad he is, but I don't want him distracted, thinking about me while he's at work, trying to save lives.

I move to my closet, reach into the darkness, and pull on the string that dangles from the ceiling. The light bulb clicks on, and for a moment I feel a pinch in my chest at the sight of my clothes. My jeans and pants are neatly folded in the built-in wooden shelving. My sweaters and blouses and dresses dangle from hangers. My sneakers and dress shoes are all lined up in the shoe rack. Besides this, all I own are my laptop, some books, notebooks, and pens. I didn't own much before, but all my things are here now, and I realize I'm never going back to living in an apartment.

This is my home now, my old home.

The place I grew up in, and the house my mother left to me, same as her mother left it to her, and before.

I return to the window. It's still night outside. I slept some, maybe two hours, but the dreams woke me again.

"What does it mean?" I speak to the window and to the bare, spindly rose vine outside. It's like a finger bone. "Keys and gates and locks and thorns"—those words that were spoken to me from my mother as she lay dying, and those words that appear to me again and again in these feverish dreams. I linger on the sound of each letter and each syllable as they tumble out of my mouth. My words hover in the air before me, existing between here and there, in a span and space of forever.

Mother often called our house "the forever house." I asked her why, and she said it was because it felt as if this house had always been here in this very spot, forever, and that it would continue to exist here, just a short walking distance from Jackson Park and the Midway Plaisance on Chicago's South Side. Mother would say that many ghosts lived in this part of town. She said some had always been here, many others came around the time of the World's Columbian Exposition, and many remained. I often brushed away my mother's talk of ghosts, her sweet and fanciful mantras, observations, and tales. Mother's head seemed to be all fairy tales and ghost stories, stars and dreams and hope and wonder. I envied how she looked at the world with such awe and saw beauty in everything.

Mother was very much like a little girl, believing in things like superstitions and specters. On Halloween she would prepare a fire in the fireplace in the living room and tell ghost stories as told to her by her mother and her mother's mother before her.

There'd be bowls full of popcorn and candy, miniature Snickers bars, M&M's, Reese's Pieces, and more.

With the lights dimmed low, Mother would clap her hands as if commanding the attention of a great audience, when it was just me seated on the rug. She'd smile that sly smile. Her eyes glowing from the nearby roaring fire. She'd then look from side to side, scrunch her nose in excitement, smile again, nod, and begin—

"Many say when you're driving down Archer Avenue at night, you should make sure to keep your car doors locked . . ."

In Chicago, a city of tragedy and fancy, sorrow and joy, we are raised on ghost stories. Chicagoans often claim to see the ghosts still on patrol from the Battle of Fort Dearborn in 1812; specters of crying women and children outside in Death Alley, burned to death at the fire at the Iroquois Theatre, now the Oriental Theatre, in 1903; and the apparitions of Al Capone's gangsters standing, playing lookout at the site of the Saint Valentine's Day Massacre on Clark Street; and more.

Mother was open about her belief in ghosts. She thought some monitored our movements, closely watching and following us along our day-to-day. Others, she believed, were doomed, trapped to replay their final moments again and again. Stuck, like a record, like a song playing on a loop. That sounded like hell to me.

What people don't really tell us about ghosts and death and dying is that when a loved one dies, a part of you will die too.

I wish Mother had told me that, and maybe, in a way, she had been preparing me for it my entire life by telling me these fantastical stories. I just never expected that grief would feel like this, like my entire world was fading away from me.

Maybe that's why grief is so difficult for some, because we are gripped in mourning someone we loved while also processing the pain that who we were when they were alive no longer exists either. I guess that means a part of us becomes a ghost as well?

Since Mother died, I haven't really been able to sleep long stretches. I wake up crying. I wake up screaming. I wake up trembling and confused about where I am, because the shadows in this house are not the ones from my old apartment.

The shadows in this house move. The shadows in this house talk.

When I wake up, it takes a moment for my eyes to adjust to this darkness, and another moment still for my brain to adjust to the reality that my mother is no longer here and I am the last living member in my family.

My bedroom door creaks open, and a white snout appears in the crack. My little gray-and-white pit bull wagging her tail.

"How'd you guess I was awake, Prairie?"

Prairie enters the room, wagging her tail. She sniffles along the carpet. She sits next to me. I kneel and gently rub behind her ears. She playfully paws at me.

I shake my head. "You're not going to trick me. I'm sure Emily let you out before she went to work."

After Mother died, my best friend and roommate, Emily, moved in here with me. I thought I could handle death—the funeral arrangements, burial, death certificate, various bank and billing accounts to close, and this house—but no. It was so much, so fast, that I lost myself instantly, missing deadlines for my articles, and now missing sleep.

I didn't know what was happening to me, but I started reading more, specifically about dying, about living, about the mind, about our health tied to grieving, and I learned that the living, too, suffer from the effects of death. In the days after my mother's death, even constructing sentences became difficult. I would be talking, and midsentence the words would drop, and my mind would go blank, and I would forget where I was and what I was doing. The science was all there. Grief was rewiring my brain.

And so it made sense, for many reasons, for Emily to move in here, because I needed help, and I couldn't do this alone. She wouldn't have to pay rent elsewhere on her own or find a new roommate. Plus, I had more than enough room in this house.

Prairie whimpers and I groan. "It's freezing out there," I say, dreading the cold outside.

Caring for the house seemed an impossibility when I couldn't even care for myself. This house is as massive for just two people as it is for a single person. This house is an entire planet.

Prairie whimpers again. I sigh and stand. "You're not going to trick me so you can run off and play in the snow?" I ask.

Prairie whines, and I can't deny any of her requests. "Fine, we can play in the yard after coffee."

I grab the book from my nightstand I was attempting to read the night prior—C. S. Lewis's *A Grief Observed*.

I walk down the dark hallway, and when I reach the large window in the middle of the floor, I pull back the heavy curtains and allow the sun in. Clouds of dust motes are suspended in the light in the hallway now. From here I look down and see the greenhouse in the garden.

When I was little, it felt like a playhouse, this gorgeous house made of glass and steel and copper. Today I can appreciate it much more, its Victorian-inspired roofline, and its deep-copper surface that has weathered so many years. The colors, in part, ranging from russet brown to vibrant greens. Some glass panes have been repaired and replaced over time, and as the years draw on, other pieces of glass will be fixed too, but still this structure will remain, an extension of our forever house, and the gardens.

I continue, and Prairie paws along beside me. Her feet make soft tapping sounds against the hardwood floor. In this house she is my little shadow.

When I went to Chicago Canine Rescue, I spotted her, cowering in the back of a dark crate. I asked the volunteer how long she had been there. I was told she was the dog at the shelter who had been there the longest.

"Well, not anymore," I said. "She's coming home with me." And like that, I plucked her from the darkness, and today she is helping to bring light to mine.

Emily doesn't hear the music that the house plays; only Prairie and I do.

I reach the landing and stop and again push back the heavy curtains from a large window to allow the golden rays in.

"It looks like another dreary day," I say to Prairie.

It is early December, and we're moving toward the long stretches of darkness. Soon a collection of consecutive sunless days will bring gloom. I worry about those upcoming days, when everything is muted and cast in shadows, the colors of confusion, when I'm already feeling so unwell with grieving.

Time became muddled after Mother died. When I am sleeping, I feel like I should be awake. When I am awake, I can't distinguish between sleep and dreams.

I'm downstairs now, and I pull back the curtains on this floor to allow in the light.

The foyer opens into the large family room. To the left of the family room is the living room, which looks out over the boulevard. To the right of the family room is the dining room, and then the library. From here we walk to the kitchen. My office is next to the kitchen, but lately I've worked mostly from my bedroom. My bedroom is on the second floor, as are Emily's bedroom and an empty room that used to belong to Mother. There's also another empty room on the second floor. That used to be Mother's sewing room. Each bedroom has its own bathroom.

Then there is the attic.

After the funeral Emily asked me if I would consider selling the house, and that question hurt me so deeply she hasn't asked again since.

Selling this house would be like abandoning a starving child in some wood. It wouldn't survive for long.

I throw on my coat and slip on my shoes and take Prairie out to the yard. She's there just a few minutes, dashing and rolling around in the new-fallen snow. The tip of her nose and much of her body are covered in white, which she quickly shakes off. She soon complies and comes inside.

In the kitchen I make some coffee and add milk.

Prairie pads over to the living room, and I follow. The furniture here is mismatched. Vintage items and antique pieces that have been in the house forever or that my mother collected over the years. Red. Velvet and gold trimmed. Hand carved and handmade. Floral oil paintings. Landscapes. Things commissioned with the design and the spirit of the house in mind. Empty crystal vases on side tables, in various styles— fluted, trumpet, urn, jug, pedestal, and more. In spring they're filled with fresh-cut flowers from the garden. In the winter I don't bother to store the vases, because they look pretty sitting there even without flowers, catching the sun's rays. I know that one day they will again be full of fresh water and pretty flowers I pick from my garden stroll.

There is a timelessness to the Chicago greystone. This house is antique elegant maximalism. Dark walls adorned with beautiful old things. Special things. My mother said that special objects had the ability to store magic and that being in their presence could transport you back in time.

Pretty and delicate things fit in with this house. Most of the original details of my home have been maintained as best as my family could over the years.

I don't remember my father. When I asked my mother whatever became of him, all she ever said was:

"This is a reverse fairy tale."

I didn't know what that meant for many years until I realized that in many fairy tales the real mother abandons her children. Here, I suppose Father abandoned us. Mother never loved anything or anyone beyond me, her work, and this house, as far as I knew, and I didn't mind that at all.

My father died before I could ever meet him, and the only thing he ever gifted me was a package that shocked my mother when she found it sitting on the front porch. I remember her shock when she opened the front door to find it sitting there.

"I can't believe he bought this thing," she said, standing there, her mouth hanging open. Her hands on her hips.

"Well," she finally said after a spell, "help me carry it, Bri."

We dragged the wooden contraption inside, slowly and carefully, making sure not to bump it against the walls. She directed me over to the living room, and it was there next to the fireplace we set it.

"What is that?" I asked, trying to catch my breath. Perplexed by how strange it looked. It was made of wood. There was one large wheel and another, a pedal, and gears.

Mother plucked a note that was affixed to it.

"'A spinning spindle for my daughter, Briar Rose. Love, Father.'"

She rolled her eyes and never mentioned him again.

Throughout the years, updates to this house have been to the kitchen and to the bathrooms and to things that require a technological refresh, like some light fixtures here and there. The quiet and thoughtful things, those have remained as untouched as possible, as much as this house requires.

While there is a lot of red in our home, there is a lot of green as well, particularly the library, which we call the green room. There are green velvet curtains and pictures of lush green landscapes.

Our ancestors came from Ireland, Mother said. She told me how they set about to make their ideal of a grand home, mined from their memories, of towering, majestic homes that dotted the verdant landscape. That's why many of Chicago's greystones look like castles in miniature, because those who came from Europe built something that reminded them of their homes.

The house features a turret, which is my bedroom. There are also gothic windows and a massive entry mirror, and the fireplaces are all original. There is feathered glass in some areas as well as lacewood trim in the doorways and more. Much of the intricate woodwork that sweeps through the house includes floral motifs, like roses.

I curl my feet underneath me on the sofa as I sip my morning coffee, and I turn back to my book. I read the lines:

"I think I am beginning to understand why grief feels like suspense. It comes from the frustration of so many impulses that had become habitual."

Prairie walks over to the window and stands, her two front paws on the windowsill.

I continue reading and turn the page. "Prairie, get down," I say, but she ignores me, which is unlike her.

She barks, a deep guttural bark, which startles me, jolts me from my pages. I set the book down and meet her at the window.

"What is it?"

I look out the window, and I see a man standing across the boulevard. He is looking directly at me.

A heavy feeling grows in my stomach.

I reach for the curtain and start pulling it closed.

Prairie continues barking, snapping at the window, trying to hop up on the glass.

"Come on, Prairie," I say calmly, trying to move her from the window. I don't want to bring any more attention to us, but she jumps again and again at the glass. I look again, just from the corner of my eyes, and he's still standing there, watching.

I want to hide, to cover this entire house in a curtain. "Prairie, please," I plead, and she finally moves away from the window so I can close the curtain.

I collapse on the floor with her. "That's not him," I say. Thinking about the man in the gray car. "I don't know who that is. I've never seen him before."

She's licking my chin, and I'm petting the top of her head. My hands feel shaky. "I know," I say. "I didn't like the feeling of being watched either."

Chapter 3

There's a soft hum, slow and steady.

I sit up on the sofa. I don't know how much time has passed.

I fell asleep.

Prairie stands.

I look to the window. The curtains are still drawn. I shake my head, walk to the kitchen, and pour myself a new cup of coffee and return to find Prairie's ears perked, little triangles atop her head, and her eyes directed toward one of the many radios on the built-in bookshelf.

I sit on the sofa, take a sip, and remember Mother talking to me about those radios.

"This was one of the last Zenith radios produced before World War II. A 1941 art deco, vintage Zenith tube radio," Mother said. "Your grandfather's business then transitioned to wartime production. Things were fine for a time, and then . . ." She paused and never finished that thought.

Both of my great-great-grandparents worked at Zenith many years ago. Mother took immense pride in that. She said that the money to build this house and the land surrounding it came from the radio business.

There are a lot of old things in this house collected by my great-grandfather and the family members who later took on the house. I never really found an interest in these old antiques when Mother would try to tell me their history.

At least now I can appreciate the value of these things. That radio that Prairie is staring down, I can now admire its wooden cabinet, black metal dial, and brass pointer that indicates the station.

I look closely at the face of the radio. It's an impossibility that it can be on. It would need to be plugged into an outlet, and the cord is wrapped behind it on the shelf.

The tone of the soft hum increases, and Prairie turns her head back to me as if asking, "How is that playing?"

I shrug and she faces the radio again.

"Don't pay it any attention, Prairie," I say. "There's got to be an explanation for it. Electrical? My exhaustion coupled with yours? Something else? Who knows?"

I hear a click, and the humming stops.

I lean back into the sofa and return to my book. "Keys and gates and locks and thorns," I say, turning another page. Then I pause. "Keys. There must be a key." If there's a key, then what does it open?

After Mother died, I opened every door. I opened every bathroom and every closet. I inspected every dusty and cobweb-covered corner of the basement. I took inventory of everything in the attic.

To my knowledge I had opened and inspected everything to make sure I knew what I was taking on, acquiring such a large home. I opened everything. And now I remember the trunk.

"I opened everything except the trunk," I say to Prairie.

Prairie lets out a soft snore from the rug a few feet in front of me.

The trunk. It's locked. Secrets are stored away in trunks. Isn't that how these things work?

I didn't think anything of it after Mother's funeral. I just assumed since the trunk was located with her sewing, maybe those were old projects she was working on—knit sweaters, gloves, and hats. But why lock it?

Maybe that's what Mother was trying to tell me with her last words. I could hire a locksmith. I rub my temples and groan. The thought of hiring a locksmith makes this all sound so official. I'm a homeowner. I didn't want to necessarily be a homeowner right now, and of this house?

I feel like Mother knew exactly where that key was, just like she knew exactly who that man is who parks his gray car across from our house and watches. He is never there long, just a few minutes. He is not one of the neighbors, and in all the years he has been doing this, he has never gotten out of the car.

And the man I saw earlier certainly wasn't the man from the gray car.

When I asked Mother about the man in the gray car, all she ever said was, "Maybe he's looking for something?" Then she'd change the subject.

Of course I was wary and fearful of the man.

"Mother, he could be dangerous! A killer!"

"There are dangerous things out there, but I assure you this man is not one of them," she'd say, brushing it aside. "Please ignore him."

Ignoring a stranger outside one's home never seems like a safe thing to do.

"In time," Mother would say, "he'll be gone."

In time.

In its time.

All things have their time.

She had all her little sayings about time and destiny.

Mother talked a lot about fate. Her voice was airy, bright, but contemplative too. Even though she'd talk about these big ideas, these concepts that I sometimes struggled to grasp, Mother always had a smile on her face, her features soft and serene as she talked about the past pressing into the present, and the stars above serving as witness to all.

I always worried. That's what I did, fixated and ruminated, sure that everything I'd worked so hard at—maintaining an apartment with Emily, managing my freelance writing workload—would all collapse on me, and I would find myself back in this house.

I guess it's one of Mother's sayings becoming prophecy: "What you focus on will grow."

I worried so much about my finances as a freelancer, about not being able to afford living on my own, that I would eventually have to come back and live at home, and here I am. Me worrying about what I didn't want brought that very thing to me.

I can hear Mother now: "You manifested coming back home because that's the signal you kept sending to the universe. The universe doesn't hear the negative charge. It only hears the positive. All it kept hearing again and again was 'come back home.' And here you are. This is why when you think and speak things, you must only think and speak what it is you do want. If you think about what you don't want, you may cause that very thing to happen."

I could see my mother seated beside me, a teacup cupped in both hands, blowing over the steam. A movie reel, a memory playing.

"Bri, you have to believe fully that what you want to happen is happening, right here and right now, not in some distant future. It's not about wanting the thing to happen. It's about feeling it's already occurred. That's how you manifest the thing that you want in life."

Energy. Vibration. Manifestation. Mother believed in all these things, and the more she did, the more I moved away from them, turning instead to science. I double-majored in journalism and science, and then I started working as a freelance science reporter, covering everything from NASA space launches to groundbreaking cancer treatments. I wanted to know how *things* worked, how *we* worked, how rules dictated so much of it all, but now, with grief, I'm starting to believe that maybe science doesn't have all the answers.

Maybe my mother was right to believe in some of these fantastical things.

My mind keeps taking me places, to past memories, and playing them back for me so clearly. How?

Like that memory of when I was a child, seated on the rug before my mother, my dolls scattered all around me. I must have been around seven.

Little me closed her eyes tight and then blurted out, "I want a new Barbie!"

She laughed and then took a sip from her teacup.

"My princess, not quite like that, but you'll see." She set the teacup on the side table, stood, and then met me on the rug. Mother lightly tapped the side of my head with the fingers of her right hand. Her nails were painted a vibrant red, matching the depths of the roses that grew all along our property.

"Your mind contains the universe, and you can do anything you want with your thoughts: create worlds, find answers to all of your questions, find solutions to your problems, more, and all with your thoughts." She tapped the side of her head.

In Mother's world, magic was very real. She'd conjure up a parking space right on Clark Street minutes before a Cubs game just by saying the words "Everything works out for us. We'll find a parking spot." And just like that, it'd happen, and an empty space would appear. She'd find five dollars, ten dollars, and more, in random jacket pockets at home, or looking down at the sidewalk along her stroll. Mother believed that the universe was always working in her favor, and she repeated this aloud to me regularly.

After the disease came, she fought it with science and her faith in the stars. It took time, but Mother eventually went into remission. We had some wonderful years, and in that time she was the most radiant she'd ever been. She'd laugh so hard and dance so much, she exuded an energy that felt otherworldly.

It was as if she'd been touched by divinity.

The cancer returned last winter, and as Emily, Daniel, and I opened Christmas presents in her living room, I caught Mother looking out the window, her face glowing against the holiday lights. She looked like an angel. There was a calm and a peace in her features that signaled she'd accepted that this was a part of her story.

Mother never believed the end was the end.

"Did you hear that?" I say to Prairie.

I sit up on the sofa. Prairie hops to her feet. Her ears and tail erect.

I listen as the heavy creaking groan of a gate swings open. It sounds like knives scraping against rusted metal.

There is now something scratching against the living room window. Prairie starts growling.

"Get away from there," I loud-whisper, and direct her over to me. She hops on the sofa. I set the mug of coffee down on the end table beside me. I take her in my arms. I hug her tight, all the while feeling a pinch beneath my rib cage. Then I remember the rosebush.

The rose garden.

Our flowers and trees.

They're all still there alive, but not.

Dormant in winter yet ready to burst and bloom again in spring. True beauty cannot die.

Prairie squirms in my hold and I shoosh her. "It's nothing," I say.

I think of our little greenhouse and how I've neglected it since Mother's death. That was Mother's special place; yes, she loved her sewing room, and restoring things, but it was in the greenhouse where she brought life, where she seemed happiest.

I've been unable to make my way there, but maybe soon. For now I admire it from the outside.

Keys and gates and locks and thorns, I think, and I am back in the memory of that dream. A slick black road, a black ribbon, stretching on into infinity. Off in the distance there are little squares and rectangles of white marble and white limestone. Markers of rest for some, distress for others.

The scraping and scratching against the window grow louder, more intense. It sounds like thousands of claws trying to break into my house.

I feel myself slipping, further, further down, into sleep or something else, and then I shout: "No!"

Prairie ducks her head and I kiss her.

"I'm sorry," I say. "I didn't mean to scare you. I was talking to the window."

My heartbeat quickens. I exist on the edges of fear and sorrow.

Prairie eyes me for a moment. "I miss her too," I say, "and I wish she were here so I could talk to her about my dreams."

"Keys and gates and locks and thorns." I repeat it like the chorus of a song. "A black road stretching on into infinity, and a pretty white ball gown splattered in blood."

Prairie raises her head.

"What?" I say. "But that's the truth. That's the next thing I see in my mind's eye." And because of that, I am worried. What is it that I'm truly seeing? An image? A dream? A memory? I close my eyes for a moment and take a deep breath.

I can smell the books on the shelves and the wood smells of this old house. Cedar. Oak. Pine. In the air too, there's a hint of roses, and I remember how the rose vines grew so rapidly last season, sharp thorns sprouting all along the plant. The green spindly arms spreading over the fence, eventually stretching up and across the house until they fanned across the windows.

On windy days and windy nights, I'd have to remind myself that the soft tapping that sounded like fingernails against glass were our rose vines. I'd look over at the windows and whisper a soft "Shhh" as if the rose vines would grow still to my command.

I gaze over to the window. I stand and pull back the curtain, just an inch, but see nothing but night breaking into day.

Time tricks us.

Keys. Gates. Locks. Thorns.

Roses.

A pretty white ball gown.

Nighttime roads and headstones.

The memory of a sound comes to me: an old song, an endless song, an eternal song, soft and buzzing.

I yawn and return to the sofa with Prairie. I breathe in slowly, counting—one, two, three, four—and exhaling—one, two, three, four—just like the hospice nurse showed me when she saw me having a panic attack near my mother's end.

"It's the fourfold breath," the nurse said.

I smiled between gasps, because my mother had tried teaching me it once, but I told her I didn't think meditation did anything. Yet there I was as she died, succumbing to the power of a meditative state in order to find peace in all the pain, and it worked.

I hear keys jangling in a keyhole, and that noise is like a castle bell announcing to all the kingdom's occupants that a great transformation is about to take place.

"Bri . . ." I hear Emily's booming voice in the foyer. She's returned home from work.

"I'm on the sofa," I say.

She shuffles and shifts, taking off her work boots and uniform. Emily changes into clean clothes in the foyer, leaving her blood- and brain matter–covered uniform stuffed in a plastic bag she will wash later. She will then go upstairs, take a shower, and change her clothes again.

When she enters the living room and finds me, she has a disappointed look on her face.

Prairie hops down to greet her.

"Did you at least try?" she asks, her hands on her hips.

"I slept some," I say, proud of myself.

I feel so small next to Emily. I am slender with long blond hair and fair skin. While Emily is tall and strong, with short brown hair. Her arms are thick and muscular from hours in the gym, lifting and pressing. She has always been athletic, having played college volleyball and lacrosse, while I've avoided all physical activities, except maybe helping Mother in the garden or going for long walks or hikes.

I adjust myself on the sofa, sitting straight. "What about you? How was work?"

She's chewing the inside of her mouth; then she says, "Another woman was found."

I feel a tightness in my throat. "Another one?"

Emily shakes her head, and I know what that means. Boundaries. It's difficult for her to talk about what she sees at work. "Just be careful when you're out there by yourself, Bri."

I nod and don't say anything else. I remember the woman in the alley by the house last year. It's awful to think that something like that happened so close.

Emily's job demands that she be strong. In her work she's rushed people of all sizes down flights of stairs. She's hopped over fences and helped to lift a turned-over car from a victim. Her strength is that of a half dozen people, I'd imagine. And as a paramedic, she's seen more death than I can imagine.

"I was just asleep," I say.

She squints, presses her lips together, and turns her head. "Really?"

I nod. "Yes."

"You're not a very good liar, Bri."

I laugh. "I really did sleep . . . some."

"All right," she says, not entirely convinced, I'm sure. "Bad dreams still?" she asks.

I give her a weak smile as my answer.

She looks down, as if searching for the words to say, when there's a loud bang against the front door.

Prairie barks.

Emily flinches.

"What the hell was that?" she asks, already heading to the front door to inspect the source of the noise.

Keys and gates and locks and thorns, nighttime roads, and headstones, I say in my head.

Maybe it's a door that's always been there but just needs to be opened, I think, *like the trunk.* But opening the trunk doesn't answer the question of who the man is in the gray car, or who the man was standing across the street last night.

There are questions, but there must be answers too, yes. To open the door, but better yet still, to open a portal, and not just within a house, but within ourselves, takes bravery to relinquish all we believe is real about flesh and blood and life and death.

I press a hand against my head. I'm starting to think like Mother. To believe in the great beyond, to believe in ghosts, something more.

The door opens and then closes, and Emily returns. She's shaking her head. "There's nothing there."

"Did you make sure the door's locked?"

"Yeah, Bri. I always make sure the door is locked."

I didn't hear it click. "Can you check again?"

Her eyes are wide, and she opens her mouth to say something, pauses, and then says, "Okay . . ."

I hear her in the foyer. I hear the doorknob turn and nothing else. "It's locked!" she shouts.

When she returns, she asks, "Are you all right?"

"Yeah, it's just . . . you know, with what's been happening on the news . . ."

"Right."

The house begins to groan, and as always, only Prairie and I hear it.

I wonder now what my belief in science this entire time has done, because I am hearing things. I am seeing things. I am experiencing things that I cannot explain, but I know they are real.

Some houses seem to forever have been haunted, but this house became active after my mother died.

Why?

Emily plops down on the sofa next to me. "Daniel said he messaged you, but you didn't answer. He figured you were asleep."

"I'll message him later after he wakes up. I didn't sleep well."

Emily yawns. The daytime is when she sleeps. "Maybe try melatonin or chamomile tea?"

Or warm milk, or meditating before bed, or a different million sorts of drinks or pills or tonics or potions or remedies to encourage sleep, but there's no encouraging sleep when the dreams and the house keep me awake.

Do I tell her anything about the wallpaper moving or the music playing or the man across the street? No matter what I say, she will worry. These aren't just nightmares. It's like I'm awake, but not, with my eyes open living in that nightscape. And sometimes when I pull that fairy dust with me into the awake world, I don't feel like it's a dream. I feel like what I'm seeing is really happening.

"I feel like there's something wrong with my mind," I say.

Emily reaches over to the end table and picks up the book I was reading. She reads the title aloud: "*A Grief Observed.*"

She looks at me with sad eyes. "There's nothing wrong with your mind. It's grief. You're grieving, Bri. Rest will help. That's your only job right now. Rest."

I wonder whether it's something more than grief. Maybe this house is more than a house; maybe it's a dream house, one in which people are meant to sleep for a time and wake for another. It all feels like nighttime here, no matter whether the sun shines.

We all exist with this greater possibility nestled inside us. We look up and face the stars, that sparkling sheet of wonder before us, and we ignore the miracle of it. We turn away from reality, and we ignore the messages brought to us in sleep.

Maybe we are all sleeping. Maybe we were all cast to a deep enchanted slumber by some wicked, cruel, and envious magical being.

Death and grief. This house and me. And the women popping up in the news whose murders are dotted by questions that have many of us worried, me included.

Emily adjusts her body so she is facing me on the sofa. "I'm serious. Rest, Bri."

I take a deep breath and exhale. "I'm resting. I'm just . . . reading."

"Are you writing anything right now?"

"Just researching an article."

She chews the inside of her mouth and nods. "About?"

"Dreams."

"Okay." She's nodding, looking up to the ceiling. "Did an editor assign that?"

I scratch my head. "No, I just . . . wanted to learn about what our brains do to us when we are grieving."

She's talking, but I'm not really listening anymore. I'm thinking about the house. My mother. The music the house keeps playing, the man outside, the man in the gray car, keys and gates and locks and thorns and what it all means.

Chapter 4

Their golden hair.

Their pretty voices. It all spins in my head. Spin. Spin. Spin. I've seen the spinning machine. A long time ago. It reminds me of a spiral. Of time. Kept in a tower. Kept in a house. Made out of wood. Metal. Some gears. Mechanical parts. A wheel. Another. Feed in some thread. There we go. Watch it spin. Watch it move. Round. Round. Round. Like a life stuck in a loop.

Their lives are trapped in a twirl.

Until they meet me. I am their dream.

"You dreamt me," I whisper to Lilly. I am seated beside the window. I am reading an article on my phone. I am waiting. It is late at night. Lilly and I are in a house. A pretty little house. I am waiting.

Sometimes these things take time.

"Do you like this house, Lilly?" I look up from my phone and admire the living room. She is resting.

I answer, anticipating what she is thinking. "You're right. The peeling plaster. The flaking paint. It must have been a beautiful home. Once."

She never told me her name, but I know it's Lilly. I know many things.

"I'm sorry I mentioned Briar," I say. "It was insensitive of me." Women don't like when I mention other women.

Insensitive, yes. I couldn't help it. All I think about is Briar. Her past. Her present. Her future. I went to see her yesterday. She's so pretty. Prettier than new-fallen snow.

I want to know all her timelines. I want to dream Briar's dreams. I will soon. I know that.

I close my eyes tight. I picture the nighttime world and Briar there. One day. Soon. It's close. So close.

"They all sleep in glass coffins," I say.

The wind outside howls.

Lilly remains quiet.

I open my eyes.

My thoughts drift back to Briar. I think about how close we are to her. My mind begins to paint the picture of her. Golden hair. Luminescent skin. Sparkling eyes. A voice that sounds like music. More. A perfect princess.

She has many gifts.

They all do.

Six gifts and then a curse. That's how this works.

Briar. She's special. She originates from the story. The first story. I don't usually get too hung up on things like bloodlines and legacies, but this one? This is it. She is it. A storybook princess.

"Lilly, you must be cold," I say. She makes a soft groaning sound.

Sometimes it takes a few minutes for them to see.

My father told me. He said, "Mal, it takes time for the spinning to stop."

His father told him that, and his father and his father.

Father was an important man. Father did important things. Father taught me how to do these things. Father taught me that we all spin.

It was in Father's basement. Candles flickering. Him in his black suit with that white apron over his clothes. Him leaning over that large metal table, a knife in his hand when he told me: "It's when they finally go to sleep—that's when they belong to you."

The woman on the table didn't move. She'd never move again.

"How does she belong to you?" I asked Father.

Father put the knife down, wiped his hands on a towel, and walked around to the head. He placed his hands on the metal table and looked down at the woman. She was naked. Her skin bluish. Her long dark hair down past her shoulders.

"Even after I remove all of her insides, strip her of her flesh, and mount her bones back together again, she's always going to be mine. I have my way of killing, and you will have yours. We are legends, and each woman we kill will be pinned next to our name forever. There's no separating us from them. You have your fairy tale, and I have mine."

"What is your fairy tale?" I asked him.

He picked up the knife, looked around the chamber, and smiled.

"Lilly," I whisper, hoping she awakens soon.

A soft, watery rasp emerges from her throat.

They look so beautiful when they sleep. I help them. This is what I do.

I see them. They see me. Sometimes they like me. Oftentimes they don't. I really wish they liked me, because I gift them eternity. More.

Yes, there's crying. Screaming. Kicking. Sometimes biting.

Families searching.

And then the great hunt.

Posters: *Have you seen her?*

Phone calls: *Where is she?*

Newsreels.

Newspaper headlines.

News reports.

Documentaries.

Books.

Stories shared.

I'm there watching all of it.

I keep them alive, forever, or as long as someone remembers them.

They are the ghost stories that keep you up at night.

The job is sleep. I enforce sleep. They must sleep. I must do this for them. When I see them sleep, it's like pinning a butterfly still flapping its wings to a board. I capture them. I pin them. Collect them. They are mine.

They become part of my story.

I shush them as they settle down to rest, like Lilly here.

Me: Shhh. Shhh. Shhh. In their ear.

Them: Kick. Kick. Kick. Like little babies do.

They bite. They cry. I remind them that is not how pretty, perfect princesses behave.

I like to touch their hair throughout. Tell them they'll be all right as I dig my nose into the nape of their neck and take a deep breath.

I can almost smell the forest in all of them.

They get mad at me. It is okay. I understand. It takes some time to adjust. In and out. A flickering. This world. The others.

When they finally fall asleep, I feel so good.

I'm with them all night.

When the sun rises in the morning, I go to the bathroom. I urinate. I wash my hands. I brush my teeth. I shower. I wash with one bar of soap; starting at the top of my head, I lather down to my toes. I rinse. I repeat this three times. For my first rinse I like to turn the water on as hot as I can stand. Some days I can stand more. Some days I cannot. The last rinse I use the coldest water temperature I can tolerate. Sometimes my teeth will chatter when I stand in the cold water. When I have completed my shower, I step out of the bathtub and dry myself with a white towel. Then I get dressed. It is important to wear a uniform. Father wore very fine clothes. A dark jacket. Dark slacks.

I wear a similar uniform. Father liked very fine things.

There's an energy. An electricity. A vibration. People ask. Why so many? Why so concentrated? One, sure. Two? Maybe. Three. Four. More. What's in the soil? Maybe it's the land up there in the Midwest that causes that behavior.

Grisly murders. I can almost read the headlines.

John Wayne Gacy. Richard Speck. Nathan Freudenthal Leopold Jr. and Richard Albert Loeb. William Heirens, the Lipstick Killer. Al Capone. Charlie Starkweather. Ed Gein. John. Kate. Elvira and John Bender. The Bloody Benders. The Ripper Crew. H. H. Holmes. Me. More.

All of us call the Midwest home. A lethal city in a lethal land that trapped travelers and swallowed them whole.

I am anxious. This is taking so long this time.

"Lilly!" I snap my fingers.

She does not move.

I step away from the window. I hear the crunch of broken glass under my shoe. I raise my foot and see a layer of tiny sharp shards sticking out from beneath my sole. A breeze moves across the house. Broken windows and broken doors. The pungent smell of mold rises and strikes my nose.

"You know, my darling," I say to Lilly. "This entire city, in and out, it's a horror story."

I remove the black leather gloves from my coat pocket and start slipping them on.

"Did you know that in 1899 Henry Blake Fuller called Chicago a 'hideously makeshift horror.' This was long after the Chicago fire. Many thought the fire that nearly destroyed the city was divine retribution."

I look at my gloved hands and then make fists, enjoying the feel of the material around my fingers.

"The fire didn't get rid of any of us."

I remember how hot those flames fanned. I have lived here a long time. I like my home, and I like my routine, and I like to walk and drive and watch and wait.

That is how today began. I walked. I watched. I waited. I drove and drove. Sensing and feeling, and then I saw her. Golden hair. Fair skin. Like Briar, but not Briar. I offered to help her carry her groceries. I thought that very nice and kind.

She said, "No, thank you." Very cold. Tight lipped. Eyes pulled back.

I kept walking alongside her. I offered to help her again, and then she got mad, and then I hit.

I hit and hit again.

Too many hits on the face.

We left the groceries there. No need for those anymore.

Blood drizzling down her face. Bright-red dots falling onto the snow. In the car I drove fast, searching, until I found this house.

People say words like "violence" and "obsession," but many fail to realize that for some of us this is a duty. A divine calling.

I am here because my father did this. I am here because my father's father did this. I am here because we have always been, and we will always be, and this is what I must do. Each of us has different skills. I am called to them, and they are called to me, and we can never sever our connection. Them and I, and I and them, and our dedication to sleep.

To dream.

To fall away.

I help them.

I help them to fall away into that nighttime world.

That is where they are. That is where they will stay. That is the way it will always be.

I move toward Lilly. "You and me, we'll be together forever, my dear. My princess."

I study her features and can feel she's tense. "Again, I'm sorry I mentioned Briar."

Lilly remains silent.

I kneel and caress Lilly's cheek. I can sense her pulse slowing, fading.

Me capturing them. I set them in their glass coffins. Under the light of the stars and the moon, and once they awaken in that nighttime world, they are mine forever, and I will hear them scream and they will be spoken about, whispered about.

They will be legends. They will be stories that are soft-spoken warnings.

"Lilly," I say, and I hear the wind rip across the roof. It makes the same sound as Lilly did when I wrapped my hands tightly around her neck.

I stand and admire her in her brilliance. In her deathly splendor. She will be grand.

All of them will be greater in death than they ever were in life. In their sleep. That is what I gift them. They will never end.

I thought about Briar as I stared into Lilly's eyes. I thought about Briar as Lilly begged me to let her go. I thought about Briar and Briar's house and how I often go there and watch from the outside. I admire the stately home Briar's great-great-grandfather built for her, chosen from the pages of a storybook. I picture Briar standing there, in her tower. Waiting to live. Waiting to die. Waiting for me.

Some people think it's a pattern stretched back through time.

They like to analyze in their books. I like to read what they say about us in their books.

They use words and phrases like "murderers," "organized," "disorganized," "seduce victim," "take control," "cold," "lust," "preserve," "violence that is measured and coldly controlled."

They think they know all the things there are to know.

I return to my phone. I search the "Murder Accountability Project."

I click on "murder clusters," then "county clusters."

A screen pops up:

State: IL

County: Cook

Murder Group: 17031280

Homicides: 51

Weapon: Strangulation

I find an article. I smile. I click. I read.

Chicago's Unsolved Female Strangulations

Nearly two dozen DNA samples from a series of female homicides that have occurred in Chicago since the early 2000s have been analyzed, according to a representative from the Chicago Police Department. Results do not confirm that a serial killer is behind the over 50 strangulation cases.

None of the DNA samples cross match to one another, and they also do not match any criminal profiles in the FBI database.

Founded by Thomas Hargrove, the Murder Accountability Project uses research, analysis, and an algorithm to determine patterns in homicides along geographic areas. Hargrove's research has helped identify several serial killers to date.

The Murder Accountability Project alerted CPD to a potential serial killer operating in the city in 2017. Yet no immediate initiatives were made by the department to investigate. Two years later, the Murder Accountability Project released a report highlighting key similarities in many of the murders.

According to the Murder Accountability Project, the cluster of unsolved female homicides in Chicago is the largest in modern history, with presentable patterns. Almost all the women were murdered outside or in buildings that were abandoned. This indicates that the killer and the victims did not know one another.

Most of the women killed were on Chicago's South and West Sides, with a greater concentration along the north-to-south pattern along South Indiana Avenue in the city's Bronzeville neighborhood.

Hargrove does not believe that these 51 women were killed by 51 separate people. He believes most of these women were killed by someone who has killed before.

Community activist Raymond Rodgers says the longer the investigation is delayed, the more difficult it will be to make an arrest.

"We are leaving a lot of people hurting. These women were people's mothers, sisters, cousins, aunties, more. We have to do better, Chicago," Rodgers said.

The books have told me that "a serial killer is a person who has killed three or more people. Long stretches of time between killings also indicate a serial killer is operating."

That is what they called Father: a serial killer. America's first serial killer, in fact.

The newspapers, the media, the police, they don't want to believe that I am real, because believing that I am real brings on a new fear. It tells people that there are people like me who do horrible things and that those horrible acts bring people like me pleasure. They do.

What will bring me more pleasure is Briar. Briar and me in the nighttime. One day soon. I put my phone away, and I listen to what sounds like the wind, but it's the sound of Lilly fading.

I am here and I sense Lilly's pulse stop.

I am here and I see Lilly's ghost materialize in the corner of the room.

I am here and I see Lilly's ghost mouth open in shock as she sees her body on her back on the living room floor of this abandoned home.

I am here as I see Lilly's ghost scream. Her ghost hands pulling at her ghost hair.

I stand and I feel so warm inside. So good.

I am smiling.

I extend my hand, but ghost Lilly is screaming, screaming.

"It's time to go," I tell her.

Screaming Screaming Screaming Screaming.

I take Lilly's ghost hand and I feel her shaking against me.

"It's time to go to our nighttime world."

As soon as I touch her, we cross and find ourselves here. Surrounded by thick dark woods.

Lilly's screams echo across the treetops.

Screaming Screaming Screaming Screaming.

She is so afraid.

I shush her. "You're another story. Another legend. Another warning that will be told." She should feel honored, I think. It makes me mad they don't realize how special they are now.

Her face is twisted in pain, but it is no longer caked in dried blood and bruised and swollen from my hitting.

She looks up at the forever black sky.

Screaming Screaming Screaming Screaming.

Her screams are so beautiful. It's like an alarm bell, awakening the others in their glass coffins.

All their screams erupt.

My beautiful missing and murdered. My princesses.

Chapter 5

TIME: 10:00 a.m.
DATE: Monday, December 4

A cloud of dust erupts from atop *The Encyclopedia of Chicago*. I set the duster down, reach into the pocket of my bathrobe, pull out a dust mask, and place it over my face. I bought a box of them before moving in, and an impressive amount of cleaning supplies. I really believed for a few minutes that I was going to give this house a full scrubdown. That's yet to really happen.

In grief, we often have these lucid moments, points of clarity so overwhelming, and mine was that I was going to clean and dust and polish this house new. Once I brought those cleaning supplies into the foyer, the blue window cleaner and yellow sponges and new mop and broom and dustpan, the more the immensity of this house and the grip of my mother's death stunted me. I set the cleaning supplies aside, still in the plastic bags, and that's where they remain, in the foyer.

Even if I wanted to fully remodel the home, I couldn't. I can barely afford to live here as is, and the quick math I did in my head after my mother died calculated that I barely make enough as a freelancer to pay for the house's yearly taxes, groceries, and keeping the lights on, at minimum, and the heat low, very low, in winter. There's barely any money for anything else.

I can hear Daniel now. "What if I moved in? My lease is up soon. I can help you with the upkeep."

I know he means well, but I worry. Daniel is just so nice. What if after taking on all this responsibility with me, it just winds up pushing him away and I lose him? I can't lose someone else, especially him. He, Emily, and Prairie are all I have.

I live in an area on Chicago's South Side occupied by millionaires, the exteriors of their homes well kept, their lawns manicured. Their interiors remodeled every few years, and yet here I sit in a crumbling mansion.

We know what it's like to look at something and tell ourselves: "That thing must have been so beautiful once." That's my house, and it feels like my entire life right now.

I do what I can. In some ways I have embraced that the house is decaying, and I am decaying with it, because that's the natural course of a life. There's just one direction we move toward, and that is toward the end.

When I die, I will be the last of the Thornes to have lived in this house built for our family, by our family, with instructions that it primarily be occupied by our family. What will become of it after I'm gone?

I do not know.

For now, I'm focusing on this blue poofy duster at the end of this yellow wand. I tell myself I can do this. I can complete at least this small task.

I repeat in my head over and over, "I am dusting the bookshelves." Hoping that between this back-and-forth rhythm and the hypnotic voice in my head, I can finish at least something that I started.

Prairie thinks I'm playing with her. I dust, take one step to the side, dust, take another. She is following me, hopping along. I listen as her little paws rise and fall on the carpet as she follows me. The duster sweeps back and forth across Austen and Baldwin, Brontë and Dickens, Gilman and Hawthorne; clumps of gray material float off from their spines, down onto the floor, and I groan, thinking now that next I'll need to sweep and vacuum.

Even this small chore is exhausting, but it gives me something to do, something to focus on. This is a way to move out of my room, away from staring out the window, lost in thought, and placing my energy into this house that's begging for attention.

I am too tired to put up new paint, or to hang new wallpaper. I do not have enough money to purchase new light fixtures. Or to repair some of the chipping tile in the bathrooms. I do what I can, and Daniel and Emily have promised to help as well.

The light seems to dim all around me. I pause. I pull the duster back and hold it at my side. I inspect the edges of what's within my sight—rows of books, spines of dark grays and blues, reds and yellows, more.

But they're all in shadow.

It's as if something massive stands behind me. I slowly lower my hand and notice now Prairie's movements have stopped. She is seated beside me, her body pressed into my leg.

A floorboard creaks behind me, as if someone is shifting their weight from one leg to the other. My breath escapes and my thoughts go to the gate, to the front door. Did I lock everything? Did someone get in? My hands are shaking and I'm scared to breathe, to move, to do anything.

Another groan of the floorboard and I close my eyes tight and bite my tongue, scared to make a noise, hoping that if there's someone behind me, they will just keep moving, that they will leave me alone and take whatever they need.

I hear a car horn beep outside, and I open my eyes, and when I do, I once again see the bookshelf covered in light. The only shadow is mine.

I drop the duster, exhale, and spin around. There is no one there. My legs stop working and I collapse onto the floor, my hands clutching at my racing heart. Prairie licks my fingers.

"I'm so tired," I say, patting her face. "I'm just so tired."

For a long time I believed the things I experienced in this house growing up were all wrapped around my mother's fanciful imaginings. How could any of what she believed be real? The bending of time? The power to manifest things? Ghosts? More.

What my mother spoke about, things like frequency and vibration, feeling and the power of positively charged words, how could any of that be real?

But now I wonder, Were these sights and sounds manifestations of grief, or had it all always been something else?

This house was designed by my great-great-grandfather Philip. His parents came to the Chicagoland area from Ireland long ago, drawn by the prospect of work, specifically the massive amounts of labor needed to dig the Illinois and Michigan Canal.

Great-Great-Grandfather Philip grew up in a white farmhouse in the woods outside the greater Chicagoland area. The story goes that his mother, Talia, who was originally from France, would read him fairy tales and tell him stories about the great castles in Europe. Philip then promised he would set out to build a castle of his own, and so he did, building this grand home on the South Side of Chicago, and that is where my American family has lived ever since.

I look down to Prairie and remove my dust mask.

"I think that's enough dusting for today."

A house is always listening, and a house always expects one to keep their promise.

The morning of my mother's funeral, I stood in her now-empty bedroom. I felt the house vibrating behind me, and I remembered my mother's desperate plea, that I take this house on, never sell it, never abandon it, but that I live in it too until I died.

I turned my head up to the ceiling and said, "I promise to never leave you," and I meant it.

Mother said there were portraits hung in the house once, ones taken throughout the years of all the family members who lived here. Those were hung in the hallway, but that tradition was stopped sometime in the 1950s. Those portraits, I was told, are still in this house, stored in the attic. One day I plan to sift through them, to look back at faces that will look at me, a strange sort of exercise in time travel, someone from the past looking back at me while I look to them.

I wonder sometimes about the power of a picture or an antique object. Does it have the ability to transport us back in time? Or do those items have the ability to transport themselves into our present?

Mother says that the portraits were taken down because artistic tastes turned to nature scenes over the years. Something about that sounded strange. Why not just keep the family portraits up and add those new paintings elsewhere? The living room? Dining room? Foyer?

Things inside of our homes change, just like things outside of them.

Over the years the neighborhood shifted and changed in parts, like all neighborhoods in Chicago. On some blocks not too far from here, grocery stores shuttered, homes foreclosed. People moved in and people moved out, but mostly people moved out. Entire blocks went abandoned—houses with sinking front porches, weatherworn siding, broken windows, or glass panes completely missing, just dark holes looking in or out of a house.

Many houses were demolished. What remained in parts were ghost gardens. The sprigs of perennials shooting up from the ground each spring, from plants that were once tenderly planted down the walkway leading toward someone's front door. There they grow today, in a line that leads nowhere.

I live close to the world-renowned University of Chicago, and the Midway Plaisance. I walk Prairie to Jackson Park each morning, and there we linger, walking along the park lagoon, the Columbia Basin. In spring the cherry blossoms will put on their show with their darling blooms, little pink pom-poms.

The entire area is a remnant of the 1893 World's Columbian Exposition, and I like walking there because it's like I'm going back in time, just knowing that it was once crowded by a mass of people from all over the world.

There's a lot of history in Jackson Park. Just like there's a lot of history in this house.

There's also terror and sadness here, in the number of women found murdered nearby, which the media mentions fleetingly before moving on to the next story that isn't really a story, just a distraction.

Emily and Daniel have been called to homicide sites while on the job, and they've encountered many of these murdered women. I can't imagine what it must be like for them to come upon a crime scene like that. Neither of them talks about work or what they see there, but I know it weighs on them deeply, and maybe that's why we all understand each other so well, our dealings with grief and death.

I shove the duster inside the cleaning closet, and then Prairie follows me into the living room. I sink into the sofa, and she sits on the rug, facing me.

"It's something I should finish," I say, thinking of the article I had been researching, but I still don't quite have enough to tell a story, and I'm still not quite sure what story it is I want to tell.

I want to talk about grief. I want to talk about how grief changes our brains. I want to talk about sleep disturbances and what causes that and what those bring, including the disconnect of time, because that is so much a part of what is happening to me. I am both gaining and missing hours when I slip into these time warps, and is that a normal occurrence of grief? I still don't know.

Mother used to say that if we allow it, the past will seep into the present. I wonder what that means, exactly. Mother used to read a lot of works by new age thinkers. People like Marcus Aurelius, Earl Nightingale, Neville Goddard, Esther Hicks, Florence Scovel Shinn, Wayne Dyer, more. She liked to quote them:

"The way to get rid of darkness is with light"—Dr. Joseph Murphy.

"Time is conditioned by man's conception of himself"—Neville Goddard.

"Time is a sort of river of passing events, and strong is its current; no sooner is a thing brought to sight than it is swept by, and another takes its place"—Marcus Aurelius.

Mother spoke of light and dark, time and dreams, and she believed in things like the spiral of infinity and the wonder of impossibility. So when I asked her what she thought about the growing number of women found murdered in Chicago, she said: "What we are seeing right now is the repetition of a pattern, and the only way to stop a pattern is to break it."

I didn't know what that meant, but I made sure to make note of it for later.

Prairie barks, a deep guttural bark.

"We're not going outside yet."

Her head turns this way and that.

It was my fault. I said the magic word: "Outside."

"Later," I say, and then I think of Emily's warning to be cautious when I go outside.

I stand and motion for Prairie to follow me. We walk to the library. There are books and papers of Mother's that I can reference for my article.

Mother was fascinated by ghost stories. I'd often catch her reading things like *Haunted Chicago: Famous Phantoms, Sinister Sites, and Lingering Legends* by Tom Ogden; *The Ghosts of Chicago: The Windy City's Most Famous Haunts* by Adam Selzer; *Haunts of the White City: Ghost Stories from the World's Fair, Chicago* by Ursula Bielski; and more.

I thought my mother's interest in ghosts was silly, but now I wish she were here so I could talk to her about them.

My mother didn't really tell me what her favorite Chicago hauntings were, but it was easy to guess. In the library, she had an entire shelf dedicated to Archer Avenue. There were manila folders full of documents and pictures. When I asked her why she was so fascinated with a single road, she laughed.

"Archer Avenue is an energy center. A thin place. Just like this house. Archer Avenue doesn't obey the rules of our reality." She paused, her eyes turned to the ceiling, and then she said, "Great-Great-Grandfather learned a lot about the power of thin spaces growing up in that farmhouse deep in the woods off Archer Avenue. He took much of what he learned and brought it here. This house is a thin place too."

"What's a thin place?" I asked.

"It's a place where one can walk in both worlds, here and there. The veil. It's a space where both of those worlds are knitted loosely, or tightly, depending on what you want to see. There's flexibility and freedom to slip into either reality."

From the corner of my eye I think I see something. A streak of color. A swirl? A ribbon? A piece of thread?

Red, then white, and then it's gone. It happens so fast there's not even time to question it, or to be afraid.

I brush it from my mind, because anything else is a distraction.

I move along the bookshelves and remove one of the Archer Avenue manila folders. I open one, and then feel the grains of dust between my fingertips and flip through the pages, not knowing what it is I am searching for, until I find a black-and-white photograph, with old wooden shops on either side. It looks like the main road in a frontier town, hand-painted signs, and horse hitching posts. The lens is focused on the road, covered in dirt and snow, and off into the background it's bright white, as if a snowstorm is approaching, or maybe it's already passed.

On the bottom right-hand corner of the picture, there is writing in black ink, swooping letters that read:

Archer Avenue, 1885.

There's a sheet of notebook paper with my mother's swirling cursive handwriting in blue ink.

Archer Avenue is an ancient road, the route used by the original Indigenous population that lived in the area long before Europeans arrived. Chicago operates on a grid system. If you know directionally where you are—north, south, east, or west—and especially if you know that Lake

Michigan is east, you can practically never get lost in this city. Well, unless you find yourself on one of these diagonal roads: South Chicago Avenue, Vincennes Avenue, Elston Avenue, Ogden Avenue, Grand Avenue, Milwaukee Avenue, Clybourn Avenue, and Lincoln Avenue.

I turn past more pages, finding another torn sheet of notebook paper with my mother's writing:

> There is, in Chicago, a street of endless dreariness, a street curiously uninteresting to the casual glance and more and more uninteresting to the lengthening look ... It was one of the earliest streets of the city, stretching away from the center and far out toward the wilderness, Robert Shackleton, The Book of Chicago, 1910.

My mind repeats those words: "Away from the center and far out toward the wilderness." And what was in that deep wilderness along Archer Avenue? Does it remain there today?

I find another sheet of notebook paper with my mother's handwriting.

> A number of people have died along Archer Avenue, by accident, and have been murdered on that street, murdered elsewhere, or dumped there. It's a strange road with even stranger stories. It's because of that reputation that Archer Avenue has also been called one of the most haunted roads in America, and perhaps the world.

> Besides the numerous cemeteries along the route and the deep and dense forests along either side of it, there's also the abandoned Old Joliet Prison, where Al Capone once was held, the Saint James at Sag Bridge Church, the oldest operating church in northeast Illinois, and more along Archer Avenue.

> Is all of the activity because of Red Gate Woods?

"Red Gate Woods?" I say aloud and make note of it.

Until her death, my mother held a fascination with this road.

She chose to have hospice care in this house because she wanted to die in the home her ancestors built, the very ones who started their life in this country out there by Archer Avenue and would later move into the city limits.

I was with my mother at that last doctor's appointment, where they told her they had exhausted all their efforts. As we exited the building, my mother said, "I want to die in my home, in a thin place."

As her illness progressed, her conversations would become more focused on fanciful things. She would speak of sleep and dreams and forests and castles protected by what she called "those that were dead, but not really dead."

In her sleep, Mother would speak of specters that glided across the treetops, trolls who'd emerge from around creeks and streams, gnomes that seemed to pop out from behind trees, and fairies who magically appeared near flowers and bushes.

"Spirits," Mother would say. "They're all spirits, and what is a spirit but energy? Some of that energy is earthbound. Not all energy is good and kind," she'd remind me. "Not all magical things vibrate with wonder. There are things that stand beside the trees watching us, waiting for us to be distracted, by the sound of the breeze cutting through the leaves or the rumble of a passing car. Things that have always been and things that will always be. Those things hate us. They want us dead and gone. Don't forget, Bri, the book of a fairy dream. A key. A dress and dancing shoes. Listen to the music. Or it'll come for you too."

It became more and more difficult to follow her words as her illness progressed.

I remember the smells of home hospice, the stringent sickly-sweet smells from her pain medicine and ointments that kept her hands moisturized, the hint of urine that'd linger in the air from when I'd change her drainage bag, and the milky, chalky chemical scent of those nutritional shakes, which were all she could keep down there at the end.

I remember the hospital bed that was installed, and I remember the steady whirring of the oxygen machine. What I remember worse were her cries those last few nights, the pain that clamped down as the cancer spread and ate her. That's what cancer does; it's a monster that eats our loved ones' insides until their bodies shut down.

Her cries still wake me up at night. They won't leave me alone.

The house remembers and plays back memories.

I'm sitting now on the floor in front of the bookshelf, reading through more of my mother's handwritten notes. I run my finger across the page, feeling the indentation of her letters. Missing someone I will never see again is the greatest pain I've ever felt.

In time I feel my eyelids growing heavy. My contacts feel dry, and each time I blink, it stings. I should take them out, but instead I just keep reading, turning pages, and then I close my eyes for just one minute.

When I open my eyes again, I am in my mother's room, and she is in her bed with layers of blankets on top of her.

She is holding my hand.

"Only you can stop this." Her voice is so faint, a song fading. "You're the last one. Stop the pattern. The attic. The portraits. The trunk. Roses . . ."

I smell it. The air growing thick with the air of roses in full bloom. I look out and now we're in our yard. Mother and I are standing among the rosebushes and admiring the tall vines, tangled with one another and stretching over a collection of trellises in the yard.

"The rose is the key," Mother says.

"What key?" I ask, and then I am awake.

Emily is standing over me. "Bri, what are you doing?"

I awake, finding myself on the floor in front of the bookshelf. Papers are scattered all around me.

I sit up and rub my neck, which feels stiff. "I was reading here and must've fallen asleep."

"Did you need some help?" she asks, reaching for a black-and-white photograph, but I stop her.

"No, it's okay. I've got it," I say, still in that foggy, dreamy state. I hear my mother's voice still, telling me about the rose key.

Emily watches as I gather up some pictures and papers and stuff them back into folders.

"I'm heading out. I'm spending some time with Dana before heading in to work," she says. "I ordered you a pizza. I figured you'd be too tired to make something."

I nod. "Right." I try to think of something to say, anything, but my thoughts feel so disconnected. Then I just stick with work, because that's easy. "How was work yesterday?"

"Good." She scratches behind her ear. "Well, better. Not like the day before," she says.

"Do you want to talk about it?" I offer.

She gives me a weak smile. "Maybe one day." She sighs. "Also, Daniel says you haven't messaged him in days. He's starting to freak out that you're ghosting him."

"Two days?" I say.

"Yeah, that's enough days. He's worried, Bri. Just message him. He misses you."

I'm scared to message him. I'm scared for him to see me like this. I don't feel like I'm getting better. I feel like I'm getting worse. Isn't the death of someone like a car crash, and time is just you walking away from it? But I don't feel like I've walked away from it. I feel like I'm sitting inside the burning car.

I miss him too, a lot, but I don't want him to hear me, or even see me like this.

Emily places a hand on my shoulder. "Please eat something when the food gets here, and please try to get some rest." Her uniform is clean. Gray shirt. Dark-blue slacks and a black belt. A blue jacket with a patch on the right shoulder with American and Chicago flags, and on the other shoulder, a red emblem: CHICAGO PARAMEDIC. FIRE DEPARTMENT. In the foyer she'll pull on her black boots.

Her eyes follow as I stuff a manila folder back into the bookshelf. "Are you working on something?"

"Yeah, still researching this article."

I want to tell Emily about the dreams, about the nightmares, about the . . . waking dreams, about my mother and the visions of a girl in white, how I seem to pull the essence of that nighttime world with me into the waking world, but she'll only worry more. She'll only say I need to sleep, maybe even talk to someone, because my reality is becoming distorted, which it is.

I hear the wind brush against the living room windows. I'm frightened to ask Emily if she hears what I hear, so I don't say anything.

Emily reaches for her phone, checking a message. "I have to go, but I have Thursday off. Why don't you and I do something."

I think of what I'd just read in my mother's notes. Red Gate Woods. "I think I know where I want to go."

She raises her eyebrows and nods. "Good. Getting out of the house will be good for you. Both of us." She looks down. "Well, Prairie too."

When Emily's eyes meet mine, she looks stunned. "Bri, what's going on?"

I realize that I'm crying. Crying has become so common that sometimes I don't even notice the moisture on my cheeks. Emily is already reaching out to give me a hug.

No one knows what the tightening of grief feels like until they've lived it, and what it is to lose a loved one. It's the constant feeling of your heart being squeezed.

I feel like my mother was the only one on the planet who understood me. She wasn't just my mother; she was my friend.

"You know what's the worst thing about this all?" I say into Emily's shoulder.

"What?" she asks.

"That there is no coming back. There is no saying, I'm so tired of missing you so much. Can you please come back? You sit here, and you watch your loved one completely deteriorate. You watch them shrink in their body. You hear them moan in pain, and then those moans turn to desperate screams, and your name is called again and again in the night, and you become so scared to even go to sleep, because what if they need you?"

"I am very sorry, Bri. I wish there was more that I could say, but she loved you. She loved you so much."

The wind picks up. Inside the house it sounds like a great thunderstorm is about to tear across the sky above, but when I look outside, it's just an endless sheet of textures, from dark to light, moving slowly across my window.

I wipe the tears away from my cheeks. "You're going to be late for Dana."

"I can reschedule."

I shake my head. "No, I'll be fine. See you later. We'll hang out Thursday."

"If you need anything. Just to talk. Anything. Daniel too. He wants to be here for you."

I'm nodding and not really listening, and I gather she picks up on that.

"Bri . . ." Emily's voice sounds like it's coming from the far end of a long corridor. "Maybe you should think about talking to someone, about everything that you're feeling. I'm here, of course, I'm always here. I'm your friend and I love you. I'll always love you and I'll always be here for you, but I am worried, and I want to make sure you're safe and healthy."

"I'll be all right," I say, not really believing it. "I'll plan our outing. It'll be good."

Emily gives me a big hug. I press my face into her shoulder and breathe deep. She smells fresh, like lime and mint.

"Bri," she says at the door, "be careful when you walk Prairie. If you see anything strange, call me. There's someone dangerous out there."

I want to tell her again "I'll be fine," but only a year ago a woman's body was found just outside in the alley beside the dumpster.

As soon as Emily closes the front door behind her, I want to shout, "Please! Don't go! Call off work. Sit here and stay with me all day. I'm scared to be alone."

But I don't.

Losing someone you love is so incredibly painful. I don't even think any words in any human language can fully communicate what that pain feels like. The point in time in which they die draws further and further away, yet that sting, that ache, remains, and it doesn't fade; it only intensifies because they are not here to join you in your life's continuing moments and movements, the joys, bursts of laughter, profound achievements, and wonderful meals and discoveries. They are just not here to talk to and share in life with you anymore.

I stand to look out the window, watching strangers walk past, wondering about their lives. Are they lovers? Are they friends? Are they happy? I do the same to drivers in their cars, thinking about them and their stories. Are they good people? Are they bad? Are any of them the killer?

I'm scared to think of how close the killer can be. I'm also scared of what this house demands, and I'm scared of getting lost in that nighttime road in my dreams.

Chapter 6

TIME: Noon
DATE: Monday, December 4

I'm cold.

This house was always so cold growing up, and nothing has changed. I am sitting in my room with one of Mother's most prized books on my desk. I showered and put on new clothes, lounge pants and a lounge shirt, gray wool socks, and my fuzzy bathrobe over it all.

I'm scared to open the book, and so for now I just sit here, my eyes directed to the window. The red velvet curtains are secured with a gold tieback, and I listen closely, hoping that the house can replicate my mother's voice.

Is it in the wind that rushes past the windows? Or is it in the heater that clicks on and the flow of air that hums through the vents? I look for my mother in anything and everything. I look to my bedroom door. It's open, and I can barely make out the outline of her form standing in the doorway.

For people who live in houses with others for years and decades, and then one of those occupants dies, the regular movements in the home when they were alive become imprinted somehow. Shuffling to the bathroom in the morning, down the stairs to the kitchen for a cup of coffee, standing at the back door, checking for their car keys. A house gathers these impressions.

The marks that my mother left behind in this house can be felt throughout, along the banister, brass doorknobs, in mirrors, and more. Sometimes it's as if I actually feel her sitting next to me on the sofa, a soft indentation forming where she'd be sitting.

When I walk past her vanity, I can almost sense her sitting there at her stool, brushing her hair. I can almost hear the delicate tinkling of glass perfume bottles as she reaches for one, debates, changes her mind, and selects the other.

In the morning, I sometimes see her standing in the bathroom, checking her lipstick in the mirror in front of the sink. Once again at night she's there, in the family room in her lovely clothes, silk shirt, linen dresses, cashmere turtlenecks, or chiffon skirts. A lovely pressed and cleaned outfit each day.

My mother was so beautiful, and so elegant. Everything she did, everything she touched, everything she wore, felt like art. Mother was gorgeous and magical, and the house holds the imprints of her everywhere.

I still sense someone, something at the door, and so I call out, wondering, hoping, praying that maybe she'll respond:

"Hello?" I hesitate.

Silence responds, but I try again.

"Mother, can you hear me?" I feel silly as I say it.

I stand, tighten the belt of the bathrobe around me, and then open the door. It's much colder in the hallway. I look to my left and see nothing but the dark paneled hall and closed doors.

I gather the collar of the bathrobe around my neck and walk down to the room at the far end of the hallway. I place one hand on the surface, and then press my forehead against the door for a moment. I hate that sometimes things can't stay the same. I exhale and then open the door. I take a few steps into the center of the room. I look toward the door, and it's just so pitch black in the hallway.

I spin around the room. It's bare in here now. With Daniel and Emily's help, we moved all Mother's things to the attic after the burial. I don't know why I did that so fast. Maybe because it felt like I was doing something, anything, to keep my mind distracted in the aftermath. Maybe I didn't want to see her things, her dresser, clothes, reading chair, and current knitting all there, as if expecting her to just return.

I didn't want to open this room and feel her in pain any longer, so that's why I moved everything out, hoping that if it was empty and just a room again, then somehow my mother would no longer be in pain.

"Mother . . ." I say.

There's a shift in the atmosphere, warm air mixing with cool air. It feels like an electric charge. Upstairs, right above me, I hear a voice. The words are rushed, like the sound of leaves moving in a wind.

My eyes turn to the ceiling. I concentrate, trying to make out any familiar word, and then I hear something crash overhead.

Silence.

I sigh. *It's probably one of the radios,* I think. I likely disrupted their positioning when I entered the attic earlier today to place the last of Mother's sewing there, a small basket of vivid mohair yarn I found in the closet in the foyer. She liked to make bright shaggy sweaters out of this fluffy material. Mother loved to create, and she especially enjoyed sewing. She liked to hem her own skirts, tailor shirts, repair tears, reattach buttons, and when she had time, which she often did in winter, knit scarves or sweaters, hats or mittens. All those beautiful things that she wore and created are now packed in the attic. Her cardigans and pleated skirts, tailored pants and silk hair ties, and even her vanity—the things she loved are all stored away.

I turn to the door, but it's closed now. I know I left it open. I place a hand on the doorknob, turn it, and before I open the door, I hear a voice whisper in my ear.

"The king commanded that she should be left to sleep in peace until the hour of her awakening should come."

Tears well up in my eyes. All breath escapes me. My head is spinning. I wait a moment, two, three. Hours. I don't know how long. Once I feel it's safe, I turn around. There's nothing and no one there.

I step into the dark hallway, fearful that I'll be swallowed whole by the darkness and lost in the universe that is this house.

The sounds of leaves fluttering in the wind engulf me.

My heart is a car engine revving in my chest. "Mother?"

There is no one here but Prairie and me, and I'm overwhelmed with the intense feeling that we are not alone in this house. We are in the company of memories that are not so distant.

"What does that mean?" I ask the house.

There is no response.

In life, my mother worked with pretty and delicate things. She worked in rare-book conservation and restoration at the Art Institute of Chicago. She often worked for many hours alone in the museum on detailed repairs on books in her lab. Mother found wonder and infinite stories in old books, leather-bound and paperback copies, and she felt that restoring them guaranteed those tales would never end.

"They're much more than words on a page," she'd say. These actual books have been gifted, passed on, thumbed through, read, and reread, generating with each reader a sense of excitement, curiosity, and awe. That is what special objects like books did; that is what stories do.

Stories transport us.

For the first few days after my mother died, I would wake up in the middle of the night, sometimes screaming, other times gasping for air. My heart fluttered so quickly in my chest that I was sure doves would burst from my body. The panic attacks came and settled into my life as a companion I neither asked for nor wanted.

And then there was the shifting of time.

This is what life feels like without her, like I'm wandering a dark forest alone. The only thing that gives me comfort is that she lived here, but yet it's this very house that also seems to be stirring up this dread.

The lack of sleep.

The increase of dreams . . . no, nightmares.

Sometimes I'd awake to find Emily by my side, trying to comfort me as I cried into my pillow, and other times, while she was at work, I would awake in terror, utterly alone. Screaming at the walls, ceilings, floors, anything. Or worse, I'd sit up in bed, gasping for air, disoriented and confused as to who I was and where I was.

Upon waking, I'd sometimes be paralyzed with fear from tall shadows that stretched across my walls and soft music that played. There were times when my vision would adjust, and I'd note that those ghostly shapes were created by a combination of the streetlights just outside my window. The music sometimes came from a passing car, but there were times when I could not explain what it was I saw or heard.

I return to my room and I don't just feel tired. I feel drained. Not sleepy, just lacking any energy.

And what is sleep? What is a dream? What is death, and what are the thresholds of each? And how can I trust any of them?

When one sleeps, practically every part of one's body experiences a notable change.

Breathing slows.

Heartbeat reduces.

Muscles gradually relax.

Brain waves undergo changes.

Stages of sleep are then entered, from light to deep, then even deeper still, rapid eye movement, or REM, where closed eyes move quickly behind eyelids, because our eyes are somewhere, just not in the waking world. They're in that other world, observing, interacting, and seeing something not there in the very room with us.

At my desk I sit and open the front cover of the book that's been sitting there for days, waiting for me to read it, but it feels too painful to do so. Ice forms around my heart, and I close the book once again.

This was Mother's most precious object, something she found in the attic long ago that belonged to our ancestors. I adored the cover, pretty white baby's breath and striking red roses all along the frame, lovely green trees, and a beautiful woman in a pink dress. On the center the words:

THE SLEEPING BEAUTY OF THE WOOD

I move down to the living room, and before entering the kitchen, I stop and stare at my reflection in the large gold-trimmed baroque arch mirror that leans against one of the walls.

My memory takes me back to my mother standing in front of it. Her eyes wide in wonder. A smile on her lips as soon as the delivery crew dropped off the mirror from the antique shop from which she acquired it. She ran her right hand along the top edge. "This mirror is magic, Bri!" she said with such excitement. "The past speaks to it."

Normally I'd admire my features in the glass, fix my hair, adjust my clothes, but I didn't like looking at myself like this, with grief coloring my entire life now. So I turn away.

I didn't want to see my hair in a messy bun atop my head. I don't even know the last time I combed it. I didn't want to see how pale and dry my skin looked. I didn't want to see that far-off look of sadness in my eyes.

I am so exhausted with grief and overcome with worry over money. I can barely think straight, so how can I write? If I can't write, I can't get paid. If I can't get paid, I can't maintain this house. If I can't maintain this house . . . what am I supposed to do? I just feel like running away from it all, but there is no place to run away to, so I just run away in my mind.

I force myself to face the mirror, and I speak to the memory of my mother.

"Where did you get it?" I ask.

And there I see myself, teenage me. My mother hugging me from the side. "It belonged to someone very special, a girl who loved music, who loved to dance. It took me a while to find it, but it's now back where it belongs." She opens her mouth as if to say more, but she stops herself. She reaches out a hand and places it on my shoulder. "Please always take care of this house," she says.

She returns her focus to the mirror and presses a single finger to the surface, the reflective world touching the material world. "There's other worlds. There's this world and the next and the next, and another and on and on. Worlds where time is not real. In some times we sleep. In some times we dream."

The teenage me laughs. "Well, I like to sleep and I like to dream."

"My sleeping beauty, because when you were born, you did not cry. You blinked at me once, and twice, three times, and then drifted off to sleep as I held you, and I wondered where you were drifting away to already. What were you dreaming about so soon? You had just arrived in this world, and you were so eager to visit another."

We want to sometimes desperately believe that there are other realities, and even if there are, how do we get there? How do we make that journey through that deep, dark wood? How do we bend and shift and shape time? Is it with a mirror? Is it with a story? Is it with an object? Is it with a book? Or is it all within the power of our minds?

My thoughts begin to drift to beautiful dead girls and snow. I remember that day I was here visiting Mother when I saw a gold, flickering light in the alleyway across from the house. I went outside to investigate.

When I stepped outside onto the front porch, there was no gold flickering light, just the pulsating blue-and-red glow from emergency vehicles.

Some images are seared into your mind forever, and forever I will think of her. I wonder how much progress law enforcement has made in finding her killer, but I fear not much.

Detectives arrived quickly. Then came the growing memorial of teddy bears, lit glass-encased white candles, and Mylar balloons with phrases like "I Miss You."

All evidence of that discovery is gone. People forgot, and a woman was left to be murdered and dumped in an alley, and today it's just another city space. But does time change that an awful thing happened there? I don't think so. The essence, I think, of that awful thing remains somehow.

We just can't see it, but if we try hard enough, we can feel the impact.

I feel guilty that I'd forgotten about that death, for letting it fade from my memory, for being another person who heard about someone's murder and yet just went about their day like nothing happened.

Maybe also remembering these women is an act of defiance. Maybe by remembering them, we're telling their killer that these women meant something, and they, the killer, they mean nothing.

So many people are quick to push past the headlines of the murdered, but then there are some people who linger on the words "missing," "kidnapped," "killed," "found strangled" in the headlines, but luxuriating in true crime, especially unsolved true crime, makes us nothing but spectators to the murderer's sport.

Why do we push from our memories women who were ravaged, beaten, bloodied, and killed? Many people take pleasure in the details of the crime: from where she was taken to and how she died. But so few people actually use their power to do something about it.

We've always been fascinated with tales of how the dead came to be, when it occurred at the hands of another. Those stories then get told and retold, again and again, sometimes morphing into myth.

I find myself in the kitchen, and I don't even remember walking down here. I'm standing in front of the coffee machine, yet again, heaping too many tablespoons into the filter. Coffee grounds spill onto the white marbled counter. It looks like potting soil, and this reminds me that I need to get out to the greenhouse soon to clean and organize it, but . . . just not quite yet.

The greenhouse is the only part of the property I've avoided since coming back home, because it reminds me so much of Mother.

I don't anticipate I will sleep much tonight or tomorrow night, or after. In last night's dream, I saw my mother doing her sewing. She looked up at me, just for an instant, and returned to her work. A pair of black-framed glasses on her face she used when creating delicate details. A piece of red velvet glided smoothly from her hand and through the pins in her sewing machine, stamping down into the material. The machine made its steady, melodic, and metallic punching sound. It sounded almost like the keys of an old typewriter, fingers punching down on each letter steadily.

"I'm hemming new drapes for the family room," she said above the noise.

Mother didn't pause her work as dream me stood there. A bright lamp shone down on the machine.

"The book. The letter. Bri. They'll tell you all that you need to know."

I stuttered my words, trying to remember what it was she was talking about. "Which book? Which letter?"

"The letter, Bri!" She nodded in the direction of the black trunk with gold latches. "It's right there if you just look!"

"I don't have the key," I said.

The sewing machine whirred. Mother's fingers and fabric moved swiftly. "You'll find it," she said. "The baby. The curse. The book. Keys and gates and locks and thorns, Bri. You know where the key is. Stop delaying."

Blood rushed from my face. My arms shook like branches in the wind. "I don't know what I am searching for."

"Mother!" I shouted, but she didn't look up.

Punch. Punch. Punch.

The mechanical sound of the sewing machine filled the room, filled my brain.

"Mother, please, I need your help. I don't understand any of this."

She looked up. "He's looking for you, Bri. You will find her in your dreams, but he will also find you. Move quickly now."

The coffeepot starts sputtering. A ribbon of steam floats above it. My hands are shaking. I reach for a white porcelain mug in the cabinet, and I set it down with a thud. I lower my head and press my palms into my eyes. I wish things were the same way they were just weeks before.

Why do things have to change?

"Bri . . ."

"Mother . . ." I look up.

There is no response, and so I call her name, wondering whether that is the pull she needs to remain here:

"Aurora . . ."

The name is the sun's beaming rays breaking through the clouds in the morning. It hangs there in the space and energy of this room.

The house is not just a house; it is a reflection of what is within the interior.

This house speaks.

This house moves.

Emily doesn't know this, of course. Emily doesn't see the things I see or hear the things I hear.

This house is meant to communicate only with its family. I am its family, and I understand that now.

My mother exists as a real aurora, in many ways. An aurora in the sky, sweeping and flowing blue, red, yellow, green lights visible around Earth's geomagnetic poles, caused by solar wind. Swirls of colorful particles, dust and light spinning in an electric field. My mother, I wonder . . . is she out there in the cosmos, a beautiful burst of light? A galactic rainbow-colored light show?

I look beside me and notice a crack in the plaster that needs to be sealed. The house is hurting and I am hurting with it; we are each a manifestation of what it means to grieve and mourn, our broken insides exposed slowly to the outside. The house is falling into disrepair. My DNA is unraveling and my heartbeat is irregular. This heartbreak is now my universal constant. The house and I are crumbling with time. I do not know how to regulate grief, and I am not sure if it will ever be possible. This heartbreak, this heartache, is my universal constant.

I pour myself a cup of coffee, add some milk, and return to my room. I sit at my desk and look at the stack of manila folders, a collection of ghost stories compiled by my mother. Clippings and notes about Archer Avenue, the 1893 World's Columbian Exposition; writings about fairy tales, sleep, dream, consciousness, the power to bend and shape and shift reality all with one's mind; and then news clippings about a series of missing and murdered women in Chicago, referred to as the Forgotten 51 by some media outlets.

I open the folder titled FORGOTTEN 51. On the inside I see in Mother's looping cursive the words "Vanishing Daughters." I don't know why Mother found interest in these names, accounts, and crime statistics about these women.

I set it aside and return to my notes about grief. My eyes scan across phrases and words like:

Grief can cause effects within the body
Increased inflammation
Digestive problems
Cardiovascular problems
Lowered immunity
Joint pain

Nausea creeps up my throat. My stomach feels sour. There go the digestive problems. I don't remember when I ate last. I flip through more of my mother's handwritten notes. Details about these women's deaths, and I just don't understand why she wanted to know this. It all seems so grim.

I feel a breeze from the window. I stand up, push back the curtain, check the latch, and it is indeed locked. I press my forehead against the cool glass, and I exhale. A cloud of condensation blooms. A lightning flash of adrenaline jolts my heart. For a moment I think I see a familiar car driving away. I wipe the glass with the sleeve of my elbow, but the car is gone.

I return to my desk and close the folder that says FORGOTTEN 51.

I thumb through the folders on Archer Avenue, fairy tales, dream, sleep, and consciousness. For so long I found my mother silly for believing in the power of thought, but now I'm starting to feel like I don't really even understand my brain at all.

Yes, I'm sad.

Yes, I miss her.

Yes, I cry all the time, but how does grief make time disappear? How is a lack of sleep creating these memories or visions?

What is happening to me?

I hear a radio switch on, somewhere within the depths of this house.

A click and then I hear a soft hum.

A sad, silvery tune plays.

Gentle and subdued.

This song feels like a confirmation that something is happening in the folds of my mind and in this house, but I just don't know what.

There once lived a great lord who was blessed with the birth of a beautiful infant daughter, whom he named Talia. The lord sent for wise men and astrologers to foretell what fate had in store for his daughter, and after they had consulted together and cast her horoscope, they told the lord that Talia would be put in great danger by a splinter of flax. The lord then decreed that no flax or hemp, or anything of the kind, should be brought into the house; he thought that by doing so he could protect his daughter from her fate. —"Sun, Moon, and Talia," Giambattista Basile

Chapter 7

TIME: 5:00 p.m.
DATE: Monday, December 4

I hate waiting for Briar, but I have to. It's not the right time for her, but until then, there will be others.

It's cold, but nice for a walk.

Cold walk. Night walk. No lights. Just night.

Northerly Island is so dark at night. Black. Blacker still. It's hard to tell where it stops and starts, but there's a full moon on. There's some light.

Flurries float around me.

Lake-effect snow.

The sunset at 4:30 p.m.

Snow digs in my shoes, but I keep walking. I wanted to come back. To see my work. To see them see my work.

During the daytime this is a pretty park. In summer I make sandwiches and I sit here and I watch them. I watch them ride bikes. I watch them fly kites with their kids. I watch them walk their dogs. I watch them. They don't watch me. No one notices me. I like it like that.

To my left is Adler Planetarium. I like it there. Models of planets and the sky. People think they know about things, but they don't. They really don't know how anything works. How the sky works. How their brain works. We are so much more than a body. Energy. That's what we are. Energy. More.

No one bothers me when I sit here in the warm summer months and read. Most people leave me alone because they see what I am reading. I like to read nonfiction. I read books like *In Cold Blood* by Truman Capote, *The Crime of the Century* by Dennis L. Breo and William J. Martin, *The Stranger Beside Me* by Ann Rule, *Mindhunter* by John Douglas and Mark Olshaker, and more. I also really enjoy *The Devil in the White City: Murder, Magic, and Madness at the Fair That Changed America* by Erik Larson. He wrote about Daniel Burnham, the man who made the *Plan of Chicago*. He also wrote about Father too.

Today, I see flashing lights at the end of the park. There is a cluster of trees here. I step into their shadow. I will stay here, and I will watch and listen. I have many layers on. I have two pairs of pants and two sets of socks and a short sleeve and a long sleeve and a fleece. I have a heavy parka and two sets of gloves and a scarf around my face and a knit hat. I am just a neighbor. That is what I will say if they ask. A neighbor out for a stroll. A neighbor out for a walk. A curious neighbor. A concerned neighbor. Yes, that is all I am.

Up ahead I see bright lights shining down on a patch of snow. There are people standing around—paramedics, CSI, and the officers first on the scene. Those first-scene officers always look so stunned. This isn't their job, finding a body. They're just driving around one day, and there it is, something pale, not moving. A mannequin. A large doll. Seeing what a body looks like after I'm done with it isn't easy on those officers. I like to see that uneasy look on their faces when they see my work. That unease they feel, it will never go away.

I can't hear what they're saying from here, but I see white mists from their breath floating above them all, like little text bubbles from some comic strip.

My cheeks are already going numb from the cold.

"What'd we got?" I hear one of them say.

"Female. Eighteen to twenty-five. Looks like she was strangled."

I close my eyes tight and fall back deeper into the trees, and I listen. I am very good at being stealthy and listening when I shouldn't be.

"You know what I'm going to say, right?" a younger-looking detective says, his face fresh and smooth. He's got on gray earmuffs and gray gloves. The other detective's face has deep laugh lines, and sunken eyes. His hands at his sides.

"We just found a dead girl over in an abandoned house, and now this one? Our killer's back, Kowalski."

Kowalski points at the officers in uniform. "You two assess the scene?"

They give their weak affirmatives, followed by their names: Officer Ryan and Officer Jones.

Officer Jones is wearing glasses. A scarf covering his nose. His glasses are getting fogged up.

Kowalski takes a few steps out, his feet digging into the snow. He's looking all around, scanning, thinking.

I like him.

"We've got tire tracks and some footprints. We got more people coming to help. We'll need to be careful, look for signs of struggle, any unusual disturbances in the snow."

Officer Jones speaks up. "This is a pretty big scene to assess."

I laugh quietly. The crime scene is the entirety of the peninsula. I can't imagine how they are going to do that at this hour. Evidence can be anywhere.

A paramedic approaches a spot in the snow illuminated by lights.

The body is under the spotlight. So perfect. Angelic. More than angelic. Divine. Cosmic. Her face is pale. Strands of her hair are blowing in the wind. She's in a pretty white dress that clings to her figure.

That is how I left her. She will make a wonderful addition to my collection.

"We got pictures already?" I hear the question followed by an affirmative.

"We're going to need more when it's daylight. We need this whole area scanned. Footprints. Everything. I need to know who came in and who came out."

I wonder if they're looking closer, at the strands of blue and purple marks that circle her skin.

There are so many questions, I'm sure, coursing through their minds. Why her? Why now? Is she connected to the others? So many questions. Can they answer them all? I know the detectives have all thought about me. They've wondered whether I was real.

I hear whimpering behind me.

"Help me . . ."

I smile. Her voice is so small, like a child's.

"I'm so cold. Help me, please."

I turn around and see her standing there, shivering in her white dress, her eyes bloodshot. Deep purple fingerprints around her neck. Sparkling blue bruises across her cheeks. Swollen cracked lips. She asks me to help her again, and I see that her two front teeth are missing. She'll be repaired once we go into the nighttime.

"Help me!" she screams, but then she is gone. Embraced by the pine trees and whisked away into my world. I will see her soon. This one is called Magda. She will sleep in a glass coffin beside the lake, and when people talk about the beautiful girl found dead on Northerly Island, Magda will awaken. Her ghost will appear here, walking along the prairie grass. Strangers and tourists alike will hear her sobs. Some lucky travelers will see a wisp of white. Maybe one day an even luckier person will see Magda standing there in silhouette, looking out over Lake Michigan.

People will talk about the girl murdered under the moonlight on this peninsula for decades, more. They will share stories of her haunting, but no one will ever mention the man who murdered her, because that is how ghost stories often work.

Romanticize the person killed and forget who did the killing. It's in that forgetting that allows me to continue, creating another myth or urban legend.

I hear the detectives and officers talking.

Theories.

Times.

Injuries.

What they see.

What they are missing.

What many of them seem to forget about serial killers is that we have a hot period and we have a cold period. We can go quiet for a number of reasons. Maybe we go cold because we got arrested. Maybe we go cold because someone got a little too close with questioning.

None of it really matters, because even if a serial killer's gone dormant, that doesn't mean they're not still a serial killer. They're always capable of killing again, months later, years later, decades later. A cold period is just that. We are always thinking, plotting, planning, waiting for the perfect next. I went cold to make my plans with Bri.

The cold is breaking through my fingers, and they are going numb. The air is starting to burn my throat. It's fine. I endure it because I enjoy this, my work, my duty.

Some think this goes back a year, or two, a decade or three, but it's much more complex. Time is much more complex. Magda is now one of many.

I think a lot about time and where and how it exists. I wonder whether time truly exists outside me or somewhere else. I really believe that time exists inside me. I can control time. I can create my own time. I don't need to depend on watches or clocks, or those digital little numbers in the upper right-hand corner of any computer. Or my phone.

I am time.

This is much more complicated than any of them can ever comprehend.

I hear someone say: "It's the Chicago Strangler."

People like to give names to things. It's like if they don't label something, it doesn't exist. A name to bring power over it. Sometimes even when they know the name of the thing, they will still give it a new name. Everyone likes a little control.

Some of the investigators move out of sight. My focus remains on Magda's body. Exquisite even in death. Perfection in the night. I made sure to leave her eyes open to the blue-black sky above.

"No signs of fire?" one of the authorities asks.

I like to play with fire, but it's not always needed. Sometimes I like to see what it does to their skin or their hair or their eyes. Not tonight. The snow was enough.

I like to be involved as much as I can in their transition. There are procedures in this transition I never view, of course. Parents showing off pictures of daughters on their birthdays, at prom, at graduation, at weddings, or on family vacations, smiling so big and bright into a camera to homicide detectives. Parents sitting in the living room with water and ice in tumblers beside them. Stunned. Then polite conversation. Then a return to the horror of the situation. Their daughter vanished. Their daughter is found. Their daughter is dead. Their daughter is never coming back.

Authorities will search for and question suspects, boyfriends, husbands, bosses, friends. They will grow weary, and they will grow tired, and then another dead girl will sprout up in the city, and it will all begin again.

It is beginning again.

I am collecting sleeping beauties who will join me in the night.

They're as perfect in death as they are in life.

An icy breeze blows, and lake-effect snow swirls around me. I smile. I will wait here for a while still, watching, listening, thinking. Thinking of Briar and how much longer it will take until she will be one of my tales.

Chapter 8

I gather Prairie, placing her in her pink harness. I put on my coat and gloves and hat and scarf.

Layers. It's important to wear layers in Chicago's winters, and really, to at least try to look put together when I step out. I don't want to give the neighbors any more reason to worry about me. Otherwise they may come outside and try to chat me up. Of course they'd do it to be kind, but it's hard to talk to people who just don't understand.

My neighbors are sweet. The entire block came out for my mother's funeral service. Neighbors made me food and checked in on me for days after the burial. In time I just stopped answering the phone and opening the door when they'd ring the bell. People, I believe, understood that what I needed in the aftermath of her death was silence, to process and understand what death truly means.

I still don't know what death truly means.

We read about death as young children in fairy tales, but no book and no movie can really capture or communicate what it feels like to lose someone. How you're stunned for a time and confused, how soon anger seeps in, the feelings of being betrayed by the universe, and then the great spiral of despair in the form of accepting that they're never coming back and this is life now.

Prairie and I walk the same route we always do, down the Midway Plaisance to Jackson Park. The Midway is a tree-lined mile-long stretch that connects Washington Park to Jackson Park, and Prairie can happily walk this route multiple times a day. As we walk, I think of Mother's notes, especially about the 1893 World's Columbian Exposition, and I'm wondering whether that is why she compiled all those details, because this is the very neighborhood that hosted the World's Fair so long ago? Maybe that history was just another one of her many interests?

It's early morning, and Prairie and I pass brave joggers and students making their way to class at the nearby University of Chicago campus. I like walking slowly through here, admiring the beautiful redbrick buildings and Gothic architecture.

This part of my walk with Prairie never seems to grow old.

We approach Jackson Park and walk down a paved path where cherry blossoms are slumbering. In spring they will bloom, and the landscape here will be dotted in pretty pink pastels.

We walk along a bit more and find ourselves at the Nancy C. Hays Bridge. It's cold, but not cold enough for the lagoon on either side to be frozen. I feel the bite of the wind against my cheeks, but it's nothing I'm not used to as a Chicagoan. Being able to tolerate the sharp winter winds is a point of pride.

Prairie and I stand on the bridge for a moment, and then I start down toward the Columbia Basin, with its striking view of the Museum of Science and Industry, the only building that remains from that 1893 World's Fair. I learned that from Mother's notes, and I feel like I should have always known that.

A jogger passes by and gives me a nod. In the distance I hear the laughter of children. I turn and see a mother pushing a stroller, a baby inside and a toddler bouncing beside her.

I spent time last night digging through many of the books Mother had on her shelves about Chicago history and this neighborhood. In just that short reading I learned that during the World's Fair, the Museum of Science and Industry was called the Palace of Fine Arts, and artists from all over the world exhibited their work there. All the structures erected during the fair were meant to be temporary, but still, a mysterious fire tore through after the fair and destroyed all the buildings before they could be properly dismantled. The only building saved was the Museum of Science and Industry.

Just to our right is Lake Michigan, and behind us is the Garden of the Phoenix, a Japanese garden constructed on a scenic little island. We walk off the paved path onto the grass, and then find the woodchip hiking trail that wraps around the lagoon.

I think about what Emily said, to be safe and to be vigilant, and of course that is what I will do. It is daytime, and the sun is a brilliant spot in the sky on this icy December day.

Daylight, I imagine, means nothing to our killer.

Prairie and I are standing, looking out over the lagoon. The museum is reflected in the water's surface. I shift my weight to my left leg and feel muddy woodchips beneath my boots, and the memories hit me. My mother moaning in pain. The smells of her medicine and nutritional shake and just how gaunt she looked at the end. A living skeleton.

I start crying because there's nothing else I can do. No matter what comfort I offered her while she was in that state, I couldn't save her.

"Would you like a tissue?" a man says from behind me.

He is wearing dark slacks and a dark wool coat. He does not look like he belongs here or anywhere. In this time, or any. He is so handsome, with chin-length dark hair and eyes so bright blue they remind me of the lake.

Suddenly I'm self-conscious about the way I look. I didn't shower this morning or wash my face. Leaving the house with Prairie is a triumph alone.

I decline. "No, thank you," I say, wiping away at my tears with my gloves.

He crosses his arms against his chest, and we are both looking at the museum now. "I recently lost someone too," he said without turning his head.

Prairie is sitting still, panting, inspecting the man, her little head turning this way and that, trying to size him up the way dogs do, wondering, "Is this a good human? Or is this a bad human?"

Moist cheeks in this biting December wind prove much too painful. "Actually, I'll take that tissue."

He hands me a Kleenex from his pocket and smiles, a comforting smile, like he's always known me.

"Why do you think I've lost someone?"

He raises his eyebrow and shrugs. "It's the way you're crying. There's a very specific type of cry. A grief cry. The heaviness of the mourning cry. It's this deep-down sort of heaving"—he points to the center of his chest—"that possesses your entire body, because all of you is hurting for the person you've lost."

I finish patting my eyes and cheeks and shove the Kleenex in my pocket. My face feels cold and raw.

"Who did you lose?" I ask.

He clasps his hands in front of his chest. "A woman I thought was the one."

"I'm very sorry."

A police siren wails in the distance. One part of me says I should end this conversation and continue with my day, but I don't, because I'm not ready to go home to the nightmares that blend my days and nights.

He points to Prairie. "May I?"

I glance down at her, and she seems as curious about him as I do. "Sure. She's really sweet," I say.

"A rescue?" he asks.

"Yeah," I say, making sure I'm holding her leash tight. "She was in the shelter a long time. It took her a while for her to trust people."

He removes his hands from his coat pocket and motions toward Prairie. He's wearing black leather gloves. His way of dress isn't normal around here. Most of the university students are in jeans, hoodies, and heavy parkas. His dress is formal, too formal, especially for this time of morning. Maybe he's a professor, I reason.

I nod. He squats. He holds his hands out to her, showing her that he wants to say hello. Prairie is still, eyeing him carefully, taking all of him in, trying to make sense of this man.

"Do you believe in the one?" he asks as he's rubbing the top of Prairie's head. She turns to lick his hand. She seems happy, and that puts me even more at ease.

"The one?" I laugh, not anticipating this type of subject matter at all. I think about Daniel and how much I adore him. I know I've been pushing him away, but it's because I don't feel it's right for him to see me this way. *I* don't even want to see me this way. I want him in my life, completely, entirely. I never want him to leave me, and I know I will never leave him, but with what I'm struggling with, I feel like I need to do this alone.

The wind whips around my face. "Yes," I say. "I know I've found the one."

"That's wonderful. I hope they know they're your one."

I tug my knit cap farther down my ears. "I think he knows it."

"What about this? I think you should tell him. Right now. Life is so short."

I smile because it sounds so sweet and silly at the same time. "I would but he's sleeping. He's a paramedic. He was up late last night."

He stands and Prairie draws closer to me. I don't know why I'm even still here, speaking with this stranger, but it feels nice to make this small connection with someone.

There's something about him that's familiar, comforting. Is it his handsome face? His soothing voice? Those charming clothes? The way it feels as if he doesn't belong, but then he does? Then I think of what Mother said about thin places, these elastic pockets of energy that exist all around us, and for a moment I wonder whether we have both stepped through a thin place.

"That must be difficult work. The type of work I imagine would give someone nightmares," he says, and it's that reference to nightmares that just seems a little off, as if he knows something or as if he's giving me a sort of clue, a nudge that he knows something.

"I imagine you need to get back to where you were going," he says, motioning toward the paved path. We make our way there.

"I haven't been sleeping well," I admit, trusting this stranger.

"Bad dreams?" he asks.

I nod.

He continues talking, his hands clasped in front of him. "Night terrors usually occur in the first half of one's sleep cycle. You may thrash or scream or fall out of bed. My mother used to tell me that it's ill advised to wake someone from a night terror."

"Why's that?"

He tips his head to the side. "Because they'll forever remain in that similar state, frenzied and manic, gripped by an overwhelming sense of fear and dread that they'll be unable to engage with the outside world."

Above us I hear the caw of seagulls, followed by the low rumbling of an airplane making its way across the sky, heading toward O'Hare International Airport, I imagine. This moment feels still and peaceful, normal even, regardless of the painful things we are discussing.

"A nightmare, these happen in the second half of one's sleep," he says. "Now, these are dreams. These are scenarios we see during REM sleep, and we almost internalize these things as if we are truly living them."

"Isn't it dangerous to wake someone from a nightmare?" I ask.

He stops, his features lost in thought, and then he raises his eyebrows and says: "I'd imagine so. Maybe there are parts of you that are pulling those particles of that nightmare into your waking world." He shoves his hands into his coat pockets. "What are your nightmares about?"

Those images I will keep to myself. "Nothing I can consistently remember," I say.

"Sigmund Freud believed that nightmares were, in part, events people were experiencing again and again. Carl Jung, too, believed that truths existed within dreams, memories, plans, experiences, even aspects of telepathic visions."

"You seem to know a lot about dreams," I say.

"I'm a psychology professor at UChicago," he says, "and much of my personal research includes consciousness and dreams. Nightmares are scary. Sometimes they're trying to tell us something we don't want to see or hear."

We continue walking, a slow, leisurely pace.

I can hear Emily: "You met a stranger . . . in the park . . . and you just walked and talked with him? You know there's someone out here killing women, Bri?"

I want to believe I'm a good judge of character. I want to believe that my intuition spoke to me, and that feeling I had when I met someone, that sort of radar, was correct at predicting whom to trust and whom not to trust.

He adds: "What's also scary is sometimes when you're trying to wake up from a nightmare, you just can't. You open your eyes and you're just there in your bed, feeling trapped and paralyzed."

"What's that thing called? That thing that sits on your chest when you're having a bad dream? Is it a legend? Folklore?"

He nods. "A hag. A monstrous woman who sits on a sleeper's chest. It's from German folklore."

"Why does she do that?"

"The same reason all wicked things do what they do—because they enjoy it."

There's a break in the conversation. A pause. Prairie is walking happily, but my thoughts move back to my dreams. It's beyond nightmares what I'm experiencing, and for a moment I worry that the hallucinations will never go away.

"So you're experiencing grief and nightmares? That's a lot of hurting."

"Yes," I say. It is a lot, and it's nice to hear someone acknowledge that.

He leans in closer, just a little. "Grief does that, it knocks you from your center and then there is no center. There's just spinning."

I want to keep talking to him, but I need to head back home. I do feel a little bit better having talked to someone. My thoughts are a little bit clearer, and I feel a little bit more hopeful, just from this short conversation.

I point my thumb behind me. "I need to head back. I have work to do."

"What do you do for work?"

"I'm a freelance journalist."

"Very nice." He tilts his head back. "What do you write about?"

"Health." I laugh because I feel anything but healthy right now. "And science."

There's a gleam in his eye, an excitement. "What about health and science?"

I roll my eyes and sigh. "Well, I had this idea that I can't quite pull together yet. I wanted to talk about grief brain and what grief does to someone, but then I started having those dreams, and I don't know. I don't know what I should focus on. The physical manifestations of grief in our bodies, how we store that pain in our bodies, or something else."

He nods, listening. Processing what I said, which I think might sound as confusing to him as it did to me.

He takes a deep breath and then says, "Maybe grief does that. Maybe grief is held in our bodies, and maybe it does something to our brains, unlocks something that we didn't know was there before."

"Like what?"

He looks up. "I don't know. Maybe grieving does something as simple as remind us what it means to love and to connect to someone. Maybe when we're grieving, we're grieving losing the connection with that person here in the physical plane, and maybe we just need to learn a new way of communicating with them."

I laugh to myself and repeat his words: "A new way of communicating. You sound like my mom."

He pauses and stands erect. "I'm hoping that's a good thing. I realize I didn't get your name."

"Briar, but you can call me Bri," I say. "And yours?"

"Isaac. Isaac Adler. Very nice to meet you, Bri. You lost your mother, then, I'm guessing?"

"Yes, a few weeks ago."

His features go solemn, soft, contemplative. "I'm so very sorry. I know where you're at right now. I've been there. You'll likely not even remember this conversation. While grief is a universal experience, it's isolating. It's lonely. No one can feel your pain, and you cannot offload the full spectrum of your pain to someone else. There is no offloading the immensity of it. Those feelings are like an entire planet. But the hard part is, you have to feel it all. Allow yourself that."

I am still unsure what it is I'm feeling, this rush and crushing weight of emotions. I feel it in my aching upper back, in my jaw that feels tight, in my hands that start tingling when I sit down to type. It's gripped me completely. Grief, I'm unfortunately learning, is adjusting to the fact that we'll never see our loved ones again, that we must live the rest of our lives without them present for our growth and milestones and accomplishments. Grief is accepting that the pain one feels from the loss of their loved ones is a pain that is constant, forever. Eternal. There are many things that can be undone, that can be replayed or revised in life. There are many decisions that can be reversed, but death is not one of them. There is nothing more permanent than death.

"Were you and your mother close?"

"Yes, very. She was my friend. My best friend. She knew me. I could look at her and she'd just know what I was thinking. You don't have that type of relationship with too many people in this life. That bond can be cultivated with some, maybe. But there are just some people that you come across in life that you instantly know they know you and love you, and not all mother-and-daughter relationships are like that, and I had that."

Isaac adjusts the cap on his head. "When our loved ones die, many people tell us to talk to them as if they're still there. It may sound silly to do, but it brings me calm. Energy, we're all energy, and everything is energy."

It sounds so sad, that possibility, if it's true. What if I talked to my mother and she heard me, but I couldn't hear her? It seemed so unfair.

I shrug. "What if we're just speaking to the void?" I ask.

"We could be, but what if we aren't?" he reasons.

I take a deep breath and exhale slowly. I want to believe she can hear me, but I also want to believe that in some way I can talk to her too.

"Maybe," Isaac begins, "we're all asleep within these walls, and to fully understand what is happening, we need to wake up, but we cannot wake up if she is still asleep. We sleep because she sleeps. What will wake her, Bri? Is it music? Is it something else?"

It's as if the air has been squeezed out of my lungs, and I feel like he's saying something more, without saying it. A message? A code? Did I even hear what I think I heard? It's as if he knows my mind or knows me too well in this moment. I am exposed to this stranger.

I look around, and there are people in the park, walking their dogs, children chasing one another, throwing snowballs. Even though there are others, I feel as if I am alone with Isaac, as if it's just the two of us existing right here in this moment.

He continues: "What if I told you that it's possible to have two-way communication with the dead?"

I want to laugh, it sounds so unreal. "How's that?"

Isaac looks at me like the answer is so obvious. "Dreams."

"Dreams?"

He looks around us, as if checking whether anyone is listening in on our conversation. "Do you believe in ghosts?"

I open my mouth to say something, but, really, I don't know what to say.

"You think I'm silly, don't you, for believing in the things that I do, but here we are, Bri. You and I. Two people. No one can answer why we're really and truly here, where we came from and where we're going. Yes, we know how babies are made. How people age. We know of these unsaid rules and expectations. Education. Work. Family. Pay bills. Die. But is that all there is? I don't think so. I think that much of what we're taught is a distraction."

"A distraction from what?" I ask.

"The dreams. Are we asleep? Are we awake? Is this a dream? Is the dream world the real world or the other way around? What is real?"

I shake my head. "I really don't know sometimes," I say.

"For example, you're writing about grief, the physical manifestations of it. Of course grief impacts our dreams, our sleep patterns."

I nod. "I mean, that's true."

"Have you seen anything in your dreams after your mother's death that you didn't see while she was alive?" he asks.

I think of the girl. The white ball gown. The black car. And I don't know why, but I lie. "No."

"No?" He tilts his head and seems perplexed, like I gave the wrong answer.

I don't want to think about her or that car, not right now.

He looks up to the sky. "Do you believe in ghosts?" he asks me again.

"My mother worked in funerary art restoration for a long time. We spent a lot of time visiting cemeteries, and in all of that time there, I never saw anything."

"Did your mother believe in ghosts?"

"Yes."

He presses his lips together in thought. "Have you seen something *not* in a cemetery?"

I feel like he's trying to get me to admit something he already knows about me.

"No," I say, lying again.

I hand him his own question. "Do you believe in ghosts?"

"Confidentially," he says, "yes. There's so much that we don't understand. Why are we here? Where do we go when we leave? So why not believe in ghosts? Even you. I'm sure there's a part of you that wants to believe in ghosts."

"Maybe," I say.

"Maybe it's all about being receptive. Open to all communication, to all manifestations and realities."

"What do you mean?"

"I think we just need to learn to listen better. That there's more out there than we may think. Are you familiar with the concept of synchronicity?"

I smile. "More Carl Jung?"

He nods. "Indeed. More Carl Jung. The occurrence of meaningful coincidences that don't seem directly related."

Isaac points to himself and then points to me. "You and I, right here, right now, at this very park, talking about life and death and mourning and the existence of the beyond. Even the fact that we are both right here, speaking to each other. It seems like an impossibility in many ways. That two people met on a random winter morning who wanted to talk about big questions of life and death and consciousnesses and living with grief."

"How did you learn to live with grief?" I ask him.

"Simple, meditation."

I feel my eyebrows lifting. "Meditation?"

"Many people don't spend time with their own thoughts and in their own heads. They live in their phones. They allow a scrolling screen to think for them, or movies or anything. A lot of people are uncomfortable with the idea of sitting still with their own minds. With meditation, you can rewrite your reality, you can manipulate so much of what you think and feel, and even who you are. In meditation, you can find answers to questions that you've been searching for desperately your entire life, because everything you need is internal. You can't deny the power of your conscious experiences, and so don't deny the value of your unconscious life. Try meditation. See what worlds you can create. How you can bend, and shift, and shape your reality all in the universe that is your mind."

All in the universe that is your mind.

It sounds like something my mother would say. She swore by her meditative practice, that it changed her life.

"So the answer is to just sit quietly with my thoughts and my life will change?"

His face brightens. "You should look up the Gateway Project. It's a form of meditation. You can find the audio files online."

"Gateway?"

"Yes, the Gateway Project. I think they have what you're looking for. Many of the principles there have been present for a long time, but these techniques were refined in the 1950s by a man named Robert Goddard. With your writing interest and your exploration of grief, I think these meditations can help you in many ways."

My mother meditated often, seated on the floor of her room on a yoga mat, her legs crossed beneath her, her hands on top of her knees. Her spine erect. Her eyes closed, facing the window, the sun on her face. Sometimes she'd sit quietly. At other times I'd hear her humming. Sometimes I'd hear her chanting a mantra.

"What are they, breathing techniques?"

He turns around, and I see his eyes scan across the MSI, that large building built for a moment in the past but that has stood defiant to continue to exist in the present. "That and more. So much more."

He looks to Prairie, and then to me, and claps his hands together once. "I'll let you get on with your day, Bri. It was wonderful meeting you today. I hope to see you and Prairie again soon. I'm often here in the mornings around this time. Please come find me. I'd love to talk to you more about all this—manifestation, the exploration of the self, beyond."

"How do I find you?"

"Oh, just think of me, and I'm sure I'll appear. I'm kidding."

We exchange phone numbers, and then Isaac says, "Bri, can you promise me something?"

"Depends on what it is."

He smiles. His teeth are so white and straight. So beautiful. All of him is just so beautiful.

"When you dream, if anyone ever asks you for the date and time, never provide that information. Just ignore the question."

"Okay . . ." I say, so confused.

"Trust me," he says.

"Sure. Goodbye," I say, still processing his request, then I watch him walk toward the bridge.

He turns around and is walking backward. "There's no such thing as goodbye. We never end, Bri. We"—he points to me and then to himself—"are eternal."

Isaac waves. "I hope to see you in the Gateway." He turns down the path and is gone.

Chapter 9

I am sitting at my desk, reading about Chicago's murdered women. My eyelids droop and I shake my head. What is the difference between sleep and meditation anyway? And why can one cause so much change, but not the other? It makes no sense.

How many hours is the recommended number that one should sleep again? Six? Seven? Eight? Nine? What are the consequences for too little sleep? Too much?

My curiosity pulls me to check. I click a tab open and tap against the keyboard.

A search online generates summaries of issues from lack of sleep, ranging from memory disturbances to mood shifts, a weakened immune system, difficulties with thinking and concentration and more.

I huff and run my fingers through my hair.

Memory disturbances.

Mood shifts.

Difficulties with thinking and concentration.

More.

I wonder whether anyone has ever died from lack of sleep. I press my fingers against the keyboard to ask the internet that question, but then I move my fingers away. It's probably best not to ask.

My head is beginning to hurt, right between my eyes, and there's a slow, steady, dull pinch radiating at each temple. Each breath feels heavier than the last. I reach for the cup of coffee beside my computer and guzzle what's remaining there.

I return to the article about sleep. The next thing I read is as unsettling. My eyes land on the line:

> You could start hallucinating, seeing, and hearing things that are not really there.

I read further.

> A lack of sleep also can trigger mania in people. Additional psychological risks include:

> Impulsive behavior.

> Anxiety.

> Depression.

> Paranoia.

> A lack of sufficient sleep can also lead you to experience microsleep during the day. Microsleep entails episodes in which you fall asleep for a few seconds without realizing it.

I close the tab.

None of this is good, and I don't want to know any of it.

I just don't want to feel this way anymore, but neither being awake nor being asleep makes anything better. Each state of being has its cons.

I go downstairs and mix matcha tea with my coffee. Prairie finds me in the kitchen, sits, stares at me, and starts whimpering.

"Fine," I say. "Even though we had a really nice walk."

We walk to the foyer, and I reach for her harness and slip it on. I check the temperature on my phone. It's in the teens. I'm in a gray hoodie and I decide to skip the coat. The cold will wake me and keep me awake, I think, knowing that's probably not a good move.

The jolt of cold when I hit the front porch is a shock. Before Prairie and I walk down the icy stairs, I reach for the small bucket of rock salt beside the door, grab the scoop, and scatter some grains across the front steps.

Prairie and I carefully go down the stairs, and I look up and down the block. The street is silent, so Prairie and I just walk. I can hear Emily's warning again, to be careful, that someone is out here hurting women, but I've never felt unsafe in this neighborhood or in all of Chicago, well, not since the other day when that man was staring into my house. That was strange, but it could've been anything, a misunderstanding, anything.

Then there's Isaac. I wonder how Emily will react to me making a friend at the park, exchanging numbers, and agreeing to meet him again. She is a worrier, and I can understand that, given her job and given all that I've been through lately.

It's quiet, and a light dusting of snow is falling. The shimmering white flakes look like glitter being scattered across the sidewalks. We walk down the block and back, and that's enough for my limbs and joints to handle. Everything feels frozen and stiff. I'm shivering, and I admit, leaving without a coat was not the best idea, but I'm no longer sleepy.

When we return to the house, I notice that all the curtains are open.

Emily is still at work. As is Daniel.

I rush up the steps and stop at the welcome mat.

I feel myself blink rapidly, my brain trying to process what I'm seeing. I realize that I'm holding my breath. There's a single red rose on the welcome mat.

"This wasn't here when we left," I say to Prairie. "Who the hell left that?"

My legs and shoulders feel tight. I'm scared to pick up the rose. Instead, I step around it, checking the door, making sure it's locked. I dig for my keys in my hoodie pocket, open the door, and slam it behind me. My heart racing, I peek out the window, waiting to see if anyone appears, but after a few minutes no one does.

There's a thunderous moan from upstairs.

"Hello?"

It sounds like someone in heels is running across the floor above me. I'm almost relieved that it's the house.

"I'm not in the mood for this right now!"

The moan turns to a clatter, turns to a sharp wailing. A keening, almost.

"You're being a bit overdramatic," I say.

I hear the flip of a light switch.

Click.

And then another, and another, and another.

Click, click, click.

The noise starts upstairs, lights turning off now throughout the house, down the hall, making its way to the first floor to where I am in the large family room. The curtains all close with a loud swoosh.

The light here remains on.

"I don't believe in ghosts," I say, not believing it myself.

The staticky sound of a radio scanning across stations blares. A jumble of words and voices fills the room.

"Stop it!" I shout, and when I do, the radio and the voices go silent.

It sounds so empty, like I'm standing inside a vacuum, and then I hear a soft ping, like a champagne glass being tapped with a fork at a wedding, commanding the couple to kiss.

I look up and see the grand chandelier. It's detached from the ceiling, and it happens so slowly, but then not, because there's nothing I can do to stop it as it crashes onto the oriental rug.

Thousands of glass bubbles explode, burst, pulverized into sharp dusty clouds from the impact, sending teeny-tiny pieces of glass skittering across the floor.

"I'm not doing this right now!" I shout. I leave the mess, stomping my way upstairs through the darkness to my room. "I am suffering too! I am grieving too! I have this article to write. I have to pay these bills. And look what you're doing to me? How am I supposed to get anything done when you keep distracting me?"

All the way upstairs there's wailing, those keening, deep, mournful pit-of-your-stomach cries of grief.

Before I slam my bedroom door, I see the lights in the hallway turn on, just like the lights in my bedroom. I hear a shifting and the tinkling of glass, as if it's all being swept up into a dustpan. I refuse to go down there and watch the house clean up after itself.

I know I'm operating at a dangerous threshold, and I don't need this house to push me any further. How many hours did I sleep yesterday? I think back. I count on my hand. I look at the clock. Four. It was four hours of sleep. The day before that it was four as well. The day before that, perhaps three. I'm afraid to sleep, because that's when it happens—detachments, disconnections, dreams or visions or hallucinations or memories. Perhaps it's what Isaac said, a shift in reality?

When I sleep, it's as if I fall deep into a well, and all the parts of who I am stop and I become something else, someone else, somewhere else, that melding of sleep and reality where I do not know where I start and I do not know where I stop.

Then I think, again, of the glimpses of the things I have seen in those dreams, or visions that seem to skirt on memories—a dark old-fashioned-looking car, like something out of a movie from the 1950s. The vehicle is driving down a dark road, and I see a girl in a white dress and white shoes. There is something stirring in the shadows alongside the street, and when I see movement beside trees and the shape of something begins to emerge from the wood, I close my eyes tight and beg myself to wake up.

Mother was right about a lot of things, I see now. There are things that live outside in the dark that we will never understand. Fairy tales and stories warned us not to walk through the forest at night. Urban legends warned us to avoid certain roads after sunset. Both fairy story and urban tale collide as one in my dreams. And this is what is happening to me, right now, the collision of two things, two worlds.

I see Prairie. She is facing the door.

I sigh. "I need to work for a little while. I'll go down later and check on it."

I return to my computer. Minutes go by, an hour or two, and it becomes more difficult to fight my eyelids, and my body begins to sway in my computer chair.

I need more coffee.

I open my bedroom door and announce, "I'm going downstairs."

Silence.

Prairie and I make our way down to the first floor. I hear the soft electric buzz of a radio being switched on somewhere, and music begins playing. Emily is still not home. She's chauffeuring the dead and the dying. My best friend as Charon.

I reach for the filter and the coffee container and scoop, losing count. I pour water into the machine, and I sit at the kitchen table, watching the snowflakes outside, beautiful ice crystals gliding slowly to the ground, where they'll come to rest and eventually disappear.

Isn't that what humans are like? One day we're here, sparkling bright against the light, and then we're gone.

Outside seems so quiet, but inside it's getting loud. The music in the house grows louder, but I ignore it. It's useless to search for which radio the sound is coming from.

The house is full of dozens of radios, perhaps hundreds, as many models as Zenith manufactured as possible. My great-great-grandfather Philip kept as many items as his company created as could fit in this house. Eventually it became too much, so he just kept versions of ones he favored. It was said that his daughter, my great-grandmother, told him: "Eventually this house will no longer be a house, just a thing of music."

Philip's mother was originally from France. His father grew up in Connemara, and both met in Ireland, married, had children, and came to Chicago. It was Philip's father who worked digging the Illinois and Michigan Canal. Philip grew up in a farmhouse with his mother and sister deep in the woods along Archer Avenue.

As an adult, he came to work with Karl Hassel and Ralph H. G. Mathews, who founded Chicago Radio Laboratory.

The name Z-Nith, the original spelling, came from the call letters of their tiny radio station in Chicago. It later became Zenith Radio Corp. When they opened their large factory on South Iron Street, Philip figured he'd found financial stability, and he started construction of his house.

He said he wanted to build a castle, a castle in which music would be played and songs would be sung, where his family could live and enjoy this city for years to come.

I don't know too much about his children, only that he had a son and a daughter, and that daughter is the one who loved music and dancing so much she encouraged him to bring all these radios home. I've seen pictures of Philip and his wife and his son, but never his daughter. When I'd ask Mother, she'd just say that it was up in the attic somewhere, stacked with those portraits that were taken down.

The coffee finishes brewing, and I pour myself a cup. I hear a tapping against the window, and after the chandelier dream, something tells me not to look out the window right now. My mother would say that there are things that exist outside that function to tempt us into their holds when we are weak, when we are tired, when we are vulnerable to their advances, and so I ignore the outside sounds.

It is a forest out there, with treacherous roads and magical beasts, and only in these castle walls am I truly safe.

There's tapping again, and then my name is called.

"Briar!"

I ignore it.

"Briar! Briar!"

I don't acknowledge it. I don't look. I keep moving as it keeps calling my name. It never stops, even as I walk up the stairs I hear it, calling me, over and over.

I reach my bedroom door, and just before I close it, I hear it:

"Briar, I see you!"

I slam the door and then the music intensifies.

It booms all around me, as if every single radio in this house has been tuned in to the same channel.

It roars from the attic, where the majority of the radios are located.

It's a jazzy, upbeat song. I can pick out the saxophones and the trumpets and the trombones. There's a piano now, and drums, the strumming of a guitar. It feels like a story, like someone sleepwalking.

I face the door.

"Please just let me get some work done," I plead.

The song ceases, and I feel as if something inside me unravels. A seam loosens, and I need to stitch it back together before I come undone. I clutch at my stomach. I feel the wind knocked out of me.

The house grows quiet.

Outside, the wind howls, rattling windows, and I hear a car driving steadily along the boulevard.

The doorknob rattles.

"Bri!"

I'm watching as it turns. I slam against the door and lock it.

"Bri, let me in. I need to show you something."

"Please stop!" I scream.

My heartbeat thrashes in my ears. I feel lightheaded, dizzy. Black spots fill the outlines of my sight, and then the doorknob stops moving. I catch my breath, feeling the blood return to my face, and only when I feel safe do I return to my computer chair.

"I'm going to get back to work," I tell myself.

A text appears on my phone from Daniel, and my heart feels as if it falls to my feet.

Daniel: I miss you.

My hand shakes as I reach for it and stare at those three words.

Another message comes in.

Daniel: I know you're awake. Emily said you haven't been sleeping. Please, Bri. Don't push me away. I'm here for you. I promise. I want to be here.

Bri: I'm just so tired.

Daniel: I know.

Bri: How's work?

Daniel: Nothing overwhelming tonight. I can come over when I'm done?

Bri: That'd be nice. And, I'm sorry. I'm just not OK right now. I miss her.

Daniel: I know. We're getting a call. I'll see you soon.

Before my mother died, everything was going great. I'd wake up in the morning and feel so good, so hopeful. I was writing steadily. My thoughts were clear and focused. I could complete small and complex tasks. I could finish writing articles. And now, even just sitting here, I am exhausted. I'm tired all the time. My days are all blending together, and I feel like I'm losing a grasp on all of it. And I'm scared. I'm scared I'm going to lose everything and lose myself.

My mother's illness was so aggressive that I felt like a part of me died with her too. All those late nights caring for her, sitting in that chair by her bedside, watching her sleep while I myself was too afraid to sleep, because what if she needed water? What if she was in pain? What if she was cold and needed another blanket? I was on alert. High alert, and now I feel useless because no matter what I did, no matter what I do, she's still dead.

Now I feel like I'm wasting away in this house. Planning the smallest task, like going to get groceries, will wipe me out for days.

Sometimes when I'm talking to Emily or reading, everything goes blank and I forget what I'm doing, or I forget what my next thought should be.

Then I remember that this is part of grieving, my brain and body adapting to the fact that my mother is gone, and when I finally accept that, then there will be a new expanse of grief to cross.

I've kept Daniel away because I'm afraid for him to really see me unwell. I'm afraid to talk to him about the house. I'm afraid he will worry, but I know that the dreams and the house are all interconnected, and I need to work on this alone.

I don't know what I'll tell him when I see him later. I'll tell him I am scared. That I miss my mother, and that I will mourn her until my own death. I don't think I'll tell him about Isaac. I don't think he'd understand.

In terms of sleep, I will tell him not to worry, that I've returned to writing.

My phone buzzes again.

I look down to the screen.

Daniel: I just need you to know that I love you. That's all. Back to work.

I take the phone in my hand and, with the other, brush away tears that have formed in the corners of my eyes.

"What if I lose him too?" I say.

Prairie patters over to me and lies beside me. Her eyes wide.

"What if everyone I love leaves me?"

She's sitting straight up now.

"Okay." I laugh. "Promise me, then, you won't leave me, Prairie." I pet the top of her head; then I place my hand on her side. "Fine, then what if he breaks my heart?"

Prairie grumbles.

"I just can't take any more pain," I say. And it is, it's painful to mourn, the headaches, the tension in my jaw, the heaviness in my chest, my aching joints from the stress of it all.

Prairie snorts.

I sigh. "You're right. I should get back to writing."

I look at the book on my desk and smile. "Daniel and I have known each other a very long time," I say. "And it all started with that story. In high school, one day, we went on a field trip to the Auditorium Theatre. They were performing *Sleeping Beauty*, and before you say anything, most people haven't read Charles Perrault's *The Sleeping Beauty of the Wood*. Everyone assumes they know what happens, how she's awakened, but not everyone has read the story."

I knew the story because Mother read it to me again and again. The teachers didn't want us whispering throughout the performance, so they paired us off with someone we didn't normally talk to. That's how Daniel and I met.

"Anyway, on the bus back to school that day, Daniel said he was moving. He looked very sad. I held his hand and told him he'd be all right. We reconnected recently when Emily started working as an EMT and she told me how wonderful her partner was. When she invited him and the rest of her team over for a Fourth of July barbecue, he looked at me and said, 'Sleeping Beauty!' And he's been in my life since."

The music turns on again. It's a faraway song from a faraway time. The lyrics are sad and beautiful.

So far away and so long ago
One day I dreamed a dream
Now I see that dream is right here beside me

I look toward the wall before me, the green-and-gold wallpaper, following those golden loops and swirls. For a moment I catch the sweet scent of an evening in spring, and there it is, the smell of velvety roses and fresh-cut grass.

I know there's a secret here I'm meant to find, in this house, in these songs, in these dreams.

"I promise I will help you," I say to the house, "but you need to help me too. Maybe if we both find what we are looking for, we won't be so sad anymore."

Chapter 10

TIME: 3:00 p.m.
DATE: Wednesday, December 6

I don't know when it happens, but it does.

I'm standing outside with my coat over my pajamas. My winter boots are on. I'm in the snow on the boulevard, looking at the front of my house. My eyes draw up to the turret, and there I am, my other self, standing in the window. I am watching myself watching . . . me.

Two points converging.

Both versions of me existing right here and now. Is it even possible to split your consciousness and send it outside, away from your body? I don't know why that question comes to me. It sounds like something Isaac would ask.

Isaac. The things he said sounded so magical, otherworldly. I am starting to hope that maybe the supernatural is possible.

I look down at my hands.

This is beyond my consciousness. This is another me. I am standing outside, and I am watching myself standing in the window watching me, and I am now shouting "Briar!" to myself.

As I yell my own name, my mind tries to make sense of it all. Which is the real version of me? Is one real and the other the dream self? If so, which one am I?

I hear the wind but don't feel it. I see the snowflakes cascading down from the black sky, and as they land on my eyelashes, I don't even feel them melt into my eyes.

I feel myself being tugged across the street.

There are no cars outside. All the lights along the houses on the boulevard are off. It seems so quiet. It seems so still. Just as I begin to wonder if I am the only person in this world, I see two bright-white spots approaching. Headlights. The car is driving slowly toward me. I stand beside a tree, hoping I'm not spotted and wondering why I'm hiding. There's an internal alarm ringing inside me, telling me to run, telling me to hide, telling me that if whoever is in that car stops and sees me, it will be bad.

The car slows just as it approaches my house. It's black. The lone occupant is a man. He is wearing a dark coat and a dark hat, and I cannot make out the rest of his face because I cannot tell whether his features are obscured by the moisture on the glass from the melting snowflakes that cling to the window or if his face is obscured only to me.

I stare closely until I make out the shape of a smile, and for just a moment all I see is the shock of sharp white teeth and bloodstains. The man's head turns in my direction. He sees me. He knows I'm here and I know I am in danger.

"Do you know what date and time it is?" he asks, leaning out the car window.

My internal alarm is screaming. Time. There's something about time and dreams that should never be asked, that should never be spoken.

He stops the car in the middle of the street, pushes the door open, and my heart feels like it's about to burst into flames.

He's smiling, and it's not a kind smile, no. It's a predator locking in on his prey, and I scream. I close my eyes and scream again. I scream so loud the intensity of my own voice pierces my ears. I hear windows shatter, and it sounds like the loud rush of wind through the forest canopy.

I open my eyes and he is gone, and the car is gone, and all I see is a flickering white light ahead of me in the alleyway.

Shadows dance across the redbrick walls of the exteriors of buildings as I approach the alley. I see nothing but black trash cans for regular garbage and blue trash cans for recycling and, at the mouth of the alley, two large blue dumpsters.

There's singing. A woman's voice.

I continue moving, more and more, the squishy, crunchy sound of wet asphalt and snow beneath my feet.

I turn around and look back at the house, and there is my double, still watching.

In the alley I follow the soft dancing light, yellow and gold, to between the dumpsters. I inch forward, turn my head, and there's no fire. There's no flame. There's just her. The woman in the white dress from my dreams. She's seated against the brick wall. She's not wearing a coat. She's not wearing a jacket. How is she not completely shivering in this cold?

"A girl died here," she says.

"Yes," I say. "A long time ago."

The girl in the white dress looks to her hands on her lap. "A lot of daughters vanish in the night because of him."

Her blond hair is pulled back in a high ponytail. Her skin is so fair, translucent almost. Her dark eyelashes are long and swooping. "It's an awful way to die. Your thoughts are in the clouds, thinking about all the joyous things you will do at home, books you'll read, music you'll listen to, dances you'll attend."

Her face is glowing, and a sweet smile spreads across her lips. She's blushing. "And maybe in those thoughts are wishes that a boy whom you fell in love with at a dance will call you one day."

Her eyes meet mine, and they reveal infinite sadness. "Take me home, please. I'm tired. My feet hurt from so much walking. I just want to go home."

"What's your name?" I ask, reaching my hand out, and just before our fingers touch, I hear footsteps approach. I spin around and see him standing at the entrance of the alley, a black silhouette, but I know that frame, and I know that hat, and I know those sharp features. What is he doing here? Why is he in my dream?

"Isaac?"

"Bri," he says. "You have to bring her home. The only way is through the Gateway. Change your thoughts. Change your reality. Sleep. Find her in the Gateway."

The girl is standing beside me now, whispering in my ear. "Please take me home. Please take me home. Please take me home."

I keep my eyes on Isaac and reach for the girl's hand. Electricity courses through my body when our hands meet, and it's as if the screams of a million women rattle inside my head.

I am back at my computer desk.

Back in my chair.

Back in my house.

My feet feel heavy, and when I look down, I'm wearing my winter boots, and there's melting snow all along the edges.

I feel warm light falling against my cheek. I turn and see that the curtain is open and the sun is setting.

I think back to what Isaac said to me.

"You have to bring her home. The only way is through the Gateway."

Keys and gates and locks and thorns, I think.

Isaac spoke of meditation. The Gateway Project. Worlds and time. Consciousness. Things that creep in our sleep that are trying to send us messages.

Whoever that girl is in my dreams, she is trying to send me a message.

How did he appear in my dream?

How did he know her?

How does he know I need to go to the Gateway, whatever that is, to lead her back to her home?

I look out my window, across the street to that alley I was just standing in. "Mom," I say, "who was that girl?"

I hear the front gate opening. I look down and there is no one there, just the air pushing the front gate in.

My focus remains outside, and then I see it, that familiar gray car I had not seen in some days. My chest feels like there's a block of ice resting there. My breath escapes me.

The old man parks his car and remains sitting in the driver's seat for a few minutes, gazing at my house. I stand to the side of the window, hoping he doesn't see me, and just as I tire of standing there, he touches the top of his cap, nods, and drives off.

"Keys and gates and locks and thorns," I say softly to the window. "What does this all mean, Mother?"

A dream with a kind man I met at the park.

The appearance of a man who likes to visit our house.

Should I be worried about either of them? Someone else?

I spot movement through the corner of my eye. I watch the door to my bedroom swing open quickly. There's no noise.

I let out a yelp and then cover my mouth.

The hallway is pitch black. Something skitters across the floorboards, and in rush a few dried, weatherworn leaves.

I rush to the door, and I hear something stomping up the stairs. I lock the door once again.

My cheeks go cold. "Who's there?" I call out, but there's nothing.

The noise in the hallway ceases.

This house is always moving.

My shoulders ache with the tension of being on alert. There's no one I can talk to about this.

I look down at the cracked, dried brown leaves around my feet. The outside has been creeping inside for some time.

Regardless of how often I sweep the leaves from the back porch, they always seem to be blown back into the house when I open the kitchen door. It's not unusual to find leaves and twigs in the kitchen or living room, family room, and now upstairs, I suppose.

The house feels very much alive, something organic, that needs the rhythm of the sun and the moon, and beyond.

Yesterday I spotted a rose vine that had snaked its way through a hole I thought I'd covered up in the stained-glass window on the landing. A small rosebud resting on its tip found salvation inside, away from the night air. I didn't know what to do, so I placed some tape along the hole and allowed the vine to remain in the house.

I hear water running now, and a voice.

"I'm just going to let her sleep, but if you want to drop off food, I'll let her know you stopped by."

"Emily!" I call.

I didn't even hear her come in.

"Yeah, I'm home," she says. "I hoped you were sleeping." She tries the doorknob. "Your door's locked."

I unlock it. She's eyeing me. "You all right?"

"Yeah, I must have done that by mistake."

She's wearing a bathrobe over her navy-blue Chicago Fire Department sweats. "Daniel's going to stop by. He picked up some food."

"That's really nice of him."

She hangs the towel over her shoulder. "I think he wants to ask you something."

"What?"

Emily is chewing the inside of her mouth. "His lease is up soon, and he was going to ask if he could move in here."

I exhale. Nervous at the thought. I don't want him to see me like this all the time. All jittery and confused.

Emily holds her hands up. "Look, it's a good idea. I'm fine with it. We need the help around here. You have the space."

My head is in my hands.

"What is it? Don't you love him?"

"Of course I love him. Of course I want him here all of the time, but"—I sit back and motion to myself—"I'm not okay."

She crosses her arms across her chest. "Uh, yeah, that's clear as day. We all know that. And we're both still here."

I start tearing up, but I catch myself and shake it off. I change the subject.

"How's Dana?" I ask.

Dana, Emily's longtime girlfriend. She was with me when my mother died, because both Emily and Daniel were at work.

"Residency hours are no joke." She laughs to herself. "We're going to make it work. I'll do whatever I can to make it work. If I see her for a few minutes on a break. If I can take her dinner. Whatever, I'm going to make it work, because I'm marrying a doctor." She hops on my bed. "Either that or I'm stuck here living with you and Daniel."

"Daniel doesn't live here . . . yet."

"I am tired of shoveling snow, Bri. Daniel can do it when he moves in."

We both laugh.

"You are absolutely ridiculous." And this is why she is my best friend.

"Can I ask you a work question?"

Her face goes serious anytime it has to do with work.

She hesitates. "Sure."

"What do people say right before they die? Like, when they know they're going to die?"

"Ahh." She throws her head back, then lies down on my bed and says: "Usually they call out for someone. The person they loved the most."

I close my laptop, and I'm looking away from her now. My thoughts drift back to the dream and the house and Isaac.

"Have you ever heard anyone mention something called the Gateway as they're dying?"

Emily props herself up on her elbows so she can see me. "Gateway?" She looks around the room, thinking. "Like the gates of heaven?"

"No." I rub my eyes and then yawn. "I don't think it's like that, at least I don't think so. It's like something with your brain, some place you reach with meditation."

She scratches behind her ear. "You're talking states of consciousness?"

I nod. "I guess so. I've been reading a lot about it for this article I want to write."

"And this is what you do during the day? When you're not sleeping? Thinking about sleeping?"

"Emily . . . I'm being serious."

"I'm just joking," she blurts out. "Look." Emily sits up and holds her hands out. "Stay with me here. There's gamma," she says, holding one finger up. "That's when we're concentrating, reading a book, or studying for a test." She raises another finger. "Then there's beta. Here we're a little more relaxed," she says, shimmying her shoulders. "Not fully engaged. For you, maybe that means you're on one of your walks with Prairie. Or a hike." Another finger goes up. "Alpha. Here you're super relaxed. Well, not you right now, but you know what I mean. You're not really paying attention to your surroundings."

Emily lowers her hand. "Now these last two, these are where you're furthest away from being focused. There's theta. That's the state you hit when you're in deep meditation. Everyone enters this stage before they fall asleep. They're also in this stage as soon as they wake up. That's that fuzzy, foggy twilight state you're in when you're opening your eyes in bed."

"So we're in theta twice?" I ask. "Before we go to sleep and when we wake up? Night and day."

She raises her eyebrows. "Right. The brain does a lot of weird things in theta. Very often when people see ghosts or shadows or weird things, it's because they're in theta, falling asleep or waking up."

They're in between worlds, I think.

"What's the last stage?"

"Oh, sleep. Your delta stage. This is when a person is completely asleep. The slowest recorded brain waves are when we're asleep. To this day, literally no one can tell any of us why we sleep. Yeah, they'll say rest, restoration, but why? Why does the body even need to sleep, and sleep a certain amount of hours? We don't know. We understand so very little about why we even biologically need sleep."

I find myself yawning again.

Emily stands. "Speaking of sleep, why don't you close your eyes for a bit?"

"I slept . . ." I start . . . and she's giving me that look like she knows I'm lying.

And then I hear it, music playing deep within the house. It's gentle, like a lullaby. Emily doesn't hear it. I can tell.

"Just sleep for a bit. When Daniel gets here, I'll wake you. We'll all eat, and then he's got a shift tomorrow, and you and I will go on our adventure."

"Adventure?" I say.

"Bri! We just talked about this. We were going to hang out. You don't remember?" She's shaking her head.

"Yeah, I remember. Sorry," I say, clearly not remembering a discussion we had.

Emily finally notices the stack of manila folders on my desk. "Those are from the library, right?"

"Yeah, just things my mother kept and wrote about."

Emily is closer now, leaning and reading the tabs. "Consciousness, then? That's what you're writing about?"

I nod. "Consciousness."

"Ugh, huh." She nods and then pats me on the shoulder. "Get some rest."

"It's a good-paying feature," I say. "Plus, I need the distraction. Like I told Isaac . . ." I start, and then I immediately regret saying his name.

She looks from side to side. "Who is Isaac?"

"A man I met at the park."

"Briar." She says my full name, like my mom would when I was about to get in trouble for something.

I take a deep breath. "It's fine."

"You very well know they found a woman dead not too far from here in some abandoned house. And now Northerly Island."

"Northerly Island?"

"Yeah. It's all unfolding. Just be careful."

"It's fine, Emily. I'm fine." I stand, not knowing where I'm going to go, and that's when she notices I'm wearing my boots and the puddle of water around me.

"Why are you wearing boots in the house?"

"I . . ."

I don't have a good answer.

"Bri . . ."

"I forgot."

"You forgot because you're tired and you need to sleep. Maybe we should reschedule."

"No! I want to go. I need to go. It'll be good for me to get out of the house."

Tears fill my eyes, and I know it's because my mind and body are tired. I think about my mother, and I think about the gray car and the black car and the girl in the alley.

Keys and gates and locks and thorns and I just want to scream because it's not all coming together fast enough.

Emily places a hand on her hip. "You know, maybe meditation would be good for you."

Meditation. Gateway. Maybe I should download the meditation audio Isaac mentioned and try that out?

Emily taps on my desk. "Rest and then we'll go on that adventure . . ." She looks out the window. "Where are we going on this adventure?"

I scan the manila folders, and the answer is right in front of me.

"Archer Avenue."

"Archer Avenue?" she asks.

"Yeah, I'll give us a ghost tour, courtesy of my mother's notes here."

Before Emily makes it to the hallway, I ask, "Can you make sure the doors are locked?"

A look of concern spreads across her face. "Yeah, Bri. I'll make sure."

Chapter 11

TIME: *1:00 p.m.*
DATE: *Thursday, December 7*

Emily drove down I-55, passing billboards that flew past so quickly there was no way to know what they were selling, so I suppose the marketers only hoped that these sales messages seeped into the minds of drivers subliminally.

Then it was past industrial corridors, shipping containers and refineries, until we left the city limits and entered tiny towns and villages that Chicagoans ignore. Places with names like Justice and Summit and Willowbrook. The entire time, Prairie whimpered and whined. She doesn't like car rides.

I instruct Emily to drive up the small hill. A church peeks out from the top, and as we turn, the headstones and cemetery grounds come into view.

"All of Archer Avenue," I say, "is a thin place."

"What does that even mean?" Emily asks as she parks and turns off the car.

"My mom told me thin places are places where the veil between the spiritual and material world are somehow thinner. They're places with strange sightings; people claim to have experienced miracles, see visions, or see . . ."

"Ghosts. We're ghost-hunting, aren't we?"

I look out the driver's-side window and see those rows of granite and limestone blocks. Many are aged, pockmarked, and worn away by years of rain and snow and sunlight.

She's looking out the window, and then behind us. "Bri, there's no one here."

"It's fine," I say as I reach back. Prairie's tugging at her seat belt, ready to bolt out.

On our drive here, I told Emily about the accidental deaths I read about in Mother's notes, many of them along the Illinois and nearby Michigan Canal. I told her about the spectral black carriage and horses with fiery eyes that were reported by village residents in this area for over a hundred years. I told her about the shadowy forms that rose above the church at night and how people fell to their knees at the sight of those terrifying monks. And I told her about how this place was where my earliest ancestors in Chicago died.

"This entire area is legend, folklore, and myth central for Chicagoans," I say as I slam my car door and point at the church. "Much of that starts here." Behind me are tombstones jutting out from the ground, fluffy white outlining their edges.

"What's the difference?" Emily asks. She is kneeling, adjusting Prairie's bright-orange winter coat.

"Difference between what?"

"Legend, folklore, myth?"

The church is closed, but I direct her to the cemetery, where we start walking, snow beneath our steps.

"We're not going to get in trouble for being here, right?" She looks behind her shoulder. "I don't feel like getting arrested in Lemont, Illinois."

"No one's going to come up this hill, and if they do, we'll see them from afar. Don't worry, we're not going to get arrested. The gate's open; that means the cemetery is open and we can be here," I reassure her.

It's the first time in a long time I feel a little clearer headed. Maybe it was the drive, being out of the house, or maybe it's this cemetery. It reminds me of the beautiful work my mom did when she was alive. She even restored some monuments here. There are pictures of some of them in her folders.

The cemetery is small, and so it's easy to take it all in visually. The snow on the ground is fresh, and we're the first ones to leave behind our footprints. It's also quiet here, above the town, and we can barely hear the cars passing by below.

I clap my gloved hands together. "All right, let's get started with the tour," I say. "A legend is something that's said to be tied to history, but it doesn't have any proof behind it. Folklore is a collection of tales about people and animals that just aren't true. A myth is a story that tries to answer some of life's big questions, like how the universe was created. Things like that. And an urban legend, that's a story we're told about something that happened. Just think of stories someone tells you when they're like, 'Hey, you have to hear this. It happened to a friend of mine. It's wild.' Think of the man with a hook who stalks young couples making out in their car—"

"Or," Emily interrupts, "the vanishing hitchhiker."

"You got it." I nod.

"It doesn't look much like a castle," she says, hands on her hips, her face directed to the stone church. "But you're right, it is very pretty."

Emily takes a step back, her boots crunching in the snow. She raises her phone and snaps a picture of Saint James Church.

"Monk's Castle," I say. "All good Chicago-area hauntings have good nicknames." I continue my mini tour for her. It gives me something to do, something to get my mind situated back in this reality. "The church was started by people who worked on the Illinois and Michigan Canal. They'd haul limestone along that steep hill we drove up."

"When did your family come to the Chicago area?" she asks.

"Eighteen hundreds," I say. "My great-great-great-grandmother Talia and great-great-grandfather Joseph. Talia was from France and met Joseph in Ireland. They had a family, came here, and just out there by the water is where Joseph died. Talia and her kids moved down Archer Avenue to a small farmhouse in the woods."

"That's such a sad story," Emily says. "But it's impressive. A woman living alone at that time."

"I'm sure it wasn't easy. Leave home with two kids for another country. Your husband's killed within weeks of arriving."

"Is he buried around here?" she asks, scanning the graves.

"No. He was carried off by the current."

"Oh, that's messed up. I'm sorry."

"A lot of people died digging the Illinois and Michigan Canal. What's even more messed up is there's really no official record of who they were, how many were killed. There's nothing."

All I know are stories, bits and pieces of broken accounts passed down from one generation to the next, our way to remember our ancestors who emigrated here; even if no one else remembers them, we at least have our tales. Maybe that's what part of our memories are, records of the ways in which we keep the dead alive.

Emily has spent a lot of time with death. I often wonder how she remains so calm and still, considering all the horrors she is forced to witness. She told me it is all about focus, that's what keeps her together. Being so focused and in the moment while she is at work, and when she isn't at work, she lets it go.

She rarely speaks of the things she does on the job unless I ask. It is as if it were another Emily who left the house each day and climbed into that ambulance and spent hours driving around the city, cutting through traffic, rushing out of the vehicle and racing upstairs, flanked by family members pointing and screaming, "This way! This way!" Bursting into living rooms, bedrooms, backyards, and garages. I've seen her face in the early-morning hours right when she's returned home and is trying to transition to her life here, and I know the face of loss when I see it. Her eyes lost in thought. I can picture her playing out scenarios in her mind: "What if we had driven a little faster?" "What if I had moved quicker?" I see regret in the tension forming around her jaw, her eyes unfocused, her rubbing her fingers together. Death is such a difficult opponent to fight.

"Sometimes there's nothing you can do when there are so many holes in a person," she once said while she was slumped in a chair in the family room, her face blank. "It just won't stop, the blood flow, and I put gauze on, and I apply pressure, and if it's winter and they're wearing a heavy coat, it takes time, even if it's just seconds, that's too long, because it's just blood pouring, seeping out so fast. I try to do what I can."

I point to a headstone jutting out of the ground, the writing on its surface completely washed away by decades of rain and snow. "I've talked to you about limestone, right?"

"Little bit," she says, admiring the church.

We continue walking, our movements slow and careful, so as not to slip and fall. We weave between monuments, our boots crunching beneath us.

"Limestone is made up of all of this marine waste. Whatever falls to the seafloor. Think of little sea creatures. Anything with a hard shell. When they die, that tough part that won't break down just collects on the bottom of the ocean, river, lake. Oh." I raise a finger. Remembering.

"Some limestone also forms on land." I point at the church. "Tons of this stuff eventually gets buried under the sediment, and it all gets compacted and pressed into rock. Just look at those layers. It all contains millions of teeny animals, corals, and clams and things."

Emily's eyes move up over the old church. "You're saying it's made up of dead things?"

"Yup. Limestone and things that are made of limestone are all made of dead things. That's probably why somehow it all got connected to paranormal activity."

We approach a small mausoleum on the property. Emily takes a picture. "I think we're kinda obsessed with dead things," she says.

"Maybe dead things are obsessed with us," I say.

"That could be true too."

The name above the church's doorway is THOMAS COBURN, and the copper doors are a bright green, in parts, from the oxidation over the years.

"There's a trail nearby, but I don't think we'll make it there today since I want to make sure we have enough time to get to our hike. My great-great-great-grandfather Joseph wasn't buried, but other people who died working on the canal were, and even before that, there were burials here. So way before the church was even established, this hill was used as a burial place. It's believed that this was the cemetery of the Indigenous population."

History books I pored over at home said that this piece of land stood out to French missionary Father Jacques Marquette, who traveled through the area with cartographer Louis Jolliet. They stopped here for a time, and Father Marquette gave mass here. But the dates are all fuzzy as to what happened here and when.

The capstone over the church doors lists the date as 1833. The memorial arch reads 1837. The cornerstone reads 1853.

Maybe the dates are all over the place because those immigrants were all trying to adjust to life in a new land, in a new climate, and maybe recording things wasn't a priority, like the date the actual church was built or when burials here first started.

From what I remember, the earliest recorded burial here is for someone named Michael Dillon, who was buried in 1816. But even then, we know there were burials here before records were kept.

There's just so much mystery about this place.

All of Archer Avenue, really. It's all murky. Names and dates. What was seen. What was said. Who died out here? How?

Emily looks toward the cemetery, her hands in her pockets. "Why have you been so worried lately about making sure the doors are locked? Did something happen? Is it that Isaac guy you mentioned?"

I adjust my knit cap on my head. "No, just with what's been going on on the news, with the murdered women," I say. I will never tell her about the rose, the man in the gray car. Any of it. I don't want to worry her.

"I'm serious, Bri. There's something going on in this city. Community organizers keep talking about a serial killer operating here. If you see anything weird, say something."

I look up and take a deep breath. The cold air chilling my lungs. "I will."

Continuing with my tour, I say, "We can't forget the obvious, that there were people living on this land when Marquette came here, and just look at this place? It's a bluff, overlooking his land, and yeah, it's just the outskirts of some small town, but way back then, this was a strategic lookout for the Indigenous peoples here."

Emily gives me that silly smile of hers, as if she's fighting back a laugh.

"What?" I ask.

"Nothing, you just kinda seem good right now. Happy"—she raises her arms—"and strangely, all we needed to do to make that happen was bring you to a cemetery." She spins around, and then gets tangled in Prairie's leash, reaches down, and unhooks Prairie from her leash to straighten out the material.

We continue walking, Prairie ahead of us in her pink harness, matching coat and boots, her little feet making indentations in the snow.

"Now why this area is called Monk's Castle varies as well. It's thought one of the earliest reverends, Reverend Aschenbrenner, would chase graveyard thieves away at night, shouting at them from a bullhorn and waving his flashlight at them. Even Aschenbrenner knew about the belief that this area was haunted. Here, I even have a few quotes."

"Look at you," she says. "You came prepared."

I reach for my phone, remove my right glove, and scan through my notes app until I find my details on the Cal Sag Church. "Ah, here we go: In 1973, in the Lemont centennial book, he said: 'There are many legends and tales about the Sag which whet the appetite of the historical minded.' One of the weirder ghost stories from this place comes from a Cook County police officer who filed a two-page report about what he saw here."

"Now listen to this quote: *'After Thanksgiving, Officer Herb Roberts said he was on patrol out here and he saw nine hooded figures floating up the hill. He went to retrieve his shotgun and ran after the figures, but when he got to the top of the hill they were gone.*

"'More accounts emerged over the years, of people being chased out of the graveyard by dark figures. One account by Father Ploszynski claims when he would look outside of the rectory windows, he'd see the landscape of the bluff rising and falling, as if the land was breathing. He'd also later go on to claim he too saw hooded figures walking among the headstones at night. Back then at least, they could have been grave robbers and not ghosts, but who knows?'"

Emily rubs the tip of her nose with the back of her gloved hand. "That's completely wild. Why don't you write about stuff like this?" she asks.

"Like what?"

"Like ghosts and stuff. Folklore. You love this stuff," she says.

I know what she means, that I should probably be writing about something that's not so heavy right now.

Emily sighs and shakes her head. "You know what's best for you, Bri. I'm just here because I care."

"And because it's cheap rent."

"Of course it's cheap rent! You don't even have central air."

We laugh and continue on our walk, our feet digging into the snow and Prairie bounding behind us.

I tell Emily more about what I learned from Mother's old books. How reports of monks walking around this area spiked in the 1970s. How people have claimed to see all sorts of things, black-robed figures rising above the church, crawling out from behind the tombstones, appearing with all sorts of things, books and candles in hand. Often said to be chanting, but no one could ever recount what was being said.

There are more stories, not just about monks. There are stories of people saying they've seen the large statue atop the hill change position. That they've seen flashing ghost lights floating across the area. My favorite claim is people having encountered a black carriage pulled by two shiny black stallions with red fiery eyes, galloping across the grounds.

I've always wondered how these stories come to be.

Is it that someone sees something and tells someone, and the accounts morph from person to person, shifting and changing over time? I'm very well aware that all these stories existed way before the internet. They were shared by word of mouth, or in newspapers or official reports. So which is it?

I'm staring down a headstone of someone who died over a hundred years ago, and it's so hard to comprehend that here I am over a century after that person took their final breath.

"Why do you think all of these accounts get repeated again and again? Is it because multiple people encountered these things? Or do you think it's just because people want to believe these things?"

Emily is admiring a picture she took of an obelisk memorial on her phone screen. "Honestly, Bri, people just want to believe in this stuff. It's death too, you know? That fear of death. They're trying to understand it. Create stories about it. Maybe in hopes it'll all make sense somehow. Life and death. When you think about it, there really is no making sense of either."

She shoves her phone into her pocket. "Your house is made of limestone, right?"

"Yes."

I always remember Mother talking about that, about the house being made of limestone. She'd say, "Our house is like a radio. It can pick up different frequencies." And I never understood that until recently. She'd say that and more strange things close to the end. She'd just babble and talk, these long conversations with herself. It was like I was watching in real time the synapses of her brain firing away.

I realized later that her behavior was all part of the dying process.

When my mother would be in those moments, I wouldn't say anything. I'd just sit there and listen. It was scary at first, then sad, and then I just accepted it. She was undergoing a change; she was visiting some place, testing it out before she made her permanent move there, and for now I could not join her.

What I do know is that whatever was happening to my mother in that house, in my house now, as she died, it was peaceful, beautiful, divine, supernatural.

Emily puts her arm around my shoulder. We come up to a simple white headstone on the ground. The edges are stained black with time by rain and snow and dirt that get blown with the wind. A Latin cross is embossed in the top center with a Gothic arch that reads BRIDGET. There is a marker standing right behind it:

ERECTED BY THOMAS BURNS IN MEMORY OF HIS WIFE BRIDGET

ALIAS

MCMANIMAN

WHO DEPARTED THIS LIFE

FEB 23, 1856

AE. 20 Y's. & 1M

NATIVE OF THE PARISH OF

DUNAMORE COUNTY DONEGAL

IRELAND

MAY SHE REST IN PEACE AMEN

"She was so young," Emily says. "We're just a few years older than she was."

I wonder what age is the cap to be too young to die? I feel like at any age there's something someone would want to do, see, live. Twenty. Forty. Sixties. Beyond.

"Here, what about this one." I motion Emily over toward a monument I've admired here for some time, sculpted in the form of a tree trunk. The faded engraving takes a moment to read, but the words appear with some effort:

MARY, WIFE OF JOSEPH BROWN

AGED 39 YEARS, 7 MOS., 19 DAYS

"Here," I read. "She died December ninth, 1872. A lifetime ago. But she was almost forty. And then there's her." I point to a headstone made of red rock. The surname written across the top is:

McGINTY

And just beneath that is her name:

HANNAH

1810–1880

"Hannah was seventy years old. Did she feel like she had enough time?"

Emily admires the sculpture and says: "No amount of time is enough."

I notice more and more how women tended to die much younger, little girls and teens, women in their early twenties. I imagined the environment here was difficult; the weather and sickness, and even childbirth, were major causes of death for many women.

I really admired my great-great-great-grandmother Talia, who lived out here alone so long ago, as a widow with two little children. She was so far away from home. She must have been scared in these woods at night, a place so foreign and a place so strange.

We make it to the end of the cemetery. "Is this the end of Archer Avenue?" Emily asks.

"Guess that depends on who you ask. It could be the beginning or the end."

This road started here, with a history of ghost stories stretching all the way into the city. Archer Avenue is dotted by stories of apparitions throughout the years. Legend and folklore, myth and murder. The stories told about this road are infamous, and while it's not in the very city limits, each and every one of these sites, nearly every Chicagoan grows up knowing these tales. We hear about them on Halloween, in school from kids trying to scare us with tales of monsters, and at pubs, that one drunk guy recounting what a friend of a friend saw.

Chicagoans know their town has some weird stories, and all Chicagoans know about this road, and most of the eerie sightings along its way. Many, however, aren't familiar with where I'm going to take Emily next, a place my mother muttered to me about in her last days, in her transition from here to where she went.

We make our way back to the car. Prairie is moving quickly, ready to get out of the cold. Emily opens the driver's-side door, turns on the car, and starts warming up the engine. I open the door right behind her and buckle in Prairie. It's when I walk around to the passenger side that I pause, noticing something. There are footprints. My chest tightens. I want to jump in the car and scream for Emily to *Drive! Right now!* Tell her we have to get out of here.

I follow the footprints and see they came from down the hill and stopped right at my door.

"Are you staying here with the ghosts?" Emily shouts, oblivious to the footprints.

I open the passenger door, sit down on the seat, and kick off the snow. She's talking to me, but my mind is a jumble of possibilities.

"Let's go," I say, trying to not sound so urgent, trying not to scare her. I lock my door.

She turns to me. "You all right?"

"Yeah, just tired is all," I say, even though I know we were visited by one of the famous ghosts, or monsters, that live along Archer Avenue. I don't want to tell her, because we need to visit this next site, and I don't want her to be scared. This isn't just for my research for my story. This is for me, to prove to myself that there is something more after death, and so far I'm seeing little glimmers of that.

As she backs out and drives down the hill, I keep scanning the grounds for anything, any movement, anyone, but there's nothing.

Chapter 12

TIME: 2:00 p.m.
DATE: Thursday, December 7

There's planning involved.

There's thinking.

There're ideas.

There's waiting.

There's time.

I saw you with him. I hated that. I hate how you smiled at him. I hate how you spoke to him. I hate all the happiness he gives you. Only I can give you that. I can give you what you need. What you need is sleep. Rest. Eternal. Deep.

I came for Aurora, but she reminded me of the deal. "A daughter's daughter," she said, standing in the doorway of her beautiful home. She looked down at her stomach. She was pregnant with you.

Numbers work that way. Bloodlines and lineage. Not the mother. The daughter. But aren't all mothers daughters? No. There is a skip in time. A beat. I lose them there in that break.

Aurora's face was not happy.

I bowed my head, covered my heart with my hat, and stepped away. "I will return one day, for your daughter."

She slammed the door.

There was a party after your birth. I stood outside in the shadows. I watched through the window. All the people there, singing, dancing, eating, drinking. You in your pretty little white dress and how they handed you from person to person to hug and to hold, to kiss and to tell you "I love you."

I love you too, Bri. I love you the most.

I watched you play in your yard with your big pink ball. I watched you through the windows. I watched you. And I waited for the right time, and when that time arrived, I visited your home, but you were gone.

"Leave her alone," Aurora said, meeting me at the door again.

"Time" is all I said.

You can't stop time. You can't stop what is meant to be. You are mine. This is how it works.

I collect them. I place parts of them in this box in my home. An identification card. A passport. There are hairpins and concert tickets. There's a shimmering purple scarf. I have these green dangling earrings. An engagement ring. A journal. A tube of bright-pink lip gloss. A hairbrush. A pretty pink pen. More. Pieces of them that sit with me in the day. This holds me over until I can visit with them in the night, unlock their glass coffins, and take pleasure in their terror.

Father knew that is when the important work would be conducted. At night. Father's work was more involved than mine. But I do like my work. We each have a style. A preference. A motive, as they call it. An MO. I like those letters: *M* and then *O*. But what I do is more complex than that.

"Modus operandi."

Do you know that word? Briar?

My MO: Find the beauties. Put them to sleep.

My signature: I like to put them to rest outside. Under the stars. Beneath the moonlight.

Where they can hear the trees. In a forest is best. There's no forest in Chicago, but I make do.

Sometimes they call people like me a "person of interest." That is a funny term. I am not a person. Not really. I have no interest, except in them.

Person of interest: Someone to be questioned. Someone to be monitored. Someone connected to a crime.

They are a little different from a suspect.

Suspect: Someone suspected of committing a crime.

Law enforcement has many rules. They have many measures. It is easy to know what someone is thinking when they think of the same thing each time. It's so easy to get around authorities. They are always thinking about what it is I can possibly be thinking, but they do not know what is in my head.

I think of some ways police use to apprehend suspected criminals:

- Observe the location of the crime. Try to remember if they have seen the suspect elsewhere.
- Record the time as precisely as possible.
- Observe if the suspect is carrying anything that can be considered a weapon, knife, handgun, revolver.
- If the suspect left the scene of the crime, note the time.
- If the suspect left the scene of the crime in a vehicle, note the vehicle make and model.
- Watch out for accomplices or decoys.

Police aren't very smart, because I am always thinking around these things. It's so easy to adjust my movements when all their tactics can be found easily. So many measures.

They also like to record the description of the suspect:

- Sex.
- Race.
- Origin.
- Age estimate.

- Weight estimate.
- Build.
- Face—what does the face look like? Describe.
- Clothes—what do the clothes look like? Describe.

No one can describe me because I am easy to forget.

- Average face.
- Average build.
- Average clothes.

I do not stand out. I am just an average, everyday man. I am the man in line at the grocery store. I am the man behind you in traffic. I am the man who stands next to you in the elevator. I am the man seated across from you in the airport terminal. I am the man you walk past in a restaurant. I blend in anywhere. I blend in everywhere.

I'm in my apartment. It's small. It's clean. I don't own many things. I don't like a lot of things. I like their things.

I'm reading. On the computer. Scroll and click. Scroll and click. This is what most people do all day. Like mice on a wheel. Going round and round. They're not thinking of time. They're not thinking of beyond things. They're just scrolling and clicking, but I am looking for their names.

I stop.

Aurora.

What happened to my beautiful Aurora, whom I dreamed about too often at night? Who I wished was a daughter's daughter? How did I miss this?

Aurora Thorne died today in her home in Hyde Park. She was 61.

Aurora was a world-renowned artist and scholar. For years she was a funeral arts restorer, traveling the world to consult and rebuild statuary. She was a professor at the School of the Art Institute in Restoration. In recent years, she worked at the Art Institute as their lead book historian expert.

Aurora is survived by her only child, Briar. Funeral services will be held at Resurrection Cemetery followed by burial.

My face feels wet. I pound on the desk. I am mad for Aurora. I am mad for me. If I could have just put Aurora to sleep, she would be with me forever and not a rotting thing in the ground.

Briar. I stand. Briar. I think. Briar. Briar.

Little Briar Rose.

"I will see you when the sun goes down!"

Screaming. Screaming. They are screaming in their glass coffins. In their golden towers.

I will let them out in the nighttime, and then they will scream. And then they will walk, and then they will repeat their ghostly patterns.

But it is not nighttime, and I will not see them for some hours. In the day I am here. In the night I am with them. That is how this works. The flip-flop of time. Topsy-turvy. What is real? I am real. They are real.

My princesses.

Briar is my princess. Aurora was my queen. I lost Aurora. Dead in the ground. Not for me.

I will visit Briar. She will see. She will be happy to meet me. I will tell her about her mother. I will tell her about her grandmother. I will tell her about her aunt. I will tell her about all of them. I will tell her not to be scared, because it's just a little hurt. A little pinch. I do like when it hurts. But after it is over, she will open her eyes again. She will see me. She will always be with me. I keep them there. In my nighttime world. My father did a little bit of this.

Preserve.

When the sun sets, I will let my beauties out. When the sun sets, I will go to Aurora's, now Briar's, house. When the sun sets, I will begin my planning. I will squeeze Briar's throat tight, too tight, and I will feel her body tremble against mine. I will enjoy her life evaporating in my hands like mist. I will enjoy the feel of her soul pulling apart from her body. I will enjoy when she wakes as a ghost and screams. I will enjoy when I place her in that glass coffin in my nighttime world. I will enjoy making a new legend.

She had no sooner touched the spindle when the magic curse was fulfilled, and she pricked herself in the finger. The instant that she felt the prick she fell onto a bed that was standing there, and she lay there in a deep sleep. And this sleep spread throughout the entire castle. The king and queen, who had just returned home, walked into the hall and began falling asleep, and all of their attendants as well.

—"Little Brier-Rose," Jacob and Wilhelm Grimm

Chapter 13

TIME: 2:30 p.m.
DATE: Thursday, December 7

There is an extensive network of forest preserves along Archer Avenue, starting at the Saint James at Sag Bridge Catholic Church. There are Henry De Tonty Woods, Buffalo Woods, Paw Paw Woods, Columbia Woods, Willow Springs Woods . . . and then there's Red Gate Woods.

The east end of Archer Avenue begins in Chicago's Chinatown. The road then passes through the neighborhoods of Bridgeport, McKinley Park, Brighton Park, Archer Heights, and Garfield Ridge. Outside Chicago, Archer Avenue moves through a collection of villages— Summit, Justice, Willow Springs—and just reaches the southernmost edge of Lemont before ending in Lockport.

It's not a long road, just over thirty-three miles. But this stretch of pavement contains a collection of histories, myths, and legends, from ghostly sightings to missing and murdered persons, so that when anyone in Chicago hears a story beginning with "Over on Archer Avenue . . . ," they know it's going to be about something in the realm of the unexplained.

There are two trails, and Emily parks right beside the one with the large informational sign. Prairie is hesitant to leap from the car, but I'm not surprised. These woods have a reputation for giving visitors strange feelings. It's likely because of what's buried at the end of one of the trails.

"I know," I tell her. "It's an odd place. It was odd even before the Manhattan Project chose it."

"What?" Emily slams the car door. Her mouth is open wide. "You didn't tell me all that."

I gather Prairie's leash. "I figured it would be an interesting story for our hike."

"You sure this is safe?" She looks around. "There's just our car and one other. Probably belongs to some serial killer," she says, joking, but that alone is enough to set off my anxiety. My face starts to tingle and my heart rate quickens. What if this is a bad idea?

When she turns back and looks at me, she can tell she went a little too far. "I'm sorry"—she shrugs—"but you're the one bringing us out to all of these places where there's no one . . . or fine, someone, but you get it."

"Yes, Emily, people hike. They do that."

"They also kill people. You remember the news about what happened to that woman in Midlothian Meadows?"

I do. I remember the news reports because of how gruesome it was. Ariadna Ojeda was hiking with her mother in the Midlothian Meadows, a short drive from here, when she decided to return to their car and rest. Her mother continued along the trail, and Ariadna headed back toward the parking lot.

She was never seen alive again.

After an intense search, her body was later discovered in the very woods where she'd gone missing, which made no sense. Investigators had scanned the area with dogs, so they believed the body was brought back and dumped there after search crews left. Ariadna had been beaten, raped, strangled, and set on fire. No leads were ever fully developed, at least none that authorities shared with the public.

"It must have been the Chicago Strangler," Emily says. "He always strangles his victims. Sometimes he does other things too. I'm nervous, Bri. It's us two, Prairie . . . and we're looking at a hike that's over a mile, alone, deep in some woods close to where a woman was murdered."

I'm growing nervous too, because Emily is nervous, but we are here. We made the effort to come out here, and it seems unfair that our movements should be stopped just because we fear something, fear a man.

"We'll be fine," I say. My throat feels dry. I reach in my backpack and drink some water; then I wipe my lips and say, "We have Prairie. We have pepper spray. We're going to be fine. We can't think otherwise. We have to say that and believe that."

Emily smiles. "You really are becoming like your mother, in a good way. She'd always say all of these just super nice things."

We stop at the beginning of the trail and read the sign.

DAWN OF THE ATOMIC AGE

ON DECEMBER 2, 1942, SCIENTISTS AT THE UNIVERSITY OF CHICAGO PRODUCED THE FIRST CONTROLLED NUCLEAR CHAIN REACTION IN HUMAN HISTORY. SOON AFTER, THE REACTOR WAS RELOCATED TO "SITE A" IN THE PALOS PARK FOREST PRESERVE, WHERE SCIENTISTS PERFORMED EXPERIMENTS AND BUILT AN ADDITIONAL REACTOR AS PART OF THE MANHATTAN PROJECT, THE U.S. NUCLEAR DEVELOPMENT PROGRAM DURING WORLD WAR II.

This was something else I had read about in Mother's books about Chicago and Chicago-area history. I'd learned that when Site A closed in 1954, the two reactors were buried, and a decades-long environmental cleanup by the Department of Energy took place. The area was deemed safe and reopened for public use years later. I'm sure some people are still nervous about spending time out here, where deep in the woods, the world's first nuclear reactor is buried. I believe it's fitting in some ways, that these devices—which later taught men to create machines of death and destruction—were put to rest along Archer Avenue, amid all its stories.

Emily takes a step back from the sign. She tilts her head. "Really? There's a nuclear reactor buried out here?" She drops her hand. "I'm going to be so pissed if you expose me to radioactivity and get me murdered."

"Emily," I whine.

"I'm kidding . . ." She takes a deep breath. "We'll be fine, right?"

"More than fine. It's a short hike."

And so we begin a hike that I've wanted to do since I spoke with Isaac. After talking to him, I thought more and more about synchronicity, about time and how it bends in on itself, and since then I've been needing to come out here.

The ground is muddy and covered in leaves, and while the trees are bare, there are so many of them closing in around us. Claustrophobia begins creeping in. Branches twist and curl into one another, along and across our path, and it feels like the extensions of each are like claws inching toward us, to snatch us and drag us in.

I pause. For a moment I feel like telling Emily, "No, let's turn back. We can do this another day," but I've already convinced her to come this far.

"You all right?" She's holding Prairie's leash, and the dog is panting, eyeing me.

"Yeah, I was just checking for my phone."

I'm just a few steps away from Emily, and I turn around one last time to watch the parking lot fade out of sight. We're on this trail now, to the end and back.

Emily asks me more about the article and my research. She asks when I'm aiming to complete it, and I'm not entirely sure. "Before the end of the month would be nice," I say as I start to feel suffocated by the surrounding trees.

I can only imagine that in spring the foliage must be so thick it would be impossible to peer through the wall of green. What if wildlife were hiding behind that layer, or something else?

I catch up to Emily and Prairie, whose head is low, her eyes focused ahead, her tail dipped behind her. Usually on our walks she's rushing ahead, but not here. Here, she's keeping close.

The air begins to thicken. A musky, deep scent of earth and decay and leaves stings my nostrils. I hear Emily talking, but I'm not listening to her. What I am listening to is the wind, the rustling leaves, and there, the snap of a twig behind me. I gasp. I turn around so fast the toe of my shoe catches in a gnarled tree root across the path. Emily has her hands on my shoulder before I crash to the ground.

My chest feels like it's being squeezed on either side by boulders.

There's something there. A blur in the woods. Then it's gone.

"You all right?"

I nod. There's a rolling, fluttering sensation in my stomach. I inhale. "Yes, I'm fine," I say, trying to distract myself from it all.

Prairie approaches and I kneel. She's licking my hand. I gently rub her head. "I'm fine," I tell her, but she knows I'm lying. When I stand, her head snaps in the direction where I'd seen movement.

"What is it?" Emily asks.

We both stand, scanning trees lined in snow, but there's nothing else.

"Nothing. Let's keep going."

Snow and twigs and dead leaves crunch beneath our boots.

Emily tells me about park rescues. It's a way, I think, for her to avoid thinking too much. It's hard to not notice how our voices and movements echo along the hike. I'd imagine if someone were out here, it wouldn't be very difficult to trail us, given all the noise we are making.

"Trying to find people in a park sometimes can be an exercise itself, because we'll get a call and only be told the name of the park, but not the street or any other marker that gives us anything useful about where we need to find this person. So we get there, with our gear, and we're just running around, trying to find a crowd of people, shouting out, 'Who called for a paramedic?' It's the worst feeling, knowing that someone needs your help immediately, but you can't find them, and I'm just running, panicking, shouting, 'Who called for an ambulance?' because if they die, it's our fault."

"It's never your fault, Emily, or Daniel's."

She smiles sadly, her eyes on the snowy, muddy ground in front of us. "I'm trying to work to feel better about it, but I know it's that urgency that keeps people alive. Move fast. Assess what's going on. Stabilize them. Get them to the vehicle. Get on the road. Get them to the hospital. That's our job. Especially if someone hurt them and they're lying there in pain, I want to make sure that the next face they see is a comforting one, mine, because I'm going to take care of them. I'm going to make sure that I can do all I can to keep them alive."

We hear the snap of twigs before us, a soft crack and a fluttering of some object falling from above to the forest floor below.

"I know you heard that." Emily stops. Her eyes dart around. "Where'd that come from?"

I'm scared to look behind us, but I do. There's nothing there. Just a tunnel of trees and the narrow path we were walking. We listen, waiting for something else, but it's quiet, eerily so. "Probably just a bird landing on a branch," I say, explaining it away.

I feel every emotion coursing through me as we walk. It's cold outside, but my back and neck feel sweaty. Maybe it's because this entire area has something to do with my ancestor, who braved the seas with his young family, only to find himself doing grueling work, breaking up dirt, moving out stone, and within days his body was so weak that his legs gave out and he fell into the river and was swept away.

His young wife and children then moved alone to that farmhouse deep in the woods, and one of those children later built the house where I live. And my mother, she's buried in a cemetery not too far from here, along Archer Avenue.

These woods. That road. My house. It all holds the essence of my family.

I start telling Emily more about the area, information I learned from my mother's books, just to distract myself from the fear this space is generating.

"Around World War II, a lot of people in the area said they'd run into military police throughout here. There's no military base anywhere close. Neighbors were never told what was happening in these woods. They'd assumed it had something to do with the conflict. I don't think anyone could imagine at that time what a nuclear reactor even was, and that it was being buried in these woods. After it was buried, the military left, and then things got even weirder."

Emily gives me the side-eye. "You mean weirder than now?"

Twigs snap overhead. Birdsong follows. It echoes through the treetops.

"Remember that car?" Emily asks.

"Yeah," I say, looking above, trying to find the bird that's singing.

"They're in here somewhere and we haven't run into them."

I avoid meeting her eyes because I don't want her to spot worry in mine. She's right. We haven't run into anyone yet. "Maybe they're at the end of the trail?"

"Fun. I'm looking forward to running into someone even farther away from our car."

"We'll be fine. You have to believe it. We have to believe it."

She huffs. "Sorry, it's just . . . creepy out here."

And it is, but I don't want to agree with her. I don't want to say that it feels like someone's been watching us this entire time. That each footstep I take feels like someone is drawing only closer to us.

I don't want to say that I can almost sense someone's eyes on me. I just want to get to the end of this trail, because I know this place is special somehow in the context of space and time, and I think of my conversation with Isaac and how it seemed strange, but so well timed. This place and what's here, it's just calling to me right now, and I know I have to get to the end of this trail, regardless of the fear I'm feeling.

"It's just a strange coincidence that after they buried the nuclear reactor here, people began reporting more unusual activity, seeing things, hearing things. It was around the 1970s too, that reports spiked at Cal Sag Church, Bachelor's Grove, and other areas nearby. Spectral horses, floating orbs, fiery blue lights, voices, and—"

"I'm going to say it again because I know my Chicago ghost stories . . . vanishing hitchhikers," Emily said.

"Exactly . . ." I say, feeling the air squeezed out of me. "Everyone knows that story."

"The first time I heard that story, I must have been like in sixth grade. And now look at us"—she stops and motions around us—"deep in the woods. When did you first hear about it?"

"Around the same time," I say, remembering now when Mother told me that tale. It was also when she found that book, *The Sleeping Beauty of the Wood*. "My mother used to say our Archer Avenue vanishing hitchhiker was much like Sleeping Beauty . . ."

Emily turns her head. "Why's that?"

"Because she sleeps for a time, and then is awakened. It's like she's always present, in ways, but she's in a deep slumber, and we just need the right person to shake her from her deep sleep. It's a really sad story when you think about it. It's a ghost that's forced to repeat the same pattern, over and over, finding herself on a lonely road at night, begging and pleading people to take her home—"

I stop and it feels like I'm hit by a car.

Emily holds a hand out. "You all right?"

I think back to the dream of the girl in the alley and how she asked me to take her home. I shake my head and take a deep breath. That can't be the same person, can it?

I push it from my mind, for now.

"I just remembered something I forgot to do is all."

"Do you need to head back? Because if you say, 'Hey, let's get out of the creepy forest because I forgot to do something,' I'd go along with it and be so happy."

I adjust my knit cap on my head, bringing it down to cover the tops of my ears, which are growing cold. "It's fine," I say. "I'll take care of it when I get home."

She stomps at the ground playfully. "Fiiine. Anyway, back to vanishing hitchhikers. What are you saying, then? That we just need to 'wake up' our vanishing hitchhiker for her to find peace?"

I focus on the path in front of us, branches and leaves outlined in snow. The deeper we go, the more it seems like we're in another world, the grounds of a fairy kingdom. But even though the fantastical feels just within reach, so does the grim. "I think so," I say.

We continue walking in this snowy landscape. "There's a lot of versions of 'Sleeping Beauty,'" I begin. "Even different names for the story. 'The Beauty Sleeping in the Wood.' 'The Sleeping Beauty in the Woods.' 'Little Briar Rose.'"

"Sleeping Beauty" wasn't just my favorite fairy tale; it was my mother's as well, and she read it to me, and her mother read it to her, and so on.

I wrote an article about "Sleeping Beauty" a long time ago. I became so fascinated with this dreamy story, and how some variations of it were so violent. In some we see how Sleeping Beauty was hated and cursed when she was just a few days old, because of a slight her parents made. Then later we see how her finger is pricked, blood forms, and how she is damned to sleep, and in this state her body is abused. Violence upon violence upon violence on someone so innocent.

And we remember this story. Recount it. Buy picture books of it. Watch the animated adaptations, and still, many of us know how some of the variations go.

All the versions contain our princess.

I tell Emily how in my research I learned it's a story with seeds that stretch back to 1300, perhaps even before. There was an Arthurian chivalric romance called *Perceforest*. In it there are glimmers of what later came to be the "Sleeping Beauty" story we all know today.

In *Perceforest*, a woman with supernatural powers gets very angry because she feels she has been disrespected by an elite family. The woman then places a curse on the baby girl of those who hurt her. The curse makes it so that when the baby grows, she'll prick her finger on the needle of a spinning spindle.

I think about the spinning spindle in all these versions like the sharp point that stabs Sleeping Beauty operates sort of like a poison dart. That wound that breaks her skin causes her to fall away into a deep sleep.

"You didn't tell me," Emily says. "How did you even learn about this place? I've never even heard about it."

"My mother. She told me about Red Gate Woods. She said there were a lot of superstitions around it."

In all the versions of "Sleeping Beauty," she's placed on a bed, in the tower of her home, and that home is surrounded by a massive forest.

Around the same time *Perceforest* was written, a Catalan poem titled "Frayre de Joy e Sor de Plaser" was published. In it, the daughter of an emperor collapses. It appears as if she's died, but she's not dead. She's still breathing.

Time goes by and her body does not decompose. She's fallen into an enchanted sleep. Her parents refuse to bury her because they know she's still alive, and so they move her to a tower surrounded by a dense and deep forest.

Stories were told about her for years, and one day a wicked prince heard the tale of the princess in a tower who sleeps. The prince traveled to her home and assaulted the sleeping woman. In her sleep, her body grew a baby, and when she awoke, she gave birth and was later married to the prince. That isn't a tale of happily ever after we're accustomed to.

There are threads of truth in some fairy tales, and as Emily, Prairie, and I maneuver this trail, being careful and cautious along an icy stretch of the route, my mind begins to wander.

Emily is holding her arms out, trying to maintain her balance as we walk over a section of gnarled tree roots jutting from the ground.

"Careful here," she says, and I tighten my grip around Prairie's leash.

Prairie hops over each root. I step carefully, watching my boots, but my thoughts are somewhere else. I'm thinking, what if out there, beyond the trees, far away from what we can see, there is a structure, and what if inside that structure is a woman hidden away in a tower, sleeping, waiting for someone to set her free from her curse? I wonder, then, what does one dream in a cursed sleep?

I wonder even further, how did this story originate? A beautiful woman locked away in a castle, cursed to sleep?

I continue: "Three hundred years later the story of Sleeping Beauty appeared again in Giambattista Basile's *Pentamerone*. What makes Basile's *Pentamerone* so special is it's the first fairy tale to be collected into a single book."

In *Pentamerone* there are fifty stories all connected by a bigger story, the frame story. Many of the stories Basile wrote were later adapted by the Grimm brothers, including "Rupunzel," "Puss in Boots," "Hansel and Gretel," "Cinderella," and "Sleeping Beauty."

In *Pentamerone*, the story of a sleeping princess is titled "Sun, Moon, and Talia." It also details the assault of Sleeping Beauty, but this time by a king. This is one of the darkest versions of "Sleeping Beauty." Sleeping Beauty, here named Talia, births two children after her assault; they are named Sun and Moon. The queen learns of her husband's infidelity and orders Talia killed and her children to be cooked and fed to the king. The children are saved, and Talia and the king go on to marry.

I realize that my great-great-great-grandmother's name is Talia. I wonder whether her parents knew the fairy tale. I wonder whether Talia read *Pentamerone* or the adaptations that came later.

The brothers Grimm knew Basile's version, but they later heard Charles Perrault's adaptation, *The Sleeping Beauty in the Wood*. Perrault's was later dictated to the Grimm brothers, and they went on to adapt Perrault's into "Little Briar Rose."

There are more versions of Sleeping Beauty—Italo Calvino has a variant—and the Grimm brothers also have a variation titled "The Glass Coffin."

For hundreds of years, people have been fascinated by a woman who sleeps, who is awakened. Why?

Even the idea of a glass coffin . . . it's so somber and beautiful at the same time. An outsider can observe you, but you cannot observe them. It's so strange and sad.

In some stories she has no name. In others she's Talia or Rosamund . . . or Briar Rose.

Emily pauses. "Well, we know where you got your name," she says.

We hear a bird singing overhead, high pitched and sweet like a flute. It repeats its song.

"Also, don't forget the Disney version," she says. "Maleficent."

"That's right! Disney." I stop and flip around my backpack. "That's where Maleficent appears! The wicked fairy."

"Such a creepy name," Emily says.

"It makes sense," I say. "'Mal.' Those first three letters translate to 'bad' in almost all of the Romance languages."

"Ahh." Emily throws her head back. "Makes sense. Also, what are you doing?"

"Don't laugh at me," I joke. "I just don't want to forget about this." I pull out a notebook and pen, and I'm balancing both in one hand while my other fumbles with my phone. I notice then that I have no signal. I start waving my phone around in the air, trying to locate any bars. When I do, I stand still, afraid to lose my connection to the outside world. I start searching on the browser. "You mentioned Maleficent. So, Disney's *Sleeping Beauty*, and I want to check the year it came out and write that down before I forget."

The search engine tells me 1959.

I jot the name "Maleficent" and the year "1959" in my notebook.

Emily rubs her nose. It's turning red now, just like her cheeks. The temperature feels like it's dropping, but we should get to the burial place soon. Hopefully we can rush back before it gets too dark.

Emily is rocking on her heels. "I'm so confused right now. Are you going to explain what just happened?"

"You're just helping me write my article is all."

"You're ridiculous, and I adore you."

The path narrows a bit, and I note the sun hanging in the sky. I'm walking more briskly now, trying to focus on the trail ahead, hoping for an opening to a clearing soon, but all we pass are thousands of thin, bare trees. I hear birds chirping, the muffled beats of our boots hitting the ground and dirt and snow, and the shoosh of walking over last season's fallen leaves that cover it all.

Something is going on here; like all fairy tales, there are layers, complexities, and we just need to pay attention to each stitch in the fabric. The air shifts. It feels denser. Earthy undertones get stuck in my nose. I think I hear something behind me, shuffling, footsteps, someone. I stop. Turn. There's no one there.

"Don't you think it's odd?" Emily's voice is low. "That we haven't passed anyone yet?"

"They could be at the other trail across from us."

She makes a sound like she doesn't quite believe that's a possibility, but I can feel she's tense, and her head continues moving left and right, her eyes sweeping across the forest.

My thoughts return to the stories of Sleeping Beauty. What is consistent among the tales of a sleeping woman in a tower is that there is a woman who falls asleep, sometimes by some supernatural force, like a curse, but she always falls into a sleep that is much like death, and eventually she awakens from that state. But that's just a fairy tale. Someone who is in many ways dead waking up? There's no coming back from death.

"Wait?" Emily pauses, hands on her hips. I see the clouds of condensation as she breathes in and out, catching her breath.

"This is all just clicking for me." She snaps her fingers. "Are you sorta connecting the buried nuclear reactor out here to all of the weird paranormal stuff that's been reported in the area?"

I was worried at first to tell her what I thought, but I'm too tired to pretend.

"That's exactly what I'm doing," I say. "I feel like there's some connection. Energy. Vibration. Strange occurrences have always been reported all along this stretch of road; as long as there has even been record of Archer Avenue, there's been reports of something being seen or heard along Archer Avenue that people just can't explain. Then in the seventies there was this spike of incidents. There were tons of newspaper articles written about it, reporters came down here and interviewed people. Ghost hunters and ghost tours in the area. I know it doesn't make sense right now, but there's something here. I know it. It all just makes me wonder, does this thing being out here almost make the area more magnetized to this sort of stuff?"

As I speak, my voice shakes and my body trembles. Then I remember what my mother said: thin places. If we can step through a thin place and see and feel and experience something not in line with the rules of our physical reality, doesn't that mean that other things can do the same? Meet us here at this crossroads?

Emily is looking at me. She's smiling.

"What?"

She takes a deep breath. "You just sound like her. Your mother. She believed in all of these big things, and you never really wanted to believe in any of it, so it's just sweet is all. To hear you want to believe in something."

Maybe it happened after talking to Isaac. Maybe it happened before. But I feel a change happening.

I look down and around me, and keep feeling as if we are being watched, or followed, but it is too difficult to tell what is ahead of us or what is behind us. And then we come up to . . . a road, a road at the end of the hiking trail.

A road in the middle of the forest.

"You know, when I said we should get out for an adventure? To get you some air? I was expecting something fun. Not terrifying," Emily says.

I hand Emily Prairie's leash and step out into the middle of the road. The asphalt is cracked and buckling along the edges. I look left and then right. I can't tell where either end winds up, with one way stretching up, and the other going downhill.

"There's something about this road and there's something about travel and there's something about the specters that have been spotted around this place for a long time that seeps into the hearts and minds of Chicagoans."

There's an air of restlessness here, similar to what I feel in the house. There's something off center. The ground is loose, shaky, unsteady.

I look right and left again, and that's when I notice the orange reflective arrows hammered into a tree stump, pointing left, uphill.

Prairie starts to whimper, and Emily squats and pats her head. "It's okay, honey," she says, and digs into her backpack to retrieve a treat. "We've been walking for a long time." Prairie takes the treat gently from her hand. "I don't remember seeing this at all on the GPS."

"It looks decommissioned," I say. "It was probably just used by the military, and then when they buried the reactor, they closed it off."

I point left. "Guess this is the way." We continue, walking deeper into the woods down a ghost road, something that doesn't even exist on maps.

"I don't really understand what a nuclear reactor does anyways," Emily says.

"The simplest explanation I found is that it's a machine that produces a lot of energy, and then that energy is released as heat."

"Okay, so what about the weapon part? Manhattan Project. Bombs. All that. Isn't that what we're visiting here?"

"It was the Manhattan Project that would go on to make nuclear weapons."

Emily's face grows stern. "I can't even imagine why someone would want to do something like that. Kill so many people."

"That's because you're a good person. I think the massive amount of energy this thing can produce just kinda shook this place up."

Emily raises her eyebrows. "Disturbed the dead, you mean?"

"Sure. I guess? Maybe? Like, I just can't believe that even if it's turned off, decommissioned, whatever, that there's still not some sort of pull this machine has to attract or generate energy? Even something residual?"

Emily blinks rapidly. "It's a stretch, Bri. It's a stretch to say paranormal activity picked up along Archer Avenue because a nuclear reactor is buried here."

It feels silly to admit, but: "Yes, there must be something to it. It generates a massive amount of energy. What are we? What is life? It's all energy. Everything is energy, and you can't destroy energy, it just changes form . . ."

"Ghosts, then?" Emily asks. "I guess I never asked if you believe in ghosts."

As of now, I don't know what I believe. I know that there are different states of consciousness, and I wonder whether death was just a different state, like delta, which is sleep. Is there something deeper? Just another way of being?

I struggle to find the right words. I stare down at my feet and then say, "I don't quite think we become ghosts, though? I guess I don't know, but I don't believe death is the end." It's like sleep, and I wonder, is death just another way of existing?

Emily remains silent and then opens her mouth to say something, but pauses. We are here. Finally.

"I feel like this is it," she says.

The road opens to a wide, snowy clearing. An undisturbed, immaculate winter wonderland. To the far left I see what looks to be a frozen pond, the surface like glass, reflecting the gray sky and low-hanging clouds. "I think you're right."

Out in the center of the field are two large blocks of stone and a man standing between them, his back to us. He's in a heavy winter coat and boots and hats and gloves. He just appears to be another wintertime hiker like us. He's standing at one of the monuments. Both Emily and I walk to the opposite monument, away from him.

"I think we found the owner of that car in the parking lot," Emily says quietly.

"We'll be fine," I say, even though I'm hearing screaming inside my head. There's a tightening around my neck, as if someone's hands are pressed there, squeezing.

The man doesn't seem to notice us as he backs away from one of the stones. Prairie sees something skitter across the field, a small mouse. She tugs, and I trip forward as she leaps into the snow, wagging her tail and barking. I pull her back, and it's at that moment the man turns just slightly, but I can barely see his face. The mouse darts away into some bushes.

"Prairie," I hiss, but then feel guilty as soon as I do. She lowers her head. "Forget it," I say, feeling sorry.

"Look at this." Emily motions me over to the monument. It reads:

CAUTION—DO NOT DIG

BURIED IN THIS AREA IS RADIOACTIVE MATERIAL FROM NUCLEAR RESEARCH CONDUCTED HERE 1943–1949. **BURIAL AREA IS MARKED BY SIX CORNER MARKERS. 100 FT FROM THE CENTER POINT THERE IS NO DANGER TO VISITORS.**

US DEPARTMENT OF ENERGY

1978

"Why tell people not to do the thing you don't want them to do?" Emily laughs.

"I think it's safe to assume people have tried to come out here and dig. Nuclear grave robbers, I guess."

"Don't forget to look at this one!" the man shouts.

His voice sounds like shattered glass, like a shadow that's being cast by nothing, like all the shrieks from all the nightmares that have ever been.

Emily and I eye each other. I know what she's thinking. How could he hear us? We're standing so far away.

We both look over in his direction, and he has an arm extended, pointing to the rock he was facing. Then he begins to walk back toward the trail.

I feel a sense of relief, a loosening around my neck the farther away from us he gets.

I move toward the marker he indicated.

"Are you serious?" Emily loud-whispers.

"He's leaving," I say, keeping my eyes focused on the path.

I can feel Emily beside me, her hand in her jacket pocket, clutching the pepper spray. I keep my eyes on the man. I hope he keeps walking, moving away from us. I hope he doesn't stop and turn around and want to talk. I hope . . . he doesn't want something else. My arms feel shaky, as do my legs, but it was my idea to come out here, so I try to remain calm.

I stop in front of the second monument on the field.

The stone in front of me reads:

THE WORLD'S FIRST NUCLEAR REACTOR WAS REBUILT AT THIS SITE IN 1943 AFTER INITIAL OPERATION AT THE UNIVERSITY OF CHICAGO

THIS REACTOR (CP-2) AND THE FIRST HEAVY WATER MODERATOR REACTOR (CP-3) WERE MAJOR FACILITIES AROUND WHICH DEVELOPED THE ARGONNE NATIONAL LABORATORY

THIS SITE WAS RELEASED BY THE LABORATORY IN 1956 AND THE U.S. ATOMIC ENERGY COMMISSION THEN BURIED THE REACTORS HERE.

"Huh," I say to myself. My mind begins to race when I see the year.

"What is it?"

"Nineteen fifty-six—that's the year the Grimes sisters were found dead along Archer Avenue."

She looks from side to side. "You're saying that like I'm supposed to know who and what you're talking about?"

"It's a famous cold case." It goes back to what I was saying, Archer Avenue, how bizarre this area is, dotted with synchronicity, with coincidences you can't really say are connected. The road. The sightings. Activity here absolutely boomed between the 1930s and 1970s. Why? What is it about this place?

"That's the nature of Archer Avenue!" the man shouts, adjusting the scarf around his neck.

"How the hell can he hear us?" Emily whispers, her lips barely moving.

The man continues: "It's like a Twilight Zone. Some people might even call it a thin place," he says, and my insides twist when he says "thin place."

The man proceeds back to the trail from which we came, and our eyes remain fixed on him.

It's like Emily and I are holding our breath, watching, hoping he disappears from our sight.

When we no longer see him, it's like we both exhale together.

"I would have been so mad if I got murdered out here with you," she says.

"I told you we'd be fine." I'm leaning on her now for support, because my legs feel weak from the anxiety of it all.

"Isn't that weird?" she says.

"What is?"

Emily removes her phone from her pocket and starts taking pictures. "That he mentioned 'thin place,' just like you were talking about. Totally random and weird, don't you think?"

I look back, making sure he's gone. I'm starting to accept that everything is a bit blurred between the lines and we are living in a dreamscape without even really knowing it.

I stand straight and shake my arms out. "Well, we weren't murdered. Let's change the subject, please."

Emily puts her hands together, the leash between them. "Fine. Fine," she says, thinking. "You never really told me what superstitions your mother believed about this place."

I take a deep breath, remembering her words. "She said fairies lived in the woods along Archer Avenue. Some fairies are good, and some fairies are evil, and it is not a good thing to anger a fairy."

Chapter 14

TIME: *4:00 p.m.*
DATE: *Thursday, December 7*

We make it back down the trail, Emily and I walking fast, speaking minimally, and just on high alert. I know that both of us don't want to mention the man we encountered and how frightened we both were.

At the parking lot we find another car having just parked. Inside there are two men and two large border collies. They exit the car, and the dogs are all paws and wagging tails. They stop and say hello, and we tell them all about the nuclear reactor, and then they go on their way.

In the car, Emily pulls on her seat belt and places her hands on the steering wheel. "It wasn't just me, right? That guy back at the end of the trail, his vibes were off, right?"

We are in our car, and we are safe, and I don't want to upset her, and so all I say is, "I think we were also on edge." I say this even though the entire hike back I kept fearing we would encounter the man, and he'd have a knife or gun in hand. My thoughts wandered to such horrible places on that trek back. Would we never return again? Would our family and friends hold vigils for us? Would our stories fade? Would we eventually become tales of warnings that other people share many years from now? "Don't go into the woods, because one day two women entered and didn't return . . ."

Emily starts the car and turns right onto Archer Avenue.

The trip to Monk's Castle, Red Gate Woods, all of it, has me exhausted, and I'm looking forward to being back in my house.

We drive down Archer Avenue, and a few minutes away from the forest, Emily asks, "Did you want to visit your mother?"

I have not visited her grave site since her burial, and I do not think I am capable of visiting it now. I make an excuse. "The sun is going to set soon, and we'll just get locked in there and have to call the groundskeeper to get let out and it'll be embarrassing. So, no."

Emily looks at me through the corner of her eye, and my friend knows I'm just not ready to revisit the spot in the earth where my mother's remains are stored.

For now I would rather just go home and sit in my room, in my house in which my mother lived for so long, and surround myself with her things, her pretty perfume bottles, the lovely scarves she knit, the books she collected and the books she restored and all the things she did to the house, the gardens, to make them beautiful—her knitting, and her books.

To my right I see the stone wall and iron fence, headstones and funeral monuments, obelisks, and weeping angels, and then we pass the entrance gates and the engraved stone that reads:

Resurrection Cemetery

I really don't want to believe where my thoughts are drifting to, the connections my mind is making, so I push those ideas from my head. I'm conflicted with thoughts of fairy tales and fairies, ghost stories and other worlds, and how we're all energy and in turn manipulated by it.

Emily shoots a quick glance out the passenger-side window: "This is where people see her, right?"

"Yes," I say. "At night."

"Do you believe the stories?" she asks.

"I don't know," I say, feeling a pinch in my chest. "My mother believed those stories, though."

There are a lot of things people tell you after a loved one dies. Things like "Well, remember the good times," "Be glad you knew them," and all of that feels so empty. It's almost like hearing these things hurts more because they insinuate, in a way, that we should just move on.

It feels so simple.

I'm sorry for your loss.

It feels so small, like a teeny bird's song in the treetops somewhere. I hear it, it's there, but that's all.

What am I supposed to respond with?

Thank you.

Am I thanking you for saying sorry or am I thanking you for saying anything? In either case, what is "sorry"? It's sorrow. It's sympathy, and so am I then supposed to thank you for taking on the burden of sorrow and feeling the sadness of sympathy? It's so strange.

Before anyone says to me "I'm sorry for your loss," what I really want to say is:

I am broken.

I am unraveling.

Time is slipping.

Time has stopped.

I am coming undone, and no matter how many times I try to stitch and weave and knot these words of condolences together, and process people's wrapped-up-in-a-bow sympathy, I feel like I want to shout. Because none of it—no words, no care packages or cards, none of it—equals the whole of the person I lost.

I wonder whether people tell you these types of things to make themselves feel better, as if imparting some recycled wisdom absolves them from feeling any of the pain you are experiencing.

My mother spent a lot of time alone. That's the type of commitment conservation work requires.

Dedication.

Detail.

Long hours alone to focus.

She enjoyed her own company and the company of the beautiful things that she worked tirelessly to revive. She enjoyed holding a book that had been read and reread so many times over the years. The feel of the paper between her fingers, the sound the pages would make as she turned them.

Books came to her in all sorts of conditions, damaged over handling and use, speckled with mold, spotted with curious stains, damaged by flood, or singed by fire.

"I don't think people understand the power of books, Bri," she told me one day as she was seated at her workstation. "These are words on a page, and when we look at these words on this page, we slip into worlds. Come." She waved me over and pointed to a line.

"Read that aloud," she said.

I looked at the text on the yellowed page and read:
You would have thought her an angel, so fair was she to behold.

Her eyes danced with delight. "Do you know how many people have read that very line from this very book?"

I gazed at the words, hoping the answer was hiding somewhere tucked within the loops and shapes of the letters somehow.

"A few," she said, "including a great-aunt of yours."

"Really?" I say. "What was her name?"

Mother looked from side to side, and then lowered her voice. "We can't speak her name in this house, at least not yet, but one day I will tell you the story. Her name is a secret everyone knows."

Grief is long-standing. Grief comes in waves. Grief is those silent moments when you look at your phone and realize they're not going to call you to wish you a happy birthday. Grief is that amazing roasted chicken recipe you pulled off that you can't talk to them about. Grief is waking up every morning and going to sleep every night knowing that when the sun rises again, they will not rise with it.

Grief is also knowing that our planet is full of the remains of every single person who has ever lived. I think of cemeteries, bodies in boxes, or ashes scattered across lawns. Material that was once human. Seeds planted that cannot grow, yet they lived once. They were real and their dreams were real, and their laughter was real, and the things that they loved were real. So where does that intensity, that joy and energy, go when they die? I refuse to believe it all just completely ends when eyes close, never to reopen. One day we will end, and for some of us our death will take on new life in the form of a ghost story.

My mother would say, "Everyone is asleep," and for a long time I thought it meant that everyone is oblivious to the world around them, but I think the meaning is deeper.

And then there are people in the world who make ghost stories by killing people.

Emily is hitting the right-arrow button on the steering wheel and scanning to find the next song. "You're quiet," she says.

We're driving down the expressway, and the great Chicago skyline is stretched across the sky in front of us. Those black-and-silver gleaming horizonal shapes, wise sentinels welcoming us back home. On either side of us, neighborhoods pass us by, and I know that shadows exist there, tucked in corners and hiding in cracks.

"The Chicago Strangler," I begin. "Why do you think he does it?"

Emily raises her eyebrows. "Because he can, Bri. That's why bad people do these sorts of things. They're just evil. There is no rhyme or reason to it. There is no dissecting it, understanding it, it just is. Some people just enjoy torturing and killing other people." She takes a deep breath and then says, "I've seen what these people do to other people. It's ruthless. They're monsters."

We get home and Emily sleeps and I stay awake, making coffee, staring at my computer screen, wanting to write, but unable to. I'm sad, even though we had a nice day, visiting Monk's Castle, visiting Red Gate Woods. I feel like all the sunshine and the air did nothing to make me feel better long term, because the fog has returned, clouding my thoughts.

I try to write a little, but nothing comes out quite right. I down a mug of coffee quickly, and when I open my bedroom door to go down to the kitchen to pour myself another cup, I'm surprised. When I step into the hallway, I see Emily standing at the edge of the stairway. She's in shadow, and she doesn't move or say anything at my appearance.

"Why are you awake?" I take a step and then another, and still she does not move. She does not speak. She's turned away from me. She's in dark clothes and her hair is in a ponytail.

"Emily . . ." I stop, the empty coffee mug dangling in my hand at my side.

She speaks, but it's not Emily's voice. It's not any voice I have ever heard before.

"You would have thought her an angel, so fair was she to behold."

Emily turns around, but it's not the front of her face I see. It's still the back of her head.

I press my hand against the wall, scanning the surface, searching for the light switch. I find it. Flip it.

The hallway is empty.

The coffee mug falls to the floor with a clunk, the handle breaking away.

The room is spinning. Blood rushes away from my face. I saw someone just there. I heard someone just there.

The hallway begins to sway, and I sway with it. I lean against the wall. "There's nothing there. There's nothing there," I'm telling myself, hoping my brain catches on, and that this house catches on and neither shows me something that's not there again.

It's just an old house with a lot of windows and corners, rooms and doors, and all of it casts shadows. I gather the mug and broken handle.

When I approach the stairway, I notice that the curtain to the large window is open an inch. I close it. "It was just shadows," I say to myself, mostly just to hear my own voice, to hear anything in this house other than silence.

Downstairs I stop in the kitchen and toss the mug in the trash can beneath the sink because I want to check if the curtains in the living room have been fully drawn as well.

In the living room I stop at the spindle and shake my head. What a strange gift, and it was even stranger for my mother to accept it and keep it here.

Why?

For a long time I thought of it as just another antique piece of furniture in this house, this dusty museum of dust-covered mirrors and light bulbs and crystal chandeliers, sinking velvet armchairs and sofas with springs digging into one's back and sides.

I count the number of wooden spokes. Tapping my finger against each. Twelve. Like the hands of a clock.

For all the years this sat here, Mother never once used it, but she did keep it clean and polished and free from dust. Mother didn't spin yarn, and that's what spinning spindles do.

One could use a drop spindle, which is a handheld tool with a hook on the end that would attach to a bundle of wool, and then they would spin the tool, and it would create a long thin strip of yarn.

That's what a spinning wheel did, but it is much larger, faster, and thus can produce more yarn quicker. The craftsperson would sit beside the spinning wheel, and a bundle of wool would be fed into the spinning wheel, while the craftsperson would press their foot against the pedal, or treadle, which goes up and down. And with their hands they would slowly tug the long strips of yarn that the spinning wheel had produced.

In "Sleeping Beauty," the princess pricks her finger on the needle, and that is what drives her into a century of sleep.

Modern spindles don't have a needle. That section, the very front of the machine, is usually covered by the flyer arms, the bar where the yarn enters from the wheel and where it would actually be wrapped around and collected. However, my spinning spindle had a very sharp and exposed needle. Perfect to put Sleeping Beauty to sleep with.

None of the "Sleeping Beauty" variations ever really talked about what they saw in their sleep. What were their dreams like? Were they pleasant dreams? Or were they nightmares? One hundred years is a long time to sleep, to dream. Did she live another life somewhere else in those hundred years? And was she even truly happy when she awoke, considering her parents were dead?

There's a soft buzz, like a fly inching toward a light bulb. It stops. My focus remains on the spindle.

"It's just a house," I say, and a house cannot hurt me. I look to the living room window and think of the man who was standing out there just the other night. "But a man can." I walk to the window, peek out from between the curtains, and feel relieved to find no one standing across the street or parked in a car watching my house.

I hear a woman hum behind me.

I spin around. Another woman's voice joins, and then another and another.

A group in harmony. It's a doo-wop beat.

Each night
My dream lover comes to me
A girl all magic and charms
I want
Her
To call
Her
My dream lover
I just want to dream with you

The music intensifies.

Where are you, dream lover
You are my love so true
I held your hand under those lights
I want you here as I grow old

My head throbs. "I do not understand what I am supposed to do."

That sound of a fly buzzing returns, sharp this time, and then just as it begins to sting my ears, the music ceases.

I turn to the window and see light glowing along the edges. It's daytime again somehow, within seconds.

I hear a key in the front door.

That can't be. Emily is here and I am here. Who can that be?

I step into the hallway leading into the foyer, watching the door-knob turn.

The front door swings open, and it is my mother. She's holding a stack of mail in her hand and something tucked beneath her arm. She's shuffling through the mail, reading the senders' names aloud before setting the stack of letters and cards on the entryway table.

"I'll deal with that later," she says, shaking snowflakes from her hair, and then slipping off her dark wool coat and hanging it in the coat closet.

She stops right in front of me and squeezes my shoulder. "What's wrong, darling? You look like you've seen a . . ."

"Ghost . . ." The word comes out in a shallow breath.

She is young and healthy, wearing a lovely black dress. I see now what was tucked beneath her arm. A pink book. She hands it to me.

"I got the job, Bri." She kisses me on my cheek, hooks her arm in mine, and leads me to the living room. We walk past the mirror. I see her, and I see me, and I am so young, a teenager.

In the living room she sits on the sofa, and I sit cross-legged on the oriental rug, facing her.

"What about your application?" I ask, turning over in my hands the book that she used as her application. I inspect the cover like it's the most precious object in the world.

"This was just to show them what I could do to restore old books. I showed them pictures of what it looked like before, and I took them through the process of how I restored it. I attached a new ribbon; I built a new spine. I cleaned the binding edges, and of course all while cleaning and maintaining the original cover. Now it's yours."

"Mine?" I say, lost in the colors and pictures and shapes on the cover, a forest scene, greens, golds, and yellows.

I open the front and admire the text.

My mother leans forward. "It belonged to her, Bri." Her eyes move up to the ceiling. Upstairs a radio plays. "This was her book. You must take great care of it. Promise me that."

"Whose book?" I ask. The lights turn off, and my voice is just a sad, lonely echo that dances around me. The only illumination entering the room is from a streetlight outside the window.

"Mother," I call, but she's gone.

I look down at my hands and they are empty.

I move to the wall, turn on the lights, and walk over to the bookshelf. There are rich leather bindings, some vibrant and polished, others with a mellow and warm patina. Some book bindings have embossed details, delicate florals, and gold leaf details. Other spines display a rich, worn elegance, softened corners and gentle creases that tell stories of years, decades, hands, and fingers, and of wonders read and reread.

There is the faint layer of dust that lingers on the edges of the bookshelf and trim, even after my recent dusting, indications of the past and how it's difficult to leave.

This house is just so large I cannot keep up with its demands, the pace of cleaning every detail, and so I accept that growing worn is part of its new character and part of its new charm. The beauty here may be faded, it may speak to another time, but the opulence hangs in the air like the voices of the occupants of this house who have come and gone, and many of whom I still hear in the night.

I search through the collection of rare and used books my mother carefully restored over the years for pleasure. Her interests were classic fairy tales: *Grimms' Fairy Tales*, *Hans Christian Andersen's Fairy Tales*, *Charles Perrault's Best Known Fairy Tales*, and more.

And then there I find the very book she used decades ago as an example of her craftsmanship and care, a book she gifted to me. I remove it gently from the bookshelf, and then I hear a radio click on.

"How?" I say. "This was just in my room."

After my mother died, I removed this book from its place on the bookshelf, took it up to my room, curled up with it on my bed, and cried. I remember how happy she was to get that job, the love and care that she put into bringing this book back to life, and I just wanted to hang on to that moment, that happy moment, forever, even though I felt utterly lost in this wood.

I hear birdsong. The knocking of a woodpecker dutifully at its work. Another woodpecker responds nearby. I hear the soft shoosh of bushes swaying, dancing with the wind.

The house doesn't just feel like it's in the middle of a dense forest. It feels like it *is* the forest. I smell earth and fresh green leaves. I hear whirring, warbling, chirping, an orchestra of birds, calling and responding to one another. Then I feel it, the breeze lifting my hair, gliding across my forehead, nose, and cheeks.

The feel of the forest disappears.

The house plays another song.

A twangy guitar. Golden melodies paint the room with the hues of nostalgia. Blue notes of a saxophone flow in, wrapping around me like a comforting embrace.

The house is sad. It's suffering. It's wailing now.

Warm tears roll off my face and drip from my cheeks.

Above, I hear Emily stir in her bedroom. The springs of a bed. Feet hitting the floor and walking down the hall to the bathroom. I hear the rush of water from the sink. She'll be ready and dressed for work soon.

I've lost several hours, not to sleep, but perhaps to something like a dream but not a dream.

I carefully open the book and turn the page:

This book belongs to

There is no name written here.

"Whose book is this?" I ask the house, and the music stops.

A new song plays.

I want you in my arms
I want all your charms
Whenever I want you near, all I have to do is
Dream

"I do not know what I'm supposed to do with this information. What am I supposed to see?"

The lights turn off. The music pauses, and above me something bright shines. A pinprick of light in the darkness.

A disco ball grows and hangs suspended from the ceiling. Tiny mirrors along its spherical surface catch and reflect the surrounding light. It spins slowly, and bright shards scatter and sprinkle across the room, aglow in glimmers and sparkles.

I repeat my question to the house, to its windows and doors, floors and wallpaper. To all of it. "What am I supposed to see?"

Mother is standing beside me. I see her outline through the corners of my eyes. I cannot move my head. I am frozen here. My body goes stiff and numb. My eyes trained up to the sparkling sphere above. The music continues to play.

Mother speaks: "The evolution of a ghost story, or an urban legend. Did each tale weave its way in and out and along, depending on who was telling it? Who is to say what is real in a ghost story, one that has been told again and again, by different people? One person in one bar tells one person one story, the haze of alcohol is present. The story is then taken elsewhere to another gathering in another part of town, it's noisy, some words are chopped and sliced. That person then takes that story and shares it at a family gathering, and over a dozen versions of that tale it becomes something else, a patchwork, something like the original but not. But listen very clearly, no matter the story, no matter who tells it, her name never changes. Her name is always and forever the same."

My fingers begin to move, and I have feeling in my arms again. I don't understand any of it. "What am I supposed to see?"

"Bri," she says, looking forward, not looking at me. I cannot turn. I cannot move, but I see from the corner of my eyes her lips moving. Her voice is a soft whisper, a violin. "In order to see it, you have to expand your thinking into what you believe can be possible. To believe in a ghost story is to believe that there are so many other things in the world, and beyond. To peer into the thin place, you must be open and receptive to all possibilities."

The drapes hanging on the windows fall. Outside is no longer outside, the boulevard is gone. The city gone with it. Pressed against the windows are shrubs—just beyond, dark-brown trees. I can see the textures of the bark, ridges, and furrows, each tree's individual fingerprint.

I hear the hooting and screeching of evening things, bugs clicking, night birds announcing their presence. A full moon shines down on it all.

"I want to wake up."

The wind blows and the branches scrape against the windows, like the claws of some giant troll trying to break in, and then a hand appears. White, porcelain. The palm slams up against the glass, rattling the window. The hand pounds on the window again and again.

I pinch myself. I tug at my hair. "I need to wake up," I say. I search the room, and I see the spinning spindle. The needle that juts out from the bobbin. A sharp point onto forever. Maybe if I slam my hand against it, I'll wake up. No. I can do this on my own.

"Wake up, Bri," I say.

I need to wake up.

I scream, "I want to wake up!"

It's now daylight and I'm in the living room. My mother is gone. The disco ball is gone. The dark forest outside of my house is gone. The book is out of my hand and on the bookshelf.

I find myself not standing where I was just moments ago.

I'm leaning forward over the spinning spindle. The wheel is turning, fast, as is the pedal, as if there is someone there guiding it.

The flyers are turning, imaginary wool being spun, and there I am shocked, bright-white terror, witnessing it all from so close.

My right eye is inches away from the needle.

Chapter 15

We speak of haunted houses as if they're grim and gruesome things, but what makes a house haunted?

People.

A person dies.

A soul is restless, and I do not know if I believe in souls or spirits or ghosts, but what I do believe is that I'm slowly losing parts of myself.

Emily is in her uniform, and she finds me standing in the darkened living room, staring at the spinning spindle.

My words come out shaky, my eyes fixed on that wheel. "Do you see it moving?"

"Bri." Her voice is shaking. She looks from me to the spinning spindle.

The wheel is moving. I point. "You see it now, don't you? Please tell me that you do."

She walks toward me. Her palms out, like she's scared I'll dart off or something, like some lost cat found, but I won't. "Let's get you to bed."

I throw my arms up. "No!" I take a seat on an armchair. I am seated in the shadows, clutching the book. Wake and dream are blurred. I am accepting I'm just a weary wanderer between both. The ticks from the grandfather clock are the sharp cries of dying time.

"I don't need sleep. I don't need dreams. I am fine. Everything is fine."

She follows my gaze to the book in my hands.

"It was one of Mother's first projects. Her application, she called it. She took it with her to the Art Institute the day she interviewed for the book conservator job. And . . ."

Mother worked there for sixteen years. I wonder how many books she touched. I can see her now, in her dimly lit studio. The air is imbued with the faint undertone of bookbinding adhesives. Her soft hands are moving with delicate precision along a worn bookbinding. There are tools set neatly beside her, organized by need and style and size. Paints. Tiny brushes. Even tinier scalpels. My mother works in silence, and all I can hear are the whispers of parchment meeting her skilled fingers. My mother wasn't just a technician, she was a guardian of stories and a keeper of memory. Each artifact that came through her hands transported her through time, past and present meeting at no point and every point, all at the same time.

Then there was this book. This book has always been here, but who did it belong to first? Why is the name missing? Why is the owner's identity secret?

House, I wonder, *what are you keeping from me?*

Emily's voice is distant. She's saying something. I don't know what, because it's just me and this book, me and this story, me and a fairy tale that had been told and retold, adapted, and reshaped. What does it mean when a story is told hundreds of times, millions? That there are people both living and dead who know this tale. We carry these stories with us in life and death, beyond.

Emily's phone begins to ring. She looks at the screen, tilts her head, and answers. "Yeah . . . she's with me right here. She called you? What'd she say?" Emily takes a deep breath and exhales through her teeth. "Yeah, I'll see you at work in a bit. I'll tell her." She ends the call and looks at me. Her lips pressed tight. Her eyes searching. "Daniel said you called him."

I shake my head. My voice cracks. "I didn't call him."

"He said you told him you were going to Archer Avenue. That you needed to bring her back home. Then he said you hung up, and he kept trying to call you back."

I run my fingers through my hair. "I don't remember doing that." I reach over to my phone on the coffee stand, look at my missed calls, and see ten from him. I also find the one outgoing call to him prior.

She clears her throat. "I forgot something in my room. Come on, I'll walk you up to your room," she says, even though I can sense she didn't forget anything in her room; she just wants to be sure she gets me to mine.

I yawn. "I'm really not sleepy," I say when we get there. "I'm just tired."

Her eyes widen when she sees my desk covered in empty coffee mugs. I don't remember those. I just remember the one that fell and broke.

"You've been up all night, Bri. It's not healthy for you. You're hurting yourself at this point by keeping yourself up."

I sit at the edge of my bed. Emily's phone rings again. She looks at it and says, "I'm really sorry, Bri, but I have to get to work or I'll be late. Please get some sleep. I don't know what else I can say other than you need to sleep or . . . I don't know what can happen. Just that it won't be good."

After Emily leaves, I go downstairs, take the pink book from the shelf, and once again curl up on my bed with it and cry. Too tired to even close my bedroom door to keep the chill from the hallway out.

Are the hallucinations a part of grief? Or are the things I'm seeing appearing because of insomnia, the house, or something else?

The music returns. It's loud this time, and my body is aching with so much exhaustion I'm too tired to even shout for it to stop.

My mother walks past my bedroom. I sit up, and my brain is screaming, begging for rest, but I set the book down on my bed and follow her.

I find her in the kitchen, standing at the stove. The teakettle is sputtering, and there's a white porcelain mug on the counter with a tea bag resting in it.

She says, "The dead often return, or just remain in the place that they loved, because those are the surroundings in which they felt peace, and where they felt cherished. We think of haunted houses as homes with gunshot blasts in the walls and where bodies were once packed in basements and where blood oozes from between the cracks in the wallpaper, but no. What if a haunted house is a loving thing? A record. A memory. A being itself that longs and loves. Maybe haunted houses aren't scary things. Maybe haunted houses are extensions of your family, *are* your family. And maybe those hauntings, those things that you see, are little loving messages, reminders, or warnings. A house loves you like a mother loves you. We should all believe in something beyond death, if even story, because stories keep us connected to each other and the fabric of space."

"Ghosts . . ." I say.

"They're very real. Ghosts." A smile crosses my mother's lips. "They're here, listening. Shimmering spots you see beside the window, or a translucent shape out of the periphery of your eyes, a drop of temperature in the room, where the tip of your nose grows cold, of murmurs of a melody, fragments of conversations that were once spoken in this very living room, but still hang in the air as particles somewhere. These things, all these things, are signs of the other realm, but sometimes some of them get stuck, like a vinyl record skipping on the turntable. They're caught in a snag, caught on a thought, and they can't let that thought be. And maybe that thought is a mission, needing to say goodbye, or simply finding one's way home."

They sound like restless spirits.

The teakettle whistles, and Mother grabs a pot holder and tips the boiling water into the cup. "They're not quite restless," she says as if she were reading my thoughts. "They're not all here to frighten. They're not all snarling in the folds of shadows. No, what I'm speaking of, my darling daughter, is memory. And I'm here with a warning: one's murderer can keep them pinned in the ether if they know how. But"—Mother eyes me, those bright eyes the color of Lake Michigan on a clear day—"we're not going to allow him to do that anymore. You're going to find him, and you're going to stop him, and then . . . finally, her story can be told the way it should have been told a long time ago. Her tragic story."

"Whose story?"

"I can't tell you her name. No one can tell you her name. It's something you must remember. It's in your mind. Focus, Bri. What is her name? It's there along the highways of your thoughts. Find her name."

I look out the window, new snow is falling, and I continue listening to my mother's hypnotic voice.

"Many people die too soon, their lives stamped out because of violence. Sometimes when that happens, they come to us and ask us for help. They're not here to hurt or harm us. They're not monsters. They're just looking for someone who can save them even in death, because even in death one can suffer."

Mother reaches into the cupboard and removes the sugar canister. She drops a square of sugar into her teacup.

"Mother, I don't understand."

"I know you don't, but one day you will," she says, the teaspoon clacking as she stirs the sugar into the hot liquid.

I approach her and I beg. "What am I supposed to do, Mom?"

She presses a hand against my cheek. It feels like a cold morning mist.

"Find her. Bring her home. Stop the pattern. That will stop him."

When I was growing up, Mother told me to be careful when I was outside. To be careful when I walked home alone. To always look behind my shoulder and to note the cars that slowed down a little too much, and all these warnings and all the cautions I felt were unfair to adapt my movements to, because how is that fair? How was it fair that

I had to change the way I moved about in the world just because I'm a woman?

When I moved out on my own for college and then with Emily, Mother's worries remained. She said to never trust the world fully because there were pockets that were not safe.

"One must always take care along their journey because that is where one often encounters treacherous traps and gruesome beasts. All it takes is a few seconds, tiny snapshots in time in which things can never return to what they were, and where you will never see home again."

I hear a click followed by a soft, staticky noise. Before the radio locks into a station, there's a symphony of silent crackles.

"I don't know what I'm doing," I say, and I feel the house grow angry with me. Another radio turns on somewhere in this house and then another.

A mix of sounds and songs.

Crackles. Beeps and snow.

Vocals begging a lover to return.

My voice

Your time

Our steps

Forever

The smooth voice of radio personalities introducing an ad:

"And we've got to keep the lights on somehow. Here's a message from our sponsor . . ."

I feel completely fatigued.

I am holding a hot mug of coffee in my hands. I don't remember pouring it.

The house is still. My mother is gone. I am fighting with my eyelids, begging them to stay open, these drapes that keep the nighttime world away. I don't want to see that black road anymore, and I don't want to hear these radios playing anymore, and I just want this all to stop, but I know it's already started, and there's only one way to end it.

Find him before he finds me.

I feel like I'm fading away, maybe into this house, slipping into the walls, detaching from my own body and blood. I see the windows, and I see the doors, and I hear the drone of cars outside, but I cannot sense myself in many ways, and I begin to wonder again, *What does this all even mean? What is happening to me?*

My mother's words, her final words, play in my head again and again.

Keys and gates and locks and thorns.

Maybe it's a lullaby? No, maybe it's a fairy tale.

I am so tired, but I cannot sleep. I am scared to sleep. So I go upstairs to my room, and I sit and think and piece together quotes and locations, victim details.

I groan and rest my head in my hands. "What am I supposed to do, Mother? Help me, please." I'm so tired of her being dead. She'd know what to do. She'd know what was going on. She'd know how to help me.

I hear the wind again, or maybe it's not the wind, maybe it's the drone of a car. I hear engines now, vehicles accelerating, decelerating. Tires screeching. I look out the window, but all I see is a single black car driving slowly down the boulevard. The black paint is shiny and polished. I see the gently rounded curves of the exterior, silvery chrome accents, a gleaming chrome grille and trim that catches the sunlight. The fenders are sculpted, seamlessly flowing from the front of the automobile to the back. I can barely make out the interior from this distance, but I see upholstered brown seating, and the lone occupant, the driver who looks straight as he drives. His face is melted snow.

This car is very, very old. Something from a 1950s song, drive-in theaters, milkshakes at a hot dog stand, big band music, Elvis Presley and Audrey Hepburn, polka dots, and swinging poodle skirts that fall right beneath the knees, leather jackets and jeans for the rebels, tailored suits and ties for the others.

The car is a time machine in ways, and I feel myself in parts slipping away with it.

I hear that familiar tapping against my windows, the sharp thorns pressing against the glass, begging to get in.

"Bri . . ." I hear a woman say.

I don't look. Instead, I say, "I'm thinking."

"Bri, but what if we could bring her home?" the house says.

A tap against the glass.

"Bri, if you let her in, it'll stop. Just let her in."

I turn to the window, and there's a reflection there, a woman. Snow continues to fall so heavily, and I cannot really see her face. I try to focus, I try to see, and for a moment I see that she really does look a lot like me.

Chapter 16

I like to visit them. They like it when I visit them too.

I hold my camera high, and I say to myself and say into the eye of the camera: "Today I am at Holy Sepulchre Cemetery in Alsip."

Alsip is a small village. I've found some beauties here before. A long time ago.

I like Chicago. There are more beauties there.

In Alsip the houses are very old. Not a nice old. A worn old. A sad old. Even when it's sunny outside, Alsip feels gray. Cold. Somber. Mournful.

There are small taverns on corners with square white, red, and blue OLD STYLE beer signs hanging over the door. There are pizza restaurants with sticky floors. There are too many car dealerships and auto body shops. I remember, when I was little, I asked Father what an auto body shop was. He answered that it was a place where people took their automobiles to be repaired. That is not the picture I imagined in my head.

In my head I saw severed legs stacked in heaps on the floor. Arms bent in bunches. Torsos piled on industrial tables. Heads arranged on shelves. Not automobiles.

Holy Sepulchre Cemetery feels a lot like it belongs in Alsip. No one cares about Alsip like no one cares about Holy Sepulchre Cemetery.

There are many cemeteries within a two-mile radius of here.

The cemetery is bordered on all sides by major streets. It is surrounded by commercial and residential zones. The businesses right outside the cemetery are Premier Auto Works—I am sad it is not called Premier Auto Body Works—Jenny's Grill, Jack & Pat's Old Fashioned Butcher Shop, and Nicky V's Beef Dogs.

This town is dead. There are no beauties here. In this town there are just headstones with names of people that other people forgot, and auto body shops and bad pizza.

There are more bodies underground in Alsip than aboveground.

I parked my car at the main office. No one came out to greet me. I like it that way. I do not like to be bothered when I remember.

Many of us like to remember.

Ted Bundy liked to remember. He confessed to returning to the scene of his crimes. Sometimes the bodies were still there. He'd pose with the bodies and take pictures. Sometimes he'd do other things with the bodies too. Dennis Rader, BTK, would leave messages behind at the places where he killed people. He also liked sending letters to the media. One letter from BTK read:

I'm sorry this happen to society. They are the ones who suffer the most. It hard to control myself. You probably call me 'psychotic with sexual perversion hang-up.' When this monster enter my brain I will never know. But, it here to stay. How does one cure himself? If you ask for help, that you have killed four people they will laugh or hit the panic button and call the cops.

I can't stop it so the monster goes on, and hurt me as well as society. Society can be thankful that there are ways for people like me to relieve myself at time by day dreams of some victims being torture and being mine. It a big complicated game my friend of the monster play putting victims number down, follow them, checking up on them waiting in the dark, waiting, waiting . . . the pressure is great and sometimes he run the game to his liking. Maybe you can stop him. I can't. He has already chosen his next victim or victims. I don't who they are yet. The next day after I read the paper, I will know but I to late. Good luck hunting.

YOURS, TRULY GUILTILY

P.S. Since sex criminals do not change their M.O. or by nature cannot do so, I will not change mine. The code words for me will be . . . Bind them, torture them, kill them, B.T.K., you see he at it again. They will be on the next victim.

The Green River Killer, Gary Ridgway, liked to go back to the sites where he killed people. To relive those acts.

David Berkowitz, the Son of Sam, would return after shooting his victims to watch the police investigate. He said he got pleasure from the looks of fear and confusion on their faces.

John Wayne Gacy buried many of his victims in the crawl space of his home. He said he liked spending time there.

We like remembering because it feels good to remember.

Many people like to study us. They say we return to our crime because we feel a thrill. They say we want to relive the act. They say we like the feel of power over the victims. They say we return to leave behind little trinkets or collect trophies. They say we fantasize when we return. They say we get gratification being back. They say we like to talk to people there who are grieving. They say we will talk to authorities at the scene of the crime. They say we feel an emotional connection to where we killed a victim. They say. They say.

It's all true.

Funny, when I read about serial killers, there's always the idea that what is being published is to teach the public. That what is being written about us can help protect people from becoming our victims. It's funny that the public forgets we like to read about ourselves and about other serial killers too. We know all that the public knows. We know all that law enforcement knows.

We know all of that and more.

It is cold but very bright outside. There are a few cars here. I see some people standing in front of headstones. Their heads are down. Many headstones are covered in a layer of snow. I like the way the trees look when they're lined in white.

I hear the crunch of my boots against the snow, and it sounds like someone chewing lettuce. Many grave sites have little Santa Claus dolls or plastic poinsettias. I forgot Christmas is near. I don't celebrate any holiday. My life is simple. Wake. Read. Wait. Sleep.

It's quiet. I first stop at the Mausoleum of the Archangels. I raise my black scarf over my face in case there are people here. I don't like when people look at me. It's fine if they do. They won't remember me anyway.

In the mausoleum there are statues of archangels—Michael, Gabriel, and Raphael. They are missing Uriel. Uriel is the fourth archangel. The archangel of wisdom.

This is a garden crypt. It's not like a traditional burial vault. A burial vault has an inside. This crypt is all outside.

I take some pictures.

I think of people. I think of Father. I think of the work he did and his father and back. People die. People stick them in the ground. Or make them into dust and stuff their ashes into an urn and set it on a mantel somewhere and forget them. Some people like to throw ashes in the ocean or in the woods. How much different is that from dumping all sorts of body parts there? That's what ashes are. Little microscopic pieces of body parts. Bones. One clump of dust an eyeball. Another clump of dust a tongue. A few clumps a thigh.

They are all going to die. They will all find themselves here or dumped somewhere else. Everyone will rot and decompose, but not me.

I leave the mausoleum and continue walking. I see an elderly couple adjusting a floral arrangement that announces MERRY CHRISTMAS. I would say that the living leave decorations to make themselves feel better, but the dead can see. My dead can see and hear and feel things. That's what it's like to live in the nighttime world.

The cemetery is quiet. I'm in a section now made up of mostly lawn-level markers. Each marker is a little rectangle. Those rectangles mean "Here lie the remains of a person."

Most of the headstones are flush with the ground. As years pass, many of these sections will shift and rise. This will all grow uneven one day.

For now, lawn markers make it easy for mowing and groundskeeping.

It is possible to have upright markers for family plots. Family plots require purchasing multiple grave sites and using a single larger marker dedicated to an entire family. This is very expensive. My father is buried in an unmarked plot. My father was buried ten feet down. Not six feet. He didn't want people robbing his grave. Superstitious people believed him supernatural, didn't want him crawling out of the grave. Father is still in the ground, but for some reason I am still here.

The older part of this cemetery has upright headstones and markers. Those come in many different styles—fanciful and artistic, slanted, flat bevel, benches, wings, memorials, obelisks, or sculpture markers, angels, crosses, and more.

Holy Sepulchre Cemetery was consecrated on July 4, 1923. I've been visiting it since then.

When a Catholic cemetery is consecrated, that means a bishop, or his designee, blesses the land where people will be buried. When people say Catholics should be buried on consecrated ground, that's what this means. Put them in this blessed dirt. A Catholic cemetery means there is a continuation, even in death.

My beauties always continue after death.

There aren't many notable interments here, not like at Graceland Cemetery or Rosehill Cemetery. There's John Panozzo, a cofounder and drummer for Styx. Some politicians, including Dan Ryan Jr. Interstate 290 is named after that guy. I know it well, driving up and down the South Side of the city. Then the man who ran Chicago for decades, former mayor Richard J. Daley.

I didn't come to visit Ryan or Daley.

I came to visit my two beauties, fifteen-year-old Barbara and twelve-year-old Patricia Grimes. I see them at night, but I miss them now.

I take a few pictures of the flat marker on the ground where both girls were buried. I like taking pictures of them when I visit.

Bodies feel energy. Bodies experience energy. When a person dies, their body can no longer feel, but we are more than our body.

When people die, they are pumped with embalming fluids, placed in a casket, and that box goes in a concrete container. Another box. Into the ground. A burial vault.

Caskets weren't always buried in burial vaults. Some were placed right in the ground. Dirt and worms around them. When it would rain, water would seep into the caskets. When that would happen, decomposing flesh would mix into a stew of rainwater, turning bodies into sponges. Most burial vaults are only expected to last one hundred years. In time, all elements will reach a human body.

It doesn't matter what my beauty's bodies look like in the dirt, because in the nighttime world, they are perfect.

I read the names on the grave markers.

On the left it says:

BARBARA
1941–1956

On the right it says:

PATRICIA
1943–1956

In the center at the top of the marker is their last name, GRIMES, with flowers etched at either end. Their names are engraved in the outline of a book with a cross in the center. Beneath the cross are the words MY JESUS MERCY.

Their murders are called cold cases.

I remember the images from their funeral. Two closed white coffins, each with a picture of the girl inside it set on top. I remember a little boy kneeling at one of the caskets. His eyes closed. His hands in prayer. I think he was just ten. I wonder if the parents told the little boy what happened to his friends.

My memory is so very good. I remember the women at the funeral and how they cried. I remember the little children and how they looked confused. I remember the church service. I remember it was rainy and people were wearing dark clothes. I remember the girls' mother, Lorretta Marcela Hayes Grimes. She collapsed over her daughters' caskets and had to be held up by the crowd.

I even remember a newspaper clipping of that moment.

NEAR COLLAPSE: Mrs. Lorretta Grimes is supported by members of her family as she leans over caskets containing the bodies of her daughters, Barbara, 15, and Patricia, 13, during burial services in Chicago. The sisters were found slain in a roadside ditch recently. Police are holding on a slaying charge Edward L. Bedwell, known as "Bennie the dishwasher." Since his arrest Bedwell has recanted his confession of complicity in the murder of the two girls.

Lorretta Grimes is buried beside her daughters. Her headstone reads:

MOTHER
LORRETTA M. GRIMES
1906–1989

She died in 1989. She lived another three decades without her girls. Thirty-three years. That's a long time to live in agony. A long time to go without seeing your daughters.

I see her beauties every night.

I remember that night a long time ago. The stories told and retold.

On the evening of December 28, 1956, the two sisters left their home. They walked down Archer Avenue, in Chicago's Brighton Park neighborhood. Barbara and Patricia Grimes were big fans of Elvis Presley. They told me. They left to see the singer's first movie at the nearby Brighton Theater: *Love Me Tender*. They adored Elvis.

People think of the 1950s as an innocent time. In some ways, it was. Children would often wander great distances alone. People wouldn't always lock their doors. Today people keep their children close. People look over their shoulders when they are walking at night. People look for the monster who is hiding.

People are looking for me.

Their mother told them it was too cold outside. That they should stay home. The girls begged their mother and promised that they would stay warm. Their mother loved her daughters so much. The girls convinced her. She said yes.

The girls promised they would be home by the time agreed. They were seen at the theater that evening with children from the neighborhood. As the neighborhood children were getting ready to leave, the girls said they were going to stay and watch the film again for the last screening of the night.

By ten that evening, the mother sent her son, Joe, and her oldest daughter, Theresa, to the bus stop to wait for the girls. The children watched three buses pass. The girls weren't on any of them.

While they were outside, the children saw a police car down the street. They walked to it, and the officer told them that he would drive toward the movie theater.

The girls didn't come home that night.

Days passed without the girls. The problem wasn't that they didn't have enough leads. The problem was that the authorities had too many. So many girls in those days looked and dressed alike, like my beauties.

During that time, all young girls looked alike, and so people claimed to see the girls everywhere, on trains, in the city. There was so much media attention around the missing Grimes sisters. Even Elvis Presley put out a public plea to the girls to return home. Their mother later received a ransom note asking for money. The date and time for the meeting arrived, but it was a hoax.

That wasn't me.

I've watched every single interview with Lorretta Grimes I could find. I helped in the search. I attended the funeral. I now come here and visit their bodies.

I see a newsclip in my mind. Black and white and grainy, and Lorretta's voice is so soft:

"Whoever has them against their will, if they'll please let them go, I'll forgive 'em from the bottom of my heart. Just help my girls get home."

On January 22, 1957, twenty-five days after the girls went missing, news reporters alerted the family that the girls had been found. A resident of the area was driving to do some shopping, and he saw what he thought were mannequins by the guardrail on the other side, on the westbound side of Archer Avenue.

The black-and-white newsclip shows a man in a coat and hat, shaking. There's snow on the ground in the background:

"I went home and told the missus about it. I says I think I discovered two bodies lying on the side of the road by Devil's Creek."

The girls' father was brought to the scene, and he identified the girls.

When the police chief was asked how long he thought they had been lying in the snow, he said:

"There's snow in between the bodies. There's some snow under the bodies. And from the position and condition of the bodies, I would say they've been here a matter of days, three, four, five days."

People say, before this moment in time in Chicago, in Cook County, nearly all crime centered on the mob. These were the high-profile crimes that were happening, organized crime. Or crimes or murders that were domestic in nature.

Stranger murders were . . . rare.

Stranger murders of young women, of children even, this was very rare, but still not impossible. People forget the history of this city and the history of a man. They like to forget my father busily working in his chamber.

The coroner's official cause of death was "secondary shock due to cold temperatures."

It doesn't matter how they really died, but they died, and they died cold.

Their mother warned them to stay inside. That it was cold out. When they went outside, they found me. I found them. They were too beautiful to let go.

People had many questions. Were the girls left in the woods without their clothes? Were they taken somewhere? Given to someone?

As the newspaper clippings indicate, there was a suspect: Edward L. Bedwell. He was held for a time, but later released. Even Lorretta Grimes insisted Bedwell had nothing to do with her daughters' murders. Old newsclips can be found of Lorretta and Bedwell's mother holding hands in court. She believed that Bedwell was just picked up because police wanted to close the case swiftly, but no evidence ever tied Bedwell to the girls.

That is where the investigation really ends.

Every few years it comes up. A cold-case detective. A curious sleuth wondering, *Who killed Barbara and Patricia?*

No one has any true leads, but it's been me this entire time. No one can ever find me because I do not exist to them.

I am looking for the ghost stories. I am looking for those myth-makers. I am looking for those beautiful women who sleep, who drift, who dream, and they will be mine forever.

I am looking for Briar.

Chapter 17

I'm at the park with Prairie when I see him. We meet eyes, and it's a wonderful sense of familiarity.

Even though we've only met once before in Jackson Park, still we hug, and it feels so good, and it almost feels odd to think that I'd miss him, but I do.

"Bri!"

He smells so nice, like a lovely winter garden.

"Hello, Isaac," I answer, and I smile against his shoulder.

He releases his hold. "That's a lovely scarf. Red is very beautiful on you."

"My mother knit it," I say.

He looks to Prairie and seems pleased to see her. "Prairie." He kneels and gently pats the top of her head, and she seems just as happy.

Isaac digs into his coat pocket and pulls out a small dog treat. "May I?" he asks, and I say yes. She takes it happily and he stands.

He looks as excited to see me as I am to see him. He points to my arm, and I nod.

Isaac hooks his arm in mine. "She was a knitter. I love that."

I smile. "Yes, she loved crafts."

"That is incredible." And then, "How are the dreams, Bri?"

I can't lie to him, so I answer honestly. "They're getting worse."

"Hmm," he says, lost in thought. He rubs Prairie's head once more and then stands. "I knew I would see you both again today."

"You could've messaged me," I say.

He smiles. "It's comforting to see when fate brings a friendship together and fosters it," he says.

I feel so good being with Isaac. It's like I've always known him.

"The bridge?" he asks, and I nod, and we walk toward it.

"Have you ever heard of Red Gate Woods?" I ask.

"No, what's that?"

"A forest preserve along Archer Avenue. I was there with my roommate recently, and we had a strange encounter. There was this man there at the end of the trail, and I couldn't really tell what he looked like, but . . . there was something about him. He scared me. Just his presence."

He pats my hand. "I'm very sorry to hear that, but I'm glad you're both safe. Archer Avenue. It's a very mystical street, isn't it? The home of so many classic Chicago hauntings. You have heard of the most famous one, the vanishing hitchhiker . . ."

A vanishing hitchhiker, and then I think of vanishing women throughout our city. Where do they go? Who is taking them? They are not leaving on their own. They can't be. Not that many women.

"Yes," I say, and something within me stirs.

"Is everything all right?"

"Yes, I was just trying to remember if I locked the front gate of my house. I had something weird happen the other day." I rub my head. "I feel like something weird is happening every day. I feel like grief has just flipped my entire reality."

I take a deep breath. Sigh and smile. "I don't know what's happening."

He gives me a sympathetic look. "You're doing all right. You're doing everything you're supposed to be doing. Did you take me up on my advice? Meditation? The Gateway Project."

"I looked up the Gateway Project and it seems . . . interesting, don't you think?"

It seems wonderful in ways, the possibility of it—that just simple meditation can start me on my path to peace, because I hate feeling this way—disjointed, disconnected, and confused, afraid to sleep, yet so utterly exhausted.

I longed for a sense of normalcy and stability in the world, but my baseline shifted. My baseline dropped.

"Since you spoke about your trouble with sleep," he says, "I thought it could help. Maybe your dreams are trying to tell you something, and maybe through meditation, or even manifesting with the Gateway Project, you can determine what your dreams are trying to communicate."

I sigh. "I'm considering it." I know I need something to help with the dreams and this feeling.

We walk slowly, the same route we walked before, toward the pretty bridge over the water. Today it's one of those steel-gray days in which the sun is hidden behind dense clouds.

"I think you'll figure out what it is you need, Bri."

I laugh.

"What's so funny?"

I feel the wind at the back of my neck and adjust my scarf, covering my skin. "A lot of really bizarre things are happening in my life."

"Then maybe these are little signs, little synchronicities that you need to listen to."

"I feel like I don't even know what's real some days," I say.

"Maybe it's all real," Isaac says.

"What do you mean?"

"The strange things that you're speaking of. I'm assuming you're seeing things, hearing things, feeling things. Maybe all of those things are real."

He speaks so carefully, smoothly. With care. Isaac is so beautiful. Angelic. Serene. His features are smooth. His electric eyes are kind. He vibrates with this intensity of joy. Being with him just feels like sitting outside in the park with your best friend in summertime. It's so natural.

"People speak of things, like time and space and dreams and reality and fiction, like they're all different somehow, but we're still experiencing something when we experience an oddity. Time shifts. We grow up from little children to adolescents to adults. Time bends. We forget things, misplace things. Then find them again and wonder, 'I could have sworn I looked there, but there is this thing I was searching for again and again.' In that instance, time shifts. I'm just saying, be open to believing that there are things in this world that are more complicated than what we imagine to be so."

I think about the nuclear reactor buried deep in the woods. How the purpose of that device was to manipulate energy and about the spike in oddities along Archer Avenue after it was buried.

"Is it all fiction?" I ask as we approach the bridge. "Am I just fooling myself to believe all this?"

"If you believe it's all fiction, then it is fiction. If you believe it's real, then it's real. That's how it works. We know that all possibilities exist as one, but what everyone doesn't know is how to get there. How one can travel. How we can walk through the veil, step into thin places, speak and listen to people and things that exist in places we just cannot see with these eyes . . ."

"And how do you get through them?" I ask.

"With your mind, Bri. It's all in your mind. You can do whatever you want, you can figure out whatever it is your dreams are telling you, you just need to focus and find the answers and you can do that in the Gateway."

We're standing at the bridge now, looking over the pond. It's not yet cold enough for the water to freeze over, but it will be soon, when arctic depths arrive in January and February. For now, there are snow and ice crystals all along the edges.

"Where'd you learn about the Gateway? Your research?"

"Yes, some of this thinking, about the power of the subconscious mind, comes from Jung. Some of it comes from Robert Goddard, who created the Gateway Project. He was a radioman who studied altered states of consciousness. He later founded the Goddard Institute, where he applied his ideas. He developed hemi-sync. Hemispheric synchronization. You can also call it brain-wave synchronization. What hemi-sync does is stimulate the brain functions of the left hemisphere and the right hemisphere. By stimulating both hemispheres, your brain waves become synchronized, and that is called hemi-sync."

I picture a brain in my head, both sides of it beating as one, but I'd always assumed a single brain would act as a single machine with a single purpose. "I didn't think I'd learn about brain synchronization on my morning walk, but here I am."

He laughs. "It's really fascinating when you think about it."

"What exactly does hemi-sync do?"

"Lots of things. Promote mental well-being, out-of-body experiences, or trigger altered states of consciousness."

"Wait." I hold back a laugh. I'm sure my face displays my skepticism. "Out-of-body experiences? Really, Isaac?" My face is hurting from smiling so much. It all sounds so silly.

"Have you heard of binaural beats before?"

I nod. "Yes, well, I think so?"

"Sound waves. Vibration. It all has the power to manipulate energy. To manipulate consciousness. You can search online right now and find a collection of binaural beats on music streaming services and on a number of platforms. It's music that is set to be played at certain frequencies. Delta waves for deep sleep, pain relief. Things like antiaging and healing. Theta waves for REM sleep, meditation, and creativity. Alpha waves for relaxation and focus, stress reduction, positive thinking, and learning enhancement. Beta waves for focusing your attention and improving problem solving, and gamma waves for things like memory recall. You wear headphones, you play the frequencies, making sure the music is playing in each ear, and you enter a meditative state, thus your consciousness is altered."

I remember my conversation with Emily at Monk's Castle about consciousness. We spoke of this very thing.

"Goddard later took these ideas and created a program, a training series dedicated to exploring and applying expanded states of awareness . . ."

I look at him. "The Gateway Project?"

"Exactly. I've studied it quite a bit, and it's a very effective way to get people to alter their consciousness. The program has a series of eight progressive levels, and within each level there are ten exercises. Each level is designed to lead you to an expanded state of awareness, and from there you can develop creativity, solve problems, obtain guidance . . ."

"Wait, obtain guidance, from what?"

He takes a deep breath and looks up to the sky and holds his arms out. "I don't know how to explain it without sounding completely insane . . ."

"What I'm living through, or sleeping through, feels completely insane. I'm listening."

"Good." He clasps his hands together. "The program was proven to work," he says.

"By whom?"

"The CIA."

I feel my eyes widen. "Like the CIA, Central Intelligence Agency?"

He smiles. "Incredible, right? The CIA investigated it along with the help of Liam Weinstein, an inventor and a scientist. Weinstein believed consciousness permeated everything. Essentially, Weinstein confirmed everything that the Gateway Project started to accomplish. The CIA published a report: 'Analysis and Assessment of the Gateway Project.' It's public. You can search for it online and read the full report on your own if you need more proof. Everything Goddard says the Gateway Project could do, the CIA and Weinstein confirmed."

Prairie begins wagging her tail, indicating she wants to keep walking, and so we do. She tugs at the leash as she sees a squirrel bolt across the sidewalk, and both Isaac and I laugh.

"So what exactly did Weinstein and the CIA confirm?"

He pauses, his eyes focused on the ground, thinking. "It's a little complicated to explain, but follow me. Let's believe that human consciousness has a frequency—"

"Like a radio station," I interrupt.

He points at me. "Brilliant. Exactly. According to the CIA, if the frequency of human consciousness drops from ten to the power of thirty-three centimeters per second but remains above a state of total rest, it can transcend space-time."

I shake my head. "I think I understand what you're trying to tell me, but can you give me an example?"

"Think of a radio example. Imagine that human consciousness is a radio playing a certain music station. Well, if you move that dial and start searching for another station and just land on nothing, on that fuzzy place we call snow, that is total rest. That is where you can transcend space and time."

Those words sound like a wind chime—"transcend space-time."

Isaac digs his hands in his pockets and raises his shoulders up to his neck as a gust of wind blasts us. We lean into each other and continue walking. "Gateway allows humans to achieve this state and establish a clear pattern of perception in dimensions. Human consciousness brought to a sufficiently altered state can obtain information about the past, present, and future, since everything happens simultaneously. Our consciousness is an all-knowing and infinite continuum."

This all sounds too fanciful for me, too far stretched beyond what I can touch, taste, smell, and see, but still I ask, "What could I even do with this? Why would anyone want to do this?"

"Like I said, you can manifest the life you want, you can obtain knowledge, and you can communicate with other beings, energies that have always existed, or energies that once existed . . . like the dead."

I open my mouth and hear myself say, "Ohhhhhh." It's making sense now.

"Where's Professor Weinstein now?" I ask.

"He died, on Flight 191 here in Chicago in 1979." I suppose he notices that blank look on my face. "You don't know about it, do you?"

"No," I say.

"It was the deadliest domestic aviation accident in American history. Flight 191 took off from O'Hare Airport, and after thirty-one seconds in the air, an engine detached, and the plane crashed into a field."

I feel like I should know more about it. There's something, however, in the stretches of my mind that finds a single string of familiarity, like maybe I had heard about this somewhere, seen mention of it on some program or read a line about it in some book. It's one of those things that one feels like they should know more about, because there's an instant connection to it, but I just can't catch hold of that flowing gauze in the wind.

"A lot of people don't know about it. There wasn't even a memorial erected to all two hundred and seventy-one people who died until 2019, forty years after the accident."

"All right, so, how can this help me now? Technically there is no bringing my mother back. There is no bringing anyone from the dead back. So what do I do with this?"

"Maybe you just need to shift your reality a little bit, shift your perception and your thinking. Maybe these dreams, these visions, they're something more and you need to listen closely. The Gateway Project will help you become more perceptive. We are all antennas, but sometimes we need to learn how to tune in to the right channel, in to the right music. And sometimes we just need a little bit of help. This will guide you to manipulate the energy around you that you're experiencing and maybe finally find the answers to all of the secrets you're searching for."

"Again, maybe I'll consider it."

"But Bri . . ." He pauses.

"Yes . . ."

"When you begin the Gateway Project, you have to be prepared for something."

"What?"

"Reality distortion."

I laugh and rub at my eyes. "Isaac, I feel like my reality is already distorted."

He nods. "I understand, but this is different. Energy cannot be destroyed; it can only be converted to something else. Everything and everyone remain, even after they're gone. And again, there are things out there that we don't really understand, but they understand us. But I do believe this will take you where you need to go."

We walk some more and pause at the lagoon and admire the Museum of Science and Industry.

"We should visit the Japanese gardens tomorrow," he says. "They'll be frozen over in parts, but they'll still be very pretty."

He points across the way to a brownstone. "I'm just right there. On the first floor. You can meet me there if you like. Message me when you arrive, and we will walk right over. Enjoy the Gateway."

"Okay," I begin, gathering my thoughts. "What can it really help me with?" I think of my grief and mourning, I think of the article I'm trying to write, I think of my dreams. The strangers outside of my house. "What can meditating do about any of this?"

Without hesitation, Isaac says, "It will give you all of the answers you seek."

At home, I am still not sure how I feel about starting the Gateway Project, so I decide instead to sit on the living room sofa and close my eyes and just meditate on my own, in silence, with deep breathing. The fourfold breath. I know that. I can sit with that for a bit before I graduate onto something else. The Gateway Project.

I steady myself.

I take a deep breath, the length of the intake, counting to four in my head. I hold my breath when I can no longer take in any air, and

I count again to four in my head, and then I exhale out my mouth, slowly, counting once again to the count of four. I repeat this pattern.

I try to let go of the thoughts that are pulling my brain in all sorts of directions: Cleaning the house, writing that article, what to do with all my mother's things. Grief. The dreams. The nightmares. Emily. Daniel. Isaac. Strange men looking into my windows. The bodies of women being found outside.

Daniel—my eyes open because I forgot to call him. He's probably asleep by now. The challenge of our different schedules. I send a message, hoping it doesn't wake him up.

Bri: I'll see you when you wake up. I miss you.

I set my phone aside on the sofa.

I start the fourfold breath again. Breathing, holding my breath, exhaling. Repeating. I see my thoughts, and they return to a collision of my mother, the house, Emily, Daniel, the Chicago Strangler, cold cases, and Isaac . . .

My eyes open and I feel my heart rate take flight.

Who is Isaac Adler? I think. *Who is he, really?* I like our talks, I do. I don't get to speak with many people. I'm in my house all day with Prairie, but why does he care to tell me these things? Maybe he's just as lonely as I am and seeking a connection with someone. And isn't that what many of us simply want? To connect? To feel seen and understood? And to love and be loved?

I hear a soft lullaby playing from down the hall. I know if I stand to search for it, I will not find it. That's how the music in this house works. There's no pinning it down. It exists everywhere, within these walls, the plaster, the baseboards, the light switches.

This house is a music box.

Most people would be fearful of these things, of lights flashing on and off. Of music playing with no known source, but I believe now what my mother said about the house: maybe these are all messages, and not the house trying to hurt me. The house will not make me afraid. The house cannot hurt me, I think and hope.

Keys and gates and locks and thorns.

Warm tears run down my cheeks. I take another deep breath, close my eyes, and say, "I love you, Mom."

I feel a cold hand on top of mine, and a soft hiss, as if someone is trying to make out words, but cannot. I try to open my eyes, but I can't. The cold hand begins to squeeze my hand, and it feels as if my entire body is being squeezed.

"Stop it. Stop it!"

When I open my eyes, the sky outside the windows looks darker, the light of the sun more golden. Morning stretched to sunset in the blink of an eye.

Prairie approaches me, her tail wagging, with something in her mouth. It's long and white and shiny.

"Where'd you get this, Prairie?"

I reach for the long, thin piece of fabric dangling from her mouth. It's a hair ribbon. A white satin hair ribbon.

I stand.

Prairie sits at my feet.

"Where'd you find this?"

Emily's hair is short, and she'd never wear a hair ribbon. Still, I walk to her room to inspect whether the door is locked, and it is.

There's only one place I could imagine something like this being.

I kneel. "Did you go to the attic?" I pet the top of Prairie's head. I see the door leading upstairs open. A narrow dark stairway that leads to the attic.

My heart feels tight.

I wonder what most people do with the things from their loved ones after they've died. These objects that defined their life. Hats and shoes and socks and hair combs. What about personal things, like jewelry or makeup or hair ties? What does it feel like to throw those things away or distribute them to family or friends, or pack them up in a box and send them away to a thrift store?

I'd imagine for many people, what they do is just pack these things up and hide them somewhere, holding on to them like precious gold in a pirate's chest, burying it deep within their home. They're too frozen with pain to throw away any of these contents, and they're equally conflicted about giving these items a new life, so what do they decide to do?

They decide to store these items that were precious to this person in their house. There these things will sit until another person's death. It's just a way of putting off the grieving process. But one day these things owned by people now dead will be tossed or sold, in garage sales or antique shops, and they will take on a new life.

I enter the attic.

A sad in-between place with two entire walls covered with radios: radios on shelving, radios in boxes, radios stacked on top of one another. Then there is all my mother's sewing, the cabinet full of yarn and fabric and needles. It's a burst of color in that corner. I can still feel the whimsy of her. She was magic, and every room she entered I knew she was there without even needing to turn around, without even needing to hear her voice, because that was her energy, this pulsating, brilliant star.

There is furniture covered in white sheets, old love seats and settees and armchairs, dressers and boxes written with Sharpie:

Mom's Shirts
Mom's Pants
Mom's Jackets
Mom's Dresses
Mom's Shoes

There is also the large trunk beside Mother's things. When I look down at my hands to find the hair ribbon, believing it must belong among Mother's sewing, I find that it's no longer in my hand.

"How very odd," I say, looking around the floor. "I must have dropped it on our way here."

I walk around to the boxes, reading what else is written on their sides.

Baby Clothes

Christmas Decorations
Light Fixtures
Photo Albums
Family Portraits

I've just reached for the box that says Family Portraits when I hear the low whir of a radio turning on.

Radios. I think of Robert Goddard and what Isaac said. That Robert Goddard was a radioman who believed that frequency and sound had the ability to shift our consciousness. I wonder now whether that's what the house is trying to do by playing music. Is the house trying to transport me to some other time by playing these songs?

I hear Prairie panting and I look down at her. "I know. I can't explain any of it either."

I walk over to the radios; I know most of the model names.

A gorgeous wood-finished Zenith Model 5-S-220. It's a little cube with a round dial face, and in the middle it reads Zenith. There are three dials beneath and in the center. We have a very rare Zenith 6D030 from the 1940s. The dial looks like an upside-down half-moon, and while it isn't as pretty as the others from this decade, its style is distinct. One that I enjoyed playing with when I was a little girl was a 1941 Zenith 6G501 Universal Portable Tube Radio with Wave Magnet. I liked the cream-colored case it came in.

There are so many in this little museum, and my mother didn't know what to do with them all—nor her parents, nor her grandparents, and so they remain.

Every single room in this house has a radio, even the bathrooms. It's always been that way, so I leave them there. I dust them, and sometimes I move them in a more convenient spot, but still, in each room there is one. I was told by my mother that this is just the way things were and had been for a long time.

I imagine the house likes it this way, and so they remain.

I fear making any updates to the house. It's time consuming and costly, and if I shifted something just so, or painted something slightly wrong, would the house grow upset with me? One thing I was always told to take caution with were the radios and to never move or disturb the radios no matter what. When I was much younger, I remember accidentally breaking one, and I was so fearful Mother would get angry.

"It fell," I said. "I'm terribly sorry, Mother." I had been reaching for the radio when it tipped over and crashed to the kitchen floor.

My mother looked at me with such love. I should have known she could never be angry with me: "Do not worry, my beautiful darling. Help me with the broom and the dustpan?"

I rushed to the cleaning closet and brought them to Mother. She took the broom, and I held the dustpan steady as she swept.

"Did you know, Briar, that everything has the possibility of being heard again, broadcast across waves and time?"

Mother swept the bits of plastic carefully into the dustpan I held in my hands. "I fear one day the house will ache so deeply and the music will play so loudly, and that's all you'll hear and know too."

"I don't understand, Mother."

Mother continued sweeping, moving carefully so that the broken bits collected into the dustpan. She began saying something, as if she were singing a song, but then I realized she was reciting a poem.

> She sleeps: her breathings are not heard
> in palace chambers far apart.
> The fragrant tresses are not stirred
> That lie upon her charmed heart.
> She sleeps; on either hand upswells
> The gold-fringed pillow lightly prest:
> She sleeps, nor dreams, but ever dwells

Mother paused her sweeping. "'The Sleeping Beauty,' by Alfred, Lord Tennyson. There are many variations of this story, of all of our stories, of the women who came before you and me. There are realities within realities, my beautiful Briar Rose. It's all unfolding, and maybe somehow we will find her wherever she is, and we will bring her back home, like she's been begging and pleading for decades." Mother returns the broom and the dustpan to their place, and I find her looking out the back-door window.

"Do you hear that?" she says.

Before I could say anything, Mother put on her coat and stepped outside. I watched her walk toward the greenhouse and enter. She was a blur behind glass, bringing a bright-red rose to her nose, and a smile crossed her lips.

It was then that I first heard it. A soft hum. A buzzing sound like a swarm of bees. It started with the crackle and the static of a radio somewhere in the house, and it wasn't until my mother died that I began to fully hear the music.

Now I'm sure when she was alive, she heard it too, and with her death the music was passed on to me, a secret that I need to decode.

Downstairs I hear the front door open and slam shut. A stampede of footsteps running across the floor and up the stairs. I hear something shifting in the dark hallway leading up to the attic. It's all happening so fast. I have no time to think. To move. To hide.

I hear footsteps rushing up the stairs.

"Bri." It sounds like the wind, but I know it's that and more.

I'm tired of feeling scared in my home. I walk to the entryway, and there is my mother, in the dark shadows of the stairwell. A finger to her lips.

"When you see him, you must be silent. Silent like a sleeper. Like a dreamer. He's coming for you."

When I open my mouth to say something, anything, scream, my mother's form dissolves into the thick black shadows along the walls.

Another memory and another vision. The house is speaking firmly to me now.

"Mother?" I say, but there is no one here but me. I hear the creaking of wood and move downstairs.

In the living room I see the spinning spindle, spinning again on its own.

Chapter 18

I slept five hours last night, and again I dreamed of Isaac. This time both he and I were standing in the middle of a street, about ten yards from each other. It was dark outside, and on one side there were commercial businesses, a tire-repair place, an old dive bar, and on the other a cemetery. He pointed behind me, I turned around, and there she was, inches from me. In a white dress and white shoes, a white ribbon in her hair.

When my phone rang, I was still disoriented with sleep, but when I made my way down to the front door and opened it, I was happily reminded of my date today with Daniel. Our schedules finally aligned.

"Emily!" I shout toward the stairs, awkwardly holding a bouquet of red roses. "Daniel's here . . . with FLOWERS."

Emily laughs from her bedroom. "I wish Dana would bring me flowers."

Red roses. Elegant. Classic.

They match the house.

He rubs his hands through his hair. He looks tired. I feel tired. We can both match each other's energy today.

Daniel is in a dark-blue long-sleeve shirt and jeans. He's got light stubble, and there are dark circles under his eyes. He worked last night, and I insisted he get sleep, but he wanted to take advantage of his day off with me, he said. Daniel and Isaac couldn't be more opposite. Isaac's hands are soft and manicured. Daniel's hands are calloused and nicked from working on cars, his pastime. Daniel likes Chicago White Sox games on spring nights, sitting in the foldout of his truck and looking up at the stars after a day of hiking in northern Wisconsin. Isaac, I imagine, spends his leisurely time reading, researching, and lecturing.

"How's work?" I ask him.

He smiles a weak smile. "Exhausting." He runs a hand over his stubble.

I touch his face. "I can see that."

I don't know how he and Emily do it, but I know they are good people who care, who want to save lives, and whoever is in their care is lucky.

Emily meets us in the kitchen. She's dressed in a light-blue sweatshirt and sweatpants.

"Where are you two off to?" she asks as she fills her water bottle.

Daniel leans into me. "It's Bri—take a guess?"

Emily gulps some water down, her eyes trained up to the ceiling. She then pulls the bottle away from her mouth, wipes her lips on her sleeve, and says, "Cemetery."

"Am I that predictable?" I ask.

"No . . ." Emily says, reaching for her car keys. "Never." She laughs. "I'm off to the gym and then spending the day with Dana. You two have fun. Text me pictures."

"This doesn't look like a cemetery," Daniel says when I ask him to park in a small parking lot in the Rubio Woods Forest Preserve. I tell him to trust me. He unbuckles his seat belt but looks hesitant.

"I'm not going to murder you," I say.

"Yeah, that's usually what someone who's going to murder someone says *before* they murder them."

I shrug. "You got me."

Daniel smiles. "You're ridiculous, Bri."

I stretch and point across the road. "It's about a quarter-mile walk down that way," I say.

"Hiking in winter to a cemetery. This feels pretty good." He laughs. "Totally normal."

I raise my hands. "What's normal? Also"—I lean into him—"I took Emily to a cemetery recently, so it's only fair I now take you."

"Ahh, so you took your best friend someplace cool before you took me? Got it."

"Exactly."

We carefully cross 143rd Street to the South Side, where we find a CLOSED sign hanging on a cable between two wooden posts on either side of a dirt road. There's a single path that stretches past our view, flanked by trees whose branches look like wrinkled and knotted troll fingers.

The snow looks undisturbed. So no one's made it out here since last night's snowfall.

He looks to me for guidance. "You've been here before, right?"

"It's been years, but yeah, my mom brought me out here once before."

"Is this illegal?" Daniel asks as we step around the cable.

"Maybe?"

"What?!"

"I'm kidding." I laugh. "The cemetery is open to the public during normal forest preserve hours. The sign just means closed to vehicles, but it's a usable footpath. The road was closed in the late 1970s."

"Why was it closed?"

We walk past the sign and start onto the trail. "The last burial here was in the seventies. Then slowly after that it just became a place kids would come, drink, hang out, then . . . they started doing not-nice things like knocking over headstones and digging up bodies."

"Yeah, grave robbing is definitely not a nice thing."

"The place then just got a really bad reputation. During the Satanic Panic of the eighties, people said there were satanic rituals being conducted here . . . people being killed here, just wild things . . ."

"Why'd people think that?" he asked.

"Well, visitors out here started finding small dead animals, scattered across graves, strung up in trees. Headstones smashed or completely gone. And yes, bodies dug up, the caskets empty."

He raises his eyebrows; his mouth falls open. "That's completely insane," he says. "What next? You're gonna tell me this place is haunted?"

"It's supposed to be. Some people say it's the most haunted cemetery in America. Other people say it's the most haunted cemetery in the world."

"What do *you* think?" he asks.

"I've never seen anything strange here, but it has always just felt like a really sad place to me."

A gust of wind blows, and he zips his coat all the way up. He then reaches for my hand. "Unfortunately, I feel like you and I know a little too much about what it's like to be sad."

He puts his arm around my waist, and we continue walking.

I think about the people who were buried here. I'm sure they had friends and family visit them for a short time. But people die, and so, eventually, I imagine many people out here stopped having friends and family visit. I wonder if most of the visitors here for these grave sites were just tourists and ghost hunters, and that thought makes me so sad. But that's the reality of life and death, that one day there will be no one who remembers us in life.

Daniel presses his lips together. "I know I don't talk much about work, because it's hard to, but I can understand a little of what you're feeling."

We continue walking down the deserted path covered with dried thorn bushes and a few fallen branches.

I watch what leaves remain fluttering atop the trees. The sky is a low-hanging gray and white sheet. The thin trees sway, side to side; the textured tree bark looks like the scales of some monster. I stare deep into the wintry forest. It seems terrifying, yet magical, as if a great mythical beast could emerge from within the wood at any moment, and if so, I almost wouldn't be surprised. A few bright-red berries remain on branches, but the scene is mostly browns and golds and bronze.

A few birds flutter overhead, and some land on branches. Everything seems in motion, and everything changes each second as the sun shines this way, then lowering that way. Minute by minute, more shadows, longer and darker, stretch across the forest floor.

The first European settlers came to this area in the 1820s, people of English, Irish, and Scottish descent. After the 1840s, most of the new settlers were German. Plots of land were divided and named after the families who acquired them: Walker's Grove, Cooper's Grove, Blackstone Grove, and of course where we find ourselves now, Bachelor's Grove. There are two thoughts about the origin of the name, some believing it was originally named Batchelder's Field, after a family who settled in Rich Township in the 1840s, or that it was named Bachelor's Field originally, because the land was purchased together by several single men, or bachelors.

What I know for certain is that this is the area where my widowed great-great-great-grandmother settled with her two little children, nestled deep in this forest, all alone, without her love, and far, far from her home.

We come upon a small field and a chain-link fence with a sign that reads BACHELOR'S GROVE CEMETERY.

Daniel looks around. There is no one else here but us, but it's not scary so much as quiet, and peaceful. It feels like it's only the two of us who exist in all the world right now, and maybe that's true; maybe we've stepped into a thin place in which just he and I and ghost stories and urban legends exist.

"I almost expected a stone fence or an iron gate, not a chain-link fence," he says.

Bachelor's Grove doesn't really feel like a cemetery so much as a little piece of land where some people were buried deep in the forest. It's got the feel of one of those family cemeteries planted in front of a farmhouse you pass by in a blur on country roads.

Here, there are just a few remaining headstones, scattered far apart from one another. "Here," I tell him. "I'll give you the tour. Cemeteries are the kind of thing that don't change a lot over time." I direct him to the largest monument on the grounds.

He tells me about working as a paramedic in the city, its pressures, and anxieties.

"There's always something, every shift. It's never a quiet day," he says. "I hear the sirens all the time. It's like they're in my head."

"I'm sure people are very happy when they see you arrive. Relieved almost. It's hard for Emily to talk to me about it too, but she does like to tell me about helping people and how happy they are when they see you."

"It's our job to care," he says. "I see how scared people are when we get there. They know we're there to help, but you see this terror on their faces too. You can't do something like this without really caring about people. There's an energy to it all, from the moment a shift starts to when it finishes. The adrenaline kicks in and we just have to go, move fast. Think fast. Don't mess up."

I sympathize with Daniel and Emily; the pressure and stress they live with each day weighs down on them. Their presence literally dictates whether someone lives or dies.

My gaze moves up to the towering trees and the skeletal branches. "You're racing against time," I say. "I guess many of us are just trying to understand this all—life, death, what it means, what else is out there." I look at him. "Thank you for being here."

"I'm always going to be here," he says.

"I'm dealing with a lot right now," I say.

"I know. You don't have to explain it, and when I say I'm here, I mean it. I'm here for all of it."

He reaches out and takes my hand in his.

For the first time in a long time, I feel like my fall into grief is halted, for at least a little while. Like I am caught and being held carefully in the air. It's in this moment I'm starting to realize that no one can fix you, not instantaneously, when you're feeling so many emotions, but it's nice to have people there for you, who will not abandon you to the darkness. And while they can't hold that darkness for you, they can at least hold your hand as you navigate the treacherous path through thick brambles and thorns that tug at your clothes in the deep wood. That's what real friends do; they do not abandon you when you're at your lowest, suffering with an intensity in which you cannot even breathe steadily because the pain of losing someone, of losing so much, has rocked your life, and has jolted your entire DNA.

Daniel looks around to the scattering of headstones and funeral monuments in the cemetery. There aren't many. Over the years they've been vandalized, broken, and taken away bit by bit. There were only around eighty total burials here before the graveyard was decommissioned, and there's way less than that many markers here today.

He adjusts his dark scarf. "You're right, it's not as scary as I thought."

It's quiet and haunting and beautiful here this time of year. The tombstones are weathered and worn. For the first time ever, it hits me how lonely this place actually is, how many cemeteries are. Yes, we all will die, and I imagine many of us will think about what our own funerals will look like at some point, but do any of us ever think of this? That one day everyone we know will be dead? That one day, if we choose to be buried in a cemetery, the pieces of stone that mark where our bodies lie will sit there quietly and alone, past the seasons, rain, snow, shine, without visitors. Maybe there will be some people who walk past our remains, but one day everyone we know will be dead, and if we're lucky, some stranger will walk past our grave markers to say hello.

For a moment I think I hear it, the soft crackling sound of a radio trying to find the right station, the right song to play. Daniel catches my look of confusion.

"You all right?"

"Yes," I lie, and then I continue talking about anything just to distract myself from that sound. "The first burials happened here around 1834. These were workers who died while digging the Illinois and Michigan Canal." As I say that, it registers. Illinois and Michigan Canal. "Workers digging the Illinois and Michigan Canal were also buried at the Saint James Cemetery, just a few miles from here," I say. "My great-great-great-grandfather died while working at the dig site."

"Is he buried here?" Daniel asks.

"No, his body was whisked away by the river, and his wife settled around here somewhere, in a white farmhouse that no longer exists." And as I say that, something else connects.

The reported hauntings at Saint James Cemetery, of ghostly apparitions.

The reported hauntings here at Bachelor's Grove, of all sorts of strange things.

It's there, screaming at me, and I've been ignoring it for so, so long:

My family is connected to some of the most famous Chicago-area hauntings.

"That sounds awful and terrifying," Daniel says.

My throat is dry, and I feel dizzy for a moment, but I try to pull myself together and just keep talking.

"It was dangerous work, digging out that canal. Lots of people died, and we don't even have records of all of them, which is even sadder."

The Illinois and Michigan Canal connected the Great Lakes to the Mississippi River and thus then to the Gulf of Mexico.

My brain catches a new thought and begins to spin that needle and thread.

Limestone and moving bodies of water. The folklore and belief that limestone activates paranormal activity. Perhaps that's why the area all along Archer Avenue is so magnetized with urban legends, ghosts, and monsters. Energy, it's all energy flowing, and unfortunately, my ancestors did not know that they were stepping into a thin place when they arrived.

"What's wrong?" Daniel asks.

"Nothing—it's this connection I was thinking about, how limestone is thought to increase the amount of paranormal activity, and how areas with moving bodies of water are thought to also generate paranormal activity. Limestone and water, and that's what exists all throughout this area, all along Archer Avenue."

He gives me a wide smile.

"You think I'm being weird, right?"

He shakes his head and laughs. "Bri, I think we're all weird. We're all unique. It's okay. I love you. I like this. Spending time. We can't let so much time pass before we spend time together, Bri."

I lower my eyes. "I know."

He touches my chin and gently raises my head.

"I want to spend every free second I have with you. I know you're not feeling well." He takes both of my hands, and he looks me in my eyes. "Bri, I'm going to take care of you through this, more. All of it. I promise you."

We embrace and it feels like forever.

I place my hands on his chest. "We need to keep walking or we'll freeze to death."

I direct him to the largest memorial on the field, beside a tree. It's a massive upright granite structure, with natural stone details that blend into the environment. There's an intricate column sculpted into its side, and embossed on the front is the word FULTON. Beside this monument is a much smaller upright headstone that reads:

FATHER 1838–1922

In front of the larger stone there's a small little upright grave marker that reads:

INFANT DAUGHTER

"Do you know who they are?" Daniel asks.

"It's for the Fulton family. They were one of the first families to settle in what is today Tinley Park. FATHER is John Fulton, who died in 1922. INFANT DAUGHTER is Marci May Fulton, who was the grand-daughter of John and Hulda. She was born and died in 1914.

"People like to make stories up about these monuments for some reason, like who was the infant daughter? How did she die? It's all speculation, and maybe sometimes people want a scary story, and I don't know why. Because some people can just die of illness and natural causes, and those deaths are just as traumatic for family and loved ones, because someone is still lost and will never return."

I walk Daniel over to a large square-shaped stone with checkered markings. There's no name here to indicate who is buried at this spot. I imagine whatever did indicate the name of the person here was part of what was vandalized and stolen some time ago.

"There's this famous picture," I say, reaching for my phone and searching for an image, "of a ghost people have long called the Madonna of Bachelor's Grove."

I find the picture of a figure, face obscured, wearing a sheer, trans-lucent white gown. She's seated on this stone, glowing, but somber all the same.

The woman in white. The vanishing woman. She has many names and seems to be everywhere yet nowhere.

"Can I see?" he asks, and I offer him my phone. He zooms in to the image and shakes his head. "Who knows, right? I want to believe that we go somewhere else when we die, that we become something else. Do you think that picture's real?"

"I think that there are a lot of people who are hurting who want to believe that it's real, and sometimes I don't know what I'm fascinated more by, the fact that something like this *could* exist? A ghost. Or the fact that there are people out there who *want* to believe in ghosts."

"What do you believe?" Daniel asks.

"I know there are strange things that happen that we can't explain, and we can't pretend to know everything that there is to know. Scientists don't even know everything there is to know about everything. Even our exact location in the universe. People don't really think of the scale and scope of all this. Just imagine, Earth exists in the Milky Way. Great. But beyond that we don't really have a full concept of how large the universe is, so how can we know where we are located in this vast thing that is the universe if we don't even know how big the universe really is?

"The universe doesn't have a start or stop. The universe doesn't have a center or an edge. So how can we even conceptually pinpoint where we are? We know where we are in relation to where we know other things exist, but in terms of where we are in space and time? No one really knows. So what is space, really? What is time? It's all made up, and no one really knows anything, and if no one really knows anything, who is to say what is real or not? Who is to say if we're even truly conscious? Am I dreaming you? Are you dreaming me? What does it even mean to be awake?"

I look to him and feel I've lost him. *This is weird,* I keep thinking. *I'm weird.* I preoccupy myself with death and concepts of ghosts and time.

He opens his mouth to say something, and I'm panicked by what his next words will be.

"Bri, you can tell me anything. It's fine. I'm listening. You're weird. Your house is very weird"—he laughs—"but that's why I love you, because you are your authentic self, and you in turn accept me for my authentic, weird self."

I exhale and finally feel much more comfortable. I feel a lightness come over me. I'm being held up, I think. I'm not falling. Someone else is listening. Someone else actually cares. I'm not alone in this grieving process. I have people who are supportive and accepting of me.

I feel myself blushing, and then I direct Daniel over to the murky pond. It's dark and green and thick with sludge.

"At one time, people used to come here and picnic. Little kids used to play in this pond. Can you imagine children doing that today? That's the thing about time, how something was done once and how it can no longer be done. But there's an essence of that time that remains here, I think. You can feel it when you walk down that path and enter this cemetery. You can just feel that life once lived here alongside death, but then something happened, some great terror, and since then the energy has been disturbed, disrupted, and we all feel it when we enter this space."

Daniel reaches out and squeezes my shoulder lightly.

"What?"

"You're sounding like your mother in the bestest way. I loved sitting out in the backyard with her at night. She'd pull out her telescope and just talk about how big everything was. It was magical. I miss her too, Bri, but there's pieces of her here, within you. You just gotta look."

I feel the tears coming, but they're happy tears this time. I wipe at my face and say, "Okay, back to the tour, because I'm getting cold. Thank you, by the way."

It takes me a minute to find my train of thought, and then I remember the murky pond.

"The rumor is that Al Capone's North Side Gang would dump bodies here. It's just a rumor, but in Chicago, there's always some truth to some awful string of gossip. There was some activity around this area during Prohibition, but nothing with Bachelor's Grove or the pond directly. What's also another strange story is that people have reported seeing a horse struggling to break free from the pond, and when it finally does, they see it's dragging a plow with a man. It's said that a farmer nearby was plowing and something scared his horse, and it raced here and plunged them all into the water. So dead bodies; the remains of a horse, a plow, and its owner; and even some of the missing headstones are said to be at the bottom of this pond."

Daniel's staring at the pond, hands in his pockets. "You think anyone will ever drain it to see what's at the bottom?"

"Doubt it, but I'd love to see what's down there."

The pond is fenced off. There is a tear in the fence, but neither of us gets close to it.

We walk back to the main cemetery, and I tell Daniel the remaining stories I've picked up through my mother's books and her research folders. The Deck stone, where husband and wife Joseph and Jennie Nikias are buried after dying in a car crash in 1928. They're buried with Jennie's parents and brother. Then there's the Moss stone. Thomas Moss and his first wife, Elizabeth, are buried there. He married three times in his life, and each of his wives died before him. After the death of his last wife, he lived another twenty years. He also had fifteen children, and only seven made it past infancy.

Then there's the moving stone that belongs to the Patrick family. People have claimed that this stone mysteriously changes location, and not by human involvement. One day it will be in one section of the cemetery, and a few days later it will be in another. At least that's what people say.

"I feel like you knowing something about them, who they were in life, is important for you," Daniel says.

"I think so. Some of them died of old age. Some of them died of sickness. Some of them died of tragic accidents. Either way, they're here, aren't they, and many of them don't have loved ones to visit them, so I'm happy we were able to visit them today. These places hold our remains. They should look beautiful, they should be peaceful, they should be loving and calming. The dead deserve that. The dying deserve that. Life is so hard as it is, work and paying bills, figuring oneself out, figuring out other people. Hell, the last thing anyone wants or needs is to come across someone who will do them physical harm and end their life. And the last thing we'd want for ourselves is to be further hurt in death." I wave a hand across the cemetery. "Like having your final resting place forgotten and destroyed."

I'm realizing now that Emily may be right, that maybe the way to spend more time with Daniel is to have Daniel move in. His lease is up.

It makes financial sense for him. He and Emily are coworkers and great friends, and I could use the help. I'll think about it more.

"Do you remember what I told you?" He laughs to himself. "On that school trip . . ."

I smile because I think it's so sweet that he holds on to that memory from so long ago.

"We placed bets," I say.

"We did. I bet you the princess would save herself."

"I thought she'd die."

"She didn't, though," he says. "She saved herself."

I squeeze his hand.

"You're going to get through this," he says. "It's going to be difficult, but you're not alone. You have me. You have Emily . . ."

"You're forgetting someone," I say.

"And Prairie."

At the fence on our way out, I turn and look at the stone one more time, the one where the woman in white appears. I wonder what the rules are for ghosts for when they should appear.

As we walk back down the trail to our car, I tell Daniel about the ghostly farmhouse that appears only in the moonlight, and as I'm telling the story, I stop and laugh to myself.

"What?" he says.

I sigh. "I think the white ghost farmhouse that people have talked about for years is my great-great-great-grandmother's house."

"This sounds good! Tell me the story," he says.

"People who've seen it claim there's candles lit in the windows, and the scariest thing about it all is the rumor that if you walk up onto the front steps and the front door opens, then you'll never be seen again."

He looks from side to side. "So you're saying you think you're related to the people who lived in a farmhouse that takes people away?"

"Yeah." I nod. "I think that's what I'm saying."

I tell him about the blue orbs that are reported at night, floating along the tree line, and even a phantom black car that's said to appear mysteriously and chase people. We return to the main entrance and take some pictures and send them to Emily.

Her response:

Emily: At least there was no creepy guy there waiting.

Bri: Funny.

Emily: You know I'm kidding. Happy you had a good time.

And I am having fun, and I am happy, and I feel good and glad that I am able to find a spot of light in all the gloom. I think about my mother and how this is what she wanted, for me to live.

At the trail's entrance, we pass a group of four people arriving. They nod hello and ask us if they're close, and we tell them it's just a short distance yet.

In the car, Daniel asks, "So what happens then?" as he's putting on his seat belt. "Let's say a person walks up to that ghostly house, or they're touched by one of the blue orbs, or that phantom car catches up to them? What happens then?"

That's a good question. All these ghost stories are tales about what was seen, what almost was, a close brush with something supernatural, and none of them speak to an actual physical encounter with the unexplained.

I look toward the trail's entrance, and I swear I see something—movement, a shape—and then I see shoes, legs, someone, a man. He's dressed in dark clothes, and he's looking in our direction, but we're so far away I can't see his face.

"You all right?" Daniel follows my line of sight.

I open my mouth to say something, but I don't want to worry him further. I don't want to worry *me* any further. What am I supposed to tell him? I feel like someone's watching me? I feel like I'm being followed? I almost don't want to believe it.

"Yeah," I say. "I'm just tired."

Trembling in his admiration he drew near and went on his knees beside her. At the same moment, the hour of disenchantment having come, the princess awoke, and bestowed upon him a look more tender than a first glance might seem to warrant. —*The Sleeping Beauty in the Wood*, Charles Perrault

Chapter 19

TIME: 7:00 p.m.
DATE: Sunday, December 10

I open the back door and a gust of wind blows in behind me, a scattering of gold and bronze leaves skittering across the floor. After Bachelor's Grove, Daniel and I went out for dinner, and for ice cream and then for coffee. We seemed to keep adding things to do to keep the conversation going, but it was time for him to get to sleep to get ready for work the next day.

When I turn the lights on, I see vases covering the kitchen counter, full of bursting red roses. I enter the living room and there are more glass vases with red roses. The house smells of rot and decay, of graveyard dirt and stagnant pond water.

It smells like Bachelor's Grove.

I pick up a vase with one hand and the card with the other.

One rose isn't enough for you. I hope you will visit me again, Briar, in the thin place. There's a pretty white farmhouse here for you to live.

I drop the vase. Glass shatters. Water splashes across the floor.

My entire body begins to shake. I reach for my phone to call 9-1-1, but what do I say? It sounds so mad. Roses appeared in my house.

No. It's a break-in. That's what this is. A violation of my space. Someone broke into my house. Someone is watching me. Someone is following me. Someone knew I would not be home.

Someone. Someone.

Who did this?

I dial. The operator answers.

"Nine-one-one, what is your emergency . . . ?"

My voice is shaky. I don't even sound like myself. "Someone broke into my house . . ."

"What's the address . . . ?"

"I . . ."

My thoughts are scattered, pinging and shooting in all directions. What is my address?

"Ma'am, what is your name?"

It's hard to breathe. I'm hyperventilating. "My name . . . what is my name?" I find myself sinking, down, down. I'm on the floor.

"My name is . . ."

The room is spinning. Music is playing. There's shattered glass all over the floor. Bright-red blooms on the counters.

My fingers are shaky. I set down the phone and stand.

"Ma'am?" I hear the person on the phone say.

"Who delivered these roses?" I ask myself.

Keys and locks and gates and thorns.

My name. My name is Briar Rose Thorne. This is my house. He came into my house. Who is he?

I rush up to my room to check if anything was disturbed. My laptop remains. I check Emily's room, and it seems undisturbed. The door to the attic is closed, but still, I open it. There is a surge of music. Mother's things are where they should be, as are the radios, but each and every one of them is blaring music now. A different song plays on each.

I check the trunk, tug the padlock. It is still locked.

Prairie and I continue checking each room and closet. The bathrooms and the basement. The house seems curious about why I'm moving around in spaces I rarely visit, so I explain myself.

"Who did you let in?" I shout. The music roars.

"How dare you let someone in," I say. The music shuts off.

"I apologize," I say. "I thought you had let them in. Who was it?" The music once again plays, loud and vibrant, echoing down the hallway.

Prairie and I return to the living room. The pungent smells are gone. The house once again smells of roses. It's then that I notice the book on the coffee table.

I look to Prairie. "I know what it is. It's a fairy tale and what Mother warned about long ago. A wicked fairy."

Prairie turns her head. She sees something. I hear voices. Small at first, and clearer.

Then I see it. I see her. I see me. I see my mother. In a memory.

"What's the difference, Mother?"

"Well, a good fairy wants to help you. A bad fairy doesn't really want very nice things for someone at all. They don't mind being naughty or mean. Moving your things or even stealing them. They don't mind kidnapping people or replacing children with a changeling. They've also been said to have murdered people, particularly targeting travelers."

Prairie's ears perk up.

"Yes," I say. "Like women walking all alone outside."

Mother's voice continues. "A wicked fairy also doesn't mind condemning an infant to death, because they are jealous, and they are mad, and they are cruel, and they are hateful."

The memory fades and I rush for my phone.

I dial Daniel and I tell him about the roses. He stays on the phone with me as he rushes to my house. When he arrives, he throws his arms around me.

"Did you call the police?" he asks.

"I . . . I don't know," I say, still stunned, wondering if the police can help with this.

He calls the police, and it takes a long time for them to arrive. When they do, it's two detectives. One older, one younger, both seeming as if they're on the verge of laughter and annoyance. They introduce themselves. The older is Detective Kowalski, in a suit and wool coat. The younger is Detective Rodriguez. He's dressed more informally. Jeans and a parka.

"Flowers?" Detective Kowalski says and points his pen at Daniel. "You sure you didn't send these?"

Daniel clenches his jaw, then says: "If I bought her all of these, don't you think I'd admit to it?"

"All right, just figured I'd ask." Detective Kowalski scribbles away in his black notebook. The younger detective is reading through all the cards pinned to the bouquets.

"Do they always send detectives right away for a break-in?" Daniel asks.

"We were in the area," Detective Rodriguez says. "There was another break-in recently."

"They all say the same thing," he says. He flips over one of the cards. "There's no information about which florist they came from, but I can call around and see if anyone placed this order, if that helps you feel any better."

"Yes," I snap. "If they could break into my house, what else are they capable of doing? I want to know who did this."

Both detectives make their way to the door. They say they'll be in touch. They say they'll investigate. I don't believe anything they say.

Daniel stays the night, as does Dana with Emily. We stay up late and order food, and we try to ignore that a strange person entered the home for a short while, until Emily brings up installing new locks and calling the security system company in the morning to check why the cameras didn't capture anything.

It grows late, and Emily and Dana head to bed. Since we are all on edge, Daniel decides to sleep on the sofa downstairs, just to listen out for noises, in case whoever delivered the roses returns, and to make sure I can get some sleep.

"Do you want me to throw all of those away?" he asks of the roses, and it's a shame to discard something so beautiful, but because they were brought in with such ill intention the way they were, they don't feel special. And I feel bad for the roses themselves.

Daniel gathers a garbage bag from beneath the kitchen sink and carefully grabs each dozen and dumps them into the bag. It pains me.

When the last of the roses have been set outside in the trash, Daniel enters the living room and finds me setting out pillows and blankets for him on the sofa.

It is late, and we say good night, and I realize as I climb the steps that I've been awake too long, and I do feel tired and I do want to go to sleep.

Prairie follows me to my room. I sit on my bed, my back against the headboard. I slowly lower myself and reach for her, petting the top of her head and thinking about that farmhouse and that story Mom told me of fairies; and the stories Isaac told me of time, realities, manipulating energy, speaking with the dead, or something else.

I fall asleep with my hand out, patting Prairie's head, thanking her over and over for always being there for me, always protecting me. And then someplace in between telling Prairie how much I love her, I'm somewhere else.

I am here, but it's not here. It's somewhere else.

Above me a giant crystal ball shimmers like a thousand diamonds strung together. There are brilliant streaks of white lights glowing across the surface, like sparkling confetti spinning around me. Or maybe it's the shimmering dust of the Milky Way. I smile, and my chest feels so full and so bright because the radiance before me feels like it's beaming out from my eyes. And then there's music.

Laughter.

The tinkling of glasses as they clink together. I see a young woman pulling along a man by the hand as they run off to the center of a dance floor that's brightly lit.

More people, dancers, gather in the center from all directions. I am seated at a round table covered in a white tablecloth. There are empty glasses, and there's a white beaded clutch. I reach for it, open it, and inside there's a few dollar bills, a single key, a mirror, and a tube of pink lipstick.

The back of the mirror is gold with the image of a red rose. I point the mirror to my face, but it's not my face, but still, I am beautiful. Fair skin and golden hair. I close the compact and tuck it in my clutch. I focus on the musicians, who all look so lovely in their black suits. I notice now my legs are crossed at my ankles, and I'm wearing a white gown, the skirt made of taffeta. I'm bobbing my foot up and down to the music, and I'm wearing pretty white dance shoes.

The music is all I need, right here and right now. My legs are crossed, and I'm admiring the white skirt and how it brushes just so against my ankles. How my white shoes match exactly, and I just feel good, good, and here and now, and there's music, and I feel like I could live this night forever. This complete, utter feeling of joy and perfection, and I hold this capsule of gratitude in my chest, this precious moment, this summer night when everything is perfect and the night is still, and then I hear him call my name. That voice. I know him. I love him. I've been waiting for him my entire life. What took him so long?

The lights dim.

"Would you like to dance?"

When I turn around, I am no longer in the dance hall.

My eyes are open, but I am in my room.

I am in my bed.

There is a chill to the air.

I feel stiff and tight in my body.

I cannot move my arms. I cannot move my legs. I cannot move my head. I cannot open my mouth. I cannot scream. But I can see her, green and gangly, a wicked smile on its monstrous face. Noxious odor fills the room; the smell of meat and decay hangs in the air.

It's a nightmarish silhouette standing against the door, bathed in the glow of the streetlight. Two luminous eyes pierce through the gloom, fixed on me. Its features are distorted, twisted and bulbous, indiscernible as anything other than a horror from a deep, dark wood where the air is thick, where moss and fungus grow, and where fallen logs are occupied with the carcasses of rotting animal remains, and where daylight cannot penetrate.

The air crackles, and a low, guttural growl reverberates through the air. I hear whispers pinging off the wall, and I don't know if it's the hag trying to speak or the house. I try to move my fingers, my toes, lift my shoulders, my head, but it's useless.

I am stone.

I breathe in the thick and heavy, gamy musk, and it curls like tendrils into my nostrils. The stench intensifies as it draws closer and closer to me.

I am paralyzed. I cannot move. Daniel, I remember Daniel is here, and I strain to open my mouth and call out for him, but my lips are shut tight. I cannot even close my eyes; they remain open wide and focused on the nightmare before me.

The silhouette places her hands on the bed and slowly crawls over me. She's hovering on top of me now, and I feel a weight on my chest, pressing, pinching.

I struggle for breath.

Those eyes are wide, fiery orbs. Its teeth are green and chipped and collapsing into her mouth. The face is a fierce, shocking smile as she moves her head lower and lower, inches, centimeters, from mine. Her hot breath is on mine, and it smells like moss and rot and animal remains.

The scream within me bubbles to the surface, but it cannot escape. It is trapped there in my voice box. I am scared, and I do not want to be touched, not by this thing, and I do not want this thing in my house. I want the lights on, and I want this thing out of my home. I want safety and peace, and I don't want to feel this.

I don't want to feel this scared.

I cannot close my eyes. My chest feels as if it is being crushed under tons of weight. I'm struggling for breath, and the hag does not move. She makes no noise. She's just staring at me as I suffocate, watching me die. Each and every muscle in my face is locked. I cannot move. I cannot call for help from Prairie or from Daniel. They will wake up in the morning and find my body here, and no one will ever know what terrors I lived through to my death.

My body begins to tremble, from the weight and from the panic that air is not getting into my lungs.

The hag opens her mouth. A snarling sound escapes that smells like the murky pond at Bachelor's Grove.

"They're all sleeping. They're all dreaming. All of my beauties," she says. "And you will dream too."

I feel the hag press something into my hand. It stings and burns and hurts. I cannot move. I cannot breathe, and just as my vision becomes a long tunnel, and I feel myself falling, I hear a loud gasp escape my mouth. I release a scream, kick at my bedsheets, and sit up in bed. I scream and scream. Prairie is jostled awake and begins to bark at the door, but the hag is gone.

The lights turn on, and my room is a loud rush of music and the lingering smells of a deep forest.

I scream again, in pain this time as I realize there's a long sewing needle that's been stabbed into the center of my palm.

I inhale deeply, exhale, scream, and with the other hand, I yank it out, feeling the pressure release in my body.

I drop the needle to the floor and wrap my hand in the bedsheet.

Daniel knocks on the door.

"I'm fine. I had a nightmare," I say, and move my hand to the side of the bed, so he won't be able to see I'm injured.

Daniel opens the door a crack. It's dark, but I can make out his shape.

"Want me to get you some water? Anything?"

"No, I'll be fine," I say. "Sorry, it was a nightmare. I'll be fine."

"All right, you scared the hell out of me." I hear him catching his breath. "If you need anything, let me know."

Daniel leaves, and I get out of bed and turn the lights on. I will not sleep tonight. Archer Avenue will make sure of that, pulling me into dreams of girls at dance halls and nightmares of ancient hags trying to kill me.

I think back to what my mother said, of good fairies and bad fairies. Fairies exist, in the trees, in nature. They're there. Listening. They don't just exist in the pages of fairy tales, but within our homes, in our back-yards, perhaps even along cemetery walls. But they're not always good and they're not always kind. They exist in the world in which we live, but they have always existed. They are earthbound spirits and entities that are eternal. And they know that we're different than they are, and sometimes they grow jealous because we can breathe, and we can love, and we can eat food, and we can feel, and they cannot.

And maybe they are jealous of us. Maybe their jealousy can cause such hatred and such rage that they can curse a king's daughter to death. Maybe, then, that jealousy carries over centuries and years and finds itself glimmering within the lines of books and pages, a fairy tale read to a child again and again, on a ship, and across the sea, to a new country where a young immigrant family comes to America to find work and build a life, and so they do.

And maybe that's part of what Mother was trying to get me to remember, a fairy tale she told me very long ago, about a young family, in a new country, and an enchanted forest.

Chapter 20

TIME: *Bedtime*
DATE: *September 9, 2010*

I am in bed. Mom is going to read me a bedtime story, but she sets the book aside.

"I'm going to tell you a different bedtime story tonight, my little Briar Rose. An important fairy tale." She brushes the hair out of my eye and adjusts the teddy bear beside me on my pillow. Mother kisses me on my cheek and then says, "Please remember this story."

"I will, Mom."

"The name of this fairy tale, Briar Rose, is 'Keys and Gates and Locks and Thorns.'"

Once upon a time, a mother and young father named Talia and Joseph left their home in Europe. They traveled across the seas in a ship with their two young children, Philip and Rosamund. Joseph found work digging the Illinois and Michigan Canal, toiling under the onslaught of limestone and water. One day he lost his footing, and he was washed out by the river.

His young widow, Talia, was so heartbroken. She was here all alone, with no family but her children. She had no money to return to Ireland, but a man in town who was moving away offered her his aging farmhouse, a creaking little house far, far from town and deep within a dense forest with no one else around, all in exchange for her caring for the property until he returned.

So, Talia and her little babies moved into this white farmhouse, and they were all alone; even the forest seemed too quiet to be a forest, because there were no sounds from any critters, which seemed odd.

Talia ignored this and set out to tending the land and growing fruits and vegetables and caring for her babies. Spring came, then summer, then fall, and an unkind winter approached.

One day Talia awoke to the sound of music and a pulsating light. She entered the children's room, and there she found a beautiful woman dressed in a long black dress. The dress was so black that it looked like the sky on a moonless night. She flipped through the pages of the pink storybook carefully. "You read of Sleeping Beauty," the woman said. "Do you wish to be a part of its story?"

"Get out of my house!" the mother demanded, and when the woman turned to her, Talia saw that her eyes were fiery blue orbs.

"You're living in my wood, and you did not ask for my permission. I feel slighted by your insult," the woman said.

"I did not mean to insult you. I only mean to raise my family in peace. Please be gone, witch."

The woman set down the book and approached the children's beds. "How dare you, child. I am not a witch," she said looking down at young Rosamund, ever so cherubic as she slept. The woman revealed her long black nails and brushed a single black nail gently against Rosamund's fat cheek. "I am but a fairy. I look different to others, but this is what I look like to you." Her focus returned to the children. "Your son and daughter are so beautiful as they sleep."

Talia lowered her eyes because she knew that bad fairies were to be feared more than any witch, for fairies were eternal. "Let us be, please."

"I will leave, but I will take the two children with me."

"No!" Talia shouted and stepped forward.

The fairy raised a hand. "And you dare to raise your voice to me too. Remember, you are in my wood, and you have neither asked for permission nor offered apology."

"I'm sorry, dear fairy, for having offended. We only want to live in this forest in peace."

The fairy turned to Talia. "But you have not offered a price, and I have offered you a solution. I will take your two children and you may live here in peace."

"Please," Talia sobbed. "Not my children."

"Fine, then." The fairy turned to Rosamund. "Her children."

"Not my grandchildren!"

The fairy looked at Talia with her wicked eyes. "You make the choice. I will take your daughter. Or I will take your daughter's daughter."

"I . . ." Talia began to cry, knowing that either choice was a tragedy.

"Very well," the fairy said. "I will take this one now!" She had leaned over to scoop up Rosamund when Talia shouted, "No!"

"And so you choose," the fairy said. "You've made your choice. I will return here for your daughter's daughter one day."

And just then, little Philip erupted in a loud cry that rattled the wicked fairy.

She pressed a hand to the side of her head. "What music to my ears. You will make beautiful music, little one."

The fairy crossed her arms over her black cloak. "You will live in peace, Talia, as will Rosamund and Philip." The fairy leaned over and kissed Talia on the cheek. "I grant you this in exchange for your daughter's daughter."

The fairy disappeared, and the young mother squeezed her children tight and cried through morning, knowing of the cruelty of fairies.

"And that, my dear Briar Rose, is the story of your ancestors who first came to this country. Theirs is a tragic fairy tale, one of horror, and I'm so sorry to have to tell it to you, but it's important that you know."

"Why's that, Mother?" I asked.

"Because fairies are deceitful, and there's no way to believe a fairy's bargain. She may return one day looking for me, looking for you. Maybe she won't even appear as she did so long ago. A fairy can appear in any shape, color, age, or size. Who knows? But be vigilant. We're all Rosamund's daughters. All women from Talia's line. So we should take care when we enter the woods."

Chapter 21

Daniel leaves for work, but before he does, he hands me a card. "This is Detective Kowalski's number from last night. If you see anything, just call him."

I shove the card into the pocket of my bathrobe, wait for him and Emily and Dana to leave, and then I go into the attic.

The lights in here are dim, and dust particles are suspended in the air, and as they catch the light from the bulbs overhead, they emit an ethereal glow. The lace curtains my mother sewed are yellowed with age. Against the eaves, there is her workstation, my mother's prized Singer sewing machine adorned with delicate golden filigree. Spools of thread in muted hues. The wooden sewing table is scarred by decades of use, with knicks and scratches and dents, and there I see my name carved onto the surface: BRIAR ROSE.

I run my finger across the rough edges of those letters. When I etched my name there so long ago, I could never have imagined that I'd be standing here one day without her in this massive house.

I look down and see Prairie wagging her tail.

"I did have a nice time with Daniel," I tell her. "I would have told you that sooner . . . but you know, there's been a lot going on."

She paws at her snout. "I wish he were here all of the time too, and maybe that'll happen soon. I just need to think about it."

Prairie sneezes. I know it's not the smell of aged wood or the faint scent from the fabrics of old furniture or the aroma of dust that permeates the air. It's just my loving Prairie being a little dramatic.

"Well, I know your answer is you want him here too."

I walk over to the radios and turn one of the dials. It clicks, but no music plays. I admire how the radios are all positioned there, relics of a different era arranged meticulously. I admire their polished wooden cabinets, adorned with designs that reflect craftsmanship that doesn't exist as widely anymore. I look at my reflection in the gleaming brass accents.

We're radios, in a way, tuned to a song. Sometimes there are people who can connect to the station we're playing, and they linger here with us for a while during this life. Sometimes the song they want to listen to changes, or sometimes they turn off altogether.

I look at the radios collected by my family over the years. But just because that moment in time doesn't exist does not mean its influence isn't being felt somehow, I think. And what is it to think? To breathe? To live? To feel? To suffer? We move about our day, and we are worlds, galaxies, walking among other galaxies. My internal world is infinity, and Emily doesn't know that. Daniel doesn't know that. No one knows my thoughts, but I know they are there because I am thinking of them. And where do my thoughts come from? No one knows. No one really knows. No one can tell us whether our thoughts come from our brains or whether our thoughts come from someplace else. Most people can't even fully understand or explain what consciousness is.

I look down at Prairie. "We are all here existing with each other, right now, but maybe Isaac is right. Maybe Mother was right too. Maybe we don't end."

I face the wall of radios in the attic. I start flipping their switches. None of them are turning on. "Why don't you play when I want you to play?"

Click. Click. Click.

There is no sound. Just silence.

"If you're really here, if someone or something is really here, then communicate with me? Don't just play your stupid music and whisper to me through these crumbling walls. If you can hear me, then prove it! Why make this one sided? What's the point in that!?"

I lift a radio off its shelf. It's caked in dust. I turn it this way and that. Wires dangling. "How do you do it?" I ask the house. "How can you make this play when you want, but when I'm asking you, you're not helping me? Tell me something. Tell me anything. Tell me I'm not alone. Tell me that when we die, we don't end. Please."

Nothing. Silence.

I turn and launch the radio against a blank wall and scream.

"I want this to go away. This feeling. Someone take this away from me!"

I collapse into the chair in front of my mother's sewing desk, and I don't know what to do. How to move forward.

I hate these feelings, and I want to take them out of my body, but I don't know where they're stored. Where are thoughts stored? In our brains? In our bodies? In the Milky Way somewhere? I wondered then if that sadness calmed in sleep, but it didn't. When I'd sleep heavily after my mother's death, the dreams grew more vivid, the terrors at night more real, pulled into the daylight, and that is now why I fear sleep. I question sleep. I distrust sleep. No one can tell me where sleep exists. No one can tell me where we go, and like Sleeping Beauty, no one can tell me where those worlds are planted in which we drift off to at night:

We all sleep. We all know the folklore and superstitions around slumber.

Never wake a sleepwalker. If you do, they'll be doomed to live in that dream world.

If you sleep with a worry doll under your pillow, she will carry your worries away.

If you hang a dream catcher above your bed, it will catch your bad dreams.

Don't sleep with a mirror positioned across from your bed, because you could get pulled into another dimension.

Don't sleep with your bed in the "dead man's position," the head of the bed in line with the door. It's called the dead man's position because that is the same way a body is removed from a room.

I know how a body is removed from a room. I sat there with my mother, watching her final breaths that morning until they slowed and stopped at 3:43 a.m. Daniel was at work. Emily was at work, and Dana didn't arrive until after her shift at the hospital a few hours later.

I was alone with her in the house. All alone with my mother's body. All alone with the woman who dressed me for my first day of kindergarten, made me my dinner, introduced me to fairy tales, buying me any and every fairy-tale book she'd come across at a used bookstore, who'd take me to the great Chicago parks—Humboldt, Jackson, Garfield— and who'd take me on the elevated train when we'd go downtown, grab some Garrett Popcorn, and walk down State Street and over to the Lakefront trail, where we'd sit and stare out at the water, to forever. My mother, who would dress up every New Year's Eve in a gown she'd acquire from a thrift store and make us sparkling cocktails, and we'd count down the last few minutes of the year in our living room along with Channel 7's delightful and so unserious New Year's Eve celebration.

My mother was so bright, so cheerful, so electric, and now there I sat, with her body that had withered away to under one hundred pounds, her mouth slack because she had lost strength in those muscles days before, and no matter how often I moistened her lips and tongue with wet sponges, sores formed. My mother, whose hands were so swollen from the sickness. I hated how this illness consumed her, caused her pain and in turn made me watch it all unfold until she died.

No one tells you what death really and truly looks like and feels like.

Once the realization hit me, thirty minutes, an hour or two, later, I proceeded to tell her thank you for loving me, thank you for being such a good mother to me, thank you for making me who I am today.

I squeezed her hand that couldn't squeeze me back, and I told her I was so sorry, sorry that we didn't have more time.

I cried and knelt by her bedside, kissing the top of her hand, telling her how much I loved her, over and over again, feeling somehow that she could hear me in this desperate farewell, like we were at O'Hare Airport and she was just about to go through security and I needed her to know all these things before she got on that plane and never returned.

I called the hospice nurse, who arrived within the hour, declared the date and time of my mother's death, and called the funeral home, who were there within minutes. The funeral director, a woman in blue pants and a blue shirt with a gray hoodie, was accompanied by a young man in a black suit. They wheeled in a black gurney that had a black bag on it. They positioned the gurney next to my mother's bed, and they asked whether the fitted sheet could go with her. I said yes, so we removed the fitted sheet from the corners of the bed, and I helped slide her stiff body across to the gurney, lifting her gently and placing her into the bag. The man in the suit zipped up my mother in the bag, adjusted the gurney into a seated position, and then they wheeled her to the front door. At the front door, they unfolded the gurney, and I followed them into the street, and I stood there and watched as they wheeled my mother into the back of the black hearse.

I looked up at our house and felt it watching. I felt the entire boulevard watching, the grass and the lampposts, the pavement and the asphalt, the city. All of us recognized that this was the last time my mother would ever leave her house.

Inside, I was in a daze. I collapsed in the living room, on that oriental rug where I'd play with my dolls and my mother would sit nearby on the sofa, reading me fairy tales.

And then I heard it, a song playing from somewhere within the house. And then I fell into a deep sleep where I encountered a road, a car, a woman, and it's been that way since—music and sounds and sights in this house I cannot explain since her death.

"Keys and gates and locks and thorns," I speak to the attic. "Mom, help me. What is happening? I'm scared to sleep, because when I close my eyes, I see her . . ."

Behind me, something tumbles and falls. I turn around and see the stacked boxes.

I walk over to the large box titled FAMILY PORTRAITS, open it, and start flipping. These are framed black-and-white pictures of people who look like me and look like my mother. Some I know, grandmother and grandfather, great-great-grandmother, and great-great-grandfather. There are some cousins, and there are some aunts, some uncles, and some dear friends. I flip again and again slowly until I find her, and she is as beautiful in a portrait as she is in my dreams.

I gasp, so overcome with how gorgeous she is. I carefully pull out the gold-framed portrait of a beautiful young woman whom I've seen over and over again in my dreams. It's all starting to come together now, stitch by stitch, a family quilt, a family story, a family fairy tale.

Chapter 22

It's freezing outside. I'm standing under the streetlight and shivering.

I'm looking around me, and I'm counting sheep—one, two, three, none of them. None of them are worth any sleep. Four. Five. Six.

They're not all perfect.

They have to be perfect.

Because where I take them is special. Where I take them, they'll last forever. In that place. Father didn't have the right gift. Father was skilled, yes. He was excellent with tools. Trained as a surgeon. Scalpel. Scissors. Sharp, shiny things. Dissection. Articulation. Take them apart and put them back together again. That's what my father did.

Father was good with people too. He could make people do things. Build things. Father had people build him his castle, one the South Side of Chicago has never seen, nor will ever see again. It burned down to the ground after Father died. No one knows how the fire started, but I do.

I set the building on fire.

That was on Father's orders.

"If they find me and catch me," he said, "destroy my bloody chamber."

"You have to tell me something first?" I asked him. "What's your fairy tale?"

He smiled. That devil smile they later said he had in court.

"Bluebeard."

Later, I read "Bluebeard" by Charles Perrault. It's about a man who remarries. His latest wife goes to live with him in his castle. He tells her she can have access to any part of the castle, except for an underground chamber. One day his bride sneaks down to the chamber and is horrified to discover it covered in blood and full of the rotting and dismembered body parts of his previous wives.

"She then took the little key, and opened it [the chamber], trembling. At first she could not see anything plainly, because the windows were shut. After some moments she began to perceive that the floor was all covered over with clotted blood, on which lay the bodies of several dead women, hanged against the walls. (These were all the wives whom Blue Beard had married and murdered, one after another.) She thought she should have died for fear, and the key, which she pulled out of the lock, fell out of her hand."

In the story, Bluebeard is eventually killed, and his bride inherits his wealth.

In my story, my father, H. H. Holmes, was tried and convicted in the murder of Benjamin F. Pitezel. Some thought Father killed a handful, or dozens. Father confessed to me it was in the hundreds.

I do things differently than he did. We each have our fairy-tale methods. His was blood. Mine is sleep.

We are all different.

Another sheep walks past.

Another lamb.

No. No. No.

I'm shaking. Standing on the street corner. Shaking. Chicago December nights are better than Chicago December days. I'm hoping I will find one tonight, because it's been some time, and I feel one near.

Golden hair.

A beautiful voice.

They're talented. Each and every one of them. Brilliant. They should be pleased when I take them away from here.

Here she is. Here she comes.

"Do you have a car?" she asks.

Of course I have a car. I've got a very nice car. Black. Shiny. Polished like onyx.

She starts talking to me more and more. I'm getting excited. I know her. I know all of her. I know her insides and her history.

Past. Present. Future.

That's how this works. Inside out. Infinity swirling in her insides. She doesn't even know how special she is, but I will tell her how special she is. I will treat her right. Real nice.

"We tell each other to be careful out here," she says. "To pay attention."

"That so," I say, and we are walking. She's wearing a dark-blue parka, black tights, and boots. She's pretty.

Perfect.

She continues talking to me about how she takes precautions. It sounds nice. She's talking with her hands.

"I look for distinguishing marks," she says, chewing gum. "A beard. What kinda beard? You know? I try to remember. Does he got an accent? Does he got a wandering eye? In case I gotta identify him for whatever fucked-up reason."

"Interesting. Why do you do that?" I ask.

Her eyes go wide. "Because there's a killer."

Chewing gum. Smacking lips.

"He's been killing girls out here on the street. He killed some mom even a few months back. She didn't even work out here. She was walking to pick up her kid's report card. Whoever this guy is, he doesn't care."

She's telling me now how after a while all the guys out here just meld into each other. A mass of angry, sweaty, horny guys. She said one was so cheap he kicked her out of the car as he was still zipping up his pants.

We keep walking. I tell her the car is close.

"Sandra," she says her name is, but I know that's not her name. She tells me about her cat. But I know she doesn't have a cat. She has a dog.

They like to tell me lies, but I know all their truths. She keeps talking, and I just keep thinking about what she said, distinguishing marks. There really is no way to distinguish us. There really is no way to identify us.

Countess Elizabeth Báthory was responsible for the murder of over six hundred. Harold Shipman. He was from the United Kingdom. He killed over two hundred. Pedro Alonso López. He was from Colombia. He killed over three hundred girls. Luis Garavito, also of Colombia. He was found guilty of killing over 138 boys. That's what he was found guilty of. He killed over three hundred. Ted Bundy killed over thirty. Gary Ridgway killed over seventy-one. Andrei Chikatilo killed over fifty-two. Yang Xinhai killed over sixty-seven.

Lethal doses. Hammers and axes. Bloodletting. We all have different tools. Different goals.

We've all got our turn-ons.

- Trichophilia, a fetish for hair.
- Altocalciphilia, a fetish for high-heeled shoes.
- Masochism, arousal from domination, retraining, or hurting.
- Raptophilia, arousal from simulated rape.
- Amokoscisia, a desire to slash or mutilate women.
- Anthropophagy, a desire to cannibalize.
- Erotophonophilia, a lust for murder, accompanied by mutilation of the victim before or after death.
- Necrophilia, a desire to have sex with a corpse.
- Sadism, arousal from dominating, humiliating, or causing pain in an unwilling subject.

There are more. Many more.

All I want, all I need, all I desire, is to put them to sleep.

Sandra-not-Sandra asks if we're close, and I tell her we are. We are very close. We walk down a corner and down the alleyway. I can feel her internal alarm start blaring. Everyone has one. Not everyone uses it. I tell her it's fine. That she's safe. And she is. She will be safer with me than she has ever been in her life.

My car is parked at the very end, and she gasps because it's all shiny and antique and wow, she says, "This yours?" Of course it's mine. It's all mine.

Inside she starts to lower the window, and I tell her no. She wants to smoke, and this car is old, so, so old, and so, so special, and I don't want any burns in here. I don't mind the other things, but burns, I don't like burns.

I ask her whether she likes the outdoors. Her lips twist up. Confused. "I don't like camping, if that's what you mean."

No, that's not what I mean, but I turn on the car, and I will find us a nice place. I talk to her about turn-ons and she's nodding and listening. I talk to her about the sky and the galaxy and being under the stars. Her and I.

I drive, and she talks, and it's dark now, and I hear them screaming, and that makes me feel so happy that they are there. No one can ever take them away from me. Sandra-not-Sandra takes off her gloves, and I notice she's wearing a pretty bracelet with half-moons, and I think it will look very nice in the box at home where I keep their special things.

I find a nice place: Garfield Park. There're trees here. Branches are blowing here and there. Flurries are falling from the sky. The shadows are stretching across the snow on the ground. I can hear them screaming so loud now. I'm smiling. Sandra-not-Sandra is talking. I take off my seat belt. She starts talking about money. I don't know about things of money. I don't care. I tell her I like it outside. She doesn't look too happy about it.

"Outside?" She's turning up her nose, but she's still removing her seat belt anyway.

"Yes, it's lovely outside," I say.

"Lovely?" She scrunches up her nose. "You sure do speak different."

I wonder whether that's one of my distinguishing markers.

There's a full moon. It's bright outside, and the snow on the ground almost looks like it's glowing.

"I know this place," I tell her, and that internal alarm of hers is ring, ring, ringing like an old telephone, but she's still following. A field, an open field, so she can see the night sky and the moon so full, and the stars that seem like it will take forever to catch up to.

We are standing now in this field, in the middle of the park, and we're far away from the streets. Sandra-not-Sandra is looking around her. I see the tension in her jaw. How she's clutching her hands.

"Look . . ." she starts, but it's too late.

My hands are around her neck. I exhale because it's bright, sparkling fireworks in the night sky. My body feels electric. Warm. This is how I know peace when they start to feel pain. The force surprises her. She falls back into the snow. There's the sound of crunching and kicking. She can't scream because my thumbs are pressed into that soft part in the center of her neck, and I'm watching her eyes. I'm feeling her body against mine. Squirming. Shaking. Twisting. Spitting. *Nothing Sandra does is going to stop this,* I think. *This is what she must become. This is her metamorphosis.*

Her hands are beating at my sides. The blows are soft, and they go softer now. The kicks become slower too. Her whimpers fade. I'm waiting for that immaculate flash in her eyes when the change will take over. I'm pressing harder into her neck.

"Stop breathing," I tell her. "Shhh. Go to sleep." I give her a shake, both hands still tight around her neck. "Everything will be all right once you go to sleep."

Like the flash of a dead star, there it is. That transformation. Her body stops moving. The gurgling sound coming from her neck ceases. A signal shoots to her brain to shut off.

This body is dead now.

Muscles relax.

The bladder empties and urine flows into the snow.

I release my hands and press my face into hers, searching her eyes. I see the reflection of the cosmos swirling in them, and from behind me I hear her scream.

I am pleased.

Chapter 23

Isaac's apartment is a massive yellow-brick building on a quiet block.

He told me the front door would be open, and it is. I walk up the stairs to 2F, and I knock on the door. There's no answer. I wait. I listen. I knock again. I check the time on my phone, and this was the time he told me to meet him here.

Maybe he's running late from running an errand. Prairie is panting beside me. "I don't know what to do?" I shrug.

She stares at the door, her head turning this way and that.

"I don't think he has any pets," I say. A dog would have barked by now. I suppose a cat would remain silent.

I feel silly and embarrassed all the same. What if I got my dates and times confused? I've been doing that lately. I check my phone again. No, I am correct. This is when we agreed to meet.

I text him and wait a few minutes. There's no answer.

Bri: Hey, I'm outside your door!

"What do you suggest we do?" I look down to Prairie.

Is this wrong? I wonder, but then I send another text.

Bri: No answer. I'll wait here a few minutes. Hope you're OK.

Prairie paws at the door.

"You're right. Maybe he's still asleep."

"Isaac," I call. And knock on the door, and it's then that the door opens. It wasn't closed all the way. I look down to Prairie. "Oh dear, don't destroy his apartment."

I peek in. "Hey, it's Bri . . ." I say, and I hear my voice echo. "You awake?" His apartment is beautiful. Light wood floors. White walls. High ceilings. Simple but clean, minimalist but warm.

I stand in the doorway, thankful for the warmth.

My phone buzzes in my hand.

Isaac: Bri, apologies. I'm on my way. Will be there in ten minutes. The door is open. You're free to wait inside.

"Well." I look at Prairie. "Guess we'll wait."

I take a seat in the living room. There's a wooden table with four chairs. There is a bookshelf with a few books, and they all look like they're psychology textbooks: *Synchronicity: An Acausal Connecting Principle* by Carl Jung, *The Undiscovered Self: With Symbols and the Interpretation of Dreams* by Carl Jung, *The Interpretation of Dreams* by Sigmund Freud, *A Brief Tour of Higher Consciousness* by Itzhak Bentov, *The Power of Your Subconscious Mind* by Dr. Joseph Murphy, and more books with fancy titles about dreams and how the brain works.

I stand and walk over to the bookshelf and reach for Jung's *The Undiscovered Self*, and Prairie's leash slips away from me.

She scurries away, darting down a hallway.

"Prairie!" I set the book down and my heart drops. "If you destroy his house, we are in so much trouble."

There is a bathroom to the right. It's all white—white tiles, white claw-foot tub, white shower curtain. There are no products on the shelves. I assume he keeps everything inside of the vanity and cabinet to keep with the simple look of his home.

A door is open to my left, and Prairie is sitting there beside the bed, facing me. A light wood bedframe with white sheets, white pillows, and a white comforter. The walls, however, the walls are what snatch my breath from me. My hand moves to my chest. I feel the room spin.

"What is this?"

Inside the bedroom are large framed black-and-white headshots of women. The walls are completely covered in this orderly presentation. It feels like a gallery, a gallery of women, but they are all so different, but yet the same, because they are here on his walls.

There are no names or identifying information to accompany any of the pictures. They look like they were taken and blown up from newspapers.

I'm standing in front of one. A woman with a short bob. She seems so happy in this photograph, all white teeth and eyes sparkling.

They're all so different. Different years. Different poses. Different places.

I walk around the room, looking into their eyes, trying to find what else connects them all.

A wave of nausea rushes over me. I'm sickened by how someone can go to sleep at night with every inch of their bedroom covered in these newspaper pictures, these women staring back at them.

Isaac, is this really where you sleep? I think.

I'm scared to look up any of them on my phone, and so instead I just start taking pictures, all around the room, one by one by one. I don't want to think about it now, but it's there, lingering on the horizon of my mind. Could it be? Could he be the Chicago Strangler?

If so, how close did I actually get?

Do I call someone? Can I call someone? These are just pictures. What can this really prove? I think of Detective Kowalski's phone number. I left it at home. What do I tell him? I'm the one who's broken into a home now.

A part of my brain tries to reason that a lot of people surround themselves with curious things, curios and collections, antiques and artifacts. But who would want to surround themselves with faces of people before they go to sleep?

Something compels me to open the closet, and I do. The only thing hanging in there is a single clean and pressed dark suit, black slacks, black jacket, one white button-down shirt, and a pair of polished black shoes.

I hear Prairie's leash dragging along the hardwood floor. I close the closet door, and now I notice that there is a notebook on his nightstand and a laptop. I shouldn't, I tell myself, but I do. I open the notebook, and it's pretty recent, new. On the first page there are a series of names:

Saint James Cemetery

Bethania Cemetery

Bachelor's Grove Cemetery

Resurrection Cemetery

Red Gate Woods

Willowbrook (O'Henry) Ballroom

The second page screams at me:

"Briar Rose," followed by my address, with a note to "Meet Bri on morning walks."

"I never gave you my address," I say to myself. "Was it you? Have you been the one following me?" I'm horrified and scared, and I feel violated. I need to get out of here now, before he sees me, before . . . I don't know what.

I hear someone in the unit upstairs, walking, and I drop the notebook. My breathing is shallow. My head is swirling. I need to go, but I need to put this stupid notebook back where it was. I retrieve it and place it back.

I look at the laptop, and I know I need to run, but I also want to know more, because I am tired of living with so many questions.

I open the laptop, waiting to see the cursor blinking back at me with the ENTER PASSWORD prompt. But it's not there. Instead, it opens to a desktop, and there is a single folder titled GATEWAY PROJECT.

I move the cursor to the folder, click, and it opens to a series of MP3 files with names like:

Discover_1_Orientation

Discover_5_Exploration

Threshold_2_Problem_Solving

Freedom_2_Remote_Viewing

And on it goes. I click on a file that reads "Odyssey_3_Point_of_ Departure," and it starts with the sound of ocean waves.

"What is going on?"

I don't understand any of this.

A male's voice appears. It sounds soft and scratchy, like it was recorded a long time ago.

"The purpose of this exercise is to learn to navigate within the second body state. Move now to your preparation process . . . followed by your affirmation, 'I am more than my physical body,' and then move to your focus state, and I will join you there."

Prairie's panting, staring at the door. "Who can I call? What can I say? On what grounds?" I know the police won't investigate this. What will they say?

"What did you find? Some pictures on a wall and some meditation tapes. That's not enough to deliver us a person of interest or a suspect."

My internal alarm starts ringing, and I know we have to go. Now. "Let's go, Prairie. We'll tell him we weren't feeling well, anything."

On the way out of the room I stop, captivated by the picture of a young woman wearing white. The picture seems like it's the oldest one on the wall, just from the texture of the photograph. Her hair is pinned up in a style I've only ever seen in old movies, and in the bottom-right corner I find a name written in faint pencil: *Mary*.

My brain is racing, my heart rate increases. "Is it? She looks like the portrait," I say, "but I can't say for sure."

I can't tell if it's her, or one of the dozens and dozens of pictures on the walls, but I feel like there's someone in the room with me. I gather

Prairie's leash and we are on our way out; down the hall I feel as if someone is breathing down my neck.

I get to the door and close it and walk down the front stairs.

I look up at the building, and for the briefest of seconds, I could swear I hear the crackling digital sound of snow coming from a radio, trying to find its station.

Chapter 24

At the house, I open the front door, remove my boots and coat and Prairie's harness. I go up to my bedroom, throw on my bathrobe, and then sit at the foot of my bed for I don't know how long before realizing that Prairie's at my feet.

I walk down the stairs and to the kitchen and gather her water and food, and I place it in her little pink stainless-steel bowls, and I sit at the kitchen table watching her, still so stunned. Still so confused.

"What do I do?" I ask, not sure whether I'm asking Prairie or asking the house, but in a strange way, I am relieved when it's the house that answers.

Music begins to play.

Isaac told me to go to the Gateway. Isaac talked to me about things like time and space and dreams and mourning. Isaac found me when I was in pain, and his words soothed me. He talked to me about finding the answers I'm seeking. Yet he also talked to me about what's real and what's not. All I seem to know about Isaac is that I don't really know anything about Isaac at all. Why does he have those pictures in his bedroom?

The music is so soft now, a soft reverberating in the walls.

"Is he the Chicago Strangler?" I ask the house.

The house whispers.

"Even the most melancholic prince to ever be written about, Shakespeare's Hamlet, was fraught with questions of existence. 'To die, to sleep—to sleep, perchance to dream—ay, there's the rub, for in this death of sleep what dreams may come.'"

"I don't understand, house," I say.

The house responds: "It's a shift we cannot control. Even the king in 'Sleeping Beauty' tried to control this evolution:

"The king in an attempt to avert the unhappy doom pronounced by the old fairy, at once published an edict forbidding all persons, under pain of death, to use a spinning wheel or keep a spindle in the house."

What was then the spindle? I wondered. A device of death. But death can't be stopped. Sleeping Beauty could have died any other way throughout the kingdom, but what makes Sleeping Beauty so captivating is that her death sleep was something unnatural, caused by the anger, jealousy, and hate of another, a fairy. A cruel eternal being who looked upon an innocent mortal, full of life and possibility, and wished her death.

Because of that anger and because of that hate, it wasn't just Sleeping Beauty who would go on to suffer, but the king and queen, her parents, and her entire community, the whole of the kingdom.

That is what many of us don't recall from the fairy tale, that it wasn't just our princess who was cast away into a deathly sleep, but her entire community, people who knew her and loved her. That is what death is, it's a piece of string that, when pulled, unravels the whole of the scarf. Because while we're, yes, our own galaxies, traversing the great universe, there are others who travel beside us, and when we're no longer around, when we've been plucked from existence, those fellow planets traveling alongside us are rocked, their trajectories disturbed. Most people do not exist in silos. Our movements impact another and another, communities, and great kingdoms, and when we die, our death is felt across the land.

We mean something right here and right now, in life. Our lives hold meaning and our existence is important to others. There are people who smile when they think of us. There are people who look forward to seeing our faces at parties and gatherings. We mean something, not just in this greater design, but to each other. And when we are gone, our impact sets many of our fellow travelers on a new trajectory. An itinerary that no longer includes someone they loved. Our existence holds meaning, each and every one of us.

"Sleeping Beauty" hinted at that, at death as sleep, but it's something more, because as she slumbered, she still lived. So maybe death is just some sort of sleep, one of those levels of consciousness. Maybe, just maybe, then, we, too, are eternal like fairies?

Many people have spoken of that state akin to sleep, and how that is the place that we can manipulate and make great changes, in meditation. We speak of manifestation as if it's just a word to explain that "I want this to happen" or "I'm going to make this happen," but manifestation is more.

Manifestation is the active level, the active manipulation of energy, to bring things to us that we want to happen. Goddard believed that manifestation was made possible in this state akin to sleep. It was in that dreamy state that one could even change their subconscious beliefs, and even bring about their desires into the physical realm.

Isaac spoke to me of that too.

Isaac . . .

I want to tell myself he can't possibly be the killer, but there are many killers, and many of them have lives beyond their hands pressed deep into women's necks. Killers have spouses, children, jobs. They go to the grocery store and purchase coffee and eggs. They sit in traffic, stand behind you in line at the coffee shop, and nod hello as they pass you on a hiking trail, or a morning walk in a city park.

A killer isn't a snarling, grotesque creature stalking women in an alley. A killer can be someone with a warm smile, a clean face, nice clothes, and a kind and thoughtful smile, until they're not. That is how killers work, that is how killers get so close, close enough to touch you, to smell you, to sink their teeth so deep into you they break skin and bone, and then laugh when they hear you beg for your life that you've already lost, but you don't know it yet.

The killings started over two decades ago. Isaac would have been a child. The Chicago Strangler must be much older, unless of course there is more than one killer, but I don't believe that.

I'm not ready quite yet to listen to the Gateway audio. There's something about it that feels too absolute.

Radio signals are wavelengths that travel far distances. On the electromagnetic spectrum, radio waves have the longest wavelengths. Radio waves can range from the diameter of a volleyball to bigger than our own planet.

We use radio telescopes to map the stars, read the planets, and research giant clouds of gas and dust. It's with radio telescopes, too, that we peer into galaxies we will never travel to in our lifetimes, but we know are there. All of this is done with the power of sound and vibration, and so if we can reach into the expanse of the universe with radio frequencies with vibrations and sound, what can vibrations do for us in meditation? Can I reach out to my mother by just extending my energy somehow?

Radio waves, frequencies, vibrations, it can all see what is there. So much exists beyond what we can detect with our senses. That's what vibration is, a song, a feeling, an emotion, waves.

We are ocean waves, radio waves, electromagnetic waves. We are energy, everlasting and eternal energy, and what happens to us isn't ever truly forgotten. It remains behind as an energetic footprint, felt by others.

When someone dies in a forest or is murdered in a house, they are the shift in air, they are the fluttering of leaves on a spring day. Energy is never destroyed; it just takes on a new shape, a new form. We are not forgotten, no matter what our killers think or want or believe. And while justice is a slow-moving pendulum, what is true is nothing is ignored or forgotten in the ether.

In the collective unconscious, everything is revealed, one just needs to know how to tap into it.

All it takes is for someone to turn the dial and find the right song.

I am awake.

My eyes are open.

I am sitting in my living room.

It is my living room, but it is not my living room.

There are the familiar bookshelves and some of our books. There is even some of the familiar furniture, but I do not know who those people are in my living room.

"Hello?" I say, but they do not hear me. I repeat myself, but they do not know I am here, and I do not know who they are.

"Where is she?" A woman is standing at the window, looking out into the dark street. Snow is falling.

A man stands beside her. "Maybe she's running late?"

The woman lets go of the curtain. "Running late." She looks at a watch on her wrist. "Look at the time. She should have been here hours ago."

"She's probably having a nice time out with her friends. They all probably went out afterward to get a burger and fries. Milkshake even."

"This isn't like her." The woman walks over to a candlestick telephone on a wooden table.

"Who are you calling?"

"Beth, Rachel, Sara . . ."

"You're calling all of her friends' mothers? At this time?"

"You bet I am. I want to know where my daughter is and why she isn't here at home, where she's supposed to be at this time of night."

The woman starts dialing and the man shakes his head. "I'll get my jacket. I'll go down to the ballroom and see if she's still there or if anyone's seen her."

"Please, I'm worried."

The man puts on his coat and a hat and some gloves and leaves through the front door. The woman returns to the window, peering out the glass.

"A mother knows these things, deep within her bones. She knows when her child should be home, and if her child isn't home, then everyone, everywhere, should be out looking for her."

The woman returns to the telephone and starts dialing.

I'm back in the attic.

Night has fallen outside. One of the radios looks like it's on from the light illuminating its panel. It makes this steady buzzing noise, like a lone cicada lazily gliding across the sky in summer.

The music clicks on and it's a sad song.

> Put your head on my shoulder
> Hold me in your arms, baby
> Squeeze me oh-so tight
> Show me that you love me too

"This is her home, isn't it?" I say. I'm holding the portrait, her portrait, in my hands. She's the one who keeps appearing to me in the dreams, begging for my help. "I'm supposed to bring her home."

The song changes.

> Venus, if you do
> I promise that I will always see true
> I'll give her all the love I have to give
> As long as we both shall live
> The music grows louder now.
> Hey, Venus! Oh, Venus!
> Make my dreams come true

"But how can that be? If she lived in this house, that means she was a family member and that we're related, and no one ever told me . . . she's my relative . . ."

Then I remember, the fairy tale—

Keys and gates and locks and thorns . . .
I'll return for your daughter's daughter . . .

The music stops.

Outside I hear a car idling. I move to the window.

It's that same car, an old gray sedan with an old man seated in the driver's seat.

Today he's sitting there with a thermos in his hand, and he takes a sip from it. I wonder whether I should go down and turn on the front porch light. Maybe I should even shout from the front porch and ask who he is and what he wants.

But I'm too afraid.

What if he's the killer?

For many years my mother told me to ignore the man in the gray car, and it seemed like such an odd request. I thought when she died, he'd be gone too, but there he is, a man who has known about me and whom I've known about my entire life. We know of each other's existence, but we have never spoken.

Prairie gets down on her belly at my mother's workstation; she rolls over on her back as if she's playing with someone I cannot see.

"This is serious, Prairie," I say, but she ignores me, pawing at the air, playing with dust motes.

"I know Mother said never to call the police on him, but this is worrisome. This is not normal."

Then the man does something he has never done, in all the years I've seen him seated in his car. He opens the car door, and I stand back and wait.

Chapter 25

Each of the radios in the attic turns on, a soft, vibrating hum that I can feel in my molars.

"What do I do?" I ask Prairie.

I look up, asking the house, "What do I do?"

Music begins to play.

Oh

My angel, My angel

Please be mine?

My beautiful dear

I'll love you

For all time

"You speak to me of longing and love," I say to the house. "But there's literally someone outside. Who is he?" I'm crouched by the window and watching the man. He's perhaps in his seventies, maybe even older. He's leaning against his car, both hands interlaced in front of his stomach. He's wearing a simple tan coat and a knit cap. His face is round, and for the first time I do not feel a sense of fear about him, more like sadness.

"Who are you?" I say to the glass, my breath forming ovals of condensation.

The old man lowers his head for a moment, and I can see his lips moving, as if he's speaking to himself. I wonder what he is saying, but I'm too far up to hear.

He places one hand on his heart and reaches up with the other hand and waves to the house. Then he lowers his head for a moment and gets inside his car, where he removes his gloves and wipes his eyes.

He's been crying.

I want to run down the stairs and flag him, but I know I will never make it. So, instead, I watch as he turns on his car. I raise my phone to the window and take a picture. I have many pictures of his car from his previous visits, but something tells me to take a new one.

I dig in my pocket and find the card Daniel gave me. I dial and it goes to voicemail.

"Detective Kowalski, this is Briar Thorne. My boyfriend, Daniel Moore, gave me your card, and . . . there was a man outside of my house just now and . . . I'm worried about it."

I hang up, not even really sure how I can explain this all in a voice message. I move downstairs, taking my laptop and my headphones with me.

Isaac said I probably needed answers, and I do. There are so many questions I have, and I cannot keep going on this way, the worry of a serial killer operating, the strange man in the gray car, grieving my mother and confused by one of her last messages and by her, the portrait of a girl who's appeared in my dreams, and who I realize now is related to me.

I position myself on the sofa. My legs crossed underneath me.

Most people don't like to meditate because they say it's difficult to sit still for so long, that they find their thoughts drifting. Meditation is a practice, and part of the uncomfortableness of it is sitting silently with ourselves and watching and listening as our thoughts drift, morph, shift, change, and move.

Our thoughts are a conveyor belt of ideas and images and emotions that are presented to us. Sometimes we don't even know where these thoughts come from; they emerge from the depths like seashells spilling out onto the seashore.

I place the headphones on my ears, and instantly the outside world becomes muffled.

I pull up the audio and hear Robert Goddard's soft and steady voice.

Digital beeps and boops punctuate the background.

"This is your exercise to enhance and improve your mental state so that you can understand yourself more fully."

I don't understand what a CIA-investigated meditation practice can bring me, but at this point I'm so overwhelmed with confusion I'll try anything to feel like I have a hold of myself again.

I hear the susurration of ocean waves. Then a digital churning in the distance. For a minute I listen to the rise and fall of waves, and I imagine that I'm standing on the shore of a beach that I've never been to. The sky is blue, and the water is clear, and the sand is soft and white, and there is no one and nothing around me.

Goddard's voice returns:

"Imagine a large box with a heavy lid. Place all your physical matter, anxieties, concerns, and worries inside the box. Then close the lid and turn away from the box. You will not need any of those things for this exercise."

I do as instructed, imagining my physical belongings in miniature— the car, the house, my clothes, my grief, my worries, my fears, all of it— and I toss it all into the box.

"Now begin breathing deeply, and with each inhale, imagine you're drawing fresh, crisp white energy into all parts of your body. Begin now and continue until I call you."

I breathe in slowly, and deeply, exhaling and humming along to the audio of discordant voices that are doing the same.

After some minutes, Goddard's voice returns, and he says it's now time to create my energy sphere. Everything up until now has sounded nothing like what I thought a guided meditation would sound like, and this sounds especially bizarre, but I follow along.

"Your energy sphere is a moving field of energy that is made up of your energy. It belongs to you. Your sphere prevents any external energies from entering you."

That idea sounds alarming, but I maintain a steady breath, listening to his instruction.

"Take a deep breath and imagine your energy as light. Imagine, then, that your energy flows out from the top of your head. The energy as light then spirals down and around you, entering through the bottom of your feet and coming back through your head, spiraling down around you, through your feet and again. Do this exercise now."

While I'm imagining this, I'm hearing snow and then what sounds like an airplane taking off, a rising and then a falling, over and over again. And I think about the story of Flight 191 that Isaac told me and how immediately after takeoff it crashed and everyone on board died—men, women, and children.

Isaac said Weinstein, who died on that flight, was on his way to present some new research on consciousness at a conference.

What *is* consciousness, really?

It's not only knowing. It's *knowing* that we know. And so if there are varying states of consciousness, does that mean that our awareness could expand, and we could know more?

Is it possible to have consciousness that's so expanded, so far reaching beyond space and time and dreams, that you could communicate not just with the living, but with the dead, or the murdered, and ask them . . . what happened to you?

My thoughts remain on Flight 191. Two hundred and seventy-one people boarded a plane one day, and thirty-one seconds after takeoff, the engine detached.

Whatever words were spoken in the cockpit will never be known, because the voice recorder within lost power, and the only thing that can be heard on whatever audio was captured is a loud bang followed by the first officer shouting, "Damn!"

Flight 191 isn't a cold case so much as a forgotten tragedy.

What's strange is how it's rarely if ever spoken about. Had it not been for Isaac, I wouldn't even have known about it, and I've lived in this city my entire life. I didn't know about the disaster and investigation to follow, and I certainly didn't know about the scientist on board who studied consciousness, time, and space, who contributed to a CIA investigation about a meditative practice that's believed to help us erase the lines of the boundaries of reality.

It's difficult to connect these points:

- The Chicago area being home to the burial place of the world's first nuclear reactor. That is also the location of heightened paranormal activity.

And

- The place where a leading scientist in the study of consciousness died in a tragic flight accident on his way to share more about his findings on energy manipulation.
- What connects the two is simply energy, that Chicago is the burial place of important devices and important people devoted to the study of energy manipulation.
- The machine buried at Red Gate Woods manipulated energy.
- Weinstein, who died on Flight 191, believed in our ability to manipulate energy.

Perhaps that's why people like to visit places that are purported to be haunted, because of the possibility of feeling something, a shift in air, a change in perception. Maybe, too, that's why Archer Avenue is so powerful—people can feel that the energy along that street is different. It's all a thin place, and maybe the appeal then of thin places is that they have the power to validate something to us, that we do not end after death, and maybe not just that we do not end but we have always been.

Why, then, do Chicagoans visit the site of the Saint Valentine's Day Massacre, where sixteen men were gunned down by tommy guns, purportedly by Al Capone's North Side Gang; the location of the sinking of the SS *Eastland* along the Chicago River, where over eight hundred people drowned in a single day; Jane Addams's Hull House to look up to the top window, where two red eyes are supposed to peer out to those seeking proof of a devil baby; Bachelor's Grove in search of ghosts that sit on headstones, blue orbs that float through treetops, or a white farmhouse thought to appear in the moonlight; or Resurrection Cemetery, in hopes that they'll catch a glimpse of her?

Others visit areas reported to be haunted because they want to see a ghost, and if they want to see a ghost, that means they want proof that life continues after death.

And maybe, just maybe, the closest we can come to a thin place when not at one is when we sleep, when we dream, or when we meditate.

My focus returns to the sounds on the audio, that of the plane taking off and landing. And then snow, and then once again the plane taking off and the sound of it moving away from me, off into some distance.

A plane. What plane could this be?

And now I see myself boarding a plane, walking down its narrow aisle. I have a paper ticket in my hand. My seat number is 12F. People are sitting, clipping on seat belts, adjusting their jackets and coats, stuffing luggage in overhead bins, and when I come to my seat, I find him.

"Isaac."

"Hello, Bri."

He stands to let me pass through and sit in my window seat.

I sit and clip on my seat belt. "I don't understand. What year is this?"

"It's 1979," he says. "Flight 191."

No one really knows just how time works, but it's not linear.

One moment you're in a greystone, grieving your mother on Chicago's South Side in the modern era. The next moment you're sitting on a plane that's about to take off and crash. We live many lives; in some of them we sleep, and in some of them we drift, and in some of them we dream, but there's a place where all these lives bend together and we just need to listen, because impossibilities are actually more possible than we believe them to be. That's what makes a good ghost story.

The plane begins taxiing.

"What do you want answered, Bri?"

"Who are you, Isaac?"

He looks at me with such love. "There's a fairy tale of a little princess condemned to death by a powerful evil fairy. Well, a good fairy stepped in, and while that good fairy wasn't strong enough to completely reverse the spell of the evil fairy, that good fairy was able to reduce the sentence of death to a sentence of one hundred years of sleep. Some things stalk the forests, and they are wicked and mean, but there are other things that live in the wood that are gentle and kind. I have always been and will always be. I cannot intervene in all things, but where I can help, I will, and I do. I am the good fairy," he said.

"And the bad fairy?" I ask.

"That's the Chicago Strangler."

The plane picks up speed. "What else do you want to know?"

"Who is the girl in the portrait?"

"I think you know that already. Just close your eyes and watch."

The voice of Robert Goddard on the meditation recording returns: "Breathe normally. Relax now and feel, know, and understand the power of your energy."

"With your energy in place, move now to focus state as I guide you.

"One . . .

"Two . . .

"Three . . .

Cynthia Pelayo

"Four . . .

"Five . . .

"Six . . .

"Seven . . .

"Eight . . .

"Nine . . .

"Ten . . .

"Ten . . .

"Ten . . .

"Relax and feel comfortable in this focused state."

My thoughts keep going back to the vision of the girl in white, the man and woman in my living room, the old man, and his car.

"You will return now to full physical waking consciousness as I count from ten to one.

"Ten . . .

"Nine . . .

"Eight . . .

"Seven . . .

"Six . . .

"Five . . .

"Four . . .

"Three . . .

"Two . . .

"One . . ."

I am looking up at a sparkling disco ball. Its shimmering lights ping all around me. I advance my gaze and see glittering streamers hanging from the ceiling, shining, and catching in those tiny mirrors. Pastel colors fill the warm space. I have been here before, many times, I know.

I find the dance floor, and it is polished to a high sheen, and I smile when I see young couples twirl and glide in rhythmic harmony. Behind them, bathed in amber light, are the musicians in their sharp suits and bow ties. The brass section beams, trumpets and trombones. The saxophones sway gently, mimicking the movements of their song. The lead musician is afire, directing his ensemble with graceful gestures, and the dance floor is alive now with couples swaying.

I look down and I see my hands. I am wearing white satin gloves, but I know these are not my gloves, and these are not my hands. I hear a man's voice above me, but I cannot quite make out his words, not because it is too loud, but because his words are not translated into my ears as having meaning.

He repeats the noises again, and then it registers:

"Would you like to dance?"

I look up and see his face, and it's as if my eyes are locked with someone I have known my entire life. I am suspended in a moment I wish will know no end. His eyes are warm. His smile is soft and gentle. His suit is impeccably tailored, and he, all of him, is magic and magnetic.

I'm quiet for such a long pause that he laughs a nervous laugh. The band finishes their song, and the dancers are applauding.

"The song just ended," I say.

My friends Kathy and Rhonda stand over us now. Both have their clutches in hand.

"We have to get home," Rhonda says, smoothing out the skirt of her lilac dress. "Suzie's waiting in the car. She's a wet rag and wants to go."

Kathy is chewing gum and inspecting the young man beside me. Her long lashes swoop from him to me. A hand on her hip.

I'm trying to signal to her to lay off him with a hard stare.

"I can take her home . . ." he quickly says, and Kathy and Rhonda giggle. "What's your address?" he asks me, and I tell him.

"You sure?" Kathy asks slowly, and I give her a look that should tell her that I am all right, and I am happy, and I really like this boy. "You just met him . . ."

"Big deal!" I say.

"What's your name, fella?" Rhonda asks.

"Jerry."

"All right, Jerry. You get our girl home safe or you'll get a knuckle sandwich from me."

"Kathy!" I say. "I'll be fine."

"Nifty," Rhonda says, reaching for Kathy's hand. "Don't be home too late. Your parents will flip their lid and call our moms, and then we'll all get in trouble."

"I love you both," I say.

"We love you too. Get home safe."

I'm nervous, but this feels right. "I promise, I'll get you home safe," Jerry says, then points to the seat beside me.

I nod, and a rush of warmth that seems to begin in my fingertips spreads through my entire being, and my face begins to hurt so much from smiling. He takes a seat and we gaze silently at each other. I want to ask him where he's been all my life, and to never leave my side.

I feel a flutter in my chest because I am acknowledging that something special is happening here right now, the stirrings of enchantment and love and the promise of a lifetime. This is how it all begins, with a single fated moment.

A new song comes on. A slow ballad and he extends his hand and I take it and he escorts me to the dance floor. No one has yet joined us to dance, and so it's just him and me beneath the disco ball, and the entire room seems to fade away, and it's just him and me in our own little pocket of forever. We sway, lost in the poetry of our movement. Strings are delicately plucked. Harmonies swell and recede. Trumpets punctuate the sweet melody, and the saxophone croons with a tenderness that lingers in the air, and all I feel is him against me and me against him.

Then, everything shatters.

A commotion erupts. Sounds of men arguing.

"Get off of me!" The band halts.

There's a scuffle; one man is at the door in a leather jacket, trying to enter, and others are pushing him out the door.

"My brother . . ." he says, rolling his eyes. "I think I have to go, but I'll be back. Just wait for me. I'll get him home and I'll come back for you and get you home safe. I promise. My name's Jerry Poulos. What's your name?"

"Mary. My name is Mary."

He smiles. "You're going to be my wife one day, Mary."

The fight intensifies, and Jerry lets go of my hand and runs off to meet his brother, and I am left alone there standing on the dance floor.

The room quiets and I hear the musicians murmuring, asking what they should play next. They're flipping through their music books and seem to come to an agreement. They return to their spaces and have moved into position for their next song, clarinets at their lips, fingers on guitar strings, and the conductor's gaze ready to start the flow.

I'm still frozen, standing in the middle of the dance floor, a little shaky but I know I will be fine. Jerry will come back for me, like he said. He promised. I will take a seat and I will listen to more music, and I will wait for him. I return to the table, sit, and wait, and it's as if I am waiting years for him, more.

The night drags on.

The dance floor thins, and soon it's just a few of the musicians there and me in this giant and cold ballroom with its bright-white lights on. I begin to wonder whether I should walk home, too afraid to ask any stranger for a ride. I think and think. I know Mother must be worried and Father must be mad. I stand up, gather my clutch, and move to the door. The parking lot is nearly empty but for two cars, and it's a pitch-black sky overhead. It will take me some time, but I will get home soon, and I will find myself in my bed, nice and warm, and I will forget about Jerry and my aching heart that he didn't return for me.

I begin my walk down Archer Avenue. It's quiet and still. The road is slick and shiny, like black licorice. I'm still singing the songs in my head from the night. There's still magic ringing in my ears.

I start to reason that maybe I shouldn't be so mad at Jerry. Maybe something happened with his brother to deter him from coming back to get me. Maybe he will remember my address, and maybe he will ring me in the morning. I will still tell him I'm upset. If he has a good excuse, perhaps I won't be upset for too long.

I hear the rumble of an engine behind me and see soft white lights shining in the road ahead of me. Perhaps it's someone slowing down to ask me whether I want a ride, but I am just fine walking home alone. My home isn't too far now. A few more miles and I will be there, asleep and safe in my bed.

I hear the car stop and a door open and close.

It smells like the deep forest—cedar and musk and earth and wood. Then it smells like something rotting, like old meat that's been left out too long. I feel a tap on my shoulder, and when I look, it's a white hand with long black nails. Before I can open my mouth to say anything and before I can blink, I am awake, and I am right back in my house.

Chapter 26

I am in my apartment. I am in my bedroom. I am looking at her picture. My beautiful beauty who walks the road. She is very special. She is very special like Briar is very special.

I have been waiting for Briar for a very long time.

When Father was alive, I asked him to tell me more about how I came to be. He said he didn't know. I asked him who my mother was. He said he didn't know. I asked him where he found me. He said at the World's Fair. When I asked him why he chose me, he said he knew I was special, like him. He picked me to work at his pharmacy. He thought it would entice young women. He thought that if they saw he had a young son, they would trust him, and many did. They trusted him, and for that they died.

It was Father who told me I could not die. I asked him how he knew this. He said he tried to poison me many times, and not once did the poison affect me. Because of that, Father said he believed I wasn't human. He said he'd read about fairies who looked like humans and believed, then, that I was a fairy.

I asked him if there were more like me. He said yes. I asked him if they were killers too; he said not necessarily. I got a little older. I'm no longer a boy. I'm a man, but I've been this age for a very long time. I think about Father often and all that he taught me.

This is what I do. This is how I am. This is how I exist. In the night. In between the night. In the shade. In the shadows. In the treetops. In the songs. I am here. I am listening. I want to listen to her. The thought of her screams sets it all right. Their screams tell me I am doing a good job.

A good job was important to Father. All jobs were good jobs, but others more so. Father would say things like, "They do not mean anything. They are things and these things help us to live. To exist."

The doctors and the scientists. The podcasts and the news tell them things about us. They say this is a psychological disorder. They say this is a trauma response to abuse. They say we do this for the fantasy of it, the gratification of it, sexual or psychological. They say that we are seeking attention or notoriety. They say that this is an impulse, a compulsion, a sickness. And maybe it's all of those, some of those, or none of those.

Does any of it really matter?

We are here and we have always been here, and we will always be. They think that reading their books about us or watching their documentaries about us, studying us like we're some organism in Plexiglas under a microscope will stop us? No one has ever stopped us.

As long as there have been people, there have been us, serial killers.

And why do we do it?

Because we can.

At night I go to them. At night they will relive those moments. At night they will repeat their cycle.

Fear. Trapped. Ghosts. Legends.

But I will be there. I will hear them scream. Sometimes other people can see them too. And they will share their stories, of the ghost of the murdered woman they saw standing at the corner, or hitchhiking, or stopping a car and begging its driver to take her home. They will never go home, because I am their serial killer, and they belong to me even in death.

Ted Bundy said, "We serial killers are your sons, we are your husbands, we are everywhere. And there will be more of your children dead tomorrow."

Jeffrey Dahmer said, "I made myself a promise that I would find a way to be happy in life, to live it and to enjoy it, and this is the form my happiness took."

John Wayne Gacy said, "A clown can get away with murder."

Richard Ramirez said, "We all got the power in our hands to kill, but most people are afraid to use it. The ones who aren't afraid control life itself."

Ed Gein said, "When I see a pretty girl walking down the street, I think two things. One part wants to be real nice and sweet, and the other part wonders what her head would look like on a stick."

We all wonder what their insides will look like outside. We all wonder what noises they will make as they beg for their life. We all wonder what it will feel like to look at them when it is done.

Father would sell their articulated skeletons to medical schools. That is not what I do. We are all different. Our work all varies. My work is different from my father's, and I know I am making him proud. I know I am making me proud. I know that the night is brimming with delight. This is what I must do.

For a lifetime I've thought of Briar. The others aren't like her. They are weaker. Briar comes from a storybook family. A family whose life originated in legend.

I don't want to listen to her screams. I want her with me. She is so beautiful, in all her sadness. She's much prettier than a ghost. Much prettier than a haunting. Much prettier than a legend. There will always be more beauties. Always. But Briar, she's had her chance at life, and I want to give her the night.

I will pluck her from this life, and she will find delight in the night with me.

Chapter 27

TIME: 6:00 p.m.
DATE: Tuesday, December 12

I am awake, I think. My eyes are open. I am looking up into a black sky. I sit up. My back is aching. I am in the middle of a street, and she is standing in front of me. She extends her hand and helps me up.

I follow her, and we are now no longer walking in the middle of the road, but down a dark corridor that seems as though it extends to infinity, but before I can ask where we are going, the darkness shifts.

I see color now, green.

I feel the brush of branches against my skin and leaves catching in my hair. I smell the sweetness of pine and feel those tiny pine needle points poke into me. I am holding her hand, and she is leading the way, a bright spot in the eternal darkness of a fairy tale.

I hear night birds chirp and the skittering of creatures around us. In the deep wood, I think now that I smell a crackling fire, or smell something like spice, gingerbread.

Far off in the distance I hear the steady chopping of wood by a woodsman and then . . . the sound of a great wolf howling.

Mary reaches a door, knocks, and we enter. Another world of nighttime, and she is so flawless in it.

I see her so clearly now.

In this dream I am not her, but I am observing her.

She is radiant in her white dancing dress, with a fitted bodice that accentuates her slender figure; the wide, flowing skirt billows and twirls as she moves. The neckline is modest, a delicate sweetheart cut. There's just a hint of a floral, white pattern within the bodice, and as I look closer, I see the pattern, roses.

The dress ends at midcalf. Her hair is styled in an elegant 1950s chignon that's swept back. Her features are classic, high, regal cheekbones. Her eyes are a striking blue, framed by feathery eyelashes. She looks like Grace Kelly. She's wearing small pearl earrings, and there's a white silk ribbon that's tied up in her ponytail in a bow.

Her skin is fair and her cheeks are rosy.

We walk down a hallway and enter the ballroom, and the lights are dim and there are people dancing on the dance floor. People are seated at tables all around the space. The music is a soft number, with couples inched closely together. There's cigarette smoke in the air and the smell of roses from the centerpieces throughout the space.

I'm confused. Are we repeating a pattern? What does she want me to see?

"Mary," I call to her, but she does not turn around.

The girl in the white ball gown takes a seat at an empty table. Her eyes are directed to the dance floor, and she isn't seated alone for very long when a man approaches. He tells her something and she shakes her head, and he seems angry and reaches down and grabs her wrist. She pulls back, and her friends are now there standing by her side. The man is escorted out of the dance hall. The friends embrace, and the night moves on, and then I see Mary and Jerry, the fight with Jerry's brother, and now Mary is walking alone down Archer Avenue.

"I don't want to see this," I say. My chest feels tight, and I am scared, but I know Mary was even more afraid than I was that night.

"Mary," I plead, "please, I don't want to see this. I want to go back home. I want to open my eyes, and I want to find myself back home in my living room."

We are on a desolate street now. An oily black sky is above and pin-pricks as stars shine above. We are walking and we are walking, passing industrial zones, car repair centers, and used car lots, a small bar named Chet's Melody Lounge, and then I see it to the right of us.

A cemetery.

"I know this place," I stop and say, but she continues walking. "My mother is buried here," I say, but Mary doesn't respond.

I can see the tombstones past the black iron gates. They are silhou-ettes against the wintry night. We continue walking, and just the street-lights above illuminate the way, highlighting the edges of the cemetery. Through the dark, I can see the outlines of crosses, mourning angels, and ornate markers. Even from here the intricate details shroud the night.

They are all at rest, sleeping. And that is death. Death is sleep that knows no end. The air is crisp and cold, and the night is both haunting and beautiful.

Mary pauses for a moment, wiping tears from the corners of her eyes.

"My feet hurt," she says. "I don't even know what time it is. I feel like I'm in some type of purgatory, like I've been walking forever, again and again along this same route, and I'm just trying to get home. I just want to go to sleep, and I just want to see Jerry again, and I just want to . . ." She pauses. "I just want to wake up from this dream that seems to keep dreaming me."

I want to tell her I will continue walking home with her. I want to tell her it will be all right. I want to tell her we should walk together, because if we walk together, we will be safe, and it's late at night and it's dark outside and there's something about a beautiful girl in a white ball gown at night on a dark road that seems so magical and mystical, but also like a target for all the wickedness that has ever existed in this world.

Then I remember all of us in Chicago know how this story will end. We don't know the details of how the situation came to be, but we know what happens afterward, when flesh becomes spirit. When life becomes folklore, and when a tragic story is told and told again, over the ages, morphing and bending into something else.

We all know the story in this city. We've heard it recounted again and again. When did it happen? On Halloween night? No, it wasn't Halloween, some say. Some say it happened in the middle of summer, with the cicadas singing through the night sky. Wait, no? Not in the summer either? And it wasn't in spring, because we'd know that, that's when the Cubs play, and the White Sox play, and the city is blooming and bright. So when did this story take place? A man is driving down a lonely road one night when . . .

At that thought I see two headlights in the distance behind her. She does not see the car until it's too late. The car pulls alongside her, and I cannot see who is inside, but I see a shadow and I hear music.

Fear spreads across her face, and she shakes her head and continues walking, but the car keeps following her. The car stops and the man gets out. Mary starts running down the sidewalk. She moves into the street, screaming, shouting for help, for somebody, for anybody, to help her.

The man approaches in that moment, and maybe it's not a man so much as a woman in black, with long sharp nails and fair skin, who has come to collect a daughter's daughter.

The woman in black raises a hand, and Mary stops moving.

She is standing still.

The woman in black kisses Mary's cheek, and then she steps out of the way, and Mary's body crumples to the ground, as if she's been hit by a fast-moving car.

We know her name as Mary, and we speak her name around Halloween, and we speak her name around Christmastime ghost stories, and we speak her name around summer nights when we find ourselves oddly driving down this road that's more than a road, but what we never mention is how she died.

How did the myth come to be?

I approach Mary, dying there on the road alone, looking up at the night sky, blood pouring from her mouth and her legs askew. Her blond hair is no longer glorious and gold, but dark red in parts. When I hold her hand, her eyes roll over to me, and they see me and I see her, this beautiful girl who will be known to us all forever, whose tragic death will be whispered in girls' bathrooms and at sleepovers, whose painful demise will be the subject of documentaries and paranormal investigations, books, and ghost tours.

She is the darling of true crime, but we've never solved her crime.

In fact, many of us have never considered her death to have been a crime.

All we know is she is a ghost, but we have never asked how she was made into a specter.

If a girl is walking home alone at night and she is killed, that is not an accident, that is murder, and, to date, no one has been questioned or suspected of killing her.

Hers is the coldest of cases in a city that has known so much murder. Hers is the case on so many people's lips on Halloween nights.

We speak of her, and we laugh, and we say how fun it must be to drive down Archer Avenue to try to catch a glimpse of a ghost. But do we ever think that this poor entity is begging us, pleading with us, to please help her, to please take her home, and to please know that her killer is out there? That he will kill again? He has.

I squeeze her hand.

"I'll stay with you," I say, because I can't scream for help. There is no help. There is nothing and no one around us but a slick road and a black sky dotted by bright diamonds.

I lie down on the cold ground next to her, and I listen as she hums along to a song I cannot hear.

"I'm so sorry," I tell her, and I see that her eyes are closed now and tears are running down her face.

"Don't let it make you a myth too," she says. "That's what it does. It's a mythmaker. It collects our suffering and feeds on it, again and again; our eternal suffering is its power. It is hateful and it is jealous and so that is what it does, stamp out beauty and discard it. Our eternal sleep brings it joy."

"What is it?"

"It is a thing that has existed forever. In forests. In trees. In wooden huts made of gingerbread. In rooms hidden away in castle walls, where it stands in front of mirrors and commands to know, 'Who is most fair?' It is an infinite being that hates and harms.

"It shifts and bends time, searching and destroying. It looks for us and finds us, walking down the streets or hiking alone in forests.

"Our light only intensifies its hatred, and so it lives for nothing other than to stamp us out, to squeeze our throats, and to put us to eternal sleep, so we are trapped in a dreamworld of nightmares, and it will rejoice in our eternal suffering."

And this is the death that sets forth life to a legend, and I am here with her, a girl who died for merely being a girl, for merely wanting to love.

"How do I stop it?" I ask.

"Break the pattern."

"How do I break the pattern?"

"If one of us, any of us, can get home, can free ourselves from its nighttime world, then it loses its grasp on all of us. It's already seen you, Bri. It's watching you. It knows you are searching for the key. Bring me home. Break the pattern. Read me my letter."

"What letter?"

"You know the story, keys and gates and locks and thorns, a black road stretched onto forever? I am her and she is me. Find the key. Read me my letter."

My hands are holding her hand, but all I feel is air. I see her now standing in front of the iron gates of the cemetery, Resurrection Cemetery.

She is Resurrection Mary.

She neither sleeps, nor dreams, but ever dwells.

Stuck on a loop.

Trapped in a pattern of suffering and pain.

She walks through the bars of the iron gates, and like mist, she is hovering over the headstones now, water vapor and particles, consciousness, or a ghost that seems as though it has always been.

There's a loud high-pitched sound and Robert Goddard's voice: "Wake up now. Your meditation session is complete."

I open my eyes, and once again I find myself on the oriental rug. Prairie is hovering over me, licking my cheek, moving up to my eyeball.

"Thank you." I pat her back, but she continues licking my face until I prop myself up on my elbows and see that beside me is a book. *Sleeping Beauty.*

I walk the book back over to the shelf, but before I do, I run my fingers along the leather cover. I open it and turn a page and then another, flipping until it feels right to stop. And so I do, and so I read:

"Then the king, who had been brought upstairs by the commotion, remembered the fairy prophecy. Feeling certain that what had happened was inevitable, since the fairies had decreed it, he gave orders that the princess should be placed in the finest apartment in the palace, upon a bed embroidered in gold and silver.

"You would have thought her an angel, so fair she was to behold. The trance had not taken away the lovely color of her complexion. Her cheeks were delicately flushed, her lips like coral. Her eyes, indeed, were closed, but her gentle breathing could be heard, and it was therefore plain that she was not dead. The king commanded that she should be left to sleep in peace until the hour of her awakening should come."

Chapter 28

TIME: 10:00 p.m.
DATE: Tuesday, December 12

I am remembering more.

Is it enchanted? Is it magical? Or is it wicked?

Mother would whisper: "Listen to the wind, and that's where you'll hear their whispers. They're always there, just beyond reach. We can't see them, but they are there watching us."

She never said who was there, but sometimes when she was in the garden, tending and mending, I would sneak close and listen.

Sometimes she would sing songs. Other times I would hear her laugh. Some days she was very upset, and it was as if she were in a great argument with someone.

Then one day she called me out to the garden, where she had a blanket spread out and a pink leather-bound book with gold lettering on the front, and she told me it was time she read "Sleeping Beauty" to me.

"There's many variations of this story, or many stories. There's versions that are too cruel to recite to children. There are poetic versions that require multiple rereads to savor the letters in each word, and then there is this version." She reaches for the book. "This is the version, and this is the book that was read to her."

"Who?"

"To Mary."

"*The Sleeping Beauty in the Wood*, by Charles Perrault," she began.

"Once upon a time there lived a king and queen who were grieved, more grieved than words can tell, because they had no children. They tried the waters of every country, made vows and pilgrimages, and did everything that could be done without results. At last, however, the queen found that her wishes were fulfilled, and in due course she gave birth to a daughter."

In our garden Mother read to me about the grand christening that was planned for their young baby, and how "when the christening ceremony was over, all the company returned to the king's palace, where a great banquet was held in honor of the fairies."

"Fairies?"

"Yes, Briar," Mother said. "Fairies."

She continued.

"Places were laid for them in magnificent style, and before each was placed a solid gold box containing a spoon, fork, and knife of fine gold, set with diamonds and rubies. But just as all were sitting down to table an aged fairy was seen to enter, whom no one had thought to invite—the reason being that for more than fifty years she had never quitted the tower in which she lived, and people had supposed her to be dead or bewitched. By the king's orders a place was laid for her, but it was impossible to give her a golden box like the others, for only seven had been made for the seven fairies. The old fairy believed that she was intentionally slighted, and muttered threats between her teeth."

Mother continued reading, stating how each of the fairies then presented their gifts to the newly christened baby.

The youngest fairy ordered that she would be the most beautiful person in the world.

The second fairy said that she would have the personality of an angel.

The third fairy said that she would do everything with grace.

The fourth that she would dance to perfection.

The fifth that she would sing like a nightingale.

The sixth that she would play every kind of music with the utmost skill.

When it was time for the next fairy to present her gift, a shudder ran through the company.

"She declared that the princess should prick her hand with a spindle and die of it."

At this moment, the youngest fairy stepped forward:

"Take comfort, your majesties," she cried in a loud voice. "Your daughter shall not die. My power, it is true, is not enough to undo all that my aged kinswoman has decreed. The princess will indeed prick her hand with a spindle. But instead of dying she shall merely fall into a profound slumber that will last a hundred years. At the end of that time a king's son shall come to awaken her."

"What happened to fairies?" I asked.

Mother looked out over the garden. "That's a great question, Bri, one I wish more people asked.

"I believe, like people, there are good fairies and there are bad fairies. But unlike people, fairies exist in their form forever. Fairies have always been, and they can see us, but we cannot see them. It's like they're standing behind a lace curtain. They know what we know and more.

"The old fairy's anger and hatred didn't cease that day. Most anger and most hatred grows and grows, consuming everything in its path. And this fairy was so full of rage that her resentment continued to flame within her, a million blisters boiling. If she was fine condemning the princess to death, then she was fine condemning more, and that's what she's continued and continues to do, time and time again, finding another beauty and another, then casting her off to an eternal sleep."

It was then, for a moment, that I thought I spotted a fluttering shadow beside the pine tree. A bird? A butterfly? But before I could say anything, the shadow disappeared.

Mother continued, reading how the king had declared that all spindles be forbidden from the land. But one day, when the princess had reached sixteen, she was running around the castle, went upstairs to a tower, and found a spindle. Her curiosity drew her closer and closer, and when she reached to touch the device, she was pricked by the needle and collapsed into a deep sleep.

The younger fairy who had counteracted the elder fairy's curse as best she could was summoned to the castle. When she arrived, she agreed that there was little she could do. The one hundred years of sleep would begin, but the fairy thought how sad it would be for the princess to awake all alone. So she touched everyone with her wand and:

"The moment she had touched them, they all fell asleep, to awaken only at the same moment as their mistress.

"Then the king and queen kissed their dear child, without waking her, and left the castle. Proclamations were issued, forbidding any approach to it, but these warnings were not needed, for within a quarter of an hour there grew up all around the park so vast a quantity of trees big and small, with interlacing brambles and thorns, that neither man nor beast could pass."

I thought it sad that Sleeping Beauty's parents had to depart, leaving her to a century of slumber all alone. I also thought it sad that everyone in her kingdom, too, had been enchanted to one hundred years of sleep; all because of a single evil person, so many lives had been disrupted.

Years went by and a prince learned of the story of the princess sleeping in a tower. He believed it all a great adventure, and "impelled alike by the wish for love and glory," he set about on his journey.

"Hardly had he taken a step toward the wood when the tall trees, the brambles, and the thorns, separated of themselves and made a path for him . . . The sight that now met his gaze was enough to fill him with an icy fear. The silence of the place was dreadful, and death seemed all about him. The recumbent figures of men and animals had all the appearance of being lifeless . . .

"Through several apartments crowded with ladies and gentlemen in waiting, some seated, some standing, but all asleep, he pushed on, and so came at last to a chamber which was decked all over with gold. There he encountered the most beautiful sight he had ever seen. Reclining upon a bed, the curtains of which on every side were drawn back, was a princess . . .

"Trembling in his admiration he drew near and went on his knees beside her. At the same moment, the hour of disenchantment having come, the princess awoke, and bestowed upon him a look more tender than a first glance might seem to warrant."

"She woke up all by herself!" I said.

"Yes, she did, Bri. That's what many people don't quite remember; in this version of 'Sleeping Beauty,' she wasn't saved by a prince. She woke on her own at the hour the curse was lifted, at exactly one hundred years."

"Can people really live one hundred years?" I asked.

"Most don't. I believe the average person does, however, sleep about six total years in their lifetime."

"What happened to the princess's mother and father?"

"They weren't put to sleep in the castle walls, so they lived a normal human life, and they died long before the princess awoke."

How sad it was for the king and queen to live that long, knowing their daughter was in a sleep like death. How sad they must have been, because they could not speak with her, nor could she speak or open her eyes or laugh or dance. And so it was a death.

"What about the wicked fairy? Did she ever come back to find the princess?"

"At least in this story, I do not know, but I do know of wicked fairies that do stalk princesses today."

"Why do they do that?"

"Because they have hearts as cold as glass, as dark as coal. They see something that's beautiful and made of light and they think that hurting it, that catching that lightning bug and smashing it and smearing that glittering liquid on themselves, is the spell that will bring their own lives meaning. But light doesn't work that way. Light comes from the inside, not out."

Mother closes the book and hands it to me. "Here, this belonged to Mary, and now it belongs to you. Your job is to keep it safe until Mary returns home."

"Just like the princess in 'Sleeping Beauty'?"

"Exactly like the princess in 'Sleeping Beauty.' Right now Mary is asleep, and she's waiting for the clock to tick down so she can awaken."

"Is she waiting for a prince too?"

"Maybe she's waiting for me to figure this out or maybe she's waiting for you? Either way, one of us will bring her back home to her castle tower."

"But"—I lower my voice and whisper—"what about the evil fairy? Should we be worried that she's watching us?"

My mother looks from side to side, lowers her head, and matches the softness of my voice. "Yes, we should take care that the evil fairy is watching us. It's always watching us, just like it's always watching Mary, those other women too, and any woman outside should take caution, for there are wicked things that stalk the forest in the night."

Chapter 29

Detective Kowalski and Detective Rodriguez knock on my door less than an hour after he returned my call.

I open the door, unsure what they want to say, but I can only assume they have questions about Jerry.

"Can we sit?" Detective Kowalski asks, but he's already walking inside the house and making his way to the living room.

"Sure, go ahead, I guess."

Detective Rodriguez takes the wingback chair. "I didn't mention it last time, but I dig the antique furniture. Where'd you get all this stuff? It looks like a museum in here."

"Whatever wasn't already a part of the house, my mom acquired. A lot of it from antique stores throughout the city, or ones we'd visit not too far away, in Door County, or Galena. She liked beautiful and original things. She worked as a conservationist."

"Conserving what?" Detective Kowalski asks.

"For a long time, she worked at funerary art conservation."

"What?"

"The statues, Kowalski." Rodriguez waves his hand. "You know those pretty statues at cemeteries."

"Yeah, I've seen them, but didn't know that was a job, cleaning them up."

I ignore them.

"And in all that time, you and your mother lived here alone?" Kowalski asks.

"Since I was a little girl."

"And since that time, you've seen that man outside this house?" Kowalski points toward the window.

"Yes."

Rodriguez leans forward in the chair. His hands together. "Why didn't you tell us about this when we were here last time?"

"I . . . don't know. I just never wanted to believe that someone so close could do me harm. My mother seemed to know who he was, but she never wanted to talk about it. She never seemed worried about him. She never told me his name. It was just something that happened on occasion. He'd pull up, park outside for a time, and then leave."

Kowalski is sitting forward in his seat, eyes on me. "And you never met him formally? Your mother never introduced you to him either?"

"No." I shake my head. There's silence between them, and then I finally ask, "Is everything all right?"

"Jerry Poulos died last night," Kowalski says. "Kidney failure. He wasn't supposed to leave his house. His niece and nephew were watching over him, and they tell me that he left at some point. And I guess that's when he came here."

My heart is crushed. Mary's Jerry. He's dead.

"Again, you've never met him?"

"No," I say, my voice cracking, and I know they don't believe me, but it doesn't matter. "It's just sad, that's all," I say. "Someone dying, regardless of who they are."

"Anything else you need to tell us?" Detective Rodriguez asks.

I go silent. I don't know how to say it, but I just do. I tell them everything about Isaac. How I seemed to meet him entirely by chance.

How we'd walk in the park. How I was supposed to meet him and found myself in his apartment, portraits of women staring back at me.

The detectives look to each other and tell me they'll look into it. Then Kowalski asks: "Do you think that this person could possibly be the Chicago Strangler?"

I shake my head. "I don't know."

Kowalski and Rodriguez look at each other again.

They leave the house, and I'm looking down at Prairie. I don't even know what to say or how to process this, but the house knows how to react.

I sit at my window and think of Jerry Poulos and how I will never see him again parked out front. I regret, in all those years, not pressing my mother further to explain who the man was outside of our house and what he was doing. I realize now that this house was the only thing he had left that connected him to Mary, and I imagine that something happened that night that prevented him from getting to her. I also imagine that, if he frequented this house, sitting in his car and lingering with his thoughts for years, he was racked with guilt because since he didn't get to her in time, something else did. And because of that, he never got to see her again.

I really and truly imagine that Jerry Poulos meant what he said that night, that he pictured a life with Mary as his wife.

So he lived a lifetime with that guilt, and with that hope that was never materialized. That is what a death does, it lingers over us, a question of "I wonder how it would have been if death hadn't stopped us?"

A low, mournful song plays, and the house is full of the smell of velvety roses.

Chapter 30

TIME: 6:00 p.m.
DATE: Wednesday, December 13

Bri's Article

Mourning Chicago's Most Famous Ghost: Resurrection
Mary by Briar Rose Thorne

I've heard the story told and retold, and it starts and
stops a number of different ways. Everyone who
grows up in Chicago learns some variation of the
Resurrection Mary story.

"Mary is a well-known ghost."

"Chicago's greatest haunting."

"America's most famous specter."

"The world's most famous apparition."

"There's a Bloody Mary they set out for her every

night at Chet's Melody Lounge."

"Many years ago . . . some people went out for a night of dancing . . ."

"They spotted a beautiful girl sitting by herself at a ballroom."

"Some young men offered a lovely woman a ride after a night at a dance hall."

"After directing the driver down Archer Avenue, she disappeared."

"She's been seen since the 1930s."

"She's been seen since the 1940s."

"She's been seen since the 1950s."

"This one driver said he saw a woman run right through the gates at Resurrection Cemetery."

"People have said they've seen her struck in the road by a car."

"I heard people have seen her bleeding, actually bleeding, after being hit by a car, and then when someone gets close to help, she dematerializes."

"Some guy said he spent all night dancing with this one girl at the O'Henry Ballroom, or was it the Willowbrook Ballroom? Says he fell in love with her right then. As he was driving her home, she told him to stop the car, and she disappeared right there in front of Resurrection Cemetery. The guy lived his entire life in love with a ghost."

The most famous variation goes like this:

A man meets a beautiful blond woman named Mary. He offers her a ride home. At some point she says she's cold and he offers her his jacket. When they get just outside of Resurrection Cemetery, she demands he pull over. He does and then she disappears.

The next morning, he goes to the address she gave him, and a woman answers the door and tells him her daughter's been dead for years. When he visits Resurrection Cemetery, he finds his jacket lying on Mary's grave.

Variations of the same story have been told around the world for years. It's the story of the vanishing hitchhiker, a common story in ghost lore, and it goes back before the time of the automobile, back to wagon-and-buggy days, and perhaps even before that.

Still, Chicago's Resurrection Mary is the most well known of all our ghostly lore because of the number of sightings and firsthand accounts of her.

With a vanishing hitchhiker, the story typically goes, I heard from a friend of a friend . . . but this isn't the case with the accounts of Mary. Researchers and historians have been able to track down multiple firsthand accounts of people who say they have encountered Resurrection Mary along Archer Avenue, and it's always along Archer Avenue.

There are multiple accounts and multiple versions of this story that people hold dear, and that people do not like to stray from. There's something about people's loyalty to the first variation of the Resurrection Mary story they heard. It's like people's allegiance to the North Side Cubs or South Side White Sox. They very rarely deviate.

It doesn't matter the exact year, but what we do know is that by the middle of the 20th century, the story of the vanishing hitchhiker was embedded in American folklore. Scholars Richard K. Beardsley and Rosalie Hankey wrote an article for the *California Folklore Quarterly* in 1942.

In it, they identified several common themes that arise with the story of the vanishing hitchhiker. Some of these stories include hitchhikers who just want to get home, hitchhikers who turn into a god, and a hitchhiker who conveys a prophetic story.

What's most striking is that in the article, and for around that period, stories of the vanishing hitchhiker were rarely heard outside of the Chicago area, meaning around the 1940s, the story of the vanishing hitchhiker was largely a Chicago story, a local urban legend that existed mostly in this area.

Some of the Resurrection Mary stories include a number of common details; a woman is met at a place of entertainment, usually a dance hall or ballroom. The woman is cold to the touch. When the driver goes to her address following the incident, he's told the girl died several years ago. Sometimes when this occurs, it also coincides with the anniversary of the girl's death. Some versions say she died the night of her prom. And the driver has generally given the girl something to wear, a sweater or a jacket, which is then located on the girl's grave after the incident.

Songwriter Dickey Lee was familiar with Beardsley and Hankey's article. His popular 1965 song "Laurie (Strange Things Happen)" talks about urban legends, vanishing hitchhikers, and of course, Resurrection Mary.

The lyrics tell of a young man who meets a girl named Laurie and how they danced all night, and he fell in love with her. He gave her his sweater because she was cold. He walks her to her door, kisses her, and on a later day returns for his sweater. When he knocks on the door, a man appears and says how cruel that the young man should be doing this, on the one-year anniversary of his daughter Laurie's death, which also happened to be her birthday. The young man later goes to the cemetery, and there he finds his sweater on Laurie's grave.

In their article, at no point did Beardsley and Hankey purport that the stories of Resurrection Mary were true. What they did instead say was that maybe these stories that were now urban legend had just become what Carl Jung had called a part of the collective unconscious.

The collective unconscious in terms of the sightings of the Chicago area's vanishing hitchhiker is that, over time, a phenomenon occurred in which multiple people seemed to be experiencing the same thing. All Beardsley and Hankey sought to surmise was that all these people were encountering the same images, sights, sounds, and senses. How curious. But they never leaned into believing that ghosts were real.

The popular stories that people tell again and again on Halloween night, about a girl at a dance, feeling cold to the touch, and a sweater that appears on a grave, are not far from many verified witness accounts.

I'm saying that maybe there's some truth to the story of the vanishing hitchhiker along Archer Avenue. How can so many people across so many years be wrong? They were all from different backgrounds, different age ranges, different areas of the city. These people did not know one another, and many of these accounts happened before the days of the internet. So there were no forums or chat rooms or social media for people to exchange stories. These stories were shared in schools and homes and in pubs and restaurants and grocery stores.

What holds true over and over again is that these sightings all occurred on Archer Avenue, a weeping woman, a woman in white, a traveling hitchhiker, and no matter what you want to call her, her name holds in our minds as Mary. What the records also indicate is that stories of this being didn't just occur outside of Resurrection Cemetery, but all along Archer Avenue, and its cemeteries, starting with Saint James of the Sag Canal at the very end of Archer Avenue.

One of the earliest recorded sightings of a woman in white occurs in 1897. Two Chicago musicians, Professor William Looney and John Kelly, were asked to play at a church fair in a dance hall in the Sag Valley. After the event, they were awakened by the sounds of horses and a carriage rumbling by. The sound of the hooves drew closer and closer, and when they finally looked out the window, they saw a woman standing in the middle of the road; she had long dark hair and wore a white gown.

A group of shocking-white horses appeared, each with a "light of electric brilliancy" beaming from the tops of their heads. They were pulling along a mysterious dark vehicle, in which no driver could be seen. The horses passed the woman. She then raised her arms, holding her palms out, and she levitated over twenty feet, and a shadow began to form around her. Then she just as quickly sank down into the earth, and the horses and carriage, the entire scene, disappeared.

The *Chicago Tribune* even wrote about the incident, saying the "deep melancholy was reflected from sepulchral eyes which rolled about with that hollow intensity indicative of some soul-eating despair."

That certainly sounds like an embellishment, but it's still clear that the stories of Mary, the vanishing hitchhiker, stretch far beyond what we think, and each of them has to do with Archer Avenue. And what is also clear and very true is that the story of the vanishing hitchhiker was rarely heard outside of the Chicago area before the 1940s.

What do we know of Archer Avenue? Why are these stories concentrated here? What we do know is that Archer Avenue is a very old road. It is an old Indigenous population trail and was among the first roads in what would become Chicago. Ghosts, including Mary, have been reported in and around most of that stretch, including around all the cemeteries.

This story has been told over and over across the years, but it is very central to Chicago, and the reason has to do with the cemetery at Saint James Church and the Illinois and Michigan Canal.

So is she an urban legend or is she something more?

I know this story is true, even though most people refuse to believe in the existence of ghosts. I know she is real. Hundreds have seen her. Yes, she is an urban legend, in ways, but she is very real too, and I believe in the truth that when one dies, maybe they linger around too shocked to believe the reality of their demise. And maybe they linger around cemeteries. Maybe some ghosts can get away with stalking these graveyards. Maybe some ghosts don't realize that they're dead. Maybe a person's spirit, what's left over after death, whether you want to call it energy or a soul, gets trapped in this reality, in a pattern or a loop, searching for something, a lover or simply the comfort of home.

Chapter 31

How can someone stop themselves from being one of my victims? They can't, not if they're meant to be one.

I'm here now, in my nighttime world, and I am walking. The streets are quiet. Earth is still. There's no wind. There's no movement. There's just screaming. Their screaming. A palace world of screaming.

Time slips here. There's just moonless night and the girls.

During the day they sleep in glass coffins. When the sun sets, I arrive here. I watch them. So pretty.

When the moon rises, they wake. Every time they open their eyes, they realize they're dead and they're here with me. They scream and cry, and I smile.

They're all dressed in beautiful dresses spun with the finest yarn. They're waking up now.

Sobbing. Heavy dreams. So heavy. A maze of pretty girls, onward forever, living in these shadows and reliving the torment.

Their piercing cries. This pleases me greatly.

I call them by their names.

Elizabeth.

Caroline.

Esther.

Diamond.

Kelley.

Dora.

Florence.

On and on.

The real world says it's fifty-one, but there's so many, many, many more. They all had their chance at life, and what did life give them? They are better, safer, here with me.

They're all beauties, but there's the one I turn to each night. I approach her glass coffin surrounded by dark woods.

She lies there so peacefully in her white ball gown. Her hands together on her chest.

I place my hand on the lid, and I speak her name.

"Mary."

She opens her eyes and looks up at the night.

"Mary." I push open the lid, and now we are both away from the forest. We are now both standing where I found her so long ago. Along a stretch of road.

She's standing on the corner, the streetlight her spotlight.

"Mary, dance with me?"

"Leave me alone," she says, her voice a tiny flicker.

I take her hand.

"Behave, now, Mary. It's just you and me here dancing in oblivion."

Her lips quiver, and she turns from me. I know what she's thinking. I always know what she's thinking.

"You want to flag down a car?" I take her chin in my hands.

"Yes."

I caress her cheek.

Tears roll down her face.

"You want to go home?" I place my hand on her shoulder.

"Yes."

"This is your home, Mary. There's no going back. There's no more daylight for you. This is our fate here. This night and time bind us. We are the same, you and I. There's no return from death."

I feel the gloom inside of her grow, and she's staring, thinking, planning her escape, but there's no leaving me ever.

They are all pinned butterflies. Lightning bugs flashing in mason jars on a spring night.

People who study us say we have a vision of a victim in mind, that we're looking for a certain race, face, shape, body, build, hair color, eye color.

Maybe.

For some.

They say many of our victims are strangers.

Maybe.

For some. It varies.

Not everyone can protect themselves from us.

We select. We kill. We keep.

"I'm going to bring another beauty home," I say.

Mary doesn't say anything.

"You'll like this one. She's special. Very special. She's special like you. She'll be a legend, just like you."

Chapter 32

I dream I'm walking through Rosehill Cemetery with Emily and her arm is hooked with mine.

I feel the uneven ground beneath me. I see places where there's just old broken stone jutting out, and I think to myself, *That was once a tombstone, but it's been broken and discarded.* That person is now lost and forgotten to time, and I think about how sad it all is, a cemetery.

We take our dead and we plant them into the ground, but we know nothing will ever grow there. There will be no new memories made. There will be no new milestones achieved. We plant dead things into the ground expecting them to stay there, and there they will forever remain, but not always.

That is what death is, it's permanent. And we the living are the ones who must walk around and exist empty from those who left us, and that is the cruelest thing of all.

What does "Sleeping Beauty" tell us? That from a deep, forever sleep we can awake, but that's not real. From forever sleep there is no waking, and there is no relief for those who will mourn your loss. Your loss will be mourned by that living person until that living person is no more, until every single person who has ever known you is gone.

What do we long for the most? We long for people. We long for connection. We long for love, yet when we get it, we're often unappreciative of it. We ignore those who try to connect with us. We cancel plans with friends and family who want us in their lives. We shun and ignore people who try with us again and again, and when they are gone, it's too late.

I wake up from my nap. I brush my teeth. I shower. I make a cup of coffee, and then I sit at my desk. I pull out the notebook Mother gifted me, one of many, and I begin to write.

"Each morning, Briar, write down whatever is in your head. Get it down on paper so that it will not weigh on you throughout the day. And then, when you're done with that, you will write down five affirmations and five things you are grateful for. Do this every day, without stopping, and you will see what is floating there in your subconscious. You will see what things need to be worked on. You will realize what it is you are grateful for. Don't keep those things bottled up where they will appear as disturbances in other areas of your life. Put it down on paper, with your hands, because there's power in that. In holding the writing instrument and placing the tip on paper.

"The science tells us this. That physical paper allows for tangible permanence. Lean into the imperfection of the irregular strokes of letters and the uneven shapes of sentences, rounded and sharp corners. It's all your mind, that galaxy that is within you being explored here in the physical realm. When you wake from slumber, you need to remind your brain and your body that you are alive, my beautiful Briar Rose. If you are moving your fingers, if you are writing, if you are reading, if you are sitting in the window with the morning sun on your face, you are alive, and no one can take that away from you."

I think of how beautiful and how tragic Sleeping Beauty is. She sleeps and dreams in a sealed glass coffin in the forest, a magical enchantment herself, with the world ever shaping and expanding around her. But she's just there, frozen in time in a way.

Women in glass coffins. Beautiful dead girls who appear to be asleep. The tragedy is knowing that someone did this, placed them into their forever sleep.

I walk downstairs and find myself in the living room. I look at the spinning spindle and think of what a dreadful thing, a dreadful reminder, it is being named after a character in a fairy tale who dies by this very instrument. I suppose my father found it oddly funny. No wonder my parents didn't last.

Still, I always wondered why my mother named me what she did. Not Rose. Not Bri. Not Briar, but Briar Rose, a character who is cursed to sleep and is awakened in death by another. I don't know if that is a happily ever after, because of what was lost, but maybe that story tells us that even in death there is life. Maybe that story tells us there is hope after sadness, and maybe then that story tells us that while we sleep and while we dream, there is something going on up there in the cosmos, that there is always a spot of light in the darkness.

And maybe that's what I need to hold on to, that there is hope in the tragedy of losing my mother and that somehow she does hear my words, and maybe there is hope in the tragedy of all these beautiful dead girls and that peace does exist for them, will exist for them, somehow. While we can't bring them back, because there really is no bringing anyone back from physical death, then maybe we can stop another beautiful girl from falling into forever sleep. Maybe we can stop another wicked fairy from casting off another beautiful girl to death because of their own jealousy and hate.

Ball gowns and dance shoes. Glitter and chiffon and lipstick and rouge. Hair done up with silk bows. I smell gardenia and lavender. A mist of citrus and I hear music, perhaps it's playing from a car radio, in some far-off time.

Then I hear her, Mary.

Beautiful Mary.

I know it's her voice because she is who I have been dreaming of. She is who all of this has been about. She is the woman in the portrait. She is the woman in the ballroom. She is the woman in the white

301

dress. She is the woman in the road. She is the woman walking beside Resurrection Cemetery merely, simply, just trying to get home.

Legend. Myth. Folklore.

Why do we fear the ghosts of women who were murdered? Why don't we fear the thing that made them what they are?

We speak of the weeping woman in whispers. We giggle with fright at the thought of Bloody Mary. We watch the road closely on nights when gentle mist creates a foggy world outside, waiting for a translucent form to appear.

But these women are not the monsters.

Whatever fictions people have claimed to see or hear, of a woman put painfully to sleep, they are just ghosts—repeated patterns—stuck in a loop, begging you to "Help me," or even just to "See me," or, heart-breakingly, "Please take me home."

Because that is all they wanted in the first place: to simply go home to their loved ones. Like Sleeping Beauty who slept, and the world moved on without her. How can we even assume that she was awakened to joy when her parents were dead?

But all of that was stolen on a single night because someone deemed that they could own her.

And now I walk these dark hallways in this house, calling out to my mother, because now I know what it is I must do.

"Keys and gates and locks and thorns," I say. "Mother, I know now. I have to bring Mary back home. If not, it'll continue killing other women it encounters on their journey."

The house remains quiet, and the house remains still. Outside a gust of wind rattles the windows.

"Mother . . ."

"Mom, where is the key?" I ask, and I hear the house begin to groan. A wondrous beast coming alive, and before I can ask again, I hear a tapping against my window. Rose thorns.

"I'm listening, Mother," I say, acknowledging the signs. I pull back the curtain in the hallway window.

"I see the thorns. Now what . . . ?" I hear the front gate. The click of the latch and rusted hinges squeaking as the door opens. I press my face to the window and look down. "Okay, I see it now, the gate." I rush to the foyer and throw on my coat and slip on my winter boots and step outside.

It is dark, and I walk down the icy concrete steps carefully. The temperature has dropped, and the snow is frozen stiff, and it crunches beneath each of my steps.

"Where's the key?" I ask, but then I wonder, maybe it's not in order, because maybe signs and symbols aren't meant to come in order. Maybe people behind the veil, in the thin place, don't communicate like we do, with things linearly and sequentially? Maybe all we need to do is be patient and listen as the clues are presented to us.

"Thank you, Mother," I say, and now I'm standing outside in our garden.

The garden appears dead in winter, but it feels very much alive, pulsating, and electric, brimming with a story that I need to listen to clearly in order to be able to tell it. The air is crisp and the air is clean. Our leafless trees with their intricate network of snow-covered branches. The deep color of evergreens and the large shadows they cast across the yard. The shrubs covered in snow that look like giant poofy snowballs. The sleeping roses, dormant rosebushes that extend across the yard, bare stems and bare branches, thorny structures dotted with dried rose hips. And the greenhouse, the jewel of our lovely garden, tucked into this city.

I hear more tapping, thorny vines against the glass of the greenhouse, and I smile. "The greenhouse," I say. "I should have known."

This is the one place I avoided entering after Mother's death, because this is the place she loved so much and she adored so much and she took such great care to maintain, but I feared entering it. How could I care for something she loved dearly when I could barely take care of myself?

I approach it and see all the greenery gone brown within. I remember the fairy tale. And I remember the bargain—I will come for your daughter's daughter—and I wonder now if over the years the fairy had returned. And I see them now, my mother standing bedside the greenhouse and a beautiful woman with her. She is in a black dress that's so black it's blacker than midnight on a moonless night.

"We are the last two women in our family," my mother says. "Please, let us be, fairy. You already took Mary."

The fairy smiles a wicked smile. "I set the price and I'll revise it again and again if I choose. When your daughter finds herself on that road at night, and she will, I will be there waiting. I am there when the sun sleeps, waiting for all of them, as they walk. I am the thing that lives in the shadows. I am the thing that hangs in the treetops. I am the thing that takes joy in their screams and pleasure in their pain. There is no escaping me. Any woman who is alone at night walks in my realm, and if I choose, I can simply pull her off her path and drag her down the forest floor and make her one of mine, my eternal sleeping beauties."

The vision is gone, and I am inside the greenhouse.

The air is thick with the scent of earth, and the aroma of greenery. I follow the narrow path, lined with cobblestones. The light from my phone guides my way. It is much warmer in here than outside, and I welcome that. I am looking for something, anything that can give me a clue. I hear the gentle hum of the city beyond, muffled and echoed, but still I am here, secluded and enveloped in this magical world where I feel no one can find me.

I walk among the shelving, past the watering system and humidor. There are pots and things growing still, resilient little greens fighting to stay alive even under my mishandling. There are grow lights that are off, and things covered by frost cloth and a potting bench with empty clay pots, waiting to be used in spring. There are bags of mulch and potting soil and bulbs and seeds and watering cans and thermometers, and beside it all an iron key.

"The key," I say, and reach for it.

It's small and rusted, and I know it's been here this entire time since her death. She left it here in hopes I'd find it.

"Keys and gates and locks and thorns . . .

"And now the black road stretching on into forever. How do I bring her home?" I ask the great greenhouse, and I feel a rustling and a stirring, as if a soft spring breeze has been trapped within this space.

I remember now. The trunk. The trunk among Mother's things.

I have stepped outside, heading for the front door, when I see him. He's standing on the sidewalk. He's dressed as I've seen him each time. Black slacks. Black shoes. Black jacket. Black hat.

"Hello, Briar," he says, removing his hat and placing it over his chest. "I'm so sorry about your mother."

It's the man from Red Gate Woods. The man from Bachelor's Grove. It's the man I've seen in my nightmares. It's not Isaac. It never was.

"It's you," I say.

He smiles and holds his hands out. "I am Mal." He's wearing leather gloves. "Why don't you come here. We have so much to talk about."

I rush up the stairs, slam the door behind me, and lock it. I turn on the light, and I start dialing the police. I'm peeking out the window and he is gone.

I run through the house, heading upstairs. I dial Daniel and leave a message. I dial Emily and do the same.

"It's him," I say. "The killer's here."

I dial Detective Kowalski and leave him a message. I dial 9-1-1 and scream at the operator to send help now.

In the attic, I find the trunk. I open it with the key, and there I find a white dress and white dancing shoes and a white silk hair ribbon, and an envelope addressed to Mrs. Thorne, but I don't believe this is for me, and I don't believe this was for my mother. I open the letter and read the first few lines, and I feel as if I am invading someone's privacy. This is Mary's letter. This is for later. I tuck the letter away in the trunk and remove the dress, the shoes, and the hair ribbon.

The letter will have to wait a little bit longer for the person it was addressed to.

I rush back down the stairs and gather my car keys and head out the back.

Chapter 33

TIME: 8:00 p.m.
DATE: Thursday, December 14

How do we communicate with the dead? How do we communicate with people who are no longer here? How do we connect? Send a message? And if we send a message, how do we know it's been communicated?

Maybe my mother knew that there was a power in things, objects, hairpins, pictures, a book, a radio, or maybe even a dress.

I am driving down Archer Avenue when I approach those familiar black gates.

Keys and gates and locks and thorns.

A family history dotted by death, a curse, and a story of tragedy told and retold over and over again.

I haven't thought my plan through, but all I know is that I have to be here to see her, and if she wants to show herself to me, then she will. I believe that she will appear. I have her dress. I have her shoes. I have her silk hair tie. I park my car next to the cemetery, and I don't know what else I can do but sit here and wait. I don't believe anyone has done it this way, sit and wait for her, but this is all I can do. In each and every account in which Mary has appeared, she did so alongside the road, crying.

I wonder whether Jerry ever visited her here. Would he sit and speak to her, tell her how sorry he was for running late and not picking her up?

"Mary," I whisper, "I'm here to take you home."

The street is empty and silent. There are no cars coming toward me and no headlights behind me. It's as if I'm in my dreamworld, where nothing exists but me and Mary, snatches of memory, and the fairies.

I rub my head, wondering if this is all madness, madness in thinking that the story of a ghost from a very long time ago can somehow connect and heal the stories of dozens of women in Chicago.

To stop the killings, I need to break the pattern, and the way to break the pattern is to bring Mary home, to pull her from that loop, and to take power away from the thing that's been taking joy in the suffering of so many women for so long.

Fairy tales warn women to take caution with their journey and nighttime roads. Fairy tales warn women of the dangers of creatures that live in the forest, ready to ravage and destroy. Fairy tales have known for a very long time that there are things that live in the wood that women should take care to avoid, because these monsters take joy in the destruction of beauty and the death of innocence.

For a moment I think I see a cloud of mist ahead of me, but it is the reflection of headlights approaching. A car. A black car. The black car from long ago. It changes shape and form—that is what it does—but I will not be deterred, and I will not be afraid. It's now parked behind me, idling. I hear the door open and close. I hear footsteps approach. I refuse to give up now. This is what it wants.

There's a tap on my glass, and I see the blurred face and lecherous grin through the corner of my eye.

Its voice is rusty nails. "Hello again, Briar Rose. Is your car giving you trouble?" he asks.

I ignore it. I ignore him. I try.

I will focus on what I am here to do. I am here to bring Mary home. To take power away from this evil so that it can no longer stalk the forests or stalk parks or sidewalks or roads. To stop the Chicago Strangler.

He taps at my window again.

Cynthia Pelayo

Once again, I refuse to acknowledge him, and then he reaches for my car handle. My doors are locked. He tries, and the door clicks and clicks but does not open.

He then tries my rear driver's-side door, walks around, and tries the rear passenger-side door and front passenger-side door.

"I'm not leaving without Mary," I say to myself.

He laughs at me. "Which Mary? There's so many Marys. Dozens of Marys. Hundreds of Marys. Thousands of Marys.

"Some of them I found on the street. Others in parks. Parking lots. Some in forests. Hiking alone. Taking a pause at a trailhead. There are more names too—the Barbaras and Patricias, Carols and Jackies, Dianes and Hannahs. There's so many.

"Some I left in ditches. Others in trash cans. Pieces of them in garbage bags spread across the highway. Alleyways and in vacant houses in which the outside creeps inside.

"There's so many of them, and they are all there, don't you hear them? Last gasps and last screams, begging, pleading, but still each and every one was put to sleep, and each and every one will never again wake. They're mine. They repeat their patterns, and I take joy in their misery."

I look down at my hands. "Mary, please. I'm here to take you home," I say, again and again. "We're going home, Mary. I promise. The house is waiting for you. I'm waiting for you . . ."

I reach for my backpack, all the while still hearing my car handles jiggle, while he bangs on the glass.

"Open the door, Bri," he says now, hitting the car so hard the vehicle begins to rock. But I will hold no fear. I will control my thoughts. I will break this pattern.

I remove the white dress and spread it across the passenger seat. I place Mary's shoes on the floor of the passenger side and lay out her hair tie.

He's pressed his face against the window now. "That's beautiful. Where did you find that? I remember what she looked like in it."

And now it is not a man-shaped thing in a black suit and hat, but a woman, a beautiful woman with smooth skin and sharp features.

"A daughter's daughter," Mal says, glaring at me.

"I'm taking Mary home!" I shout. "You're not going to keep her anymore. You're not going to keep any of them anymore. Mary, please, come now! I have your letter. Jerry's letter."

And like that, Mary appears in the passenger seat. Silent and beautiful. One hand extended, a finger pointing straight. "Please take me home," she whispers.

Now it's his face. Inches from the window. He's shouting, his face twisted in rage: "If you leave here, each and every moment you step outside, I will be there watching! I will be there waiting! You will never be free from me! I will always be the danger tucked in the shadows, waiting to rip you from your path and bring you back here!"

"You can't hurt me! I'm breaking the pattern."

I hit the gas, and the car launches forward, accelerating. The car radio turns on, and the dial is searching wildly, whirring until it finds a song, a sad song, and it plays.

> You can buy a dream or two
> To last you all through the years
> And the only price you pay
> Is a heart full of tears

I drive away from Archer Avenue. My fingers gripping the steering wheel. I don't release my foot from the gas, I just keep accelerating, trying to escape this road, trying to escape this story, trying to escape history and the horrors of the present.

The road twists and I follow it, looking through the corner of my eye and seeing Mary still with her finger pointed forward. Home.

The wind whooshes outside the windows. The engine growls, straining. I ignore the speedometer because we are not there yet and we have to get there fast. We're on the expressway now, flying, passing cars. There's beeping as I'm weaving in and out of lanes. The city skyline soon appears. Black towers with sparkling lights. The song changes and plays louder this time.

We come to our exit, and as soon as I turn onto the neighborhood street, blue and red lights pulsate behind me. I bang on the steering wheel.

"No! No! No!" Not right now.

The siren whirs.

It's not a police car. It's an unmarked car. The detectives. They must have been following me. I think for a minute; maybe if I just hit the gas, maybe if I just keep driving home, but I'm too afraid I'll lose control of the car, speeding through the streets, and so I resign myself and pull over.

"Bri . . ." Detective Kowalski says when he reaches my window. I roll it down. "What's going on?" he asks, ducking his head into my car.

He leans forward and looks at the dress draped across the passenger seat. "You okay? Going out somewhere?"

My heart is racing, and I can barely speak. My words are all the falling stars in the sky. "Please, please, please. I have to get home. Trust me. It'll all make sense when I get home. Please. Just trust me. You can even follow me upstairs into the house. I just need to get her home. I have to."

Rodriguez gets out of the car and is standing outside of my passenger-side door now. I look from him to Kowalski; their faces are blank.

"I'm begging you, please," I plead. "Follow me, you'll see."

They eye one another. Kowalski nods once. "We'll follow you," he says, determined, "closely behind."

Rodriguez hops back in the unmarked car.

We drive, through the West Side and the South Side and down through Hyde Park, and I am moving down the boulevard where my house sits.

The entire time, Mary is just pointing one finger toward the window. Her face is aglow in the streetlights of a city that was once her city, that is still her city.

I slam my foot on the gas and just drive. Through red lights. Stop signs. I need to get home.

A tow truck comes barreling through an intersection, and I weave around it. The detectives' car behind me screeches to a halt. The tow truck driver stops, and a shouting match ensues, but I keep driving, and they become dots in the distance of my rearview mirror.

I drive and drive, hoping and praying that the city streets remain clear for me and for their Mary.

Please. Please. Please.

I keep saying a silent prayer to the nighttime, to the roads, to anything that is listening. To my mom.

"Please, Mom. Help me. If you can hear me, Mom, please, please, please, just help me. Keep me safe. And, Mom, if you can hear me, please let me know. Please give me a sign."

I park the car in front of the house, not caring how well it's parked, just making sure it's turned off, and I have the keys in hand and the dress. I'm carrying it in my arms like I'm carrying her, because I *am* carrying her. The detectives are nowhere in sight, but I keep moving. I have a job to do.

I feel her weight in my arms. The weight of a young woman who was said to be hit by a car and died in the road, or maybe died another way. How will we ever know? What we do know is that she was a girl of flesh and blood who loved music and who loved to dance and who found herself alone one night on a dark street and who never returned home. And she became a myth, an urban legend, but all she wanted to do was live a life of joy and of peace and of love, not be trapped in a pattern of despair.

I open the door, and Prairie leaps at me, jumping and licking at my hands, and she begins happily sniffing the dress.

We rush into the attic. Prairie is running full speed and slams into my mother's sewing table, knocking over thread and yarn, sewing and knitting needles, and more. The room is glowing in a warm, radiating light. The room is shimmering like an enchanted spell.

Hands reach for my neck and squeeze. The dress falls out of my hold. Mary collapses onto the floor.

Prairie is growling, barking, snapping.

The room spins. My hair is held. My head is lifted and then slammed against the floor. I taste blood.

He's standing over me now.

Prairie continues to bark, snarling, baring teeth.

"What did you think? I was going to let you go?" he says, walking around me. His eyes are all madness and hate. "Outside! We should be outside! Under the stars! Under the moonlight!"

He lowers his face, inches from mine. "You and I, Bri. Dancing under the moonlight. We'll dance forever."

He's squeezing my neck. I'm trying to form words. My eyes dart around the room. I see my mother's sewing machine. It's on. Punching away into nothing. The pedal moving up and down. The radios all against the wall, their faces illuminated. The whirring of hundreds of radios finding their stations.

"Mom . . ." My voice is so small.

He's squeezing. Squeezing tight. My vision blurs. White around the edges.

I hear my Prairie, barking, barking.

"Mary," I say, calling to her. Hoping she's near. *I'm sorry I failed you and me.*

Music begins to play. Loud, roaring music. I can't see anything through the tears and the pain, but I can hear my mother.

"Briar, just to your left," she says. "Feel, just to your left."

"Mother . . ."

"To your left, Bri. Just feel to your left."

I move my left hand, sweeping it across the hardwood floor, moving, moving, and then I feel something. Metal. I grasp it. My hand shoots up, and I drive the knitting needle into his neck. He releases his hold. His hands shoot up to the knitting needle lodged in his neck. He tries to grasp the slippery tool covered in blood.

He falls over onto his side, hacking, blood pooling around him. Prairie leaps into my arms. Mary is seated beside me now. We watch in silence as his movements slow.

"We have to hurry," Mary says, "if we're to break the pattern and stop Mal."

We turn to the trunk.

"Jerry said he was going to call me tomorrow," Mary says. "That's why I needed to come home. That's why I need to be home. He promised me he would bring me home safe." She looks at the trunk sadly. "But I hoped tomorrow he would ring me and apologize. I think I fell in love with him, and I think he fell in love with me, all in one dance. A single dance I have thought about, that seems like a lifetime now."

"Mary . . ." I say. It breaks my entire heart to tell her that it's not just tomorrow, but many tomorrows later. This is what a life lost loses, the wishes of a tomorrow they so dreamed of.

I reach into the trunk, and I pull out the letter and read it. Mary leans into me, listening. I am sobbing, and I hear her cries too.

Dear Mrs. Thorne,
My heart breaks at the news of Mary's death. I feel as if I have to have died. I imagined a life with her; in just that short song that we danced to, I saw our entire life unfold. She and I happy together, young, and old, and all of that was taken from me.

I'm so eternally heartbroken for you and your family. Please know that I admired your daughter greatly, and I know that she was the love of my life and that each day forward a cloud will hang over me, but I believe that one day, when I die, I will awaken in a new world, and I pray that the first face I see is hers.

My eternal sympathies.

Jerry Poulos

"I loved him too," Mary said. "In the span of a song, a universe. A lifetime."

The radios whir, searching for a new song. They settle on something soft, gentle, a perfect love song for the moment when two people who fell in love at first sight so long ago should be reunited.

And there we are, surrounded by soft pastel lights in a grand ballroom and our beautiful Mary in her white dress and shoes and her love waiting for her, as he's waited for her for too long, and finally she can hold him, and finally he can hold her, and finally our dearest Resurrection Mary can rest because she's finally, finally come home.

I'm crying. I'm sobbing. I feel a hand on my shoulder, and I'm trembling because I know that hand, and I know that perfume, and I'm heaving now. Her arms are around me, and she's holding me, and my mother is whispering in my ear, "I heard you, Bri. I always hear you. You did a good job, Bri. You did a great job. I love you so much."

I hear Detectives Kowalski and Rodriguez enter. They're gasping for air, clearly having raced up the stairs.

I hear the crackle of a walkie-talkie. I'm crying into my hand.

"Oh my God," Rodriguez says. A look of horror on his face.

Kowalski reaches for his weapon.

"He's dead," I say.

"Bri . . ." Kowalski says. "You okay, hon? You need us to call someone? You need anything?"

I turn around, look at them, and say, "I'm tired." It's difficult to see through the tears filling my eyes.

Rodriguez helps me stand. I feel so tired. "I think I just want to go to my room and go to sleep."

And when I wake up, I'll wake up on my own. A dream won't wake me, or a nightmare. I will wake up on my own because I have the others and I have saved myself.

Chapter 34

TIME: *9:00 a.m.*
DATE: *Sunday, June 1*

Daniel moved in.

His lease was up, and my house is so big, and it needed life, more life. He adopted a darling kitten, and when he asked me what a good name was, I recommended Archer, because there is something mysterious and eternal about that, and so we went with Archer.

I never told Daniel about Isaac, but he always knew that something about the park gave me a bittersweet sense. I never saw Isaac again on my walks, but when I would walk alone in Jackson Park with Prairie, I would spend some time at the bridge, and I would tell him all about my new dreams and my wishes.

"I miss you, my darling friend," I said on a recent walk, and for a moment I thought I heard his voice respond somewhere within the gentle breeze that carried through the treetops.

"The house feels lighter," Daniel said one day as he changed the light fixture in the living room. It was time to retire the chandelier for something modern.

Emily curled her feet under her on the sofa and petted Prairie, who was asleep beside her. "I told you, Bri, this house is so big. It just needed more people."

"So you're going to ask Dana to move in?" I said.

"I asked her. She's already packing."

The house seems happy with more people in it, and maybe that's why it had been so sad, because it missed life. I realize now that the house was never trying to hurt me; it was only ever trying to send me messages, to communicate with me, to tell me it was hurting, and to tell me it would help me.

That night I dream I am back there at Red Gate Woods, walking down the path. This time it is summer, and Isaac is by my side.

"May I?" he asks, and hooks my arm in his. It is a beautiful day. The air is crisp and clean, and I am so overjoyed to see my friend. "I've missed you, Bri."

"I've missed you so much too."

He stops and looks into my eyes and smiles. "You look good. You feel good. Safe. Healthy. Happy. That's all I ever wanted for you, Bri."

"Isaac," I say, "are you like my fairy godparent?"

"Bri, I think you should know the answer to that by now."

I throw my arms around him and tell him thank you.

We continue on our walk and soon find ourselves in a clearing, and it is so green and gold. The sky is a blue ocean above. The stone markers are gone, and it is just an expansive prairie that stretches down into forever with beautiful full trees and lovely bushes and tall, colorful, and vibrant prairie flowers.

There we find Mary and Jerry, together. My beautiful Mary. She embraces me, and it feels so good.

I know that this is where she always belonged, in a place of beauty and light and love, where no one could ever hurt her again.

Acknowledgments

Thank you to Jessica Tribble Wells and Grace Wynter. Thank you also to my agent, Lane Heymont.

Additional thanks go to Hailey Piper, Becky Spratford, Todd Keisling, Daniel Kraus, Max Booth III, Michael Allen Rose, Ezekiel, Och, Phaleg, and everyone who talked to me about life and death, the stars, consciousness, and existence.

Thank you to my little angels, B and C.

Thank you also to my husband, Gerardo, for taking care of me, and for guiding me to meditate when the pain of grief was too much.

Thank you to my mother, Alida Rodriguez; and my brothers, Roberto Rodriguez Jr. and Richard Rodriguez. Thank you for the ghost stories and the superstitions.

Finally, thank you to all of you who checked in on me when I couldn't sleep.

About the Author

Photo © 2023 Magdalena Iskra

Cynthia Pelayo is the Bram Stoker Award–winning author of *Forgotten Sisters*, *Children of Chicago*, and *The Shoemaker's Magician*. In addition to writing genre-blending novels that incorporate fairy-tale, mystery, detective, crime, and horror elements, Pelayo has written numerous short stories, including the collection *Lotería*, and the poetry collection *Crime Scene*. The recipient of the 2021 International Latino Book Award, she holds a master of fine arts in writing from the School of the Art Institute of Chicago. She lives in Chicago with her family. For more information, visit www.cinapelayo.com.